T0369231

USA: THE SERPENT IS CRUSHED!

9-11

IT WAS ONLY A TEST!
19 RADICAL ISLAMISTS TESTED THE SERPENT
AND
SUCCEEDED!

A DOCU-NOVEL BY KENNETH GREEN

Order this book online at www.trafford.com
or email orders@trafford.com

Most Trafford titles are also available at major online book retailers.

Note for Librarians: A cataloguing record for this book is available from Library
and Archives Canada at www.collectionscanada.ca/amicus/index-e.html

Printed in Victoria, BC, Canada.

ISBN: 978-1-4269-1374-7 (sc)
ISBN: 978-1-4269-1375-4 (dj)

Library of Congress Control Number: 2009933340

*Our mission is to efficiently provide the world's finest, most comprehensive book publishing
service, enabling every author to experience success. To find out how to publish your book, your
way, and have it available worldwide, visit us online at www.trafford.com*

Trafford rev. 9/24/2009

 www.trafford.com

North America & international
toll-free: 1 888 232 4444 (USA & Canada)
phone: 250 383 6864 ♦ fax: 812 355 4082

DEDICATION

This book is dedicated to my mother Edith Green who had a very hard life but always had a smile for everyone in her life and a kind of giving to others that is as rare as a beautiful white daisy in the sands of the hot Sahara Desert.

She was alone the better half of her life and with the deepest love for her children she watched after them as they grew to maturity, never complaining about the cards she had been dealt.

I was not always understanding and appreciative of her dedication and patience and wished that I could tell her how much her son loves her for being, Mother. If she were here I would do that every day, day after day; but she passed away some twenty six years ago. I LOVE YOU MOM.

And to my wife Ana and my children Maria and Jason who have suffered from my obsession to write this book and who loss many hours of my personal attention they rightly deserved; God bless each of you and I Love You Guys!

SPECIAL THANK YOU

It is important to recognize someone who helped me with my manuscript. Thank you Suzanne Al-Idelbi for the hours you denoted to me to correct my, shall we say, grammar flaws. You have been a blessing!

FORWARD

This book is not about good and evil.

Everyone will accept and admit that under the definitions of those two words there exist in this world both forces and based on history they have plagued mankind ever since man disobeyed GOD.

There is a spreading plague of 'Black Evil' that is growing like a cancer. Just look around and observe the changes and action of people that are committed to ruling the world.

It is not the time to <u>Meditate</u> about the growing evil, it is not the time to <u>Contemplate on the menace,</u> IT IS TIME TO <u>OBSERVE AND WAKE UP!</u>

This docu-novel is written to outline historical events and present facts that would allow the devastating events that rock the United States from coast to coast and from the White House to the neighbor next door.

What you are about to read, while it is based on fiction, could very possibly occur in the immediate future.

CHAPTER ONE

NOVEMBER, 2000

"THIS IS THE CAPTAIN SPEAKING." I jolted up in my seat as this loud and harsh announcement came over the cabin speakers in a broken crackling sound. I had been resting my eyes after the long trip from the west coast. He continued, "We are approximately One Hundred Twenty miles from the JFK airport and should be on the ground in about eighteen minutes. The weather at the airport is currently reported to be 'light drizzle with the temperature dropping now to thirty five degrees and the wind increasing to twenty four miles per hour from the northeast'. We at Atlantic Pacific Airlines thank you for choosing us to bring you to New York City and wish you a pleasant evening and stay while you are in the Big Apple."

Why do we always have to fly into the City in bad weather? I guess I'll be late for my long awaited reunion with Brada and my college friends; but to see everyone again has the adrenaline flowing and gives me a relaxed warm feeling inside. A good healthy shot of adrenaline will certainly help me confront this nasty New York weather and of course, the two glasses of scotch on the rocks I drank after dinner, are good basic fortifiers for the weather in the Big City. The Big City, I never could stand the sound of the words the 'Big Apple'. It's big all right but Apple, well I now consider myself from Washington and our Apples are red, juicy, and crisp. Nothing about New York is like an apple.

"Excuse me, but are you going to want the Newsweek and Time magazines you were reading?" I noticed from the front covers that there were some articles about the terrorist bombings on the USS Cole and the big OIC meeting in Qatar which might give me the news media's slant on the many mid-east problems on everyone's minds lately. I thought the guy sitting across the aisle from me was probably finished with them the way he had them slightly stuffed into the seat pocket in front of him.

"No, here take them with you. Are you coming back home or visiting?"

"You know it's kind of both. I lived here in the late seventies up to nineteen eighty-five when I finished my studies at NYU and then went on to Georgetown University. After finishing Georgetown, I started with the government and ended up back here in New York with a position in Internal Affairs at the UN where I coordinate my work with our State Department. Now I am assigned to the East so I live in Seattle and keep a place here on the West Side. Even though I come here every so often, this is almost like a visit because my graduating class with many of my friends will be having our fifteen year reunion this week end." Wow, I don't know exactly why I broke into a long dissertation about myself and why I'm coming to New York. Guess I'm just glad we are here after the long flight and a little conversation gave me some kind of stress release.

Being polite I went on, "Let me introduce myself, I'm Hank Brayden," I really didn't want to introduce myself but he did offer me the magazines. "Thanks for the magazines, there are a few articles I think I might be interested in reading."

"I'm Jerry Ness." He blurted his name out as though he were beginning a speech from the stage of a grand auditorium. "My company provides security for most of the major airlines here and overseas." I wonder why he told me that. I guess he feels like me, a little bored from the long ride and wants a little conversation before we land or maybe he just wants to blow his own horn, thinking that because I work at the UN I might have influential associates or some kind of special influence; who knows.

This guy had the ex-marine look to me; a ruddy complexion, a very strong frame and big hands. He wore a bulky brown sweater and tan corduroy pants that had probably been around the world more times than this airplane. Talking across the isles has always bothered me.

Either, it is a real inconvenience and hard to hear the other person or everyone can listen to both sides of the conversation. In this instance there wasn't anyone who couldn't hear Jerry talk even if they were asleep. He was looking directly into my eyes so I continued, "Do I know your company? What is the name of your firm?" I went on in a very low and almost guttural tone so I would not draw any more attention from the passengers around us. After all, airline security in these times is not only a very important subject, but any mention of protection, guns, security, or terrorism could easily lead to unnecessary passenger excitement or even panic.

He was proud of his job as he proceeded, "I'm sure you have heard of us 'ACE INTERNATIONAL', acronym for Air Carrier Enforcement; we specialize in pre-detecting any terrorist plans for high jacking, bombing, or destruction of any and all aircraft either in fight or on the ground."
Well now I did it, just the conversation I didn't want to get into.

"LADIES AND GENTLEMEN, we are about to land. Please put your tray tables up and bring all of your seats to their upright position. If you have been using any electronic devices such as computers, CD or DVD players, or electronic game players please turn them off now. Check to see that your seat belts are securely fastened and that all of your carry-ons have been stowed under your seat. It has been a pleasure to ser......" Saved by the stewardess, must be my night.

As the doors opened I took my small case complete with shirt, pants, socks, and so on and of course my laptop; oh yes and the two magazines, said Goodbye to Jerry and squeezed my way forward. I really need to get out in the open and breathe some fresh air. Even though I am tired of flying into bad weather I love to smell the air when there is a slight drizzle. I still can't get use to the massive movement of bodies in this airport and the ill-mannered people from just everywhere. "Excuse me lady, nobody can get through here!" Passing gate after gate I weaved systematically through the crowds of people. Some knowing where they are going, some just standing in line for check in and others just standing in groups but not doing anything, only blocking any possibility of an even flow of passenger traffic headed to the baggage area. There should be 'people traffic cops' giving tickets to the inconsiderate that menace airports. Not having any bags to pick up, I can be in the city in a very short time. Friday night in New York can turn out to be most interesting or it can ruin the entire weekend.

For the beginning of our reunion I'm supposed to meet Brada and some of our old friends at 'Olivers in the Village'; where we use to spend a lot of time after classes talking about politics, women, and how to re-design the world to give us the utopian life we all thought was deserved by everyone, everywhere. We knew of course it did not exist and probably never would because most people lose their idealistic desires to change the bad to the good after leaving the environment of the academia and conveniently settling down into their chosen fields. I can remember Brada and some of the other Arabic students sitting for hours over two or three beers discussing the evils of the capitalistic system and the need to change the governmental philosophies in the Western countries to give the forsaken a better life. Always theories but not much in the way of practical ideas. Still I enjoyed listening and giving my input into those lengthy, sometimes heated exchanges. This weekend will probably be exhausting with all of the activities that have been arranged.

As I was taking the long walk to the front walkway, where the taxis and limos were just waiting for their opportunity to get a traveler new to The City, so they could make their night; I reflected back on my trip here just last May. I will never get over what was one of the worst weekends that I had ever had anywhere. I went out around 10 o'clock on a Friday night to have dinner and then to troll for a companion to spent the weekend with me. After having dinner at Giovanni's where the clams in garlic butter sauce over fettuccini might just take the five star ratings away from all the restaurants in Sicily; I had walked over to Second Avenue to try one of the newer microbreweries. The rain was just starting and I had hoped I could beat most of it. Running I just got in the door and out of the on coming down pour. Redhawk was really packed and I wove my way over to a standup table near one of the big screen TV's. Three other guys were standing by the table in their 'Here I am Pose' as they verbally described the many chicks in their, 'Friday after work best'. It looked like most of the chicks were enjoying their much needed night out after their five day grind. A grind for most that was necessary to earn just enough money to live in this city of adventure – or misadventure. Most are looking for some type of action and some are looking for a man that might just be their soul mate. I, on the other hand, just wanted to find a pleasant looking but slightly aggressive woman who could hold her own while just having a casual or maybe even topical conversation.

And then from behind me, "You shouldn't be looking so hard. With those eyes so intense almost like a laser, you'll probably burn a hole right through the person you're so intent on and then only end up with a 'number three' or worse. I love your wet hair look did you forget your umbrella or do you just like to walk in the rain?"

I had just missed a real drenching but had caught some beginnings of the down pour which gave me the wet look and I was in such a hurry to find a spot and settle down for a local beer that I had ignored my rain dampened hair. And then I looked; Wow, I thought, where did this vision come from and how did I deserve this treat late on a Friday night. The gods are shining on me. I engulfed her like a tidal wave overtaking a beach hut; nothing was left to my imagination or rather my imagination sent my head on a trip, which left me with no possibilities unexplored, or that was what I thought. Her shiny brown hair fell slightly over one eye, as I had turned quickly to engulf every molecule of this vision. Slightly tanned breasts that were as natural and fully formed as any guy could ever want. Those deep blue eyes created for one purpose only, to suck you in like a whirlpool and never let you come back out. My response was slow and well thought out. "Huh, Oh like to walk in the rain? Sure, it gives me a feeling of cleansing. Lets me throw off all the troubled thoughts of the day and discard my daily sins! Now I feel fresh and ready for anything. I'm Hank, Hank Brayden. What's your name?"

"Cheryl," she answered.

Then I asked, "Can I get you a drink?"

She answered quickly with, "I would love a vodka tonic and you. What do you want or better what would you like?" Then as she used those deep blue eyes she asked, "Think you can handle 'a walk on the wild side'?" With a quizzical look I asked, "Is that a drink?"

"No, I mean are you ready for a night from out of your fantasies?"

Now I had to pause and think. I grew up in the seventies and eighties, so it should have hit me right then and there but over the years I had succumbed to the Blue Surge mentality. Where wars are won with power, power comes from wealth, wealth controls our every day functions, and those functions are manipulated by wither there is a war.

Work at the UN information center has made me one cynical dude. And now an evening on the wild side! "Why not?" I said. With the introductions over and as the waitress set our drinks down, I found myself just staring unbelieving into her hypnotic eyes.

We left after I had kicked down another house brew and Cheryl had finished her drink. "You know it's late and I've got a comfortable place over on the West Side. How about coming up to my place for a while? Do you like Sade?" She answered, yes; as she firmly put her arm around my waist while checking the degree of excess fat, then took my arm, and guided me to the front door. We were off for a 'walk on the wild side'.

Entering my Brownstone we encountered a couple politely wrapped in each other's arms and they seemed to give me a rather strange look. I thought I recognized the short guy as he stared at us, maybe I have seen both of them before, but their look at Cheryl gave me kind of a chill! In the apartment Cheryl went straight to the stereo and removed a cassette from her oversized purse. Putting the cassette into my new Bose stereo, she turned and asked if I had a bar or could I make something delicious to drink. But instead of Sade the tape started with Mariah Carey; and Cheryl danced sexily over to me, pressed her beautiful breast against me and purred, "May I have a 'Pussy Cat' on the rocks?"

I could not resist the beauty of her perfectly formed lips and the pressure of her breast on my chest. I leaned slightly more forward kissing her, at first gently, then I moved to her neck to find the sensitive part while my hand moved inside her blouse, then inside her very flimsy bra to touch her delicious breast. The warmth and curvature caused every inch of my body to grow stiff and especially bigger. As I was still kissing her neck and with my tongue gently licking the short hair at the nap of her neck she put her hand on my crotch to feel the stiffness that had arisen. I knew we were headed for bed and I realized that this would be one of my better weekends in the CITY. She could not wait to get to my bedroom so she began to slowly pull me to the floor in front of the sofa. I wanted to turn on the automatic gas fireplace so I gently rose up and stretched over to the switch. She took the opportunity to reach for my pant zipper and opened my belt at the same time. Off came my jeans, my shorts, and my socks. I really thought

I was in heaven or at least in another world! I had to take her thighs in my hands and bring her around until I could remove her panties. Raising her dress I first came across a sexy garter belt holding up black nylons. Unrolling her nylons I felt exceptionally smooth well-formed legs. Now I knew I was in heaven. Off came her panties and in the dim light of the fireplace I sawww….. What the hell is this? OH MY Lord she is a he! "Get up! What the hellll….. You're a she-he! Get out. Get out. Get dressed now. " It only took me seconds to get him his clothes and throw her-him out into the hall.

All I could hear her say was, "You wanted a walk on the wild side."

Sick, sick experience. I wanted to throw up. Then I felt I wanted to wash my whole body with Clorox. My worse weekend in the City had begun and had ended with memories I never wanted to recall, even to myself. Wow, and now here I was regurgitating that experience again. Lord have mercy!

Finally I cleared the crowds and could see the front doors. Well, this weekend will prove to be a real treat, renewed friendships, some partying, and maybe a few deep conversations. Finally pushing through the door I looked for the area marked limousine service. I needed to put a little elegance in my weekend. No limos in sight, so probably a couple minutes wait, I thought to myself. The mist was now a gentle rain and the air was fresh and pure smelling like wet concrete. I remembered when I was a little boy and had watched for the rain to finish so I could run outside just to smell the wet sidewalks.

The crisp and fresh air also had a rather heavy more unusual aroma. New York always had its own peculiar smells, sometimes the stench from drunks who urinate everywhere, sometimes from the trash and half eaten food in their dead food wrappers left by the locals who could care less, or sometimes from the homeless who leave their own odors behind no matter what.

But now as I was trying to enjoy the freshness of the wet night air the next limo appeared from across the waiting area and pulled up to the curb. I headed toward a new white Mercedes stretch just as Jerry Ness appeared walking with two small bags and yelling to the driver to open the trunk.

He caught my eye while handing off his bags to the driver. "Well hello again, it's Hank, correct. Do you need a ride into the city?"

As if this limo was his, what arrogance. "I was about to say the same thing to you. We can both share it; I'm headed to my apartment on the West Side."

"Sure", he said, "I don't mind letting the government pick up the tab. I'll never get back all the money they owe me for the miss-use of my tax dollars anyway."

"I'm paying this bill?" I questioned under my breath, hoping he would hear but not wanting a confrontation. As the limo pulled away from the airport the rain seemed to be turning into snow. Just that quickly the weather was changing.

Gliding along in the comfort of thousand dollar leather seats I drifted off into thoughts about the coming few weeks I was supposed to spend at the main offices at the UN. They had gathered a small pallet of information I was going to have to categorize and re-deploy to the proper departments in charge. At least on this trip I was going to be able to spend some time with Dad, sis, and Grandma. My mother was not with us anymore. Maybe we would get a little hunting arranged in up state NY or in western Connecticut. I'll need to pull him out of his offices at UBC. I guess he's been executive VP now for 15 years, ever since I graduated from NYU. He really loves the broadcasting business.

Then Jerry piped up, "Driver you can take me to the corner of 55th and Eight Avenue and then you can take Hank over to the Westside." Jerry seemed to want to meet with me as he continued to talk in that very robust voice. "Before we get to Manhattan let me give you my card, Hank. Maybe we can grab a little lunch down by the UN while you're in town? Since you wanted to read up on the articles in those magazines I suppose you have an interest in the problems we are having around the world. I can brief you on all the things going on in the hot spots with most of the terrorist organizations and maybe we can compare notes on what the UN thinks about the coming disasters. I only get the input from our com-padres in Washington. And that's always slanted. Either tainted because of politics, or of our president's foul-ups or from the possibility of some foreign country being embarrassed. Sometimes I think the information disseminated by our Agencies, which are set up to guide and protect us, is continuously manipulated. Hank we are living in very strange times. The truth is changed into lies and lies are purported to be the truth."

The temperature seem to have dropped and my mind left Jerry on his soap box as I watched the little flakes of snow start to fall on the windshield of our limousine; it glistened from the moving headlights of the passing cars and I could feel myself slip into the nostalgia of the coming of winter.

We had gone over the bridge and entered the city and were on Avenue of the Americas when Jerry piped up, "Driver, turn on to 55th just let me out in front of the building there on the right at the corner of Eight Avenue after you pass through the light." Jerry seemed in a hurry as he continued, "This is perfect, listen Hank, 'How does lunch on, let's say Tuesday sound', OK?"

I tried to respond with an upbeat "Sure", but it was hard, Jerry just was not my favorite type. Too forceful or I guess too pushy.

"Here", he cracked, "you have my card let me have one of yours. I hope the government saved enough money to buy you cards."

"Huh, oh yes of course, I've got one in me ID pouch, here."

He went on, "I'll call you Tuesday morning so we can pick a convenient spot. Will you be in by 9:30 or so?"

I answered loud and committed, "Sounds fine, I'll be at the number under NY", I thought he would be impressed with a firm answer.

It was almost 9:45 and the building Jerry headed toward was fully lit up from top to bottom; a real bee-hive of activity. I guess this is the only city outside of Tokyo or maybe Honk Kong that really lives twenty-four hours per day and has no sleep. "Driver, would you please take me to 303 West 85th Street? Thanks." Opening my cell phone I dialed Dad's apartment to see if ... "Hello, Dad its Hank. I'm almost to my brownstone here in the city; I thought I'd check to see if you were in."

"How do you turn this stereo down? Which panel?"

"No Dad I'm talking to the limo driver."

"Got it, thanks."

"Now look, I'm probably here for at least one month and if the work load is what I think it is going to be I'll be here through Christmas. So let's spend some time together this time, OK? All right we can have diner Monday night at the Seasons and see what's up for the coming weeks."

"There's my place ahead by that green Expedition, just park there in the street, I don't have any bags to get, how much?"

"Dad I've got to run, I'm at my doorstep so we'll talk tomorrow."

AS I entered my flat I left my shoes at the tiled entry to keep the snowflakes off of the carpet. Looking at the hall clock I realized I was going to be late to meet my friends so I dropped my briefcase, went to the bedroom and slipped on some jeans and a sweater then put my shoes back on and went out to hail a cab. "Taxi! Taxi! Taxi.... could you please take me to Oliver's in the village?"

The snowfall had increased and the temperature was dropping so it felt good to get inside. I headed straight for the bar to get a White Label and soda, as I heard a familiar and pleasant voice with a slight Asian accent calling my name. Of course it was Tiama. That voice bouncing off the walls here at Oliver's was like being here nine years ago. We had been a real happening after graduation and all the way through my years at George Town until I joined the government and started traveling. Tiama took a job with Brada at The Journal and later I heard the two of them had moved into a reconditioned loft around 32nd street. I couldn't blame her. I had never given her any kind of a commitment or even a glimmer of hope that we might have a future. She had always been my bubbly Filipino girl with the big round eyes and straight black hair almost like a Keene painting. Full of life, always smiling and never stopping in her quest to make friends with everyone. I remember the unprecedented amount of time our particular group of friends spent at the long table right between the large window looking at the small park next door and the oversized fireplace across from the bar. Many nights we closed the bar and Tiama with her Asian accent would ask, 'Hank you finished? You got world politics tomorrow at 7:45 or psychology of world leaders or law in today's world environment or whatever'. She would take me out of the bar and help me to my three room flat in the village. Boy those are some great memories.

"Hank, it's me Tiama, we're sitting over by the window."

"Tiama! It's great to see you. How have you been? It looks like the City is still agreeing with you. You must have spent the entire summer running, you're so trim and the sweater looks ...well it just looks and looks." I can remember how she complimented the look of every fabric ever made, even the cotton in her sweats. Tiama always dressed conservatively stylish but still sexy!

"Where is everybody? I don't see anybody else here!"

"Ok listen, Saja is running late and do you remember Ghassem? It's no matter he can't be here tonight either, but Alicia and her husband Howard said they would be here around 10:30. Brada is in the 'john' and he said that Cal Mason and Robbi Assaid would be here any minute. Hank! Give me a big hug and a kiss. I haven't seen you for, well about two and half years."

Oh my! I had forgotten how good she felt in my arms and her lips firm yet tender and moist. I wanted her to enjoy this as much as I. I placed my hand gently under her hair and held her neck guiding her lips up against mine at a slight angle so that we could enjoy the movement of lips on lips. I hugged her firmly with my right arm and felt every curvature of her body. She responded as if we had never been apart, like this was nine years ago. I let my imagination play quick mind games that this weekend might bring us together again.

"Hank, you move right in, don't you? So you've heard that Tiama and I are back to just good friends." I was caught off guard with Brada's return from the 'john' and yet I was hanging on to those last words 'just good friends'. He continued, "Old buddy, how nice to see you. This being our first reunion I hope we can get in some enjoyable times together again." Brada seemed overly friendly, almost mushy. I was a little confused because of those heated and passionate arguments we use to have during university days. Brada went on, "You know those after class discussions we had right here usually got the gray matter boiling over, but let me tell you with all of the input about politics, economics and social problems; I've been able to call on a lot of our different philosophical ideas in my work around the world and in organizing and planning the expansion of Hydro-electric power programs for third world countries." He turned facing towards the window, "Here we have the old table reserved let's sit down."

I casually laid my trench coat over the end chair and slid in next to Tiama dragging my half-empty glass with me. "Is anybody else drinking or are you going to eat or what?"

"Both," Tiama said motioning to the waiter, "I think I'll start with a Bailey's and coffee and let's see, bring an appetizer platter." Brada asked for Vodka and OJ and I just asked for a repeat.

"Well my friend, do you still have time to run the Worldwide Journal on Hydro Electric Power and yet travel to all the various projects?" I really wondered what he had been doing.

"Hank, I still do but I'm not the editor anymore. I have to travel too much. It all started last year so we put a brilliant political science and journalist major in as editor. He's one of our old classmates. Do you remember Yassir Jaziri? He was the roommate with Robbi our last year. And maybe you remember Saja; he is director of our Foreign Relations department."

"Sure!" I don't think anyone could ever forget Yassir. His arrogance and crude manipulation of personal relationships while not ignoring his intolerable body odor absolutely left a very long lasting memory. "I remember him and how he always thought his ideas carried more validity then any of the rest of us, except maybe yours Brada." Saja who had entered a minute or two earlier stood next to Brada as Hank answered, "And Saja I remember you were in the middle of some of those intellectual interludes."

Brada began explaining why he had been appointed as the editor of his highly recognized journal. Rambling on, he wanted us to know that Yassir had changed a lot and took on a much more realistic view of world happenings. Telling the story of Yassir's change was like asking us to accept that the Crusades were a myth. He continued to tell us about his marriage, his family, his connection to the inter circles at the Department of Commerce. However my mind was not into the remaking of Yassir. No, I could hear Brada, but as I stared through him I disappeared back in time, into some of our more heated conversations involving many controversial subjects that had at times erupted into quite emotional scenes.

REMEMBERING - One day in April 1983.
On a late afternoon after classes we had all met at Oliver"s to discuss the up coming test on Friday and to go over political views since most of the grade would be based of essay questions.

HANK – "Hey Brada, what did you think of that last lecture on human suffering in Ghana?"

BRADA – "The government has been corrupted for years by the wealth discovered in their gold mines. The foreign intervention both politically and economically allowed by the many different leaders and the wholesale sell out for money to the international corporations caused the bondage and starvation of the people. The disjointed and down trodden populace couldn't do anything while the government elite stole the mineral wealth of the country that really belonged to the people of Ghana."

HANK – "Yes, that's been a proven fact but why blame everything on the multinationals? What about the responsibility of the native Ghana leaders to honor and protect their nation and the people. What about the advancement of many other countries economically with the exportation and distribution of their gold?"

BRADA – "That's what I am always talking about! The gold brought riches to the country and it corrupted leaders that could have advanced their nation and raised the living standard for the people. But, they chose to succumb to the ways of the West and fall into personal greed and material cravings. They became errand boys of satan as Mohammed taught so brilliantly in the Qur'an."

HANK – "OH! Back to the West is the evil servant of the devil; I'm tired of that argument! It is not realistic and it is too idealistic to think that money does not corrupt. Look at what happened in Iran with the Shah or the stealing of billions from the people of Saudi Arabia by the Prince. You can not be idealistic when the Muslims are as corrupt as anyone."

BRADA – "You know Hank, you are lost! We live by a different code and for a different power. When it comes to what to accept ethically we differ greatly, you live in what you call a practical world and we live by the tenants of allah."

AND REMEMBERING – Our last evening before graduation May 1985. Eight of us were finished with the finals and preparing for graduation, so a celebration at Oliver's was in store for the night or until no one could walk. Our conversations were primarily on what we would do with our summer and then where we intended to go with our own chosen fields.

Hank had decided to go on to school at Georgetown University.

Brada would start out as a consultant in the design of Hydro-Electric Power Plants.

Tiama decided to just travel for a while.

Ghassem had already landed a job in the city at UBC where Hank's father was the National Production Manager.

Saja wanted to see what Brada was going to do as he may want to work with his cousin.

Alicia just wanted to spend her time with her husband to be, Howard Slates, and find a nice home in Connecticut to settle into.

Robbi knew he would stay in New York for the summer and continue his prowling of the Discos.

Yassir on the other hand had decided to go to visit friends in Iran and possibly study under a Muslim cleric for two years.

The scotch had gone to my head that night and I remember I was a little melancholy as I said a short farewell. "I really have enjoyed the past years at NYU and the interaction we have had with each other. No question we have each learned a lot about the differences in our backgrounds and our personal philosophies. I hope we stay in contact no matter how far away we may become separated as our careers take us to places as yet unknown. And I hope only the best for each of you, my friends."

"Hank, you have always been kind of a leader even though you have a very quiet nature," Tiama said with slightly watery eyes, "and I know we will all miss each other, especially you."

We had all had a number of drinks and with the stress and pressure of the finals over the alcohol was beginning to take different effects on all of us. Alicia was hanging on Robbi and running her hands through his thick black hair. Although, I could not see why since Howard her fiancée was so much more than Robbi. Ghassem had been talking to Saja at the end of the table about anything but school since their eyes were continually glancing at two young girls who were sitting at the bar. But now suddenly the conversation went back to our personal thoughts about these past year's studies. Saja spoke first!

SAJA – "Well from my ideas of the pass year, I really believe that the classes with Cal on 'Geo-economic Relationships for Political Dominance', has been very enlightening". Cal Mason, a New York attorney dealing with multinational clients, was our professor for two of the political science courses four of us had finished together and I had planned to maintain contact with him after I enrolled at Georgetown. Saja went on, "He gave me a lot of insight into how the western world approaches business and politics. I mean that capitalism is first among importance and then politics which is primarily controlled by capitalism and finally individual economics which allows the have-nots to suffer in their poverty."

HANK – "What are you talking about? There is more suffering in third world countries than anywhere else in the world. A major portion of the Latin countries are desperately poor and 90% of the Arabic world is beyond destitute. They especially are down trodden and kept in bondage with their dependence on tribal leaders or over-lording clerics for everything."

BRADA – "You know that both of you have a point but you are leaving out the one important element that influences all societies and that is, their beliefs and religious convictions. This more than money or politics will influence the people and the ultimate direction of their society and even the forces behind the controlling government. As an example as you are fully aware, a society such as America is influenced by the Judeo-Christian establishment. This directs the culture towards capitalism with the driving force being both money and greed all operating under the guise of love your brother while all the time everyone is only grabbing, grabbing, grabbing and exploiting, exploiting, exploiting to have more than the other fellow. This country is driven by the evil of personal desires and wants."

HANK – "Well, at least we have an open and free society where everyone can have the hope of some sort of achievement. In the eastern societies everyone suffers under some despot like Kadafi or Saddum Hussein or powerful clerics or.... and I could go on and on. Just look at the Arab world and you will see lack of personal freedom and total intolerance."

YASSIR– "Hank, you do not even understand the Arab world as all of our discussions over the past two years have shown. READ THE QUR'AN, and then we can talk about differences. The Muslim faith according to allah shows us to love our brother and to have charity towards each other and to be honest and true to our brothers. The western world's philosophy is to compete and out do each other and to get as much as you can regardless of the consequences. Satan has infiltrated all of your thoughts, intentions and plans. Look at Hollywood, the Music industry, and the most obtrusive industry, pornography. Slowly, with out you noticing it, you are becoming more perverted and more corrupt. The Jews and their incessant desire for money and business are destroying America and the rest of the Western world. There is no right or wrong, the only right is MONEY!"

TIAMA – "Wait a minute, why are you coming off with discrimination and hitting on the Jews. Look at what the Eastern World is doing with their oil. As a child I can remember in the mid seventies the oil pinch or shortage, what ever they called it, that shot prices up from $11.00 a barrel to more than $50.00 a barrel. That is over five hundred percent increase in one year and where did all of that greed go? Billions were going right into the pockets of the kings, princes, and heads of state of the oil producing countries and not to the poor populace in those countries."

ROBBI – "I for one know that is not exactly true. My family is related to the Royal Family in Saudi Arabia and what happened back in the seventies is very important to understand. For decades the large oil conglomerates from England, The Netherlands, and America sucked out oil from us and paid a faction of what it was worth. There is no question that was the greed of the western companies that took advantage of all of us. All we did was declare independence from the West and took control of what was our sovereignty in the first place. Now we are stretching our arms and flexing our monetary mussels. I can guarantee you that our Royal Family, while they all live very well, they are taking care of the people of our country and sharing the rewards of the oil income. We believe that one has to take control and administer the operation and distribution of such wealth and allah has chosen the princes to do that."

HANK – "Wow, just Wow! This is a celebration for all of us so let's lighten up and have a toast to each of our personal journeys after tonight."

"Hey, Hey, heirr's to the futre." And with that Alicia lifted her glass to begin the toast and being a little toasted herself, fell back into Robbi's arms.

I remembered my closing thoughts that night were that even though it had been a celebration of graduation it had been the birth of a different atmosphere over each of our relationships that in the future would come to affect us all.

Sitting next to Tiama, my stare had gone to the fire in Oliver's huge fireplace as I reflected on the past and I had become mesmerized by the dancing flames.

"Hank! Hank! Come back to us. It's Alicia. Howard and I have arrived. Say hello or something."

"Hey I'm sorry; my thoughts were just back in time to other times we had spent together at this table during our last year at school. I see that Saja and Yassir got back too. How is everyone?"

Saja looked at me saying "Got back? We're okay; it was just you that seemed to be a little fuzzy. We're glad we didn't need to call 9-1-1. Just kidding. How about a fresh drink Hank and we are talking about getting some more horsd'oeuvres? Come on everybody say yes!" "Yes!" "Yes!" "Yes!" "Yes!" "Yes!" "Yes!" It was unanimous. Saja called the waiter and ordered a combo fish platter and some chips and salsa. "Alright, you remembered our usual. Pointing his finger, Saja went around the table, "The drinks are on.. on… on Alicia."

That took her away from Howard for just a moment, "On no, we'll flip for it."

As the evening became more relaxed I stopped to remind everyone. "Hey, Listen up! The dinner for tomorrow night is scheduled at 8:00pm and they expect around one hundred seventy attendees so don't be late. I tried to set up an excursion in the bay to tour the Statue of Liberty and then have a brunch on Staten Island on Sunday around 10:00am. So it is a go and set for any of you that want to go. It should be a nice boat ride and a fun time. I have never done that trip but people say the views of the city are great from there. You can see the end of Manhattan with Wall Street, the World Trade Center towers, most of the taller buildings, and way up the Hudson. Let me know the count before we go home and I'll call in the reservations tomorrow."

CHAPTER TWO

FLASH BACK To August, 1990 - Rio de Janeiro, Brazil

Jonathan al-Aziz, the uncle of Yassir al-Jazziri, could see the Mercedes dealer down the street from the restaurant where he was enjoying his favorite lunch – Camerones con Arroz y Dorado Parilla, South American style. He had been in Rio for one month on this trip and spent time arranging for his opening of the boat factory in Belem. All of the local Muslim leaders had been contacted so he had brothers to work with while completing the factory. So now working in Brazil for allah and playing in the local night life was just short of paradise.

After lunch he strolled down the Ave Pres Vargas and over to the Mercedes dealer. Once inside the dealership he looked for a young inexperienced salesperson. Knowing that he was to always present himself as a wealthy business man from Jordan, he began a tight fisted negotiation for two new 450 SEL's, one in Black and the other one in Silver for himself. After writing a check for both he wanted to see the manager to arrange to have both cars delivered to his villa each completely filled with fuel.

The taxi driver dropped Jonathan off at his villa which was set back from the street approximately fifty meters and had a seven foot dark green wrought iron security fence across the front and guard box at the gated entrance. Jonathan had not yet selected a guard from one of the Muslim cells so the guard box was empty. He inputted the security code to open the gate, paid the taxi and headed up the slightly inclined floral lined walk to the villa's eight foot high solid mahogany doors. Once inside he went straight for the telephone

"Hello operator, this is Jonathan al-Aziz and I want to make a person to person call to Yassir al-Jazziri in New York City in the United States, please. The number is 202-717-1900."

Click, click. "Are you still there operator?"
   Click, click, click. "Sir I am trying to get your party now please wait."
   "This is the New York operator, who did you want again?"
   Speaking over the operator, Jonathan loudly repeated the name, "I want to speak to a Yassir al-Jazziri." The Rio de Janeiro operator quipped back, "Sir they are trying to complete the call, tranquillo."

"Hello, this is… crackle, crackle….speaking," Jonathan waited for the line to clear, "Hello, Yassir?"
   "Yes is that you uncle? Are you calling from Brazil?"
   "Yes, and I want you to know that we are settled in here and have a marvelous villa overlooking the ocean and beach. Of course the weather is marvelous and our view, well you will see. We have set up our manufacturing plant in Belem on the docks such as they are and should start manufacturing boats for delivery by next year. I want you to come down and help me through the massive paper work necessary for exportation to the States. Abu Eisa al-Hindi left here last week after helping to set up the factory operation."

Abu was born in California and spoke four languages fluently, English, French, Farsi, and Arabic. Being a United States citizen gave him more traveling freedom then most of the leaders in Usama's network and especially the in and out movement through the States. He always traveled to London where he kept a plush apartment just outside of the Soho district. He made it his permanent home which provided a perfect place to be his center of operations. His life there was a U.S. business man that did factoring of large international trade contracts. When flying he was careful to use United Airlines in and out of the States and Kuwaiti Air when flying to Middle Eastern countries. He had passports from Iran, Yemen, and Syria which he used for travel out side of the States. That way his US passport was always clean. No one would put him on a watch list. Because Adu had such freedom in traveling he became the confident of Usama and the main money man and administrator of the financial holdings of the al-Qaeda organization in the West. Later on he would be directed by Dr. Zawahiri to carry out surveillance of targets in the States for future destruction and to case out in detail each targeted location with photos, diagrams, maps and any pertinent descriptions.

"Yassir, I want you to know that it was Abu that suggested that your help would be instrumental in the success of this project."

"When were you thinking I should be there and how long will it take to complete all necessary arrangements? I will need to leave WWJHEP for a time and then you know that I have planned to go to Iraq to study under cleric Syed Ahmed Bukhan. I want to spend maybe two years there."

"Yassir, as you remember we set up operation 'ball buster' with plans to get 2,000 boats into the U.S. by 2001 and we still must set up a dealership in Miami. Will you be able to spend a year here and then work on the dealership in Miami the following year? That would mean that you could go to Iraq for studies in the fall of 1992 or no later than the first of 1993. We have the bigger plan cast and the money has already been deposited here in Brazil from our brothers. There is twenty five million here already."

"Okay, I will need to tell Brada of our plans and I can finish up all of my things there and do all of my traveling out of Brazil. I'll prepay the rent on my apartment for the next two years so that others that are coming can use it. I'll meet Brada tomorrow to tell him and I will leave in 30 days. Jonathan, how many cells are we in Brazil?"

Jonathan thought for a minute and than responded, "A total of forty one but they are not all complete."

Yassir responded with, "In the name of allah we pray for our success, Good By uncle."

FLASH BACK To October, 1992

Miami, Florida

Jonathan's boat dealership, 'Florida Flash Boats', was finished by Yassir in September 1992 right on Biscayne Bay and the Groupo Rizzo had already brought in fifty eight boats. Yassir had used all of his influence from friends he had made at NYU and those government officials he had met at the State Department while coordinating meetings with the

Ministers of Interior from WWJHEP's client countries to get the import approval for the high speed thunder boats Groupo Rizzo was manufacturing in Brazil. He was quite talented in meeting with all types of people and getting things done. He had always dressed classy in a casual way and with his dark complexion and slightly graying black curly hair he presented a demeanor of fine breeding. He had learned to overcome his arrogance and he had become quite personable and offered an especially friendly manner when first meeting someone. He had also learned something about personal hygiene and Brut after shave so he smothered his body odor.

Yassir drove up in his rented white corvette, got out and flicked out a cigarette from a silver case for himself and Jonathan who was coming around from behind an ebony and fire red 'V' hull twin engine Monster boat which was the top of their line thunder boat. As Yassir lit up his cigarette Jonathan waved off his offer and pulled out a cigar.... "Well it looks like we have the first year of our plan right on schedule." Jonathan took a long puff on his Cohiba and added, "Not only are we on schedule but we already have forty six of the 'Special Boats' here in stock. Of course they are all sold to our brothers for future delivery and listen to this, I have been contacted by the local DEA people that they want to test our boats against what they are currently running for speed and maneuverability. We will win in speed and we have a much lower sticker price so I know we will soon be a provider to the Department of Drug Enforcement. This will give us a great opportunity to build a camouflage around our operation. We have had no problems getting through customs. They tore down our first shipment and actually took two of our boats apart to the hull. Of course they are looking for the possibility of drug smuggling, that's a laugh. Since the forth shipment it has been quite simple to go through customs. Now they just do their dog sniffing and the x-ray bit and the boats are cleared."

As Yassir was quickly looking from one side to the other and staring in detail at the dealership – Jonathan assured him by saying, "Don't worry no one can see us through the tall cypress trees and no one can hear us since I have the building scanned every week for bugs. We are safe!"

"Are we? Some of their ultra sensitive microphones can hear at a thousand feet."

"Yes we know, that is why you hear that lower humming noise. It is not machinery in the building but a sound generator that varies the pitch every two seconds to jam any listening devices. We are safe."

Yassir and Jonathan went inside to say hello to the two salesmen who were Miami natives and knew the boat business up and down and back again. The inside showroom was top grade with one smaller boat on the floor and an engine display rack along side. It was completely tricked out fully chromed and it sported a high compression blower. The feeling inside the showroom was money and money was what it took to buy the big boats. Jess said hello to Yassir who had not been around for a while and offered he and Jonathan and a coffee. Extra special espresso just the way they both liked it. Just then the phone rang and Phil the other salesman answered it. "Hello, this is Monster boats, by Florida Flash Boats, may I help you? Oh yes he is right here. Jon it is for you, a long distance call".

"Thanks I'll go to my office. Come on," as he beckoned to Yassir.
"Hello!," Jonathan waited.
"Hello, this is Saja al-Hasi. I would like to talk to Jonathan Aziz."
"This is Jonathan."
"I was told that I might find my cousin Brada or Yassir there."
A pause by Jonathan and then he looked at Yassir, "There is a Saja al-Hasi on the phone asking for you or a Brada!"
"Oh yes, I told you about Saja who went to NYU with Brada and I. He and Brada are like blood brothers to me. Saja is on an excursion in Minnesota and North Dakota looking at old Indian trails. Let me talk to him. Is this line secure? Never mind I will use my cell phone." He took the phone from Jonathan. "Saja call me on the outer extension." Everyone in the top leadership knew that 'outer extension' was always their cell phone. And they all changed cell phones each month or when they felt their security had been breached.

Soon Yassir's cell phone rang and he was talking to Saja in Arabic. All calls between Muslim brothers were required to be in Arabic depending on the subject matter of the calls. Saja and Brada were both well along in the completion of phase one of the master plan and they both had superior cells in operation. Saja wanted to bring Yassir up to speed on their adventure into the northern states. "Yassir, it is just as Abu had told us; there are many trails up here that lead from Canada right into the States and for our people to get into Canada is easier than any other place on earth. It is a real joke. I believe we can have all of our faithful brothers here by our target date."

Yassir replied with a smiling type grin, "I knew we would be successful, praise allah. I want to make sure you put the information on the correct Web site on the internet, complete with maps and trail locations. Give our travelers any informative help they might need to complete their journey and an address across the border they can go to upon arrival. Leave nothing out! You know a new Web site is created every so often for security purposes so ask Brada to find out when the next web address change will happen. Than put the information on that new site and rotate it every week to a new site. The site addresses will always be from UAE until notified differently. We should all meet in New York before I go to Iraq. 'Praise Hamas', 'Praise Hezbollah', 'Praise al-Qaeda' and let allah guide you."

As Jonathan was taking out his prayer rug, Yassir had a deep serious look on his face. He asked about the timing on boat deliveries. Leaning back in Jonathan's overstuffed desk chair he queried, "Abu Eisa will want to know our schedule so when I get back to New York I want to tell our confidants of our success. When will we have all of the eight hundred 'Special Boats' here and distributed to our brothers?"

"The last boats will be here no later than fall of 2000 and I will have completed 'Operation Ball Buster' to the glory of allah." And with that Jonathan finished opening the prayer rugs and handed one to Yassir, "It is almost two o'clock; here is an extra prayer rug, let us give all thanks to Allah."

After prayer Jonathan escorted Yassir to his corvette. Yassir gave his uncle a kiss on the cheek as he was leaving and confirmed his return to New York, "Dear uncle I will leave tomorrow for New York and ask all of our brothers for prayers to allah that your venture is completed before 2001."

"Good bye!"

FLASHBACK to July 1997 - New York City

Yassir stepped off of the Concord from London with only a small computer case. Except for three quick trips he had been over seas for almost five years studying the teachings of the most religious clerics in Syria,

Iraq, and Iran while still working with Brada at the journal. He had spent most of his time studying in his home country of Iran. His views of the Islamic future for the world had been changed and most passionately embossed on his heart and into his thinking. He truly had gained a better understanding about Hadith and could see why the Muslim people had such a peace in their spiritual lives no matter how they had to endure their current existence. He fervently wanted to work for the Muslim movement and the expansion of Islam to all nations and to crush the 'serpent leader' of the western world and it's manipulation of the people. All people must be made to understand the teachings of Mohammed the Great. Although his thoughts raged in his mind; his joy and enthusiasm shined on his face. He was on a mission for allah and he knew he had to be totally dedicated to his part in the work to eliminate all infidels.

Abu was at the waiting area to meet him and they greeted each other with a traditional kiss and moved off down the walkways towards the front of the terminal where Brada and Saja were waiting in a taxi at the taxi zone. They had a Muslim brother as taxi director and he protected their position.

Yassir embraced his brothers, "Greetings to my friends. How have you been?"

"Between work and traveling I have been enjoying the city and Saja has just been traveling with our motor home. Picking up all of our friends as they come in from Canada and taking them to their various cell assignments and going on surveillance trips. We have it parked at our meeting hall across the river in Newark and we take it out on our reconnaissance trips as we add to our strategic mapping. We have the hall rented for a few years to hold our Saturday night meetings but tonight we are having a special gathering with the ten Eastern regional leaders and some of our local cell leaders to learn more about the growth of our cause and the accomplishments of our brothers overseas. And we do not have to be concerned tonight because the hall is being used for a wedding party with banners out front so we will not be conspicuous."

The women entered into a separate room at the rear of the hall to prepare a small meal for the husbands after their meeting. This was a very old VFW hall that was only big enough for sixty people. Off of the beaten path and no longer a VFW facility it was used only about once a month. "In the name of allah we are blessed with the al-Salawaat of Mohammed the Prophet." Abu went on, "We are blessed that Yassir returns with news from our home lands."

Yassir stood as he began talking and expounding on the news. "We grow stronger every year. The brothers take as many wives as are allowed and our population is growing everywhere. We now have 1290 mosques in this country and we have the money to build a new Mosque here in Newark. Our numbers are growing in France and England and by the year 2000 we will have more Mosques in England than all of the other churches there. The AMAL is sending us faithful servants of allah to help build our cells here and to be leaders in the uprising. The al-Qassan Brigades are gaining strength and will be offering us help when we call on them."

Abu took over to talk about the growth in America. "My brothers, Islam is growing everywhere and in this country we have seen the black community continue its conversion to embrace the teachings of the Qur'an and our Prophets. Brother Farrakhan is leading the way for Haq to be spread among his people. We are providing hundreds of thousands of potential Mu'mins the ways of the Muslim and the power of the Qur'an to change people's lives through the many web sites we are building. Our leaders have the long term Miraj for the world to accept the Shariah. But we must be united and cautious because the Dajin would like to break us down and have us exposed as a threat to the evil western ways. Be strong in your commitment because as allah revealed to Mohammed 'the greater good will defeat the greater evil'. Soon we will have web sites that will provide us instructions for our individual battles against the serpent. We will change the address every month or so to keep it secret and you will all be informed of the new internet address every time we change it. We will also be running a www. org web site with continual misinformation to mislead the government agencies on any surveillance and investigations of our people. Remember to stay secure and keep a low profile. In the name of allah, peace be with you."

CHAPTER THREE

Sunday November 10, 2000

I arose on Sunday wondering just what had I eaten last night at the dinner. It had been a large turn out of around 160 alumni and everything seemed to go well, but I was feeling slightly nauseated with what felt like a big wad of bread and pasta in my stomach. Not sure if I would make the cruise around the bay I decided to walk over to Central Park for a very slow jog. While there, it came to me that I should call Dad again about our getting together. I had cut him short on Friday night and wanted to make the plans to get on with a hunting trip. I stopped at a bench near the Café in the Park and dialed up his number on my cell phone.

"Hello, is that you Caroline? How have you been? This is Hank; no I have not been back for long, didn't Dad mention that I was probably going to be here for awhile? This is the weekend of our reunion and then I will be staying to work at my office here for a month or so, is Dad around? OK, I'll see you in a week or two. Dad and I are planning a hunting trip around Thanksgiving so we'll surely have dinner there. Thanks, I'll wait."

"Hello, Hank?"

"Hi Dad, I was jogging in the park and remember I had cut you short the other night so I'm glad I caught you at home. Caroline sounds great. I can't wait to see her. I told her I was counting on Thanksgiving at home with you, her and Grandma. We haven't all done Thanksgiving together since Mom was laid to rest and I really want to be together this year."

"Me too son."

"OK Dad, I hope we can get that hunting trip in for sure?" Dad sounded tired and I knew he needed some time off so I wanted to find out about work. "I guess the EVP of network production has had you stretched with the elections and all. Didn't you also go to Yemen to co-ordinate the TV coverage of the Cole bombing?"

With a deep breath he answered, "Yes Hank and we are working on a special before Thanksgiving about this silly dangling Chad thing and election fraud in Florida. As you know we will be up in the air about this election for some time and some are saying it will go to the Supreme Court. The Democrats are going to be Bulldogs about this and we really have other bigger problems."

I had to break in, "Well thanks Dad but I was just trying to set up our hunting trip either a couple of days before or after Thanksgiving. I need to work out a schedule at my office at the UN because they have given me volumes of data to sift through this next month and then pre-pare a 'UN's View on Terrorism' report to go to the CIA. So how does it look for hunting?"

"Can I call you on Tuesday and let's see how the timing is? Do you have you cell phone here in New York?"

"Dad, come on now you know I am required to carry that with me at all times. Have some more coffee. I'll talk with you on Tuesday. Relax to-day; it's your time to enjoy that soothing environment in the country."

"OH sure, sure; Goodbye."

Dad and Caroline still live at the family farm on 20 acres in Westchester County where the Brayden's had lived for four generations. The house had been remodeled about twelve years ago but the basic exterior of the two story house remained pretty much the same. The hundred year old rock wall which was hand laid surrounded the front where an old iron gate that still worked gave access to the narrow driveway. It continued down the side enclosing about 3 acres around the house. As a kid I re-member running down the full length of the wall, about 500 feet and then jumping into a large hay pile Dad kept there for our two horses. The property was covered with old oak trees that provided us with our winter firewood. My memory of the aroma of burning oak in the cold fall and winter air has never gone away. I could still smell the smoke as I began to finish my jog. I stopped for a coffee and went to my apartment to shower and change. Jeans and a blue hooded sweat shirt was what the weather called for and I grabbed a wind breaker just in case.

"TAXI... TAXI", I was able to see one at the corner and on Sunday that's rather rare. It was chilly and as the diver swung the cab around there was a lot of whitish fumes coming out from the exhaust. Probably colder than I had guessed and that means a cold boat ride. "Good morning, I want to go to the pier to catch the Statue of Liberty Excursion boat". Not even a grunt! My luck, some non talking person from some foreign country and I hope he knows where the pier is. "You know where you are going?" Just a shake of the head.

Twenty minutes later I am there and late as usual. I could see Alicia, Howard, Robbi, Ghassem, Yassir, and Saja waiting with some kind of warm drink in their hands but no Tiama and no Brada. "Are the others coming?" I looked all around at the other folks waiting for the excursion boat but didn't recognize anyone else. The boat was three decks high and had a bright white hull with four large red lines running from the bow to the stern. Most of the top two decks were open but on the lower level there was an enclosed area with all glass walls for viewing and on this day that is where I was going. I mentioned my idea to the others and we all went through the doors into the enclosed area.

Alicia finally answered, "No, and I called them but I did not get any answer. So we are the whole party."

Our little group was prepaid and we quickly went to the front and found a table and seven chairs. As we sat down I thought that it was strange that it was Brada and Tiama that were no shows. And I thought that it was over for them. Oh well I'm here and it's time for a warm drink. "I'm going to order something, does anyone want a warm drink or just some booze?"

I really did not want to get into any heavy conversations so I turned to Howard to get a little ice breaking done. Even though we had all known each other for some time at different occasions I have noticed that my Arabic friends where often quiet or you could say tight lipped. "Howard, when are you and Alicia going to have that first baby?"

"There is something wrong here", Alicia pronounced! "How would you know to ask that? I am in my second month and we wanted to wait to tell all of our friends. That's very physic Hank. Howard has been traveling so much that we were waiting and waiting. He's home for a while and so we did it."

As I was saying congratulations the waitress came with some warm drinks and said that our lunch was already prearranged. "Would you all like your lunch now at the same time?" Everyone said yes and she scurried off to go down on the tiny elevator to the galley.

A wonderful lobster bisque and Cobb salad had been our lunch and after lunch Howard, Saja and Ghassem entered into some kind of conversation over computer viruses so I went out on the deck to enjoy the sunshine. It was already 2:00 pm and the wind had died down as it usually does around mid afternoon. We had all decided not to stop off at Staten Island so we were circling the statue. To be close and look way up at her gives you a chill, a chill of pride to be an American. I closed my eyes to relax and meditated on what a wonderful place to live; such opportunity, such freedom, such peace. With so much terrorism going on around the world I am glad I was born an American. As I mused about that and the latest threat to us from Iran over our ties to Israel, Yassir appeared from inside the enclosed deck.

Yassir approached and sat down on the seat that stretched across the bow and asked, "Are you resting or meditating"?

"Well, quite frankly I was thinking about how glad I am to be an American and thanking God that I was born here". Then looking straight at him I continued, "Not to paint you in any special light I am just talking about myself." He kind of gave me an 'I don't believe you' look and I could tell he was in the mood to talk so I just listened.

"Yes you have a powerful country and many of the worldly luxuries, but so much of the time I see everyone rushing here and rushing there, under so much stress, and with out any real peace in their faces. I imagine you would agree it is obvious. I spent a lot of time over the past ten years as foreign relations officer for the journal traveling in many countries. And I was allowed some time off by Brada and dedicated myself to studying under a number of Islamic clerics. You know what I found. A reinforcement of Truth, the truth of allah that puts you at peace even though you may be the lowest person in your country or in your village. On the other hand you are not free; you are prisoners of wealth and materialism. Look around, the material ways of this country are a destroyer; but they have not taken over the minds of those of us who have 'submitted'. Dedication to allah is a submission to live in his peace and his will."

"You know, I don't want to get into a religious discussion today and why did you come here if you think we are not on the right track. Ever since we graduated I have noticed that you and Brada and Saja have looked at this country in a different way. Why don't you go back to your people and live in the peace that you say they enjoy. Don't worry about us and let us just wallow in our own life style. We really don't want yours. In this world I think you can tell which country is the best; just open the doors and look at which way the people go. Do they leave or do they come in! It's pretty obvious. There are probably 8,000,000 Arabs in this country and why did they come here?"

But he continued, "As Islam grows we must carry the truth to the world and that is our Miraj, our mission. Allah has told us that we must go to the infidels, make them a Mu"min (believer) and give them Dawa (invitation to Islam). All must have the Shahada (testimony of faith). We will continue to work for allah no matter what the cost. We are all prepared to offer our lives to the sacrifice of allah."

My inner anger was rising. I had seen and read so many reports about what is going on with the radical Muslims in all parts of the world that I was not ready for this. NOT TODAY! "So all of this terrorism by the Muslims is just to get people converted to Islam!" I was getting more steamed as I went on. "You know, that is nuts and the terrorists where ever they are have to be stopped and eradicated. We are in sympathy with the Jews that are being slaughtered by the suicide bombers. Any religion that purports killing to get converts is off the charts". We were docking and so I just turned and left him standing there. I do not really know him any more.

As I walked down the stairs I could hear his last retort. "Are you saying that if you thought that I was a terrorist you would kill me?" I showed him my right hand - middle finger!

I hurried off the boat, waved goodbye to everyone and headed home, I was frustrated and tired. Catching a taxi I was home in about 15 minutes still a little hostile. I opened the door to my brownstone and went straight to my recliner. Using the remote for my stereo I put on some light classical and tilted back to go into a closed eye state of semi-dreaming. What was I to think? What an experience! I rose up because the hall light was too bright and my relaxing with the soothing music was not working. Turning off the hall light I lit a couple of candles and settled back in the recliner to think about the coming week. So relaxing here with the flickering of the candle light......I have a full weeekk..... aand on Tuesdayyy....... it's lunch with Jerr.......... Z z z z z 's.

With a jerk I sat up and could smell candles burning but not the normal smell, kind of a blown out wick smell. Looking where I had sat each one, I saw the bayberry rust color one half twisted over and the wick had a flame 4 inches high. Wow, I jumped up and wet my fingers and put out the wick. Then I snuffed the larger cinnamon flavored candle and noticed at the same time from the flickering light that the grandfather's clock showed 3:20. At ease with the late hour I fell back into the recliner and my head was spinning with all of the past data I had been reviewing and categorizing at work the past six months. Why was I regurgitating all of this stuff again and why tonight? Maybe the turmoil over my terrorist outburst with Yassir? It was all of the terrorist events over the past 10 to 12 years that had put the world and us at the UN on such an edge. Half dreaming and with my eyes closed I began to float backwards in time.

I remember when the Shah was removed from Iran in 1978; the Ayatollah came out of Exiled in France. The fanatics had a field day. The Islamic Revolution began. There were strikes, revolts, demonstrations and riots and the U. S. was blamed for the way the Shah had brought modernization to Iran. He advanced education, gave women the right to vote, used oil money for industrial projects and pushed social reform. Too much westernization. The Ayatollah Ruhollah Khomeini came in to take over the spiritual guidance of Iran and to bring fundamentalism back to the society. Known as the 'fugih' he set up an Islamic Republic and created the Revolutionary Council that tried and shot many of the Shah's ex-officials. The new government hated the U. S., so in November, 1979 his radicals captured the embassy in Tehran and made a joke of our country. They paraded in front of the embassy burning many U S Flags and shouting 'Death to the United States'. What an embarrassment. And good old President Jimmy Carter blew it big time when he set up an operation trying to save all of the hostages. He failed miserably! Khomeini continued his raving against the States and the motto for the Iranians was 'DEATH TO THE UNITED STATES'.

I really believe that was the turning point for Muslim radicals to realize that they could do anything they wanted. And as the huge amounts of money from oil began to flow down to the fanatics they began to spread out slowly all around the world to do their dirty work and begin the Jihad as required by the teachings of Mohammed. A Jihad that was necessary to complete his dream to conquer the world for Islam.

1980, unrest in the mid-east grew as Iraq invaded Iran with a war that lasted almost eight years and the Palestine Liberation Organization (really Arafat) began it's plan to take down Israel. Suicide bombing was to be the terrorist tool to break the Jews.

All of these things were racing through my mind.

1988, Ali Atwa hijacks TWA flight # 847 and takes it to Algeria threatening to blow it up and kill all aboard.

1988 Abuji causes Kuwait Jet to crash and all aboard died.

1988 Pan-Am flight #103 was blown up over Scotland and Libyan terrorist were the perpetrators.

Iran targets Kuwait shipping vessels and the USS Vincentes shoots down an Iranian passenger plane in error while the ship was battling Iranian gun boats. Two hundred ninety passengers died and the hatred for the U. S. kept growing.

Then I remember when the attacks first came to our own land. 1993 and the World Trade Center became a target for destruction. A Muslim cleric, Sheikh Omar Adbul Rahman and three Algerian terrorist were convicted, but still we had been hit.

1995 terrorist directed by Ramzi Yousef planned an elaborate scheme to blow up nine commercial airliners flying from Asia to the States.

1996 Saudi Shiite terrorist blew up the barracks at Kho'dor Towers in Saudi Arabia and killed 19 U.S. marines and injured 500 civilians.

In August 1998 a major Muslim Fatah website calls for the destruction of Israel and terrorist blow up two American Embassies in Tanzania and Kenya.

Suicide bombs blow up three different markets and malls from July to November in Israel that killed many Jews and then Terrorist murder 56 tourist in a hall in Israel. And suicide bombings in Israel escalated.

Last year three terrorist Ahmed Ressem, Abdel Ghani Meskini, and Mokhtar Haruari were caught at the Canadian border with explosives in their truck with plans to set bombs off at LAX just before the Millennium.

As these thoughts passed so quickly through my mind; I knew they were germinated by the discourse from this afternoon on the boat and the work I had to do tomorrow on the new data. Monday would be a full day getting my staff to analyze all of the accumulated field office reports and the information we had from various member's intelligence agencies.

The White House had issued an executive memorandum to the State Department for NSA to look for any noise about terrorist activities that might expose possible plans to disrupt the inauguration. Since we were in direct contact and in full cooperation with NSA we had been requested to work on a special report offering up any information that might uncover plans for an assault on the ceremony. I was facing over three hundred forty new reports and issues to look at this next week and then start the analysis. Yassir, his face and attitude kept bouncing in and out of my mind and intermingling with my other thoughts. I knew him at NYU as a rational fellow not prone to radical ideologies; has he changed that much these last few years? I need to talk to……. Tiama tomorrow…… she work wiiith .. him…. for a tim…….
ZzZzzzzzz.

CHAPTER FOUR

November 11, 2000

It's raining out so I won't be jogging this morning but a few calisthenics will get my blood moving and I'll need my vitamins to give me all of the energy necessary to begin this week's project. Oh no, I told Jerry I would meet him for lunch on Tuesday. I'll call him and cancel.

I'm not walking to work today; I watched for a cab to come down from 7th Avenue, "Hey Taxi... Taxi...over here. The United Nations please." Opening my brief case I checked for my cell phone. Not here. Wait a minute, it's on the table. "Taxi hold it I forgot my cell phone. Back your cab up to that slot by the curb in front of my door. I'll only be a minute." There it is on the table by the stereo. Just then the phone rang. I answered as I went back to the cab. "Hello, Hank here."

"Boy I'm glad I caught you, this is Jerry, about our lunch on Tuesday, I can't make it."

Great he is calling to cancel. What a relief. Now I'll have more time this week.

"But, how about Friday? I'll be finished around 11:00 and that will give us plenty of time; we can relax and take a break from work. And I would guess you'll want a Friday afternoon off to catch your breath."

"Well you know this is the first time back to my department at the UN for over three months. I guess an early break would be nice. But it will have to be around 2:00 o'clock."

"That's OK, still at Giovanni's?"

"Yeah, that's fine."

I put my phone in my brief case as I commented on the traffic. "Looks like traffic is a little slow this morning, any problems heading to 45th Street?"

"No, I been downtown and back and even to the uptown area. Just typical Monday's. You want me to come down First Avenue for the employee's entrance or are you a visitor?"

He said that as I was calling Tiama. "Oh yeah, go to the employee side." Ring…..Ring…..Ring, no answer.

The week went by in a flash, busy, busy, busy and then it was Friday. I closed down my computer, close my office door, closed my mind to work and went for the elevators.

"Good afternoon Sir, may I find you a table or would you prefer the bar?"

"Hello, my name is Jerry Ness and I am here to have lunch with a friend, Mr. Brayden. Has he come in yet?"

"Let me see, No I see no such name on our list. Do you wish to be seated and wait for him or go to the bar? Either way when he arrives I will direct him to you."

"I'll just go to the bar, thank you"."

"Very good sir".

As Jerry waited on Hank, he started to admire this restaurant once again. This is probably one of the finest bars in New York. The decor is out of this world and the bar itself is probably eighty feet long with the finest carvings and rose wood inlay one has ever seen. The bartender was of the old school, white apron, rolled up sleeves and a handlebar moustache. "Good afternoon. What may I get for you?"

"I think some Chivas on the rocks will do just fine." I allowed my self the privilege of some good scotch and an opportunity to relax after a long week of strategy meetings at my office. I took a sip of scotch and wondered to myself while waiting for Hank; 'How is the world going to protect it's self against all of these terrorist attacks? There are too many dedicated fundamentalist Muslims to ever be identified and even then how could all of the ones that are radical terrorists ever be found, that is question number one'.

As I entered Giovanni's I looked around for a moment and the Madre

Dee was immediately on the job, "Sir, are you looking for a gentleman named Ness?"

"Yes."

"He is waiting at the bar."

I caught his eye and waved as I approached the bar, "Jerry! Am I a little late? Oh no, I am on time so I guess you were early. I went ahead and left at 1:30 because with the work load I now have I could work all night and not make a dent in the data."

Jerry asked the bartender, "What do you think, can we just sit at a booth here in the bar area and order lunch?"

"I'm sure at this hour it would be okay."

"Waiter, we want to order and sit in that booth by the fireplace."

"That will be fine and I'll find Eddie who is the waiter for your area".

We had chosen that booth to get some relative privacy and a little quietness since the early drinking crowd from Wall Street had already begun to infiltrate our space. Jerry immediately grabbed my attention. "You know Hank the whole thing is a ticking time bomb. We don't know who will be president, no one knows when the stock market will give in to the internet bubble, most of these people in here don't know if they will have a job next week, no body knows when the next devastating earthquake will hit........, and I don't know when the next terrorist attack on an airplane will occur and you, with all of your access to the flood of information at the UN, can you say you can predict with certainty any coming hot spots around the world? Really, I mean is it at all possible to know when we will suffer the next attack on our country. My friends are very anxious about the inauguration. I really hope we can exchange information with out breaking our oaths. I've got a friend in the CIA named Jack Madden who briefs me every Monday on the operations of terrorist groups around the world so we can do our best to keep the airline industry protected. So far so good, But I must say the Israelis are way ahead of us. This outgoing administration does not think we have any eminent danger."

As the waiter approached I wasn't being rude or disinterested in Jerry's wordy comments but I was hungry so I ordered my favorite, "I'll have Linguini in buttery clam sauce with a Caesar salad and some garlic bread." Jerry ordered another scotch and deep dish ravioli with hard rolls. Pretty typical cornball request but what else would you expect, he had told me he was from west Texas.

"Jerry, what exactly did you say you do or who you work for? You just said something about an oath. What are you talking about?"

"I work for ACE International. As I told you on our flight, we specialist in pre-detection of any terrorist activity or plots to highjack, bomb or otherwise destroy any aircraft, anywhere, in any country. It requires a sophisticated flow of intelligence. I wanted to meet with you to see how the United Nations was approaching this terrorist problem since it has now become a world wide problem. Being in the Internal Affairs department I imagined that you could have a different slant on the problems."

"Okay, that I understand however I am under oath to secrecy at the UN and you mentioned your oath. You work in the private sector and we don't each share the same obligations to our employers. I am in the governmental arena."

"Gentlemen, who had the ravioli? Okay and then of course you had the scotch. And you sir had the Caesar salad and the Linguini. I don't believe you ordered any thing to drink. What would you like?"

"Just water for now."

"Let's enjoy this lunch, I'm starving. The food at the UN is so-so and when I can I eat out; I really savor the opportunity. Tell me a little about your self. Any family and where do you live?"

"Sure I have a wife who is totally involved in the 'Feed the Children Outreach' and two grown children. Both boys with one in the Navy and the other is an IRS agent. Both are in the government and both by choice. Of course I had something to do with it because I told them that a career in government, if you chose the right job, would provide the most secure future you could want and the retirement was excellent. The government good-old-boys take care of each other. We lived in Jersey until the kids were gone and then we moved to a condo in Virginia near my work. She does some traveling but I needed to be near the agencies and my office. What about your family?"

"Oh, well I am not married and I haven't given it much thought. I was raised in Westchester County on the family farm. My Dad and sister are still there. The farm has been in the Brayden family for generations. How's the ravioli?"

"Very good, I have always liked this restaurant. You know it is over 100 years old. I believe that its reputation is world wide. Look Hank, here is the deal. After we met on the plane and during the ride into the city I thought that since you were interested in the terrorist activity you must in some way be in that area at the UN. Internal Affairs must have many sections and if you operate with intelligence on a world wide basis then I wanted to get the view of the United Nations on probable future hot spots or terrorist eruptions. When it comes to oath of allegiance, I was in the Marines, special opts and retired at thirty nine, twenty years of a very satisfying career. And then in 98 after the terrorist bombing of flight 103 over Lockerbie, Scotland I joined ACE which is really owned by NSA. I am part of the government and carry a NSA ID. I get all of the intelligence from our government sources, but I wondered if the UN has a different slant on the world events. I know that it is totally to the left in its thinking and future planning. The internal philosophy is for a 'One World Government'; I know that and there are many with the same agenda who have infiltrated our government. You know the ones who have an 'It takes a Village' attitude to resolve the many hurdles face by governments around the world. But I for one will never allow us to give up our sovereignty to some international governing body bent on dictating internal freedoms."

That was a mouthful and I kind of agreed with Jerry on the status of the UN and the operating philosophy. I know Dad would absolutely agree. He would say that the UN is a big joke. Small leftist countries trying to control the direction of the world. "Well, we both have some sort of clearances but what exactly can I tell you that you don't already have access to or more exactly what is your point?"

"Bear with me if you will. First a few important facts, most of which I would believe you know or at least have heard during your intelligence reviews. In 1974 the price of oil was around $11.25 per barrel. With the embargo of 1975 the price more than doubled in a few months and sent the markets into chaos for a couple of years. Let's see what happened. None of the cost to get oil to the refineries had changed; there was no doubling of drilling, pumping, storage, or shipping cost so the excess income dropped into the government's pockets of the oil producing countries. The Arabic oil producing countries sucked what….. 7,000,000 barrels per day times $12 per barrel of money out of the world economy every day. $84,000,000 dollars per day, $2,520,000,000 per month which was 30.5 billion dollars per year of found money. Then it went to around $33.00 per barrel which handed them another 43 billion dollars a year of found money. Oil resources and reserves became a world wide problem and a major political issue. Defusing any unrest and protecting the supply of oil was for the first time a front page topic with governments, politicians and the people. Especially when everyone learned by standing in gasoline lines that the blood in the veins of our civilization was thick and black. The Arabic countries were dripping with dollars and therefore the Muslims were dripping with dollars. The leaders took control of this huge windfall and under their control they built up their countries with the new money, they invested the new money, they purchased major companies and large real estate properties all around the world with the new money, they set up social programs with the new money and of course as you well know they financed clandestine operations with this huge financial windfall. Radicals now had enormous amounts of dollars for their causes.

During the late 70's with the Shah going down, tens of thousands of Iranians and other Muslims from many eastern countries entered our country under the Open Door Policy. This new policy was unprecedented and therefore they could enter our country in floods and they had money, big money. They knew they could come in unabated and we were 'invaded' so to speak. By 1980 we had over two million Arabic people in this country and the number has grown annually. Then with the Iran-Iraq war we accepted many more middle-east immigrants and by 1997 there were approximately five million Arabic people in our country. And of course these people began to blend in. Students going to universities and colleges. Families moving into cities all over the country. They bought small businesses that were cash cows. The advantage was that the money stream was mostly cash especially in the medium to poorer areas. Liquor stores, small food marts, car repair shops, barber shops, 24 hour food and gasoline franchises, small local gas stations. What irony, they produce it and now they disburse it. Plus real estate sales, mortgage loans and really any business that provided cash transactions so money could be hidden. But the real story here is that they have buried themselves into our society. Two of the leaders from countries identified by our government as fundamental terrorist nations; Kadafi and Saddam Hussein, then financed the building of Mosques in major cities in our country. Their radical philosophy purports that they must spread the word of Mohammed to everyone and for those who are not Muslims and will not accept Islam, then they must be purged from the world as infidels who they believe are the 'children of satan'. They along with leaders from other Muslim countries fathered the radical Muslims and provided asylum to the terrorist that are now spread around the world. They all believe that the West is infested with satan and is totally corrupt and immersed in decadence. Khomeini preached death to the USA, Kadafi preached death to the USA, Saddam Hussein preached death to the USA, Palestinians preach death to the Israelis, Hazbulah preaches change by terrorism, and many Islamic factions want a Ji'had. Hank they have a mission. Their plan is well set and they are very patient to carry out the will of allah as outlined by Muhammad thirteen hundred years ago."

Jerry was definitely passionate about what he was saying. He finished the last of the scotch in his glass as he continued, "Why am I going over all of this? First, let me add that there will be over seven million Arabic people in this country by mid 2001, and some estimates are eight million. Remember the fraudulent immigration ring that was broken up in Washington state where thousands of illegal Iranians had gotten into our country and our reports are that thousands more of illegal Muslims have passed over the border of Canada through the states of Minnesota, Wisconsin and Idaho. Of the seven million Arabic people here there are at our best estimates thirty percent that are either Christians or non Islamic Arabs. Out of the other four and a half million there are ten to fifteen percent that are of the radical fundamentalist belief and devout followers of Mohammed such as the Shiites and the Mujahedin or are part of Hamas or Hezbollah groups. With just half of those affiliated with some radical Islamic organization we have a potential of 225,000 to 335,000 terrorist already in the United States. Now my point is, my very good friend at the CIA Jack Madden who I mentioned before, heads up a special section on terrorist activities world wide and I hope that we can get together again to look at and compare the UN's real underlying position on these activities. And I want you to know, not only my commitment to the operation of ACE International but more especially my love of our country, the one I fought for, and the love of my family and grandchildren are the reasons I do this job. You see the radical Muslims who have entered our country have created cells for operations against us and we are all in jeopardy. As you well know they hate the West so much they are all willing to blow themselves up and become a Martyr. Jack tells me that we know that there are two major groups operating in our borders. Al-Qaeda with Osama bin Laden leading them and Hamas with a major influence coming from Syria."

Hank interjected, "The most difficult thing you have said is that from the intelligence within all of our agencies we don't really know who is who, out of those few hundred thousand radical Muslims."

"OH! We know a few like a couple of hundred, but most of the others are buried inside of our communities. I wake up daily with extreme anxiety and fear for our country. I want everyone to be alerted."

"Boy Jerry, you have just added to my anxiety and even though I have looked at some of the many possibilities I have not been as focused on our situation as you. I can see why. You are interested in our home land as well as the international arena and I have had only the world wide view in my sights and even that has been fragmented. This has been an interesting lunch, and I thought that I had been distressed by a conversation I had earlier with an Arabic classmate from NYU."

"You have some Muslim friends?"

"Well they are actually just past classmates now. We have been distanced for some time. I saw some of them at our class reunion". Looking at his watch Hank noted, "I have another engagement so I must go now. I'm sure we will be in contact again and we can talk about any information that is not off the table based on my security obligations. Maybe you can get the tab; I picked up the limo bill. Nice having lunch with you Jerry, I'll see you later."

Jerry was a good sport and picked up the bill as he added "Hey don't forget about Jack, I'll call you".

CHAPTER FIVE - THANKSGIVING WEEK 2000

Here it is Sunday morning and another whole week disappeared like a vapor. Just sitting around trying to relax was an obscene waste of time. I had already gone for a one hour jog in the park but I did not want to be alone. I'll first shower and then call Dad. This being Thanksgiving week I am feeling very nostalgic. I need company. The shower felt good but a Jacuzzi would be better so I filled the tub and soaked and bubbled and soaked and bubbled until I was able to take last week's stress down a few notches. I'll just sit here in the tub and use the bathroom phone.

"Hey, Good morning Dad, I was having one of those Sunday mornings. I need to talk to someone so I'm glad you are around the farm today"

"Hi son, is there something wrong?"

"No, there is nothing really wrong. I just had a hard week getting all of the reports at work set up with my fellow workers and categorizing them. And then I spent a long lunch with a guy from ACE International that I had met flying in last week and the conversations kind of overloaded my brain with all of the potential problems there are around the world and in our country. As I was jogging earlier in Central Park I looked at the true beauty of New York, the diversity of the people, the beauty of the buildings – uptown with corporate centers and hotels – midtown with theaters and restaurants – downtown with Chinatown, Wall Street and The Twin Towers, the streets, the traffic, the whole flow of human activity, kind of like the unceasing flow of blood in our veins, and I thought how the city has it's own personal electrifying atmo-

sphere. You know what I mean Dad. I guess I am definitely in a nostalgic mood. I think the Thanksgiving season has a lot to do with it."
Dad cut in, "Caroline and I were kind of feeling that also so I know it
will be good for us to be together this weekend. But just a minute, what
was the name of this guy from ACE? Was it Jerry Ness?"

"Yes, do you know him?"

"Of course we do, he has been interviewed on our station here
in New York twice for up dates on the security of our airline industry. I thought that the programs had gone national, didn't you watch
them"?

"I guess not. You know I am loyal to UBC but over the past three
months I have been traveling a lot and haven't seen much television.
I can tell you though he gave me some heavy things to think about,
but we can talk about that later. Just wanted to talk, and see when you
thought we could go pheasant hunting, maybe Saturday early?"

"That will work out find and I'll make all of the arrangements. I'm
not sure but I think Caroline might go shooting with us."

"Okay, that will be great. I love you Dad, have a good day, say
hello to Caroline and Grandmamma and I'll see you Wednesday
afternoon."

"Okay son and I love you. Good bye and relax today."

What a pleasure it is to have my family so close that I can spend time
with them and remember the security of my childhood. Spending some
time with Tiama today would be good for me. I hope she is at home.
Let's see her number is 871-3634, I think. "Hi Tiama its Hank. I was
thinking about you and wanted to call and see how things were going.
I missed you on the excursion last Sunday, are you alright?"

"Hank, I am glad you called. I missed the trip because I took a new
position with a Filipino group here in the city. I wanted to be there but
last Sunday they had a gathering of Filipino's for Cush so I was busy
most of the day."

"How was the excursion and lunch? Did all of our classmates have a
good time?"

"Well, you and Brada were the only ones who missed the trip and
I think most enjoyed the day. The weather held out but it was a little
chilly."

"Most? Who didn't have fun?"

"I thought that the trip was a great idea but then I got into a small discussion with Yassir which became quite intense. I was not up for his going into his ideology and Muslim beliefs so we had a little back and forth kind of thing and I came away disturbed by his attitude. I think he has changed."

"I know what you mean and that is kind of like the reason why Brada and I are not together anymore. Sometime I'll tell you about them."

I was thinking this could be a great time to talk to her so I pushed a little, "Why don't I come and pick you up and we can spend the afternoon together. Maybe go to the Gallery of Fine Arts or take in a matinee or even a movie if you would like. I would like to see you."

"Wonderful, I'm up for that today. I'll be dressed in an hour so let's say 11:30 and we can go somewhere first for a tea or something."

"Yeah, a hot tea and hot pita bread at Grecco's on Second Avenue. I'll be there at 11:30."

I got dressed in some kaki pants and my old NYU sweat shirt. Even though it was sunny I felt a chill this morning while jogging. Tiama lived on the opposite side of the park just off of Park Avenue on 67th Street so a bike ride through the park to her apartment seemed like a good idea. I had enough time and I'm quite sure she will have room for me to put my bike in her flat. Riding through central Park can be enjoyable or treacherous depending when, where and in what part. I took the 75th Street walkway and road to the east bearing a little south as I crossed different paths. The more north you go in the park the less secure it seems. I passed by some families with their strollers, some guys playing soccer, and a lot of couples just walking enjoying the crisp fall air. Coming out on 64th, I biked up to 67th and then right to her apartment. I'm glad she has an elevator. Knock, knock, and she was right at the door. "Can I park my bike in your hall"? "No, leave it in the corridor, of course Hank bring it on in. I'm all set. Did you have any kind of a strong feeling about the gallery, the theater or the movie?" "Not really, let's get that hot tea and see what is happening at each. I can buy a paper in front of Grecco's".

"Do you have any quarters? I have plenty of money but no quarters. It takes eight quarters. $2.00 for the New York Try-imes. Just a joke, it really is too big with too much advertising. Let's sit by the window, where there is more light for reading."

"Waitress, two lemon herbal teas and a basket of hot pita bread and please bring some honey. I hope that is still one of your favorites."

Smiling she made me feel good with her comment, "You still know me. We have not lost that much over the past few years. Hank, I have often thought about you and wondered how your career was going. I left the journal and Brada's place over two years ago and have just been floating. I traveled to Europe first and spent time roaming the country side from England to Germany to Yugoslavia and then after I came back here I went to visit my family in the Philippines for a month. The Filipino group I am working for now is quite rewarding. We were organized to look after the less fortunate people from my country who can't afford the many social services they need."

I wanted to tell her that I still had a thing for her but I knew this was the wrong time and wrong atmosphere. "Well let's look at the theaters. Here's the paper. I think you should select one you haven't seen. Would you like me to put some honey on your pita bread?"

"Sure, mmm....don't see a thing interesting. I'd rather take in a movie. How about some comedy like 'Big Mama' or 'A Message in a Bottle'. I think 'Big Mama' would be a lot of fun."

I wanted what ever she wanted, "Settled then. The four o'clock showing will let us out in time for an early dinner. Look I'm asking for my first date with you since I left the State Department and went with the UN. I guess when I left and was sent on assignments that left you open to join up with Brada. As I reflect back on it, it was my big mistake. How about a real date for dinner and a little wine?"

She reached out for her tea cup but really moved her hand over mine and with a touch that I sensed was a passionate YES.

"Tiama, I am really comfortable with you and so glad that we got together today. While we are relaxing with our tea do you mind telling me about Brada or more accurately about Yassir? My time on the excursion was to just remember old times and to take pleasure in the smell of the salt water and the sea breeze. However, Yassir came out on the deck to get something off of his chest or maybe to extend the conversation from Friday night, I don't know. What is certain he pushed the ideology of Islam and I didn't want the noise!"

"Of course and I remember Friday night and it was almost like a continuing saga for me. I left the Journal and Brada because things were getting weird."

"Weird how?"

"Okay. During the last two years with Brada and at WJHEP things

46

would happen that at first seemed a little curious and then very strange. On many occasions at the journals office clients would come in for meetings and Brada would ask for privacy. Of course that was not too unusual until the meetings began to start in the mid-afternoons and last till late in the evening. On those occasions he would ask me to go home early. Brada traveled mostly to the middle-east and occasionally to Africa to advise on future hydro electric programs for third world countries. Again that was not really strange since he is Arabic and he would be more comfortable working with those people with whom he could communicate and relate. The money was good and always he was getting large consulting fees but I'm not sure over the Seven or so years I was there if any projects got built. More than that, Yassir was the coordinator of foreign relations with the countries Brada was consulting with and he never correspond with them in writing. He always used a computer and sent them either e-mails or CD's. I never saw a letter generated by him to any governmental agency or person in authority. He would always travel for extended periods of time telling us verbally where he was going and I never saw any conformation of governmental meetings. I guess everything was on his lap top and there was no written documentation of anything. I suppose that was their foreign training, but I thought it strange. He took various time off to go study as he said with the religious leaders in Iran or Iraq, I'm not for sure which. During the last couple of years when he would return there would be a constant flow of their clients or friends for meeting after meeting and always different people. Of course I was let off early. It became the same scene at home when different associates would come over. I was excused from the apartment. It just became too much and the atmosphere just began to get too weird. I wanted out so I told Brada that I was tired of working and needed to take a long awaited brake, and then one week later we broke up over our religious differences. I told him that he was just too ridged in his Islamic doctrine and that I had to follow my Catholic background. It proved to be an acceptable situation especially since Muslims have little or no respect for woman. That is it. I felt uncomfortable and wanted to make a change so I traveled and cleared my head. I guess that is not a big deal."

"I'm very glad that you are free. I want to make the most of that if you will let me." I wanted Tiama to know that I was very interested in a relationship before I went on. "I guess the actions of Brada could be protective of his client base but more probably it was just the cultural differences. Muslim men do not want women involved in their business and I would have to believe that the friends or clients wanted no women around. I think Yassir has just become too radical in his fundamentalist studies over the past ten years or so and it has rubbed off on Brada. I sure don't understand him anymore. I'm going to try to have lunch with Brada and see where he is coming from. I am curious about each of their changed ways. Let's walk to the movies, Okay?"

"Sure, here comes the waitress with the check".

We both thought the movie hilarious. Tiama showed me a great deli for our dinner date and I came away chucked full of Pastrami and Swiss cheese. It was eight-thirty so we walked back to her apartment and I asked if I could leave my bike there till later. Tiama said no problem. I caught a taxi home and I knew for sure I would be back. My bike was still there!

As I was finishing lunch I thought I had better call Dad and make sure I could get a ride from the train station when I arrived tonight. "Hello Caroline? This is Hank, are you all about ready for Thanksgiving and of course for me?"

"Hank, Dad and I are going to the cape for the week end; do you want to join us there"?

"WHAT," I hollered. "THE CAPE, for Thanksgiving? ARE YOU NUTS?"

And as I was saying that she cut in, "Hey dear brother it's just a joke! Of course we are spending the holidays at home. We are holding our breathe for your arrival. When will you be here?"

"I am going to catch the 4:30 train to try and miss some of the crowd. Can you pick me up at the depot around 5:30?"

"Sure, see you then."

When I hung up for some reason as I sat back in my chair, a vision of Tiama walking into her apartment came into my mind. I wonder what she would be doing for the holidays. It only took me a second to pick up the phone and call her. "Hello Tiama it's Hank. I just got finished talking to my sister Caroline about the coming Thanksgiving Holidays. I am going up to our families farm for the weekend and wondered if you had anything planned for the holidays?"

"No Hank, I was just beginning to feel a little lonesome and I have no plans for Thanksgiving."

"I would love to have you spend the four day weekend with me and my family. Do you think you can be ready to leave so we could catch the 4:30 train to Westchester?"

"Sure I can, what clothes do you think I should take for the four days we'll be gone?"

"Well, Dad and I are going hunting Saturday and tomorrow we are having Thanksgiving dinner at home. Casual clothes will be great if you are comfortable with that. If you want to go hunting with us I would suggest bringing some older Levis and a warm sweatshirt. Even a pair of boots would be a good idea, but that is what ever you want. I'll pick you up at 3:30 so we can get to the station by 4 p.m. I'll be in a cab and call you on my cell phone. That will save us some time, is that okay?"

"Sure, I'll be ready. What about my bags?"

"Just kidding, I'll come up and get you!"

There was a crowd at the station so arriving early gave us plenty of time to catch our train. We arrived at the Westchester station shortly after 5:30 and Caroline was waiting to pick us up. As we drove towards the farm there was a pleasant crispness in the air and a nostalgic smell of smoke from various fireplaces. We headed north and then west towards the Hudson. We pulled up to the front of the farm with it's long rock wall stretching across about five hundred feet of the front of the property and down each side almost the same distance. Our property went to the Hudson but the fence ended near the old barn. Dad had built a fifty foot long carport in front of the barn for his forty two foot RV and Caroline parked nearby under the adjacent carport. Our property had a variety of trees but mostly oaks and they were old. Plenty of trees to give Dad firewood for years to come. As Tiama got her small red suitcase I extracted her other bag as she commented on the house. "This is a delightful place and I can smell something very appetizing in the air. Is there something on the bar-b-que?"

We walked toward the back of the house where Dad had added a long enclosed porch across half of the backside of the house that covered most of the outside wall that was adjacent to the living room wall. There was a fourteen foot native rock fireplace on the wall opposite the living room and that allowed us to use the porch through a lot of the winter months. "Dad what's up for dinner?"

"I'm smoking a couple of briskets, some salad, and my favorite beans. Oh and I put corn bread in the oven. Sound good?"

Tiama was the first to proclaim her hunger with a, "I'm for that; I could eat a bear or in this case a brisket. I'm Tiama Mr. Brayden; I hope Hank told you I was coming."

"Dad, I've told you about Tiama over the past years. We got together again on this trip back to New York and I wanted her to spend this week end with us."

"First just call me Tom and second, we're very pleased to have you Tiama, grab a paper plate, a napkin, some utensils and a drink and I'll cut you some juicy brisket. Medium or a little rare? Mummm, looks all medium to me, oh well here are two big slices and some beans. Salad and corn bread are over there." Tom pointed to a long table across from the fireplace where Grandmamma Brayden was sitting.

"Come along. Grandma, this is Tiama, a very special friend of mine from the NYU who is living in New York."

"Nice to meet you sweetie, did you have a nice trip out here to the farm?"

Tiama caught her self staring at Grandma admiring her firm un-wrinkled face and perfectly groomed gray hair. She thought how Grandma was an exact image one would have of a forth generation New-Englander "Well, it is a pleasure to meet you and yes we did. May I sit down here?"

"Of course sweetie. Hank can you bring me a small plate?"

Everyone had finished and discarded their plates into the fireplace when I asked Dad if he had a gun Tiama could use to go hunting with us. Looking at Tiama he offered up a positive, "Sure, we have a 20 gauge over-n-under if you would like to try that?"

"Hank had said that we will be going for pheasants or wild turkeys so that would be perfect."

"I hope you know your guns and it is only a two shot shotgun."

"Yes, I know."

"Dad she did some hunting in the Philippines and took a gun con-trol course at NYU and told me she really enjoyed the training."

"Right, well I guess you feel at home with guns, huh?"

We sat around the fireplace enjoying the flames and chatted until after eleven. Grandmamma had retired much earlier. I put Tiama in the downstairs bedroom and was going up to my old bedroom where there were many memories of my boyhood. She gave me a funny little glance which asked the question 'why my own bedroom'? I wanted her to know how I felt from my heart, "I want us to get off on a different start this time. Okay?"

She squeezed my hand, gave me a long kiss and closing the door said "goooood niiiight!"

It was Turkey Day; so it consisted of dinner around four in the afternoon with Thanksgiving prayers, an enormous amount of food followed by football games which caused Caroline and Tiama to go off to visit some of Caroline's friends while Dad and I turned into couch lizards. It wasn't until after seven that they returned to come in and wake Dad and I up from a perfectly good snooze. Caroline took out the Monopoly game as if by instinct and set it up on the game table at the end of the living room. "Alright now," she ordered, "let's go back a few years and see who can win now that we are older and wiser. Tiama, have you played Monopoly?"

"Not much, but I will try."

"Well its not very hard", Tom said rolling off of the sofa.

We played to midnight and I lost both games. Defending my abilities I told everyone that, "I'm an international affairs authority not an entrepreneur." With that we all said good night and went off to our own little places. Following Tiama to her room in the dim light of the hall I entered in to her room and tucked her into bed so I could steal some hugging and good kissing.

Friday had turned out to be a day of just lounging around watching some college football while the girls disappeared to do some wandering through the local mall. But the next day, well it's my father's great love. Even before the crack of dawn Tom had us up with some coffee and a plate of crumble cake so we would not be traveling on an empty stomach but more importantly so we would be early to the hunting fields which were on one of Dad's school buddy's farm in western Connecticut. Saturday morning and at this early hour there was not a car in sight as we headed towards the hunting ground, about 2 hours north and west of were our farm was in Westchester. Caroline had decided to stayed home to attend to her crafts; she had never gotten into hunting even though she was handy with most guns. Dad had seen to that. Marvin, Dad's school buddy let us use one of his Dalmatians to flush out our prey so we had our limit before noon. Tiama proved to be a good shot although the twenty gauge shotgun gave her a few bruises in the shoulder. After some hot chocolate at the gas station near Marvin's place we headed home to dress our kill. As we drove I told Dad and Tiama that it looked like I would be transferred to New York permanently and be closing down my Washington residence.

"Well that's great. We'll see more of you then", and Tiama's response was a gentle hug and a quiet "I love you."

I got up late on Sunday finding everyone on the porch enjoying one of Dad's toasty warm fires and many parts of the Sunday newspaper in all of their laps or on the floor. After gathering up the pieces I nestled in next to Tiama to start with the front page. I hate to go from this piece to that piece and find a page missing so I can not finish the articles I am into. "Dad have you got part of this front section? I want to finish about Cush and Bore and then this article about the Cole bombing."

"No problem. Cush says he will wait on the facts and Bore says there are no facts. The latest on the attack is that some of the terrorist are from Yemen and the count is now 17 sailors killed and 59 injured. That's it."

With an air of frustration, "Dad, let me have the rest of the articles. I don't want your editorial; I'll do my own reviewing especially on the Cole bombing. I probably know a lot more than the reporter at the Times anyway."

"What are you saying, that the media doesn't have the whole story or that they keep back information?" Dad's voice was more quizzical than defensive.

"I mean for instance that there is a lot more information inside of The U. N. and our government than gets out to the media. That's all."

"I think we have a pretty comprehensive information research department at UBC."

"Of course you do and so do the other majors ABC, CNN, Fox, etc but I don't think they put all the pieces together in the news when it is presented. For instance, so far they have said that the Cole bombing was from terrorist in Yemen and yet we already know that they are al-Qaeda directed by Usama bin Ladin and are from his terrorist camps. Maybe supported by Yemen but from the Grand Terrorist himself. Remember his 1998 statement to ABC 'that Americans anywhere on earth should be murdered' and more exactly he said 'it is the individual Muslim's duty to kill Americans what ever country they are in and that killing Americans was more important than any other infidels'! Lately I have come to understand that we have a diabolical mortal enemy; radical Arabs that have got the resources and freedom of travel and who are fixed on the destruction of our country. I just do not thoroughly understand where the battle ground is yet. They are splintered all around the globe. That is one of the operations for my department at the UN to continue to investigate. The difficulty is keeping a finger on all of this. There are eight major countries that are harboring or better yet supporting Islamic terrorists; Iran, Iraq, Libya, Syria, Saudi Arabia, Sudan, Afghanistan, and Indonesia. Not to mention the PLO in Israel, however they are fighting the Jews on a single front and don't care much about our homeland."

Caroline spoke up with some consternation in her voice, "Why can't we all just get along? I'm being a little facetious since I think that idiot Bilary really believes that we are just a Village and as soon as we are 'All One' we will just have a wonderful world. What 'cotton candy' thinking. There is usually no reality in the liberals thinking, only the here and now, totally disregarding the wisdom of the past. And look at what Clinton did to get campaign money. It looks like He really sold out secrets from our atomic energy laboratory in Los Alamos, New Mexico while claiming he knew nothing about the spy chain that existed there. It seems to me he did that to put China up on an even basis with us in their nuclear program so that they had a certain comfort level to negotiate free trade agreements and we could bring them into the 'free world common market' on equal footing with us. We all knew that there was a huge market there with a ferocious appetite for Western products and the world markets wanted to get into China. Probably his giving away our secrets eased the negotiations."

Hank looked at his sister rather surprised, "My goodness Caroline, I never knew you had such an in depth knowledge of the various world affairs! I'm impressed since I thought that being on the school board would have you more centered on all the local evens here in Westchester."

"Did you forget I am living here with the Executive Vice President of production at UBC? I get it all. Dad uses me as a sounding board."

"Not to change the subject, but have you been offered any new proposals for the purchase of our farm? I guess the developers are still snapping up what they can."

"I will never sell the family farm. It is for you guys and mother would have wanted it that way. What you all do when I am gone is a different story. I'm not trying to be morbid but I will want to retire here and die here as your mother did."

"Well I feel the same way, how about you sis?"

"Of course; the same. I could never imagine disposing of our farm and none of us need the money so there will be more generations of Brayden's here for a long time"

Tiama spoke up after we expressed our personal feelings saying, "How nice it is to see such a close knit family as you all are. It makes me reflect on my home in the Philippines. But while we do not have such a large home, we do have a very close family. Lots of love."

With that I suggested that it was time to go and I went to get Tiama's and my suit cases. "Who will be driving us to the station?"

Caroline offered, "Dad and I will both take you and then we are going stopping at the market. Did everyone enjoy the pheasant? I have never baked a pheasant before so I hope it was not too dry. And do either of you want to take two with you? We have seven in the freezer." Tiama spoke up, "I would love to have one. Will it be okay till we get home?' "Sure, and I'll wrap up two for you Hank."

"Thanks, Dad for a great week end; we will remember this one for a long time."

"Okay then, let's get in the car and see if we can't get you on the 4:00 o'clock train." Grandma followed us to the car and after goodbyes and kisses we headed down the driveway to the road.

On the way to the station I wondered if Dad would be traveling during Christmas, "Are you planning any trips soon?"

"Only the inauguration in January, otherwise I think it will be a quiet yearend for me. Things are pretty well operating like a clock and nothing radical seems to be happening." Dad pulled the car into the parking lot noticing that the train had not arrived yet, "We're a little early."

As Tiama exited the car she bent back in to say, "Tom and Caroline I really felt at home and I had such a marvelous time, Thank you very much. I think I hear the train, so we are off, and I hope to see you all later, good bye."

Going over to Dad's window I said, "Thanks for the dinner, the family time and well, just good feelings again." He understood and told me he would call next week. We boarded the train, grabbed a seat in the front car and snuggled close together. I am feeling something very special for Tiama.

As we jogged along watching the houses and their lighted windows presenting an irregular light show, I leaned over to smell the delicious fragrance Tiama was giving off. Was it Her or her. A natural smell of someone you feel very close to or a store bought scent. A little of both I thought. "You smell so good tonight; I just want to eat you." I began by nibbling on her neck. Then to her ear where I lingered and then to her chin. I gently slipped up to her mouth and she was waiting. A kiss that you dream of at night. I knew I wanted her again, but this time permanently. I had been alone too long and I was ready. I would have to find out about her feelings. I wanted to go slow so that she didn't think I was only interested in her like before. We were younger then and then all I wanted was an arm piece and a bed partner. How it was different.

She broke the moment with, "I hope that you and Brada get a chance to talk. He means nothing to me now and I want what ever relationship we have to be on a sound foundation. I enjoy being with you again and the hugs and kisses and attention."

"I was just thinking about that and I'm going to call him this week."

She continued, "And I don't know if there is anything wrong with the journal. I believe it is doing some kind of good work in the third world countries. At least it looks that way."

"Here we are, back in the City," I said handing he, her purse. "I think I'll take you home and head out to my place leaving the bike to keep you company again. But I will change that relationship soon."

She purred, "I can't wait!"

As Hank walked towards his office he felt a strange chill while looking down the narrow hallway. Monday after Thanksgiving and the halls of this institution were like a tomb. One can hear every step echo down the hall. No one here because of the holidays and all of the delegates with their aids had returned to their home countries. There was only a skeleton staff to operate the building and the communications center and those on the forth floor where a small staff of dedicated native New Yorkers were at work on all the communiqués that continuously come in from around the world. My department was on full duty in order to complete the reports on the many disturbances around the world and the required analysis. We are, but then again we are not the intelligence department of the United Nations since they officially do not have any such thing.

Tuesday and I am deep in computer read outs. My main staff is making head way, but everything must be read. Then it is categorized and the data is re-entered in more understandable and official format.

Wednesday and I'm off to get some lunch in the commissary. With so few people here the selections for sustenance is not too appetizing. "I'll have some turkey soup and a vanilla milk shake." Can't go too wrong with those items unless they're made with last week's turkey. "As I took my tray I asked for some crackers." Finished with the soup I went back to my office and sat looking out the window drinking my shake. Mum, it's getting colder outside. I could see the wind blowing the trees in a swirling motion and the sky getting gray.

"Hey Hank there is a note on your desk from a Jerry Ness. Did you see it?"

"Not yet Barbara, let me look. Oh yes, here it is. Thanks."

Strange, this is an Alexandria exchange. I remember that from my time at Georgetown University. I dialed the number. No greetings just a voice saying this is 667-2300. "I'm trying to reach Jerry Ness do I have the right number?"

"One moment please."

A transferring sound then click, buzz, a beep-beep and, "Hello, Ness here."

"Jerry, this is Hank Brayden in New York."

"Hey, hello there. Glad you called. I am going to the City and then on a ten day trip to the East. Wonder if we can do lunch again on this coming Friday. I will be with Jack you know from the CIA, I mentioned him when we met the last time. I have a special trip planned to go to Japan, Hong Kong, Indonesia, Israel, and Kuwait so I thought you could up date me on the UN's perspective on terrorists activities in these countries. I have already been through briefings here at the agency."

"Agency? I thought that I was calling your office in Alexandria."

Jerry retorted, "I'll Explain that later when we meet."

"Well OK, things are easing up for me a little now with my staff picking up more of the load, so sure."

Jerry cut in; "I still like Giovanni's so let's meet there again say at 1:00 pm."

"Okay, I'll be there."

Friday and it was Jerry calling at 1:30 to ask me what happened? "Jerry I'm sorry, but the time got away. I'll be right there."

"No problem, the flight was late and we've only been here a short time. We'll start with a cocktail without you!"

I grabbed my case, set my laptop inside, took my jacket and headed for the elevator.

Approaching Jerry and his friend Jack from the CIA I let them know I was satisfied with my arrival time, "Well it only took me five minutes so where is my drink?"

"No problem I'll buy the first one. Let's go to the table I reserved and the waiter will catch our order. Hank this is Jack Madden."

He was a solid looking guy with that total CIA look including the blue pin strip, "Well hello Jack, how was the flight?"

"Pretty standard. Where's the waiter? I could use another drink."

Relaxing in my chair I thought to my self, 'Not much on words this will be an interesting lunch'.

Jerry blurred out as usual, "How are things at the UN?"

"I'm still on my project but I've come to believe that not much good comes from all the information our department puts out in the reports we do, even though the State Department gets copies."

"If you don't mind Hank, what do you mean?"

On the cautious side I explained myself. "I am concerned that the environment within the body of the United Nations is tainted with mostly liberal thinking. So much so that the current philosophy is that the world would be a lot better if the sovereignty of all individual governments were placed in the hands of the UN. They have often used the work from my department for political reasons to show that if there was a world wide central governing body the UN could accomplish the settlement of most disputes and uprisings. That ideology from the core inside the body politic keeps them from making an earnest effort to abate any of the brewing problems identified in our reports."

"No I mean the State Department receiving copies of your reports."

"Oh, our government in DC directly supports the budget for my department and in return they receive copies of all intelligence reports. That was the agreement when I came over to the UN."

The waiter approached. "Any one ready to order or want another cocktail?"

"First bring Jack and I the same and Hank how about you?"

"A Samuel Adams please."

Jerry turned to Jack saying, "Then we have all of the UN intelligence information!"

Jack squinted, "Unless the reports get pigeon holed somewhere along the line the answer would be yes as they are supposed to be headed to each security agency after release from State."

Jerry thought for a moment, "Jack, you know better than us."

"Pigeon holed or stacked on some bureaucrat's desk, which is highly possible."

"Hank, any chattering going on right now that could help me on my trip?"

"Chattering, what do you mean?" "Oh, that's our agency talk for information received from various sources including any trapped communications from the enemy. You guys don't look at your information that way. We have enemies and so our approach is different."

The waiter brought the drinks, we ordered lunch and Jack took over the conversation. "Hank, as I have said many times before, we have big problems looming for this country. Ever since the Ayatollah caused the embassy take over in Iran the Muslims have taken liberty to challenge the United States and actually the entire world." During lunch Jerry and Jack reviewed many of the terrorist acts the radical Muslims had initiated. Jerry finished his sandwich as he started on Clinton. "You know that Clinton did nothing about bin Laden. The Taliban and al-Qaeda are flourishing and continuing to make plans to do more and more collateral damage to us in many places around the world. Bore would be a disaster for our future. He would approach these terrorist with a desire to sit down and negotiate our differences. I can just see him now as he pulls out his hanky and dusts off his chair before he sits down at the negotiating table and then gently wipes his lips before he starts to open his mouth. At the same time the Arabic representatives pull out their knives and then cut every infidels throat at the table. He just doesn't get it. It looks like we will get Cush for President and I say 'Thank You God'. Jerry is going on a special mission to meet with a few operatives who must stay incommunicado. We are concerned about more airline disasters and we are hoping there is some kind of discovery to be made on what is behind all of this chatter we are getting from our eavesdropping and other covert activities. Something is brewing and we are not sure what. Of course there are some that think an attack on our presidential inauguration is the plan. We are standing tight on this supposition until we find out differently and all of the input we can get will give us a better chance for defending ourselves. Can you add anything about activity in these Middle Eastern countries where Jerry is going or any terrorist information that has come to you through the UN's sources?" Stunned I was wide eyed when I finally answered, "You said the inauguration and you did not skip a beat. You're very serious. Well, as of this moment I can't say we have heard anything like that, but I must let you know that we are usually three months behind on our analysis of incoming data. I doubt that we have any Intel that would help."

This prognostication for January was still resounding in my head as Jerry asked the waiter for the check. "And you have no idea yet who the terrorists might be or where they will come from."

Jack's face was like a stone monument when he answered. "Oh yes we do but we have no actual intercept inside the states yet. It is absolutely Osama and it is absolutely al-Qaeda or Hamas loyalist who have been embedded here for some time."

"Already here and you can not find them?" I was shocked at Jack's cool attitude on the subject, "Are you serious?"

Jerry responded to my question, "Remember Hank I told you the first time we had lunch that there are now too many Muslims in this country to know who is who. We must wait for them to accidentally cause their own exposure."

I couldn't believe the laze-far attitude. "That's crazy. Then it will be too late!"

"Hank that is what I implied."

With gritting teeth the words rolled out of Hank's mouth, "I'll get all of my people together early Monday morning and do a through briefing with instructions for them to bring me the latest incoming information from the middle-east. Jerry, call me Monday afternoon and I'll see if anything is of importance. An attack on the inauguration would be a disaster!"

Jack reaffirmed my comment, "No question. Our flight back to DC is at 4:00 pm so we'll go over to the Hilton and get the limo."

As we got up from the table Jack put his arm on my shoulder and commented, "Hank, it was nice to meet you."

Jerry said good bye and added, "Talk to you on Monday Hank."

It was the first Monday in December and Jerry placed his call to Hank as he had planned but all that Hank had was that there were some henchmen of al-Qaeda in Hong Kong and the government there was watching them very closely. Muslims did not normally gather in Hong Kong. Jerry had not told Hank that he and Jack were both going on the mission together. That rather innocuous information from Hank seemed to fit into the other pre-trip briefings they had received but nevertheless when they left in the next few weeks Hong Kong was going to be their first stop.

Hank knew that his next few weeks would be centered around Christmas with Tiama and family. He hoped that what he given Jerry would help with his assignment. Hank thought about the Holiday plans and Tiama.

FLASHBACK to February, 1992 - Newark, New Jersey

The morning was very cold and a major snow storm was belting the east coast as Musab Yasin headed to his insurance office. He imagined that half of the employees would stay home because the traffic control division of the highway department started at 5:00am on television telling everyone that this would be a major blizzard. He knew he had too many important things to do at his office and since his drive to the office would be on major streets that would probably be kept cleared he felt certain he could make it. He drove into the driveway and saw that the snow was already about a foot deep. Since the driveway went downhill into the underground garage he paused to open the gate before going down the decline. He was correct because the snow began to pile up in front of his tires so he accelerated enough to push on into garage and then stopped. He was early so he left the gate open.

Once upstairs and into his office he took out the list of dealerships he needed to start up. Baltimore, Atlanta, Chicago, Denver, Salt Lake City, Seattle, Sacramento, San Bernardino, Albuquerque, Houston, and

USA: THE SERPENT IS CRUSHED!

Kansas City. Musab had been in the states since 1982. His family came from Iran asking for political asylum even though they were Syrian citizens. Phony documents were not too hard to get at that time and the United States government had implemented an 'Open Door' policy which really meant just fly here and you can walk right in. There were many from all over the Middle East that had planted themselves in the states. To Musab it was a joke but a convenience that was a blessing from allah. So many of his Muslim brothers had come into the country and embedded themselves into communities from coast to coast. They had claimed professional type backgrounds and were willing to take any kind of job to make an image of a good citizen. There was money for those that could set up businesses and be successful. All the money anyone would ever need. If you just asked any of the Arabic immigrates they would say they all had rich families that were helping them. What fools these idiotic Americans are with their open society. Musab had been sent to help build an integral part of the plan to take down the American 'Kuffers'. The Ji'had had started many moons ago and true Muslims had been waiting, and waiting, and waiting.

"Operator, please get me Dr. al-Zawahiri in Egypt at (962) 35-87-981...................... Not available? Okay then Operator leave a message for my Dr. to call me back at this number, it is very important." Looking up he saw Andrea, "Good Morning Andrea how was the drive to work?"

"A little scary but I only came a short distance as you know. Did you want some coffee?" "Yes, of course and I am waiting on an international call coming in from Egypt soon. Please be careful and watch for it! Also after the coffee is finished please bring me last quarter's financials and the summation of the income from our client base."

She returned in a matter of a few minutes not with coffee or reports but a call for her boss, "Sir, there is an international call on the line but it is not from Egypt, it is from Brazil, a Mr. al-Aziz."

"Please shut my door and hold my coffee. Hello operator, yes this is Mr. Yasin." Musab answered in Arabic. "Hello, is that you Jonathan, can you hear me? Good, I was waiting to hear from our Doctor friend in Egypt. I am ready to build the dealerships. Everything here is going well. How is your business going? I have heard that you are almost ready to begin the manufacturing so we can meet the established annual quotas and that Yassir will build the boat dealership in Miami for you this year. We are all blessed by allah. Our agency has grown and we have done well."

Andrea bussed in on the intercom, "Musab, your international call from Egypt is on the line. Do you want your coffee now?"

"Yes, and tell the operator to wait one minute. Jonathan, the Dr. is on the phone now so I will talk to you later after I have all of the news. He may also call you to get your report direct. Also I know that Abu Eisa will be here soon to meet with each of us. I must go. We will talk later, Good bye." Over the intercom he commanded, "Andrea bring me that coffee and let me know how many people have shown up for work." He turned on the low noise generator which actually sounded like rain and went back to his desk to take the call from Egypt when Andrea opened the door with the coffee.

"Here, careful it is very hot! Eleven so far but I think that will be it. Do you want the reports now?"

"What? Yes now, I need them right NOW! Hello operator. Hello operator. What happened? Andrea WHERE IS MY CALL?"

"Just a minute Sir, I'll see. Where do you want the reports?"

"On the desk. Get me my call and shut the door."

The phone rang on Musab's desk. "Hello opera.... "

"No this is Dr. al-Zawahiri. Musab I have been waiting for your call. Praise be to allah and his prophet Mohammed. Is everything in place?"

"Business is good and today I have begun the program 'Over-Ground Death'. But first let me review the insurance company. We have over ten thousand clients all over the states and most are our brothers. Over the past six years I have been accepted as an agent with thirteen different major insurance carriers and have built an influential business in the Newark area and I am highly respected in the industry. I report that our financials are one and a half million dollars in our business accounts and we have the ten million in the Mid-East Bank of Yemen to build the dealerships. I will have most of them operating by next year with our most reliable people in charge."

"The light shines on you Musab and all is good news. You will be able to get the first shipment of the equipment you need for your dealerships by the end of 1993 and you will have all of the product necessary for each of your locations by 2001. allah will give you continued success in the ATV and SEAWAVE business There are great plans in development stages and we must all be patient! Good bye my brother, allah's blessings go with you."

"Andrea, I want to meet with all of my business partners on this list of names in New York City in two weeks. Please type these letters of instructions on the time and place for the gathering and mail them today." This was not the normal way of contacting the Muslim brothers but it was a standard business meeting and common method for business in the states so nothing would appear strange.

I was getting serious with Tiama and we spent the week before Christmas shopping together in one of the finest shopping area in the world, The Big Apple. There is probably no other place on earth that Christmas feels like Christmas more than in New York, especially if there is a gentle off and on snow fall during Christmas week. Walking down Fifth Avenue and window shopping, venturing into the restaurants on Second Avenue and stopping by the Plaza Hotel for an afternoon drink to dislodge the chill of the winter wind; that is part of the Christmas season in New York. All of the bright lights decorating the streets and Rockefeller Center adds a lot to the season. Christmas nostalgia brings back memories of a beautiful Christmas season in Kansas City when I was there to be with some of Mom's relatives. Not quite like New York but in its own way a feeling of Christmas that was more homey and real with the spectacular display of The Plaza lights and the tens of thousands of beautifully decorated houses. I have never seen anything like it since, but New York is different and special. I planned on a white Christmas with Tiama and the family. We spent every evening after work together and we bought presents for everyone. I would have to shop for her on a different day.

It was two days before Christmas when I picked Tiama up at her apartment for our trip to the farm. My bicycle had been gone for a while and her hall had a replacement, a chest from an Indian store which made the space more utilitarian. Her apartment was decorated with items from all over with much of the furnishings coming from upper end second hand stores along 55th and 56th streets. It was comfortable and tasteful. I had spent time there for dinners and watching videos, enjoying the feeling of her furnishings influenced by her flare for both the primitive and the natural. But I never stayed over night. We had both agreed that we would not impose on each other to stay over and cause doubt as to our real intentions this time. I wanted to be sure that we were really to be a thing and not a fling. Tiama was in total agreement with me as she never wanted another experience like the last one; NO commitment and second rate status.

The train was almost completely full as was to be expected and the over heads were full. We had sent all of our Christmas packages to the farm via United Parcel and only had two small bags with us, so I placed them under the seat and we settled back to enjoy the ride through the country and the view of the glimmering lights reflecting off of the snow covered trees and buildings.

Caroline was there to pick us up at the train station and drove us through town before going to the house so she could buy some eggnog and brandy. "Hey sis do you have the cinnamon and nutmeg for the top?" I asked as she handed me the sack.

"Well of course. What would Holiday eggnog be without the topping?" She parked the car close to the back door and I carried in our bags.

"Hi Dad."

"Hello guys how have you been? Tiama, you look fresh and Christmas-y, must be the chilly country air."

"Great Mr. Brayden, and are you ready for the holidays?"

"Please just call me Tom and yes I'm ready. I took some much needed the time off before we start with the inauguration coverage's and of course all of the parties. With Cush now elected there has been a lot of positioning going on with the political leaders in the Republican Party and there are a number of congratulatory parties arranged for his cohorts to be able to meet and sway decisions for political appointments. I want to be sure we cover it all. Come on over to the fire place and sit while I get you all a sandwich and a drink. We have ham and cheese, or cheese and ham, and just ham or just cheese. I'm saving the turkey for tomorrow. Plus you name your drink."

The house was decorated in all white lights that intermittently flashed as if to some song. Maybe a Christmas Carol. In side there was the usual nine foot tree with every color light available and the tree was covered with a glistening spun glass material that reflected the lights differently from each direction the tree was viewed. Caroline had put up holly and tree sprigs around most of the door openings with a string of lights and a string of electrically operated small bells at the archway leading to the dining room. The atmosphere was perfect and Grandmamma was sitting right in the middle of it as happy as she could be. Dad had put some Chopin on the stereo and as it played softly in the background we just talked and talked and talked. Caroline about her new boy friend, Tiama about her days in the Philippines, Dad about his plans for retirement and me well I reflected back on my boyhood days here on the farm and the fun it was to grow up in this house with a wonderful family. We had finished our sandwiches earlier and talked our way through our first eggnog of the season and a snifter of Brandy. Dad offered everyone some desert; no takers so we all scooted off to bed.

I woke Tiama early to help me fix some coffee and biscuits with honey and then we woke up Dad, Caroline and Grandmamma. Dad and I started a Christmas fire. Dad had already brought in a Yule log about twenty inches in diameter and there was plenty of kindling and other smaller logs to get a good start on the fire. He had built the fireplace for winter fires to keep the living area warm without using the heater. It was one of those old fashion style fireplaces you see in pictures of houses built in the late eighteen hundreds, six feet tall, rising above the hearth that was about eighteen inches above the floor. At about three feet long the Yule log fit perfectly into the four foot wide opening and it would more than likely burn through the night and into Sunday.

After breakfast with a nice fire going we sat around the fireplace and spent about an hour to sing a few Christmas Carols which had always been the family's routine followed by opening of our gifts and a lot of thank yous Then it was the girls off to the kitchen to start the preparations for the dinner.

Dad turned on the big screen TV and put on the Macy's Christmas Day parade. It was not on very loud as all he wanted to see was how well his people at UBC did on placing the cameras and the program presentation. While he watched the TV I asked him about the election and the coming inauguration. "I think we are much better off with Cush than Bore but I'll wait on who he appoints to be with him before I make any other judgments."

Then he changed the subject to the possibility of problems at the inauguration. I decided to tell him about my discussion with Jerry and Jack but knew that what I knew he had probably already heard from the Broadcast News dogs at UBC that were always sniffing around Washington. "I have not heard much of anything at work at the UN about attacks here at home or at the inauguration but I had lunch with

Jerry and Jack Madden over a week ago and they both are very concerned. Jack is Jerry's friend from the CIA. They have each gone on assignments to gather intelligence that may lead to more definitive analysis of the situation here but we have nothing positive at the UN. I guess everyone at the agencies is working over time to get factual information on the potential threat. Jerry privately suggested to me that some soundings point towards the use of airplanes for an attack on us, but how has not been determined."

"Of course we are fairly sure that Saddum Hussein and most terrorist would rather have Bore than Cush to deal with and threats to obstruct the inauguration need to be taken seriously."

Tom, in a serious tone changed the subject, "Son, on a different note, you know one of your friends from NYU, Ghassem, works in our financial department and some agents came in to talk with him two days ago. They said it was routine and would not let any of us in upper management know what was said, but I wonder why they came to interview him. Was it because he is Arabic? And do you know if he is a Muslim? Do you see him anymore? I know we should not ethnically profile anyone but you do wonder."

Sipping on my eggnog I cut Dad short, "Whoa Dad, I saw him at the reunion but I have not kept track of him. He seemed pretty laid back at school and I would not classify him as any kind of a radical, but today in this environment who knows what is what." Hank continued, "The conversations I had with Jerry Ness and his friend Jack were somewhat disturbing. They purport that the agencies don't have any tracking on any of the thousands of Muslims in this country and so who knows who is who. You said at Thanksgiving that Jerry had been interviewed on UBC discussing terrorism and the potential danger that exist to the airlines. Well he truly believes that a Ji'had against the United States actually began with the over throw of the Shah and the capturing of our embassy in Iran. Because they were so successful in having their way and we did nothing in retaliation it gave the radical Muslim factions around the world the inspiration to come against the United States and the Jews. He says that at least ten percent of the Muslims around the world hate the Americans and have pledged their lives to kill us no matter where we are. He truly believes that the al-Qaeda and the Hamas are heavily entrenched in the states and we have no idea who they are. Using his numbers that he says are from our government's statistics; he purports that there are approximately six to seven million

Muslims in this country and since there are approximately 10% of the Muslims around the world that are fundamentalist with radical views we have loose in the United Sates approximately four hundred thousand potential terrorist. A staggering number if you stop to think about it and no way to find them. He thinks we are ultimately doomed! And that scenario is frightening."

The weather was changing as we spoke; noticing the snow flakes in the air swirling around by the wind Dad went to the log bin next to the hearth to put another two logs on the fire. As he sat back down his voice was slightly husky, "Well, all of us at the station realized that we are in a different world since the attempt on the World Trade Center in ninety three, the bombing of the marine barracks in Saudi Arabia, the bombing of our two embassies in Africa, and the explosion that almost sank the USS Cole by suicide attackers, and then an array of other plans to do damage to the United States. All of us must be vigilant in our gathering of information and communicate any suspicious stories to the authorities. But Jerry's diagnosis is one for the books. It could very well make sense."

Watching the snow outside I was a little hesitant in my next words. "I will be hearing from Jerry when he returns and I suppose that he will have been in contact with Jack. They may have some enlightenment about any operations under way to disrupt the inauguration. I don't get as much of the covert information at the UN that Jack and Jerry are exposed to at the agencies but let's stay in closer contact as January 23rd approaches. And we can all pray for a peaceful changing of the guard and security for our country."

Dad said an Amen to that as Tiama came from the kitchen to let us know that dinner was ready. Dad and I had already turned the football game on and Tiama said that football would have to stop or we could eat in the living room. We chose to eat buffet style by the fireplace and watch the game there. Tiama was okay with that but Caroline sat in the dinning room with grandmamma.

"Go Chiefs, burn the Chargers. Did you all see that play?"

Sunday evening had come much too quickly; so with the passing of the Christmas celebration our fun times at the farm came to end and the saying of goodbyes to my family was quite sad. Tiama and I were back in the city with the New Years Eve holiday staring us straight in the face and prompting us to make more plans for another celebration. I wasn't in the mood for partying this year so to not let Tiama down I asked her what she would like to do on New Year's Eve. "Hank, can I fix us dinner at my apartment and we can watch the ball drop on the television. I would rather have a quiet time and be alone with you unless you want to go out."

"Great idea, that's what I was thinking. I'm so glad you were thinking the same thoughts. I'd much rather have a quiet time at home."

Putting my arms around her I looked at her in the dim light coming into the cab from the street lamps. "We'll celebrate the start of the new year with the start of our new life together. I want you to know how much I love you!" Asking the cabby to wait for me I carried her bag up to her apartment and spent a few minutes in her arms letting my lips tell her how much I desired to be with her. She placed her firm lips on mine and together our lips made love, the longing passionate type love that would have to wait until we were married!

Christmas holidays ended and Hank and Tiama passed New Years with the engulfing anticipation of their pending future together.

CHAPTER SEVEN

January, 2001

Even though Hank had given Jerry classified information from some of his last communications report about al-Qaeda operatives in Hong Kong before Christmas; Jerry and Jack needed to run all of their information through the DOD's data base to get confirmation that the reports of al-Qaeda operatives had been confirmed and just before they left for Hong Kong they had been told that an informant was offering information on al-Qaeda to the U.S. embassy in Hong Kong. A mission to meet with the informant and to uncover the purposes of a large number of al-Qaeda people gathering in Honk Kong was of interest to the CIA and ACE. They were delayed by the internal operations department at the CIA and did not leave until second week in January. Seems that the encounter with the possible informant was put off till sometime towards the middle of January. After a short stop in Japan, Jerry and Jack hopped on a government courier flight to Hong Kong.

Their plane flew down the bay past hundreds of tall buildings, more accurately sky scrapers, and as they landed it bounced repeatedly on the runway. These 'Hot Dog' ex navy pilots brought us in too hot, Jack thought. But every pilot knows the extreme cross winds that come up at the Kai Tak airport are dangerous making landings almost impossible. Looking at Jack, Jerry who knew this side of the world very well, made a profound comment. "Hong Kong is a real dichotomy of cultures. On one side is a thriving city and one of the world's largest financial centers and across the bay is Kowloon, China; a city about as poor and treacherous as any place in the world." Jack mused to himself, 'Makes our job exciting and entertaining as we enjoy the highlife in Hong Kong and the danger that lurks on every street In Kowloon'. Jack was known to be crazy about the thrill of danger.

After leaving the airport they went to the embassy to contact Washington on a secure line, and then picking up a very important scrambled message went to decoding. It was instructions to meet not an informant but to talk to a specific arms dealer named Taug. There were suspicions that some high profile arms dealers were in Hong Kong and the word was that there had been some movement of contraband from Indonesia to the States. But a dealer by the name of Taug was unknown to any of the agencies of the state department.

Catching a San Pan Jerry and Jack headed to one of the many floating restaurants in the bay on the Chinese side. At the Bright Moon restaurant they waited for Mr. Taug. After two hours Jerry said to Jack, 'a no show'. They walked out on the porch which went completely around the restaurant and looked for one of the San Pan taxis to take them back, and just then a very short Chinese looking man in a white apron approached them from the back side of the porch. "I'm looking for Mr. Ness."

"Who are you?"

Taking off the apron he said, "I am the one you want to talk to. I have been watching for the past hour to see that no one else is around you. And I needed the time to be right to show you the goods. I only have ten minutes. Do you have my money?"

"Yes, if the information is verifiable."

"Let me see first. Is that fifty thousand dollars? I will take a moment to count." He took the plastic bag which was actually a water proof shaving kit and took out one ten thousand dollar pack of hundred dollar bills, a little more than a half inch thick. Counted the first one and then took each of the other four and slowly flipped through the packs. "OK, it's correct! Now let me tell you that the rumor you have heard I know to be a fact. There is a container of what you call ATV's, motorcycles, and water vehicles headed to Los Angeles and in the container is four thousand kilos of C4 plus one hundred Chinese MAK-90s with twenty thousand rounds of ammunition hidden in with the crated up parts that go with each shipment."

"What is that, just on your say so? How do we know that? I think your information is bogus. Anyone can conjure up a tale like that." Jack was hot and going for the package of money as Taug was putting the money back in the bag.

"Look, see that boat headed toward the Hong Kong docks. There now see that container that has two Blue stripes and SIND/POLB that is the one. It came from Medan, Sumatra in Indonesia where I personally had the crate filled with the C4."

Hearing C4 again Jack's eyes widen when he turned towards me. "If this C4 story is true Jerry, do you know what that means? It means that if this shipment gets to the states and into the hands of terrorist they will have access to the world's best high explosive plus Military automatic weapons and enough ammunition to hold off a fairly large amount of police."

Taug went on, "The vehicles were loaded in Kowloon four days ago. And now it is going to the Hong Kong docks for loadings on a freighter headed to the states. Go! Check it out. I have given you the real facts. I have worked with these buyers before completing forty deals and this time they said it was the last shipment and they told me they were ending our relationship when one of the four that had loaded the container shot me in neck. I fell in the water and they thought I was dead. I was only nicked by his shots but fell off the dock there and acted dead. Look here! The information and the container are yours." And with that he was around the corner as fast as he had arrived. Jack pulled his Glock and ran as fast as he could to catch the supposed Mr. Taug. He came back with no shots fired, no Mr. Taug, and no money.

"I think I was just taken and it is not going to happen. Get in that San Pan over there and let's catch him now! I've never had this happen before. We'll either catch the SOB or I'll kill him." Jack had the killer look in his eyes and I had never seen him like this. I've killed over a hundred people including my Vietnam tour so I was ready, but Jack would accept nothing but Taug's blood. It was encouraging to know that I had a backup I could count on and in this business you have to react now, with deliberation and absolute commitment. Our San Pan headed back north towards the docks at Hong Kong but Jack motioned to the driver to head west towards Kowloon. There he could see a small San Pan half the size of ours heading in the direction of Kowloon. "Catch that boat now"! Jack screamed at the driver. Just then the small San Pan blew sky-high in a bright flash and then came the loud blast. Jack screamed again to the driver, "Get over there now! I want to see what happened and look for the remains and I want our money!"

There were only a few pieces in just a few areas. It was scattered out too far and we could not be sure if we were at the site of the explosion. Jack had the driver circle and circle but he could not find the pouch with the money. "That was a plastic pouch and I'm sure he closed it before he took off, it should be floating." We went in wider and wider circles for fifteen minutes. Nothing that was floating looked like a pouch. "Dam-it, take us back to the docks, I see some kind of patrol boats coming, police or some authorities from Hong Kong."

"Jerry this was a set up but why? He didn't bring us out to the restaurant to get himself blown up. But who knew we came here for a meeting with him and why him and not us too? Who ever it is, they may not have known who he was meeting before but now they do and what happened to the money? It should have been there. His buddies that wasted him will be after us to find out what went down. We need less exposure for a day or two and watch who comes and goes."

As we docked Jack spotted where he thought the boat with the container had landed. "Earlier as the boat passed I spotted the name Hundi on the shipping container and a big SIND/POLB. With the two Blue stripes we maybe able to find it." Jack went on, "And Jerry, when something smells like Mackerel it stinks and to me this is one big Mackerel." We drove around the docks for forty minutes until we found the container on Pier 52B. Jack's first notion was to go in through the pier gate but then he said with a second thought, "Great, back to the hotel and we'll report in early tomorrow at the embassy."

"Marine, who has the watch today? OK, tell him Jack Madden and Jerry Ness are here." The Marine behind the bullet proof glass got on the phone and in less than a minute we were greeted with, "Sir, I'm Lieutenant Meyers. What can I do for you?"

"Lieutenant, here are our credentials. I know the ambassador and his aide are gone today and we need a secure communications room."

"Yes Sir, I'll be right back."

"Jack, I can only stay here for two days since my assignment calls for punctual appearances at my other mission locations. I will be in Israel on Friday."

"I understand Jerry, but I must stay here to check out the container."

"Gentlemen, please go to the side door over there and I'll click you in, and then proceed down the corridor to the counter on your left. Sergeant Washington will escort you to your room. Good day."

Once inside Jack was on line with his section chief. "Sir I do not know what happened exactly but our informant took the money after a convincing scenario and identifying the target. He said that he had set up forty shipments over the past few years and C4 and weapons has been in each container along with a full load of some kind of vehicles. This was the last organized shipment but he said they tried to kill him. After pointing out the target he grabbed the money and ran. He got into his San Pan and left." A short pause. "Yes I chased him and tried to shoot him but he was too far away and with the bouncing waves I could not get off a clean shot. Then a minute or so later his San Pan was blown up with him and the money, I think."

Jack was a little flushed as the chief interrupted with a "What do you mean you think!!!!" It was so loud Jerry heard every word.

"We found nothing around the site and the money pouch should have been floating there or else the money would have scattered all over the water. But there was nothing. I searched for the container we had seen and located it on pier 52B and Jerry and I are going to chase it today. I need you to get governmental approval to break the seal and open it for examination."

"Jack what is happening to you? You've made three mistakes and what if this is number four? I can't back you up if it is another mistake. You're alone on this case. We will deny any involvement."

"What three mistakes?"

"Listen to me, you trusted your informer. You lost the money. And you left the surveillance of the target."

"Okay, but it's not that easy. The money is still around and I could not stay on the pier last night due to the heavy security. I would have been stopped. As to Mr. Taug he's for real or otherwise why the termination. I'll get the answers but Jerry will need to be leaving. He must be in Israel by Friday. Get me that authorization to pop the seal on the container and listen, I didn't make any mistakes. My informer is probably dead, the money is somewhere and I've got the container. And Sir if the information is true then this investigation is about C4 and military weapons shipped to the States, I need that authorization! Good bye."

Jerry was deep in thought when Jack finished, so he had missed Jack's explanation to his chief. It didn't matter. They had a problem that needed to be solved and right now. Jerry began in a slow but direct voice. "Jack, how was it that you could not get a shot at Taug at the restaurant? He was only maybe four or five seconds in front of you."

"Because, he jumped from the front of the porch into a waiting San Pan and then the San pan went under the restaurant through the pilings and off towards Hong Kong. By the time I got back to the side where I could see, he was to far away."

"Okay Jack, think about this. We could not immediately chase him and it was maybe a couple of minutes then the San Pan blew up. What if he never jumped into the San Pan and went into the restaurant by way of a side door. We chased smoke, and Taug and the money disappeared. I think we were had but not by an explosion but by a premeditated escape plan and cover-up."

"Let's go! I'm opening that container with or without the authorization. First we can pick up a document here from a friend that will look and smell official with language that sounds official. Sergeant Washington I need to talk to a Kim Cramer in clerical."

"Yes Sir."

"Kim its Jack, Jack Madden and I really need some help. If I give you what I need over the phone can you bring it to me in the commissary? Wonderful, I'll be there having some coffee."

After Jack told Kim what he wanted over the phone we went to get coffee. Thirty minutes later Kim came in and handed Jack a couple of envelopes. He gave her a quick hug and said thanks, turned to me and said "We're finished."

As we drove towards the piers I knew we were on an unauthorized investigation. We were hoping to uncover a major smuggling operation by al-Qaeda and confirm what had been suggested as a possibility that there was a large cache of arms and explosive material already inside the borders of the States. A revelation of this possible magnitude would rock NSA and the administration not to say how it would play on Clinton's future evaluation especially since Clinton had not taken action against bin Laden. We needed this information to be accurate and provable so Jack and I were putting our reputations on the line. However the sacrifice wasn't even on our minds, just the exposure of the plot. What was the worst that could happen to us if our plan was discovered was for us to simply use denial and then escape from the area.

At the gate we encountered a guard that allowed us through when we flashed our badges. He didn't ask to see the ID's just our badges.

They looked official enough. At the pier it was more difficult because we had to request the unloading of the Blue stripped container, locate dock workers and convince the superintendent that our papers were legitimate. He called the embassy to find a person to verify our written order that Kim had manufactured but no one in the proper section could be found. Jack pushed on the urgency for the investigation claiming all kinds of contraband in the container and finally after twenty minutes he was allowed to cut the seal and begin the unloading. Holding the original embassy envelope, Jack took the document he had given the superintendent and put it back into the envelope, but then he quickly switched it with another one he had wisely brought along as a back up. The dock workers mostly Indian brought out create after create marked Awai and full of ATV's, motorcycles, Seawaves, and crates with parts but seventy five percent of the way through Jack and I realized that we had been ripped off big time. And now we had no evidence of any smuggling and a dock superintendent who was an officer of the Hong Kong government who would soon not only be questioning us further but he would probably get the security police on the dock to come to get more information on who we really were. Jack moved closer to me and nudged me to edge towards the other containers on the dock that were stacked two high and lined up in the direction of the entrance gate.

As the workers began to take the last row out of the container and they pointed to all of crates with gestures of "what are we looking for', Jack took me down the first row of containers and then between two stacks that allowed us to temporarily disappear. Running to the entrance gate Jack said what I already knew, "Let's get away now! You drive and I'll watch to make sure they don't see our car!"

Spinning the wheels I reversed the car and headed to the main street. I went in the direction of Central Street but away from our hotel and then turned right and up the hilly streets of Victoria Peak until I came to an area that had a number of shops, bars, and restaurants. I pulled into a public parking garage and shut down the engine. "WOW Jack, I need a drink and a breather to work this out".

We went straight into the first bar and sat down on the side where no one else was sitting. It was still about an hour before noon and the bar was fairly vacant. "What is going on with this gamble we just took? No Mr. Taug. No Money. No Explosives. No Smuggling." I paused and with total uncertainty I asked, "Maybe there where two containers exactly alike and the one we opened was a decoy! Or maybe Taug took the money and then tipped off al-Qaeda and we were double-crossed! Is there any truth in the story at all? You are going to have to report something and of course deny anything about this dock incident. I'm set to go to Israel Friday so where should we start; I have two days but what are we looking for?"

Jack was silent. I think he was going through all of the possible scenarios in his mind and maybe even other operatives he could find to talk to for information. I was wondering how many people he might know here? Hong Kong has many buried agents from all over the world but you need to know the right ones. Jack has been on assignments in the East for many years. He is going to have to go deep now. The al-Qaeda has no friends and they trust no one. He broke the silence as he took a sip of his scotch, "I think Taug was sending us a message. First, I truly believe that al-Qaeda tried to dispose of him and they found out they had failed, so the attempt on his life was real. Secondly, he is too smart to get caught in a trap so I think he did not get on that San Pan yesterday and he kept the money and hid out in the restaurant. I think for sure if we go to the restaurant we'll find his friend that helped him and get some straight answers. And third, he was telling us that he was the arms dealer who supplied the contraband which was headed for the States. Was this one we opened really headed to the west coast or was it a fake? Was he a decoy for al-Qaeda and decided to pick up fifty G's at the same time I am not sure. Could there be a second container just like the one we saw; it is possible but where is that one and where is it headed? But what if there is C4 and automatic rifles hidden somewhere in the States with al-Qaeda operatives or their terrorists sympathizers; we need to find out, I need to find out the truth."

Jerry do you know much about C4 and the ramifications if there is C4 in hands of terrorist in the states?"

I quickly answered, "We had some training. And in the military we used M112."

"Right and here are some facts. RDX, its chemical name is Cyclotrimethylene-trinitramine and yes in the military it is M112 plus there are other forms now being used. The military now uses it in 1.25 pound blocks, but I'll bet what we are looking for is packed in one kilo bars and wrapped in waxed paper. Jerry as you know, the most important fact is that it is a 'high explosive' meaning that its destructive power is awesome. It has two forces of destruction. On explosion the force comes from the expanding gases that move at a speed of 26,400 feet [per second or 18,000 miles per hour out ward and after that expansion there is a second force of an inward implosion because of the vacuum left from the expanding gases. The power of C4 is awesome. The suicide bombers only carry around four or five kilos strapped to their body to do the damage they do. I'm sure you remember the power of C4 but most don't keep up to date with the improvements and proliferation of the supply. The Omar Abd al-Rahman group had plenty of explosives for the attack on the World Trade Center in '93 but what if had been C4? We could easily guess that they did not have access to C4 then so is this tail from Taug true? Just what could have happened to all of the smuggled arms Taug claims knowledge of if any of his scenarios took place? We need to find out. But you know, my thoughts are leaning towards this Awai shipment was a divergence to keep al-Qaeda clear of any suspicion in case Taug had ever sold any information to other agents before they tried to eliminate him. And it's more than likely he believed that the container he identified was the real target. But I am sure as you are sitting here they have us under their microscope. The al-Qaeda network has members everywhere and we may have been observed at the embassy and then followed to that restaurant. There are so many San Pans out there we could have been seen from any number of them and that means they know Taug is not dead. We will need to be invisible for a few days and deny everything that has happened. I'm going hunting to find Taug. I must find out if this is now rumor or fact. And if it is fact then how many containers could have gotten into Canada, the States or even Mexico, and the when and the where are they. And the most important is to find the connection in the states who could have received them. Taug mentioned four thousand kilos so over the years we could be talking about two hundred thousand pounds to as much as four hundred thousand pounds of plastic explosive sold to someone and delivered somewhere and who knows how many automatic assault rifles and ammunition is in the game. I have got to treat this as a real threat and have my mission put on high priority. Tomorrow I'll call in to the chief on what we know and then I'll drop a story of complete denial about the incident on the dock to the ambassador at the embassy. Jerry, this information is top secret and I will be making a coded report to the Company before I leave here. I'm thinking that you might as well pack it in here and get on to Israel. I will need to work alone."

Jerry's meeting in Israel with the ARKIA Airline security directors provided more insight on how dangerous the terrorist threat to airplanes is becoming and how much the Israeli government has been doing to protect its passenger planes against attack or high jacking. None of Jerry's meetings or his probing in the countries of Kuwait, Indonesia, India, Pakistan and Japan provided any more intelligence on future problems or on special precautious the governments of those countries were taking against the worldwide terrorist threat. In Indonesia the attitude was that they were not threatened.

Jerry finished his mission and was home before Valentines Day. He and Anna had promised each other that they would always spend a few days together around Valentines Day and make a little whoopee ever since his work requirements kept him away so much of the time. Over the past few years this had become very important to both of them. However he had to first put the report on his mission together on each country's posture on airline protection for ACE International to present to the FBI and the CIA bringing them up to date on the precautions other countries were taking and more precisely the preventive measures that were under way to protect their passenger air travel. Each had its own layer or vigilance and actions or non actions. By far the most aggressive was El Al Airlines. They had placed air marshals on all passenger planes, secured the pilots compartments with bullet proof reinforced doors, provided Mace spray for all hostesses, trained the pilots in missile attack avoidance, and armed each plane with a missile detraction device to ward off any ground to air Stinger missiles. To protect against the Stinger missile is quite important to El Al since the Muslim terrorists in the middle-east have thousands of them from the war in Afghanistan with Russia. The Stinger can travel to an altitude of eleven thousand feet at a speed of fifteen hundred miles per hour. They get smuggled into Iran and Iraq. Israel is the most venerable and the highest level target on the terrorists list. As Jerry was working on his detailed report he thought about Jack Madden and wondered how successful he had been on finding Taug and especially his investigation into the container shipments. He hoped Jack had made contacts with other arms dealers that could shed some light on what was the truth about the cache of explosives that they believed had been shipped into the States. As he wrapped up his paper work and cleared his desk he pinned a note on his computer to find out when Jack would return.

CHAPTER EIGHT

It was mid-March when the Coastal Express truck driver of the dual-container hauler headed southwest on the 710 and turned off of the freeway on to Pico Avenue. He had been hauling from the Long Beach piers for about two years and was always in awe of the number of ship loading cranes that rose like iron monsters preying on the floating freighters that were dwarfed by their conquerors. One, two, three, six, eleven, twenty four, thirty two he could count and there were still some on the other side of the Ocean boulevard bridge. He turned right onto Avenue Pier G and then pulled in through the gate at area 32. He was immediately stopped by the storage-master and was asked for his documents; the shipping manifest, the receiving authorization and the customs releases. As the storage master looked over the paperwork he quizzed the driver, "Do you have a pick up today? Today is February the 27th and I don't see you on the schedule for this week. I need to call the dock master to find out why you are not scheduled for a pick up today. Are you sure about your dates? I see no dates on your releases. Hold on till I call." He came back in a couple of minutes. "Okay, it seems to be a late request for pickup. You're cleared, so let's see, the papers say that one of your containers is at Isle N7 and Row E8 and the other at Isle N1 and Row W6. Check your container numbers and the serial number on the seals before loading. Then stop at the exit gate and give the guard your papers and they will confirm the serial numbers. Have a good trip."

The diver found his two Hundi containers with SIND/POLB on the lower right side. One container had two yellow stripes and the rarely used Blue stripe but the other had the standard double Yellow stripes of Hundi International. He left one of his flat bed haulers at the first location and after jockeying into position with the second one he hooked up his cable and pulled the container onto the hauler, fastened it to the bed and went after the first container. Finished, he stopped at the guard gate for an inspection of the seals to verify the security of the containers and confirmation of the numbers. With the pick up completed he called in to his dispatcher to report that he had been released from the High-Seas Shipping storage yard and was on the road with his trip to San Bernardino and then Las Vegas.

It was the same day in mid-March when a Pacific-Mountain Transport carrier arrived at the Port of Oakland to pick a container being held by High-Seas Shipping to be delivered to Salt Lake City. Hundi containers were generally shipped with High-Seas Shipping which was owned by a wealthy stockholder of Hundi. The driver had never been to the storage yard used by High-Seas shipping so he was a little uncertain of the route. He pulled over to call his dispatcher. "Hello, is this Jake? Hey this is Ron and I am not clear on the route to pick up this container for Land-N-Sea Sports. Get me some directions."

"Sure, hold a minute while I finish this other call. .... Okay it looks like you take FWY #880 east from Oakland to Union St off ramp to Fifth Ave. and then go right on Adeline St to Middle Harbor Rd. and straight till you get to Ferro St and alon........"

"Hold on, I am still at Fifth and then on to Adeline St."

"That's right and then Middle Harbor RD, actually Adeline crosses third and becomes Harbor Rd. Then follow Harbor Rd. to Ferro St and High-Seas Shipping should have their storage area somewhere on the left. Got to go, you'll find it."

Ron drove down Ferro Street looking to his left as he thought to himself, 'Hum, I see a lot of containers but not storage lots and none of these areas have any fencing or security. I guess I have to just try to locate this on my own. Anyone could come in here and steal a container and no one would know. Let me see, it is a Hundi container with one blue stripe and SIND/POLB for identity. Man, up and down four lanes and I finally found it; I had better check the serial number on the seal to make sure.

He had finished loading the box and securing it when a car with flashing lights pulled up along side of his cab and a security guard got out and asked him to open the driver's side door.

"I need to check your paper work for this container before you leave."
"Sure, Okay; I didn't see anyone in control here. I didn't notice any signs telling me to check in or anything, I'm sorry. I didn't see anybody"
"The sign was on the storage area on your right as you came down Ferro but you turned directly into this area without checking in. We could see you from our watch tower way over there by the offices. You are in violation of the Harbormaster's regulations to always check in before going into the storage areas."

"Man this is my first time here am I am truly sorry."

"Well let's see if your manifest and custom's paperwork is in order." After reading every document thoroughly the guard handed him back his papers and added, "Never make that mistake again and we are required to call your dispatcher on this violation, sorry but it is the rules. Try and have a good day."

As he pulled away he thought; Wow, I'm glad Jake is on duty and he can tell them he gave me the instructions and it was not my fault.

It was the next day when Musab in New Jersey was on the phone to California. "Hello, is this High-Seas Shipping?" Musab was checking on his last shipment of ATVs.

"Yes, may we help you?"

"The dispatcher please, I want to check on the delivery date of my overseas container."

"I will connect you."

"Is this the delivery dispatcher?"

"Yes Sir"

"I have a BLD # 01-324590-02 for an overseas container I'm checking on to see when I can expect delivery to my dealership in Salt Lake City."

The dispatcher put Musab on hold with out saying a word which irritated him immensely and did not return for over three minutes. "Sorry for the wait, it looks like it was picked up yesterday by Coastal Express trucking company and they said that it will be delivered to your location no later than the twenty second of March."

"Is the contact phone number and name clearly shown on the releases and Shipping Manifest?"

"Yes it is, Desert Sports in Las Vegas, 702-098-1111"

"What are you saying? I said Salt Lake City. You have something wrong. TELL ME WHAT HAS HAPPENED TO MY SHIPMENT. Check my Bill of Lading again! Number 01-324590-02 is a shipment by Hundi from Hong Kong going to my store in Salt Lake City, Land-N-Sea Sports. You need to find my shipment!"

"One minute please, I'll double check."

Ten minutes and the dispatcher came back on the line with Musab. "We have your shipment but for some reason it was mixed up in Hong Kong. Your container is in the port in Oakland and was picked up yesterday by Pacific-Mountain Transport company. The other container I found is from Hundi and we show it in Long Beach going to a company in Las Vegas. Yours is actually in Oakland and should be arriving in about eight days or so."

"Are you absolutely sure, do you need to reconfirm while I am on the phone?"

"No I have the correct paperwork here."

Next Musab called the cell leader that ran his distributorship in Salt Lake with the delivery information and the instructions for the unloading and distribution. "Hello Akria, its Musab in New Jersey. I have just been in contact with High Seas shipping and they confirmed that our shipment is on the way with Pacific-Mountain trucking and the dispatcher said that our container was picked up from the shipping docks at the Port of Oakland in California and should be in Salt Lake City in about eight days. When it arrives call me to confirm."

"That is great news. But I thought that our last shipment was coming in from the port of Long Beach."

"No, there were some things that came up in Hong Kong so we had to do some changes in there before this last shipment left."

"So this is our last shipment. I will be ready for the delivery Musab. Praise be to allah."

On the twenty third of March, a Hundi container with ID of SIND/POLB and a Blue stripe arrived at Akria's Land-N-Sea Sports dealership in Salt Lake City. Akria was on hand when the container arrived and after having it dropped inside the rear fenced-in lot at the back of the small industrial building housing the dealership, he started his employees to unloading it. This shipment contained one hundred ATVs and fifty Seawaves. The large parts crates in the center of the container were taken off with fork lifts by two of the most trusted brothers in the cell. The other workers were un-wrapping the plastic foam from each vehicle and organizing them in the storage lot under the car port type covers.

Inside the building the crates were taken to a secure room where Akria supervised the unloading of the weapons and the ammunition and re-packing them into fifty groups of four guns per carton each with four boxes of ten 30 round clips per box all of which had to be taken with the C4 to a private warehouse. The C4 was unpacked and repacked into boxes that looked like 'dry wall' mud boxes. Ten of the one kilo wax paper wrapped squares were placed in each mud carton. Every ten kilo box had ten detonator caps inside. Then Akria had the cartons of C4 packed in wooden creates four boxes to a crate.

Two days later the empty container was picked up by the trucking company. Akria had already taken the crates of explosives and the guns and ammunition to a private warehouse in an older industrial area with lower end sixty year old rundown warehouses. Over the next month this last shipment of ATVs and Seawaves were delivered to the Awai dealers in Utah, Nevada, the Dakotas, Montana, and Idaho. The warehoused explosives and weapons were set for delivery to the cell leaders when the call to action was received.

Musab called Akria on Monday the second of April to get the report on the last shipment from Awai. The phone rang at Land-N-Sea Sports and one of the two cell members answered. Recognizing an Arabic ac-cent over the phone he announced In Arabic, "Hello I'm Musab Yasin calling for Akria."

The answer came back in Arabic. "Just one minute and we will find him."

"Ah a brother", Musab said. "Tell him I am calling from my office in New Jersey."

"Can he call you back because we think he is at the bank?"

"Yes but tell him to call me on the outer extension."

"Alright"

Akria looked more Indian than Arabic and most in the business community and his clients thought that he was from India. A long time ago when he started his account at the old Interstate Bank; his banker with whom he had built a strong banking relationship had asked him about the best restaurant in Salt Lake for Indian food. It was impor-tant for all of the cell leaders to maintain community respect and one sure way was to have a good banking relationship. Akria and the other cell leaders always maintained more that fifty thousand dollars in their accounts. Nothing presented a picture of honesty and stability like money. And they were told to participate in community affairs. He left the bank after making the deposit and stopped for a coffee and sandwich at Ruggles diner.

Back at the dealership his main man on duty in the office told him that Musab had called and wanted him to call him back on the outer extension. Akria took his cell phone out to the back storage lot and dialed Musab's cell phone. "Hello, Musab, it is Akria, how are you?" "Excellent, and has the last of our sixty container shipments been distributed and made ready?"

"Yes to both questions. Over the next week or so every partner will have the equipment necessary for the coming task and all of the candy has been properly stored in a secure location. And now we are ready and waiting."

Musab interjected, "Not waiting because we must always stay busy and maintain our image of successful businesses. We are proud to be prepared for the orders to direct us on our mission. All of the other distributors are set and each of our shipments of special candy for the 'snake' have been prepared. Jonathan has completed the importing of the last special boat and all of its contents are distributed. We have been given new orders on the use of cell phones and that will be conveyed to all cell leaders soon."

CHAPTER NINE

By July of 2001 I was back in New York. The presidential inauguration had gone off beautifully. I remember Jerry had returned after the
inauguration and he had told me that Jack had returned some weeks
after he had. Jerry and I had only talked occasionally over the past
few months but he didn't talk at all about Jack's extended mission. The
chatter as Jerry referred to it had gone silent and things seemed to be
a bit more stable. Only the Israeli's were getting a beating from the
Palestinians with Arafat telling the United Nations security council he
was pushing to stop the suicide bombers out of one side of his mouth
while he was telling his people to kill, kill the Jews out of the other
side. Saddum Hussein was paying rewards to the families of the suicide bombers that reeked havoc on the Israeli people and nobody could
get any kind of a cessation of the attacks. For the most part Cush was
off to a good start and threats seemed to have subsided. A 'Road Map
to Peace' had been structured and presented to the Palestinians and
other concerned Arab countries. Was peace possible? I wondered!

After the holidays I had gone back on my traveling assignments and I
stayed in Seattle more of the time than I wanted. I did my best to get to
New York more often than before. A special person lived there. I had
been able to spend March and part of April at the UN headquarters
and now I was called back for an up grading of our offices. My work
out of the office had always been to areas in the East and Middle-East
so Seattle made a good in between location and I enjoyed the beauty
of the surroundings offered by the State of Washington and the rain
which to me was always refreshing. July began the hottest month of the
summer season for the east coast and August was usually unbearable.

But I remember that by September the afternoons would begin to get cool breezes from the east. I could have that to look forward to if they kept me at the office in the City as I wanted.

Being back in New York I had finally gotten time to call Brada to meet uptown for a drink just to see how things were going. My intent couldn't have been more opposite. Time had gone by so fast but I still had buried thoughts that I wanted to discuss with him including some of the conversations we had during the reunion and the comments that Tiama had made to me. It was Friday the seventh around 2:00pm as I entered the small bar off of 2nd Avenue where we had agreed to meet. The place was actually a restaurant and bar that was built around a Polynesian theme. We each ordered an exotic rum drink and some pu pu's. I started off with an inquiry in a friendly tone on how the Journal was doing and was his consulting work growing. After the first drink I was rather more direct and to the point. I wanted to know what direction's his ideology was taking him? Who was he really? And why had Yassir and Saja become so fanatical in their conversations? Brada said that even though Yassir and Saja held fundamentalist ideals and feelings they were mainly based on philosophical points of view and any open discussions were rather like we had had many times at the university. Each was too busy with business to be involved with radicals. They only rubbed elbows with fundamentalist at the Mosque.

Brada was always a straight shooter with me just like when he told me about the relationship between him and Tiama so I changed the subject for the moment and asked him how his hydro-electric programs were coming. "We are doing fine and soon we will be consulting and reporting on three of the largest dams ever built that are under way in Africa and Iran; that is except the Chinese's new project. Theirs will dwarf anything else in the world. They are going hungry for electrical power like a ravenous bear after hibernation. The third world and all developing nations will be consuming energy beyond our capacity to make it available from oil over the next 14 years so a crisis looms in our future unless all of us make plans for alternate sources. By 2020 the consumption verses the supply curve on oil as an energy source will be headed in a downward exponential curve!"

Nodding my head, "I generally agree with those projections". I added, "The United Nations international resource and research section have the combined studies from all oil producing countries and the geo-surveys from the satellites that confirm those projections." Feeling comfortable about our little talk I still had to ask him about Tiama's concern about his unusual procedures of never using written correspondence, notes on meetings concerning future projects or having contractual files in his office headquarters.

After asking, Brada said "Well it's pretty obvious that we have to keep everything on our computers because all negotiations and transactions with foreign governments are highly classified and we can not reduce any thing to hard copies and stored in our offices. Our computers are very secure and we guard them continuously".

I said I understand completely and I had a much better feeling about Brada now. I could tell that he was concerned about the future of the poorer nations and pending problems for the world's future energy resources. His work at WWJHEP was a solid contribution to the betterment of undeveloped nations. We talked a bit about my work and my relationship with Tiama until Brada said that he had an appointment and must say goodbye. I congratulated him on his work and wished him well.

Brada hailed a taxi and off toward the midtown district. I went by Tiama's for some dinner and TV. Brada's taxi stopped in front of a small barber shop 'Razor Cuts' on Eight Avenue around Thirty Second and he went inside. He sat down for a trim and some espresso. A number of Arabic brothers were already in the shop when he arrived and six more entered before the barber was finished. The shop was small with a nondescript store front wedged between a copy store and a dry cleaner/tailor shop having only two work stations and five guest chairs plus a television which completed the front area. To the rear were two doors, one marked restroom and the other private. The front windows were tinted so the sunshine was diminished and so was the ability of anyone to look in. Most of the men in the shop had disappeared through the door marked private and with Brada's haircut finished he and the three remaining brothers filed through the same private entrance to a comfortable meeting room. Only the barber and one patron remained in the front room of the shop.

"Peace be to you my brothers and the light of allah be in our hearts". Brada started the conversations with this greeting and then followed with, "I have just left a meeting with an ex-classmate from NYU and while the questions were not too detailed he asked about Saja's and Yassir's radical views. We must all realize that there are eyes now looking at many of us to see who and what we are. We must be cautious and invisible as our Miraj(plans) for Dawa and Ji'had are moving patiently forward. We can not become a Mushbooh and expose our Islamic brothers to investigation. The Kuffer are all around and the most beloved Abu al-Hindi has come with news and instructions for all of the cell leaders in our movement." Al-Hindi had been sitting against the wall and was not personally known by all of the leaders in the meeting. "Brother Abu, we are blessed that you have once again arrived safely. We have set up a static generator in the walls and this room is secure."

Abu began, "My Brothers", these were cell organizers and leaders from the East coast states, "I bring great news and special instructions from our leader Osama. First a prayer to allah, 'Innaa Lillaahiwa Innaa Ilayhi Raajioon' Great is allah and his prophet Mohammed. To begin, all cell leaders are instructed to follow procedures as I tell you and to not put anything in writing that if found could cause your possible arrest. We have set up a computer in Yemen that is connected to a phone number I am going to give you and you must memorize it. Give it to all of the other cell leaders around the country on a personal basis only, face to face. With this phone number you can access the computer and input your personal cell phone number. When you dial the computer, always, yes always use a public telephone and an international calling card. This will keep the number secret and there will be no way for a tracing. When ever verbal communications are necessary then always speak in Arabic. When asked you are to input only your cell phone number with area code and your name followed by the number one on the phone pad. The next time you call go to the number two on the phone pad. The next time you call go to the number three on the phone pad and follow the sequence until you get to nine and then start all over again. You must remember the last number you used behind your name because the computer does remember and if the sequence is broken then you will be disconnected. Why? Just in case the smallest chance should occur that someone in the government here should over hear your phone number or intercept it by listening in and know your name and then try to enter our computer; they will not know your next sequence number to go behind your name and they will be disconnected. The computer in Yemen will always dial each of your phones when ever we need to contact you and pass on operational instructions. NEVER call this phone number any other way and NEVER leave any messages, only your cell phone number and name. The computer will shortly contact all cell leaders with the new address of our website. This Web site is more important then ever because we will be using it to pass on important written instructions, maps, diagrams and pictures of targets as our leaders select them and procedures to follow for your individual assignments. Be patient as the time is approaching! As always a new web address will be created every month or as needed and sent to you by way of the computer. NEVER, NEVER write down the new Web address! Now, when contacting a brother or leader to have a private conversation use the following code for recognition. ALWAYS BEGIN ANY COMMUNICATION WITH, 'Follow allah to allah' and the answering brother will answer, 'allah is your eternal peace'. Wait exactly five seconds and then add 'in paradise'. To avoid your cell phone from being tapped or monitored get a new cell phone and number every month! If you receive a phone call from a brother on a regular land line then tell him to call you on your 'outer line' or you call him on his 'outer line'. The outer line will always be your cell phone. Using the above procedure we will always have your number available to us to contact you. This will give us absolute privacy and secrecy. Next I bring to each of you our new 'military manual' for our operation in this Ji'had. It is on the disk Brada is giving you and should never be saved to a computer but instead used in view only format. It is for teaching the true followers of allah how to lead the Hadith life, and our leaders confirmations on why there is need to destroy the Infidel. Also, how to bring other brothers into the true light, how to train others, how to operate united, how to operate in a clandestine manner, how to hide financial transactions, how to hide and be secretive, how to communicate with each other using codes and how best to travel together, how, where, and when to meet, how to secure contraband, how to kill with no evidence, how to commit espionage, how to perform undetectable surveillance of the enemy, and how to avoid the enemies surveillance of you personally. You are commanded to follow all of the guidance in this manual with absolute discipline as our Qur'an teaches. If your security is compromised then immediately destroy the surface of the disk and if possible cut it to pieces. Tell all of our people in every cell and other leaders that are not present to gather together only at the Mosques, or at picnics or family barbeques. This is highly important to appear to be good citizens but everyone is to continually study the manual to make our mission a success. It is possible that some of us will be sought out and captured and martyred. This is the will of allah and praise be to allah for our service to him. I have for all of us in the movement the greatest news of all. As you all are aware we have the resources necessary to carry out all of our missions. When the United States funded the Taliban with $8,000,000,000 to fight the Russians, Osama skimmed off almost a billion US dollars and had it deposited and hidden in many places for our Ji'had against the snake. We have the funding for the final blow. Osama has been blessed by allah with wisdom and courage. The leaders in our camps in the East headed by Khalid Sheikh Mohammed have unveiled a plan that is now in operation to attack the 'Great Snake', the Dajin who fight against the truth and the Shariah. Soon we will give our first present to the United States and we will celebrate a massive victory over the Dajjael." Everyone rose to bow to Adu and then bowed down to pray and ask allah for strength to be strong and successful.

It was now dark out side and each of the leaders left the barber shop one at a time in staggered intervals. As they took different directions they implemented the evasive tactics they had been trained in so as to make sure no one was following. Two went out to smoke and keep watch out for any one surveying the shop. All was clear as one left and one reentered the shop. Brada laughed to himself as he left the shop thinking about the stupid meeting he had with Hank two hours earlier. He needed to meet with both Yassir and Saja tomorrow to bring them up to date on the latest events and give them their disk and cell phone instructions. More importantly was the coming attack on the Infidels. He chucked again for all of the stupidity of the West.

Hank had just arrived at his office and was going over the morning reports when it came in on the alert phone in the processing center. There had been an air disaster in New York City. The sketchy report said that a Boeing 767 had accidentally crashed into the World Trade Center and there was no news as to how damaging it was. The aids turned on one of their television monitors to ABC and there it was. A major amount of smoke and fire was coming from the North Tower with a gigantic gash in a space around the ninetieth floor. The pictures were from a distance and there was nothing on the reporting that said how the accident occurred. And then as we were watching and about twenty five minutes after the first crash a second plane came straight into the South Tower and exploded with a fire ball. It only took a moment for the newscaster to realize and exclaim over the air that this had to be a terrorist attack. Our section went into lock down as we were all secured in our section and soon the building alarm system went off. Over the UN building intercom we were told to be prepared to evacuate the building and security rushed to the roof to post a look out. It took almost a half an hour before any one from the government was on the air to make an announcement of what was happening when the newscaster showed a 'Special News Alert', The Pentagon had been attacked by an air plane that had crashed into the west wing and that side was on fire. Stunned, all of us just sat there for a long time ignoring the request for us to evacuate the building. Then we started gathering communications coming from around the world. The United States is under attack. New York was in a panic. Wall Street was immediately closed down. And then if this was not enough the World Trade Center towers began to collapse. In less than two hours both towers had caved in and there was nothing but smoke and rubble.

By the afternoon we learned of a fourth plane that had been destined for a suicide attack on Washington most probably on the White House but instead it had crashed somewhere in Ohio. There were phone calls from the plane's passengers to their wives and friends before the crash telling them that the plane was high jacked and headed to Washington, DC. The news was showing Muslims from around the world dancing in the streets celebrating the disaster to the United States and shouting death to the Americans and crush the evil serpent of the west, while carrying banners of 'Islam grows on the blood of Martyrs'. The country was in disbelief and New York was almost shut down. The financial markets were closed and all airplanes around the country were grounded. This was a catastrophe of a magnitude not dreamed of by anyone. Smoke and a huge dust cloud covered New York and the pile of rubble was more than one hundred feet high where the towers had once stood. TV stations repeated the showing of the two crashes and the collapse of the towers.

I finally got through to Dad at the station and asked if he knew any more about the situation and who the terrorist were? Had any one group claimed the responsibility? He could only say that all of his people were engaged in working on answers and that the first rumors were that Usama bin Ladin was responsible. He added, "More than likely or at least according to the White House this was a one time operation. Many previous soundings had been in the air that he was going to do something but no one could have dreamed of this kind of attack." "Okay I'll call later."

I said goodbye and then called Tiama at work. "Hello, oh Hank, I'm so happy you called. This is the most horrendous thing I have ever witnessed. Nobody here can believe this is real. The pictures on the television appear as though they were from some Hollywood movie. What is going to happen?"

Not knowing myself I put together an unsure comment. "It looks like they are declaring a national state of emergency and the President will speak tonight at six. I will need to stay here at the UN. I am told that New York is shut down. Stay home and relax, our entire military is on alert so we should be alright. Dad said that a spokesman at the White House believes this is a single event involving four separate planes. I'll be alright and when I'm relieved here I'll come over. I love you sweetheart."

The next day there was an interview shown on al-Jazeera TV from Qatar with bin Ladin bragging on the success of the attack and he proudly stated for the camera that, 'he was doing god's work and that it was his personal destiny'. As the number of dead began to be counted Cush told the nation that, 'we have been attacked by al-Qaeda and the Taliban and that our nation is at war; War against bin Ladin, al-Qaeda and all terrorist. The most heinous crime of our times will be avenged and all those responsible for these acts against the United States will be found and brought to justice or killed in the effort. He, the Congress and the Nation would not rest until this battle has been won'. Thank GOD Al Bore did not become our President. Between the previous pantywaist giving away highly classified secrets and our scientific data and Mr. Al Bore, we would have possibly had to kiss our country goodbye.

The financial crisis hit many major banks and Howard Slates, the husband of Alicia Banks one of Brada's classmates from NYU, was called in to testify before a special White House committee to look at the computer security of the country's internal banking system and that system's international security with all other worldwide electronic banking transactions. Wall Street was closed for a number of days and there was a big concern about the possibility of lost data or felonious transfers which could add to the internal crisis. Was there enough redundancy in place to control and authenticate all accounts and movements of funds worldwide? Howard's company Fin-Chk, Inc. had set the standards for the industry twenty years ago when computers started to take over the financial world. Most of the operating software for controls and check points was produced by Howard's company. His company now consulted with WWBCC in Brussels where all international bank transactions are cleared on super computers, DHU class4. There are eight systems on line with four DHU's housed in two different underground locations each redundant to each other. Each four unit system is capable of receiving, logging, and transferring five trillion transactions per eight hour day. It was Howard's personal design and he had recommended that the globe be broken up into three geographical segments corresponding to the time zones of eight to four, four to twelve, and twelve to eight on the clock beginning with Greenwich Mean Time. All transactions would be processed on an uninterrupted continuous time clock but the load for each geo zone would always have priority. A mute point since most transactions were completed, reported and stored within two hundred millionth of a second.

It was October and Cush had implemented a strike back at bin Laden and the Taliban by attacking the Taliban in Afghanistan. A major offensive was launched to continue until all Taliban and al-Qaeda leaders were captured or killed and their organization destroyed. As all of these events happened, the next few months ushered in major changes in our lives, our freedom, our economy and our security. For the first time since the Spanish American war we had a confrontation on our own soil. For the first time the American public had a taste of danger and uncertainty in their daily routines which is what Israel had felt for over two decades not to mention Germany, France, England, Spain, India and The Philippines. For the second time in our history we had a disaster to the financial markets that cut the wealth of many citizens by fifty per cent or more. For the first time all of us began to look over our shoulder at strange looking people and wonder just who they were and we became suspicious of all dark skinned, big nosed, turban wrapped men who spoke no English. For the fist time our personal freedom allowing us to come and go at will was being questioned and even curtailed. And for a second time in our history we had a festering wound on our society that oozed out hatred for a select group of people with no cause or justification. Citizens were mad. Citizens resisted the government's infringement into their life styles. Citizens lost their money and their income. The economy faltered and the Airline Industry was in a tail spin. And most citizens felt that there was no security in the country anymore. The reality was that it was all true. Without a solid well grounded and ethically stable leader like President George Cush the country could have fallen into a deep depression.

It was the stance that he took against the enemy, the compassion he felt towards the victims and the strength that he showed to the American people that began to build a base for reconstruction. Mayor Giuliani was equal to the task and even more than the President he healed the great city of NEW YORK. I saw the rock hard strength of our country in each individual person who took the disaster in stride and went on with their lives accepting after a short period of time the new safe guards and inconveniences now thrust on America. The administration went to the congress with a program to create a new interior department of Homeland Security. It all took time and the wheels of a government with almost three hundred million citizens move slowly and often incorrectly. Many people fussed and fumed about the whole process and the ultimate outcome; but out it did come and slowly the enforcement agencies began to get the message.

CHAPTER TEN

It was only a few weeks after 9-11 as it was now being called when Hank got a call from Jerry. "Hello Hank, I guess there is no reason for us to talk about 9-11, we all thought that something was in the air and no one could have come up with this. How is New York fairing now? I mean the people on the street. I see the work being done at the site and all of the admiration being given to the firemen and other emergency workers. It will be a long time before we have any mental peace from this attack. I hear that the New Yorkers have already pretty much bounced back."

I responded, "Yeah, it looks that way on the surface."

"Well I am calling to see what you know about the forum being put together by UBC TV? Tom is going to put on a 'TV Special' on October the 12th with a number of professional people from different sectors of business, government, military, academic and special security agencies that have been affected by 9-11 for a round table type discussion. I have been invited along some important dignitaries, government officials and others who I do not recognize. So I am coming to New York for a pre-show briefing and to work on some of the format and add my part to the agenda."

"I have not heard."

"Well, I want to fax you an open letter to all Americans and the government written by one of my buddies from the service. He is going to send it to his congress man on Friday. I would like for you to digest it for a couple of days and give me your opinion about using it on the program. What is your fax number?"

"Send it here to me at the office before I go home. The fax number is (213) 885-7718. I'll read it tonight. What day do you arrive and when does the program air?"

"I will be there on the 8th and the special will be a two hour program on the Friday the 12th. Tom will be the narrator and I am told there will be brief showings of the President's various television appearances."

Confirming my interest, "I think I'll save some time on the 10th and go to the studio to look at the script for the forum, talk to Dad and get your take on all that is happening plus I'm quite interested in knowing more about the findings of the agencies and how much will be disclosed to the public."

Jerry assured me of the legitimacy of the special as he responded with, "The agenda is going to be reviewed by the White House to edit sensitive material but other than that censorship it will be a very open forum. I'm starting the fax now, so I will call you on Friday the fifth." Wrestling with the flies on my desk to put them all away; then picking up my umbrella, I took the fax off of the machine, folded and stuffed it into my pocket and left for the day. So much has happened in such a short time, I wonder what the theme of Dad's special will be. I'll call him tomorrow.

At home I poured a much need scotch and eased into my recliner to read Jerry's fax.

OPEN LETTER TO THE PEOPLE OF THE UNITED STATES AND THE CONGRESS

DECLARATION: God Bless America, It's Citizens, It's leaders, and It's Institutions

When in the course of human events the people of a democratic government have been violated by either foreign interest or internal malfeasance, they not only have the right to seek recourse but they have an inherent duty for the sake of society to demand and bring pressure on the government to effect restitution for any and all damages done to the populace.

The people of the United States have been attacked by a foreign force and their attack has been described by our President as 'an act of war', which is of course an act against all American citizens.

However, it would appear that there are actions by certain bodies or individuals within our government, who could be accused not only of a violation of the trust grant to them by the people of this wonderful country, but their actions could even be considered seditious.

Let's first establish beyond a doubt that these actions of the foreign attackers – *Muslim Radicals* – is the most despicable barbaric act that any human beings could have ever done. But as we all thoroughly understand, these radical Islamic individuals believe they have done nothing wrong. Quite the contrary they believe very deeply that their actions will receive the blessings of the false god allah. Clearly that is their belief evidenced by the suicidal finality of their actions.

And we American citizens must realize that there are many, many Islamic factions in many countries including here in our country that have the same radical spirit. It is their driving passion to destroy the United States of America and more importantly to kill all Americans who are considered to be infidels. It is the Muslim's 'PLEDGE TO ALLAH'. With this truth in mind what is wrong with our government?

The Muslims most often refer to it as a Jihad or 'holy war' and they believe that martyrdom is one of the highest and greatest acts that a Muslim can perform to get into paradise.

Think on this example:
> If you had a wonderful home with a great family and everyone cooperated together making the internal environment peaceful and full of love and respect for each other; would you then allow a destroyer into your home who had earlier declared to ravage your home and kill your family?
> Well, would you?
> HELL NO, YOU WOULDN'T LET HIM IN !
> BUT OUR GOVERNMENT DID JUST THAT AND STILL IS.

Then here is the problem the citizens of our country now have; there are millions of unwanted people in our country without permission to be here. We all want to know exactly who is culpable and where does the blame lie. It lies within the walls of the government and they all know it.

But do we all know precisely what the problem is? Can we, as citizens identify the countries that harbor these terrorist and all of the radical factions that are to be feared. The State Department has named the countries of Syria, Iran, Iraq, Libya, Sudan, and Afghanistan as some of the sponsors and heavens for terrorist and their organizations. Some of the groups are al-Qaeda, Hamas, Hezbollah, PLO, Islamic Jihad of Palestine, Palestinian Liberation Front, just to name a few. And of course there are many more underground factions

There are approximately six million Muslim people in the United States and approximately ten percent are *Islamic Radicals* many of them operating in cells which belong to any number of the radical factions that exist worldwide. So based on these statistical percentages from the government and many Islamic web sites there are around six hundred thousand radical Muslims in the United States. From statistics used elsewhere in the world; on a worldwide basis 10 to 15 percent of *Radical Islamist* are extremist and capable of terrorist acts therefore we can thank our government for allowing between sixty and ninety thousand potential terrorist into our country.

WHAT IS WRONG WITH US???

HAVE WE LOST OUR MINDS? WE HAVE ALLOWED A DESTRUCTIVE FORCE TO PENETRATE OUR BORDERS WHO BY THEIR OWN PLEDGE DESIRE TO ERADICATE OUR COUNTRY!

How is the government going to stop these people much less find them. These factions have the advantage now and every citizen will pay the price; a price that can not even be imagined.

How did this happen? Who is at fault? Who must pay the penalty for putting the entire population of our country in harms way?

Why is our policy on immigration in such a shambles? Why does our policy of open borders in the name of fairness and equal human rights seem so foolish to us now. And still the government has done nothing to correct this indefensible policy and to secure our borders. The Department of Immigration has the responsibility of keeping out the enemies of our country and the CIA and DIA along with the FBI have the responsibility of gathering the information worldwide to keep our leaders informed and in a position to protect us. The first tenant of government is 'TO PROTECT ITS CITIZENS'!

The Liberals in this country have put every citizen's life at risk and more likely they could and probably should be charged with treason and sedition. Many of these foolish professors of liberalism are in our congress, in our universities, and other positions of power. And is it very probable that because they have advocated temperance and openness they have caused the immigration fiasco and yet they still control the regulations that are flawed due to their liberal philosophy. So then are they not truly the underlying cause of 9-11?

OK then, let's for the moment not continue on a line of accusations but let's act now to stop this stupid liberal idealism before our country is completely destroyed.

IS THE NEXT ATTACK GOING TO BE BIOLOGIAL THAT WILL WIPE OUT WHOLE CITIES or CAN THE TERRORIST SNEEK IN A NUCULAR DEVICE CAPABLE OF LEVELING LOS ANEGLES OR NEW YORK? Can they be stopped?? They are planning to destroy us !!!!

Our leaders must stop talking about the problem and they must act now. Completely close the borders clear across Canada and Mexico. Seek out now the illegal immigrants of Muslim persuasion and interrogate them. Forget the stupid political correct position against personal profiling. It wasn't Mexicans, Chinese, or Peruvians that took out the twin towers; it was Muslims. So we now declare to you that it is your problem; you made it, SO NOW FIX IT.

BUT FIRST YOU MUST BE TRUTHFUL TO ALL AMERICANS AND TELL THEM HOW BIG THIS PROBLEM IS, HOW MUCH DANGER EXIST FOR ALL OF OUR PEOPLE. TELL EVERYONE THAT WE MUST ALL BE ON ALERT FOR QUESTIONABLE ACTIONS BY ANYONE!

TELL US ALL THE TRUTH – THAT NOT JUST A FEW HUNDRED PEOPLE MAY BE POSSIBLE SUSPECTS BUT THAT THERE ARE TENS OF THOUSANDS OF POTENTIAL TERRORISTS INSIDE OF THE U. S. A.!

References:

Ahmad Abu Halabiya – Fatwa Council as stated in
October, 2000 "Kill All Jews"

Sheikh Ibrahim Madhi – Broadcasted June, 2001
"Erase United States. Erase Britain. Erase Israel"

Ziad Ibu-Aid – Fatah Leader. Announced June, 2001
"We will not quit- there will be no cease fire"

Muhammad Dhamrah – Commander of Force 17
Announced to be world in August 2001, "We have
trained our children to explode their bodies with
explosives to destroy all of our enemies."

Osama bin Laden – Leader of al-Qaeda announced
to the world that the destruction of the Twin Towers
was a great event and it was his destiny from allah."

Finished, I stared at the small picture I had of Dad and President Cush Sr. on the table next to the fireplace. The decanter of scotch set near by. After a few minutes I poured another short drink and sat down again. Could all of this be stopped? Is it possible that the security of our country is out of control? From every direction I am getting signals that things could be unwinding and the public does not understand the gravity of what we may be facing. I thought to myself 'The heck with the United Nations and their liberal structure'. I know that every appeal to the assembly made by our government is thwarted by the ambassadors of the countries who fear some sort of retaliation. I wondered, do we really have any friends around the world.

Jerry called me on Friday asking about the 'open letter'.

"Jerry with out a doubt it is a sof other mail they get. Where did he send it and did he try running it in any of the major newspapers as an editorial or any of the monthly periodicals?"

Jerry's answer was quite casual as if he knew communicating with the government or our representatives was like screaming from inside a barrel in a wine cave, pretty futile! "He told me he sent it by e-mail to Cush, Chenny, Rummey, and about twenty senators. He did not have the money to place it in any newspapers or magazines!"

USA: THE SERPENT IS CRUSHED!

"No I meant the editorial sections. Sometimes they run editorials in the 'Of Interest Sections'. Oh Well, Jerry, who knows, someone may have actually read it and resent it to the President and the agencies. I still plan to come by on next Wednesday. See you then."

In the evening on that Friday Abu walked into the Walton department store and stopped at the shoe department. There waiting for him was Yassir. Their eyes met but no other recognition was needed or expressed. After looking at the shoe displays for a minute or so Abu walked over to the belt display and observed as Yassir left his chair and started up the escalator. He waited a minute to see that no one was following him and then proceeded up the same escalator where Yassir was waiting about twenty five feet away to make sure Abu was not followed. Within a couple of minutes they went to the book section and each picked out a book to thumb through. Both had bought a coffee from the booth next to the entrance to the book section and sat in adjoining chairs. The rest of the area was empty so they were able to talk privately. Abu smiled at Yassir and said, "We have scored our first victory. There are many more to come. Tomorrow before I leave for home in London I will stop to see that Musab has secured and distributed the last shipment of the product and ATVs. We will have a total of two hundred thousand kilos of Jihad candy for our brothers when the time is right. I understand that Jonathan is still bringing in boats to keep up the front and eliminate suspicion. All eighty thousand kilos is either in place or stored and waiting for the command from our leaders. And Akria has been able to distribute all of the one hundred twenty thousand kilos including the necessary detonators and half of the MAK 90 rifles and ammunition to the area leaders in the western section and who have placed everything in the ten regional storage locations, Seattle, Portland, San Jose, San Bernardino, San Diego, Phoenix, Las Vegas, Salt Lake City, Denver, and Kansas City. The other half of the rifles and ammunition has gone to the ten eastern region leaders for distribution to their storage locations in Boston, Philadelphia, Cleveland, Chicago, Houston, Memphis, New Orleans, Ft. Lauderdale, Atlanta, and here in New Jersey. Special instructions were given to the leaders in charge of our materials. Number one they have rented the storage locations using an American name. Second they were careful to rent only at locations that did not ask for any identification. Third they have been going in and out of these storage units about once every month or so to show some activity and for those who have a small business they rented the unit under a business name. If for any reason authorities had a reason to investigate storage units in one of these cities they would more than likely only look inside of units where there had been a long term tenant and no activity. It is critical that everyone go into an invisible mode for an extended period of time until the orders are given to begin the final attack. We are patience in our quest and every cell member must be told to live a normal inconspicuous life. You will have to travel to all of the area leaders who were not at our New York meeting to deliver this message and a copy of the disk which has the manual and to inform each of them on the procedures to follow with their cell phones. They will be required to memorize the international number and it is forbidden to write it down. A warning from our leader that they and all of their individual sub-cell leaders are to stay entrenched and go into a low profile life style until called on. The Infidels will be diligent and harsh in their investigation and all brothers will need to be ready to sacrifice their cover if trapped and to reveal nothing to the enemy. Any leaders that are arrested or must run will have killed their cell. It can no longer operate. Allah is good and allah guides our hands. Blessed is the one lord allah. We shall talk soon." Abu put the book back and disappeared into the isles leading to the escalator.

CHAPTER ELEVEN

Tiama and I spent most of our off work hours together when I was in New York. Her apartment was still under rent control so under her sublease the rent was fairly decent. That was a good thing because she did not make much money at the Filipino Community Help Center and the time she had taken off to just be lazy for a while left her with almost zero savings. Nothing consistent and not much money, but she was strong and that was one of her great attributes. We met at the Plaza for an early Saturday brunch and then walked over to Central Park. There was a fairly strong breeze blowing for the month of October and a few groups of children were doing a good job of flying their kites. We sat on a bench near the open area and watched as the high tech units flew higher and higher. I spoke quietly saying, "They have changed the kite flying sport to a super kite-a-fragilistic experience. I'm in awe at what they can do and the trick flying that is possible with their high tech designs with very fragile construction. I think I will buy one of those five section ones and see what we can do on one of these weekends."

"Why don't you wait and take our first son out to learn?"

Stunned by her comment I said, which like most blundering men I shouldn't have, "Our son? Are you pregnant?"

"Well of course not. We have been good during our relationship. What are you saying?"

Boy that was wrong! Her smile which had been prompted by partly joking and mostly her love for me died like a Lilly on a desert floor. "You mean when we get married and I know we will, I'm sorry for being a man and so insensitive. We make a special team and I love you, I love children, I want you for the rest of my life. You know that!"

With her intense dark eyes she asked, "Is that a proposal?"

Whee, I'm in it now, might as well start swimming. "It's a request until I can get a ring and do the proposing properly. But until then I want you as my wife, my friend, and my lovvvver." She immediately had a new smile. Amazing what a little tenderness and attention can do to women. I wish it was a natural instinct for us hard headed conquerors of the world.

"Not to change the atmosphere but did I tell you Dad was putting a **'9-11 - The World of Terrorism'** two hour special on this coming Friday? I'm going to UBC's studio in the Trump Tower on Wednesday to see the basic format and list of commentators. Jerry told me last Friday that he was on that list."

"Jerry will be here then this week? How is he doing? And I don't re-call you mentioning his friend Jack Madden anymore, how is he?"

"I guess I never mentioned it to you. Jerry told me a couple of weeks before the terrorists attack that Jack was killed in Jakarta on one of his missions for the CIA. Jerry said that he thought he knew what the mis-sion had been about but everything was classified and he couldn't talk about it. I hope to ask Jerry about the details one day. Hey let's just head home to my place."

Putting her arm around my waist she agreed, "Okay, and I love you."

After going to the studio on Wednesday and getting a glimpse of the layout for the special I told Dad I wanted to be there on Friday for the live showing. There would be no audience because this was a discus-sion between various professionals in economics, finance, academia, security, government, and war. No outside commentary was necessary or would be allowed. Late on the afternoon of October the 12th I took a taxi to the corner of 57th and Avenue Americas and then walked the rest of the way. The taxi could not get through and I figured there was a traffic accident or some kind of jam up. Sure enough it was a traffic jam and right in front of the building. Why? And then I saw the plac-ards being carried by hundreds of people mainly Arabic type. NO PROFILING! STOP THE HATRED! ISLAM IS PEACEFUL! WE ARE AMERICANS! How did they find out about the location of this eve-ning's program and the content of the moderator's scripts? I rushed through and showed my license and United Nations ID. Then on the elevator and up to the Thirtieth floor change elevators and on up to the Fifty Third floor which was all UBC.

There are four studios each with a small number of auditorium seats. Studio four is the main studio and inside the setting was like a political convention hall with a raised platform for the participants. Red, White and Blue Banners draped across the back wall above twenty or more potted plants with two five foot high palms placed at the end of the banners and then four American Flags in standards on each side of the palms. The moderators table and chair was on a round raised section that could swivel around in a complete circle and was placed in the middle of the platform. This allowed Dad to face any of the cameras and then at will turn to direct questions or comments to those on the two separate panels. On the left side of the platform were the government people and on the right side were the private sector professionals. All of the participants had arrived more than three hours earlier for a briefing on the procedures the forum would follow and then for the personal makeup required to give the correct facial tones for the cameras.

I waved to Jerry, Dad, and some of the other people I recognized. I motioned over to Dad and Jerry to take a moment to go outside of the studio. "Hey have you two seen the mob of people on the streets in front of the building?"

Both answered together, "Nope."

They looked down from the west window on to One Central Park West to see what I was talking about. "They seemed to be peaceful when I passed by after I came back from dinner, Tom observed, "but now the crowd is at least twice as big."

Tom looked at Jerry in wonderment and asked, "How did anyone find out the content of our program? We kept the announcements about the special directed towards the disaster itself and the future of the countries economics and security. Why gather unless those in the crowd know our attendees and the theme of the program. Who could have incited this reaction to our event?"

Down on the street there was now a massive amount of Arabic people with those that looked like Indians or Pakistani's, blacks and what have you. The crowd was chanting and some were singing and some had megaphones declaring their loyalty to the United States while others were just pushing and waving their placards. It was obvious the police were adjusting their lines to break it up.

Jerry said in his usual robust voice, "I can not understand why they have gathered here; to rally for a cause or complain about the current public criticism of Arabic people. This is not the place to demonstrate; let them do their vocalization of the injustice at the site of the disaster!" Jerry's look was very cold as he turned back to the studio.

Wandering back in I saw Howard Slates talking to Mayor Rudy Giuliani, then looking around I spotted Alicia sitting in the middle of the auditorium by her self. Other guest of the participants had chosen to sit more towards the front. Director Tom sat in a chair on a raised platform in the middle of the front row so as to be seen by everyone involved; the camera operators, the stage hands, the participants, and the guest. "Everyone take your seats please, we have less than one minute!" Tom looked around making one more check on everyone's position. "OKAY, Get ready five, four, three, two one, we are on the air."

"GOOD EVENING my fellow Americans and to all of our most gracious participants, Thank you for joining us for our special program **'9-11 - The World of Terrorism'**. I am Tom Brayden, executive vice president of UBC and tonight we bring you a forum on Terrorism presented to discuss what we are now calling 9-11; the Who, the Why, and the What Now! I will introduce our prestigious panelist on my left who make up the federal government group of panelists. They are retired General Barry Mac Gaffery, NSA Chief retired General Mike Hyden, CIA director Jack Tennet, Department of Defense Section Chief Ronda Richberg, and Department of Justice Pete Lunny. And on my right making up those from local government and the private sector are Mayor of New York Rudy Giuliani, Georgetown University Professor John Esperanzo, ACE International Chief of Security Jerry Ness, FIN-CHK CEO Howard Slates, and from the Center for Future World Events Think Tank Paul Yankan.

The first item on our agenda is a short clip showing the two planes crashing into the World Trade Center on September the eleventh and then the collapse of both buildings followed by President Cush's comments two days later standing on a platform at the base of the rubble addressing the emergency crews, the people of New York and the Nation. Following the short clip I will ask for comments from the government side and then the private sector side. We have established response procedures for the panelist. Each of you will need to press your button to light the box in front of you when you want to speak about a subject and going from my left to right in each section you are seated in seats A, B, C, D, and E. When you have pushed your button a number will show next to your letter to indicate in what order you pushed the button. Feel free to express your comments but in the order of the sequence you pushed the button. I will direct each question or requests for comments to either the government or the private sector and they will give their responses first and then the other section will be recognized. The lights in front of my table on the left and the right correspond to your seats A, B, C, D, and E. You will be able to see your seat letter and the number which will indicate the order for your individual responses. I will present the subjects to be discussed or we will show different videos for comment. Four minutes have been allowed for an interactive discussion on each subject and if I feel elaborating on a subject is of benefit to the overall program I will extend the time. When it is necessary for me to ask for you to stop either due to time or an excessive dissertation on some point that I have decide is overworked; then please stop when I say time is up."

After the short video ended Tom presented the first topic for discussion. "The first topic is 'WHO is responsible?"

Retired General McGaffery opened the discussion with, "We have many enemies world wide and there are more than eighty five terrorist groups large and small from one side of the globe to the other. It is the consensus that about fifty of these groups are Muslim based. The hatred for America and Americans is held by most of these groups and our intelligence leans to the Bin Ladin group as the responsible party."

Section Chief of the NSA retired General Mike Hyden was next. "Our focus needs to be on all major groups that have the fluidity to move about the world and create chaos. We know that Hamas, al-Qaeda, Hizbollah, Arab Revolutionary Brigade, PLO, People's Mujahedin, PIJ, and a few smaller organized groups have the financial backing and the international structure to be a threat. Further many from most of these groups have crossed into the states over the past years and been lost in the paperwork. In other words we have many terrorist types in this country who are unknown to any of our security agencies."

Professor Jon Esperanzo of Georgetown University was number one on the private sector side. "My studies for the past eighteen they are years have been on the middle east and the expansion of Islam. I have found that many of the groups that the General has mentioned are radical Islamic political factions but not the main stream Muslims. This great religion of Islam is embraced by almost twenty five per cent of the world's population. Only Christendom has more followers and there has sprung from that group of religious believers from time to time some radicals and atrocities as well. Everyone condemns the acts of war perpetrated on our country on 9-11, however we should not and we can not profile all Arabic people as radical Islamic Jihadist." After some responses and interactions from both sides, Tom motioned to move on.

Tom initiated the second video of the firemen raising the flag over the destruction and then President Cush's speech to the nation from in front of the millions of tons of rubble at the base of where the towers had stood with comments from New York Mayor Rudy Giuliani. Tom then asked, "WHY on our homeland?"

Jack Tennet's number was first. He gave a loud and short answer. "Because they hate us!" Pete Lunny was number two. He started to stand up as he began to speak but the producer waved him down. "I will elaborate on that some what. Yes they hate us. They hate our life style. They hate our freedom. They hate our wealth. They hate our strength. They hate our power. They say they hate our materialistic culture. But I say they show obvious signs of pure envy!"

Howard was number one on the right platform. "I have traveled, as most on this panel have, extensively to many countries. Being so closely tied to the banking industry and the financial markets I view the problem from a different prospective and therefore the why in a different light. Radical Muslims yes, but the striking out at America, the wealthiest and most powerful country the world has ever known, comes from a deep pent-up feeling of frustration that has erupted into this violence by those in the third world economies. Be it Muslims or some other sect from where ever, Muslims just seem to have the most anger and the backing to be able to express their frustrations. And what am I getting at? Exactly this. The radicals are using their religion as a cover for the backlash that has been building, and building, and building for more than eighty years. What backlash? A simple equation of 'the haves verses the have-nots'. As a people who have been oppressed they feel that America and other European countries have been stripping them of their natural resources and not been paying them back for having made that resource available. What they needed was help to come into the era of industrialization. Instead we kicked sand on them and in a figure of speech 'left them in our dust'. No help from us to them bred antagonism. As the world became more open, the younger people began to look around and figure out what had happened. Now we have retaliation in the form of terrorism."

More interaction on this subject lasted until Tom called for a stop with forty five minutes left on the clock. We have looked at the WHO and have been offered the identity of many organizations or groups. We have discussed the WHY in depth with theories and a lot of philosophical and ideological reasoning, but now let's look at the WHAT NOW. As a nation we have to gird up our belly and move forward.

Ronda Richberg of the Department of Defense was now number one. "I think the position of the administration is correct and is needed. The immediate declaring of war on the terrorist is our first step toward recovery and healing. It would be obvious that we at the Pentagon are fully behind a routing out and elimination of all terrorist activity where ever it may be residing and it is important to acknowledge that 90% of the country is behind such actions. The country wants and needs this kind of commitment and strength in leadership."

Mayor Rudy Giuliani speaking out of turn requested to be next. With total respect Tom motioned to the Mayor to proceed. "I must say this has all been a great discourse on trying to analysis the past events that rocked our nation. From an economical stand point it has been a devastating blow to our financial markets and some of our major industries. The airlines are still shaking in their boots. I understand that Continental has cut its flights by sixty percent and have laid off twelve thousand employees. United has made a similar move and some are predicting bankruptcy. I say listen to what the President has said and done. He has encouraged the heroic citizens of New York, comforted those that were wounded and consoled the families of lost loved ones. His speeches have worked to calm those that are fearful and assured all of the people that we must be vigilant while at the same time getting acceptance for the struggle and sacrifice that will be ahead of us over the next few years. Let's get together and continue steadfast in our knowledge that we will triumph and prevail in the face of tragedy. We always have; so to all my fellow citizens I ask you to not cringe into some corner in bewilderment but step out and continue your normal daily routine. We are a resilient people!" All of the participants stood and gave the honorable Giuliani a round of applause.

Jerry's light had been on before the mayor had requested to speak so Tom now recognized Jerry. "Hello to all of you watching us tonight and congratulations to the each of my fellow panelist for being so open in your assessments, commentaries, and personal feelings about 9-11. As Tom had introduced me, I am Jerry Ness with ACE International Corp. Our company is a high tech security organization contracted by our government for the purpose of pre-detecting any terrorist's plans for high jacking, bombing, or destruction of any aircraft either on the ground or in flight. Since this special has been designed to look at 9-11 with a completely open discussion centered on (WHO? WHY? and WHAT HOW?), and since I am the head of ITA at ACE, that is Investigation of Terrorist Activities, I feel I can add considerable to what has already been said. At first you might say we did not do out job! And I agree to the extent we had directives and ample budgets necessary from the governmental powers to be looking for domestic high jacking. But first let's look at identifying four planes out of some thirty six thousand flights per day. It would have been a needle in a hay stack search. Security at our airports failed completely to stop the individuals responsible. We know where the plan was originated, from al-Qaeda and bin Laden's group. We are slowly finding out the WHO and we do know they were mostly Arabic and all were radical Muslims. Do not forget that! My work in this area of counterterrorism has provided me with an extensive knowledge of the enemy. The WHY is embedded in the Qur'an and since the death of Mohammed in 632AD the designs of Islam has been to conquer the world. Their history clearly calls out their intentions. Although many within the Muslim movements and some clerics declare that the idea to conquer is really to overcome the false religions of the world and to convert all unbelievers to Islam, I for one disagree. And on the surface this all sounds good to most laymen, but the problem arises when an 'immoveable force meets an immovable object'. Islam teaches that you can not tolerate Infidels and if they are not converted then they are enemies of Islam and must be destroyed by any means. Most all radicals believe that the West is 'The Snake' the DAJIN. We are Dajjael the Malik. The major Muslim groups listed by General Mike Hyden preach no compromise with the

West; kill the Americans when ever and where ever you can and death of all Christians and Jews. Sarah 2:191, 4:5,27,26, 5:51,91,92, 8:12,37,60, 9:5,14,29,41,111, 24:55, and 47:4 are just a few that embody the true instructions to the Muslims.

Jerry broke for a drink of water and a couple of the panelists were twisting in their seats. I noticed nods coming from the panelist in the government section but some shaking of heads form Jerry's side. I wasn't sure if those motions were partly in agreement but not wanting others to catch their true beliefs or if the head movement was in total disagreement. I think I knew which it was for one at Jerry's table. Jerry went on, "WHAT NOW! Tom has asked and New Yorkers have asked and you at home have asked? As an ex-military man it is simple. WE TAKE AGGRESSIVE ACTION NOW AND WE FIGHT THE ENEMY! Our President is strong and correct. Our people will stand together and we will go after the terrorist and completely eliminate them. The unanswered question is where. They are not a country that you can take deliberate action against. They are spread out in many, many countries around the world most of which are as the President said "The Axis of Evil". But wait no one has gone to the records to look at the domestic problem. Where did this attack of 9-11 come from? These terrorist did not slip in at night aboard a submarine. They did not parachute down out of the sky one dimly lit night. NO! They were already here. They and thousands more like them. Here on national TV and in front of the American public and those watching in the rest of the world, HERE ARE THE FACTS. Beginning with the fall of the Shah of Iran and the take over of out American embassy the strength of the Islamic movement grew world wide at an exponential rate. I will not outline the chronology of the terrorist outbreaks year by year. The history is there for all to see. The patience and devotion to their cause is one of the greatest strengths of Islam. When Khomeini took control of Iran many Arabs took advantage of our hospitality and left the Middle East to come to the United States. Immigration regulations were changed and the foolish 'Open Door' policies were established as we opened our borders to whom ever. Political asylum was as easy an excuse to get a visa to enter our country as a child asking the teacher to use the bathroom. But we became the sucker. Hundreds of thousands of Arabic people entered the states both legally and illegally. It was so easy and there were so many entering that one could just walk across the border at an unprotected area and mix with the brothers. Nobody would even take notice. Today it is estimated by our government that we have four million Muslims in our country but I think the numbers are skewed. Around thirty percent of them are fundamental Islamist. We now have over eight hundred Mosques here for their gathering places. The intelligence community knows that in the Muslim world between ten and fifteen percent of Muslims are radical believers. Now I want to state right here that all Muslims are not radicals or a threat to other peoples. Just like in any sect or ethnic group there are those that are not orthodox or aggressive in nature."

Once again Jerry stopped for water and pouring a glass he turned towards Tom as he was drinking. Tom was a little concerned about all of this commentary and gave Jerry a look like he was going to stop him. Jerry immediately continued, "Just a few moments more and I will be finished. Therefore as I originally stated, with approximately seven million immigrants from the Middle East, African Muslim countries, and the Pacific Rim in side of our borders, there are almost sixty percent or four million of those immigrates who are professed Muslims and a minimum of one million two hundred thousand of them being fundamental Islamist. I repeated these numbers so that we can see what is so very important. Worldwide between ten to fifteen percent of radical Islamist are capable of terrorist operations. AND IF JUST TEN PER CENT COULD BE TERRORIST; I say that ONE HUNDRED TWENTY THOUSAND potential terrorist are living side by side with all of you and your neighbors and only they know who is who. What do we do? The battle at home is now urgently important! You had better profile the people who walk our streets. You had better be both cautious and curious about anyone who looks suspicious. It wasn't Jews or Christians or Catholics or Japanese or Chinese or Hispanics or Samoans in those airplanes that attacked us! IT WAS ARABIC MUSLIMS, PERIOD." Jerry paused a moment and raised his finger as he went on very slowly with his comments. "And I ask you to remember this; the Bobby Kennedy assassination, 1972 Munich Olympics, 1979 when our Embassy in Iran was overthrown, 1980 American kidnappings in Lebanon, 1983 bombing of the U.S. Marine barracks in Saudi Arabia, 1985 TWA flight 847 hijacked and the same year cruise ship Achille Lauro hijacked, 1988 Pan Am flight 103 blown up over Scotland, 1993 bombing at the World trade Center, 1998 two U.S. Embassies were bombed, 2000 the USS Cole was bombed, and the Sept 11th atrocity; everyone of those events of terrorism were the actions of Muslim extremist. The perpetrators and planners of this "Holy War" are ready and have been getting ready for many years. There are more than eight hundred cells established inside our borders with any where from twenty to one hundred fifty members in each; and they have been embedded in our businesses and communities for many years. And our intelligence departments know it. They don't want you to know it. They would rather be what they think is politically correct using that dictum as a shield to cover their concern about the potential of panic or vigilante actions then the more important issue, the welfare of the lives of all U.S. citizens. We must be concerned about the more than one hundred thousand or so people living just like you in your communities who want America destroyed. While the liberals say it is not politically correct to profile potential murders, I say we must battle the terrorist no matter where they are, no matter who they are and no matter how. I leave you with this. Would you submit your personal secure home and beautiful family to danger by inviting in two wayward people that you knew nothing about except only that you were informed one of them had no moral values at all and would kill you and destroy your precious home at any instant? HELL NO you wouldn't but that is what our government has opened us up to." The government side stood up and two at Jerry's table stood up along with all of the guest audience and all of the production crew. They begun to clap and clap and clap when Tom motioned for 'private microphone', a signal to the crew person on the control panel to kill all other microphones; and he started his closing of the program. But he had to wait as the cameras panned around to see the applause from everyone in the studio and the station's employees.

"Panelist UBC wishes to thank you for your sometimes provocative and as always informative input in tonight's special program on 9-11 The Who, The Why, and The What Now. And to our Television audience I personally say thank you for joining us and I know we are leaving you with a lot to think about. I will say this to all Americans; this is the greatest country on earth and we must join together to keep it that way. Good night."

I waited for Dad to finish thanking each of the panelists and leave some instructions for the studio crew then we headed to the elevator. Jerry was coming our way from the rest room so we held the door. "Well Jerry you sure gave the public some thought provoking information tonight! I almost cut you off, then I changed my mind because I always felt like the liberals had put our people in harms way. I can just imagine that there will be hundreds of calls coming in to our switchboard tomorrow and especially on Monday; from coast to coast and even from overseas. And I'm sure some from stockholders that have completely different opinions. My feeling is that facts count and opinions don't! I was impressed with you tonight Jerry and I congratulate you." We changed elevators and then down to the first floor and pass the guard station. There were three extra guards manning the doors and a new one at the elevator control panel. Dad waved at Dan who had been a guard from the day the building was finished. "Expecting trouble Dan?" Dad asked.

"Not in here Mr. Brayden but wait till you get outside! The police doubled their force and finally dispersed most of the crowd. We could see them taking away some trouble makers. The police barricades directly in front of our building got all busted up during your program plus we did have about twenty demonstrators try to get through the front doors. Two of my extra guards worked shore patrol while in the service and I think you will see some blood on the sidewalk outside near the only double doors we left unlocked. We will see to it that it is cleaned up by tomorrow. Donald's in Atlantic City so I think we are lucky on that one. I guess you had a controversial special tonight, huh?"

Outside we had to go around the corner to hail some taxies. Jerry took the first one and shook my Dad's hand. "Once again I've enjoyed being on one of your programs. I'm not to sure how your CEO will take the heat on Monday morning. In these times any little thing can make the pot boil over. Too much heat, lots of boiling. Monday will tell. Good night."

"Oh Jerry just a second," I was curious to talk to Jerry more about his friend Jack. "If you will still be in the City tomorrow maybe we can have a coffee some time."

"Sure Hank, call me at the Marriott. I'm in room 2334."

"Okay"

Another taxi was pulling over, "Dad you take this one and I'll get the next one and call me when you get up and maybe we can get some breakfast."

"Sure, good night son," and Tom headed off towards a small co-op he kept in town for times when his days at work ran to long. Waiting for another taxi to approach Hank watched the police move the last of the people that had gathered on their way and take down the barricades and he wondered to himself how the public would take Jerry's frank and emotionally presented observations of our venerability to terrorist activity.

The next day on Saturday after Dad and I finished breakfast I called the Marriott in Manhattan and asked for a Mr. Ness in room number 2334. The phone rang about seven times before the operator came back on the line to say there was no answer which I already knew and she asked if I wanted to leave a voice message. "Yes, please." I thought a moment, where can I meet him? "Would you please have him call me on my cell? The number is 805-579-2123? Thank you."

Saturday some of the guys from work liked to spend the afternoon at O'Shaughnessy's to watch the college games, partake in the free hot dogs and drink all the beer that they had in the bar. There have been a few times they believed in their own minds they had really done it. But the next day their heads told them they hadn't made the Guinness record book yet. I walked across the park and down to 42nd street to where the famous bar that always had green beer on St.Patty's day took up the northeast corner on Second Avenue. It was quite a long walk and I had forgotten the length of the New York City blocks until my legs and shortness of breath put a big reminder on me. It was about 12:30 and the first game had not come on. A couple of the hard core guys were already plunked down in the old railed hardwood arm chairs that Washington and Jefferson once sat on, a little banged up but not as bad as the tables. That all added to the atmosphere along with the Jimmy Carter salted peanut shells all over the floor. We always joked with the first timers to O'Shaughnessy's because Jimmy Carter is the night time bar tender and Jeremiah Washington and Hugh Jefferson still come in from the Burroughs for special sporting events on TV.

"Hey guys, I was wandering around New York and thought I would have a beer. What-a-ya think, is this a good place?"

"Hi Hank, sit down and take a load off. What really brought you down here, never mind, help us out. We were looking for an un-opinionated person to break the deadlock."

"What deadlock?"

"Okay, I say it looks like Stanford won't make it to the Orange Bowl this year because Nebraska will kick some ass! What do you say?"

Three more guys showed up just then and blurted out, "Yeah, Nebraska right."

"Well I'm a Georgetown boy but Nebraska looks real strong."

As Hank announced his favorite team his cell phone went off. One of the guys waiting for the first game to commence asked him, "Hank, don't you get any time off from that thing or is it your second girl friend? Or maybe your first."

Mike the second in command in the department spoke up, "Every one knows he has to carry that with him everywhere and I've seen his girl friend Tiama and you should be so lucky!"

"Did anyone catch the special on UBC last night? You remember Hank told us his Dad was hosting a special on 9-11 and the terrorist. I think it will shake most of the country's understanding about what Cush said here on the 14th, 'We are at War'. That last guy from ACE International may have been a little overboard but the people need to know what we have believed for sometime now."

One of the coworkers added, "The truth hurts but I hope it doesn't create some kind of panic or vigilante type of retribution. What we need now is sound thinking and stability."

Hank was going to comment but, "Sorry guys but my phone is ringing again, I gotta move from the TV, I'll just grab my beer and go over there."

"Hello it's Hank here!"

"Hank, its Jerry. I was out doing some things and just now got your message. What's up?" "You know, I was curious about what happened to Jack and, well maybe you could join me for a beer instead of coffee this afternoon and exchange some conversation."

"That's okay by me but after last night I've pretty well spent all of my conversation. Where is the best beer at today?"

"Right here at O'Shaughnessy's on 42nd Street."

"Heard of it and never been there. I'll catch a cab and see you in about an hour."

They had about fifteen TVs in the bar and I guessed about four games were on. I got all tied up in the Florida State against Florida game and lost track of time. "Hey Miles, what time is it?"

"Time for three more pitchers and a chance for you double up on your bet if you're so inclined."

"Not today, my friend just showed up and we've got some things

to talk about. I'll be back to collect my winnings after we've finished."
Hank moved off of his chair and motioning to Jerry he headed to an
empty booth that was not so close to a TV. The bar still retained the
look of an Irish Pub and had the high back seats in the booths which
gave them a certain amount of privacy.

"Well Hank I think you have found the best place to be on a fall day.
Football, beer, and free peanuts and free hot dogs. Great Saturday afternoon custom!"

"It's a satisfying diversion and escape from the real world. Waiter,
my friend here needs a beer and bring me one more too. No, just a minute. Let's just get a pitcher, that okay with you?"

"Sure and can I get a couple of hot dogs?"

Hank was in the mood to talk as he went on, "After this past six
weeks or so I want to say I am confused as to what is real and unreal.
Looking at that game on TV, that is as real as anything and to the players and people in the stands it is 'real time' real. Conversely, looking at
the hole in the ground in downtown Manhattan is surreal to me and if
things continue to come apart in the world, that kind of unbelievable
reality will overshadow everything else in our lives. I think I had been
too distanced from all the turmoil and flow of terrorist information
we kept receiving from our UN sources around the world and almost
stoic to the reports we prepared for the State Department. It was all so
far away and it had been a way of life for most all of the countries for
decades. But it was not until September 11th and hearing the President
tell us that United States was at war did I begin to get the point. The
point that many other countries around the world had known for all
of those decades. There is an evil force in this world that is bent on destruction! And after the two hour special last night and the awakening
of last month I have a bone chilling feeling about our future."

"You know Hank; it seems to get more shocking every month.
Sometimes hard to accept and then you find it becomes even harder
to believe the facts. I know them, I get more confirmation every month
on them and I can not find the confidence that we will be protected
against the enemy in the future. I understand President Cush will have
a national press conference on Monday to inform us that we will be going after the Taliban, bin Laden, and all terrorist in Afghanistan. We are
now in a state of war and our economy has been hit hard."

Just then the waiter brought a new pitcher of beer and another bucket
of peanuts. Jerry clamed up not wanting any of the conversation to

go pass the booth. A different voice and a more subdued Jerry, "You wanted to ask about my friend Jack and as I told you before he was killed in June in Jakarta. I guess I mentioned Jakarta. I can only say that he is a hero, however as you know in the CIA you never get that recognition and an anonymous star goes on the wall in the building lobby in recognition of an agent's personal sacrifice. Last December as your remember we were together in Hong Kong and meeting with an arms dealer turned informant when the mission went bad. We were investigating unproven information about the movement of military contraband into the states when our informant was either wasted or disappeared and the trail died in Hong Kong. At first we believed we might have been tricked and Jack blew his cork. He had never had a negative Opt before and with the stakes so high he was determined to dig until he uncovered the facts! I went on with my own assignment and Jack stayed to dig up old acquaintances and go deep into the world of the illicit arms dealers and the transfers of contraband from one rogue nation to another. I never heard from him again but from the reports I read he was close to verifying part of the original story we were given in Hong Kong and more importantly he had reliable leads on actual deliveries of this contraband when he was ambushed in Jakarta sometime in June. He was a dedicated, honest servant of our country. He was mean and tough and I really liked the guy."

"I am truly sorry; I can see that you two were close. Let me ask a question. You say contraband, is that just terminology for Nuclear or Biological weapons? Are we that close to an even bigger disaster to our country?"

"No, I am not saying what it is and I am not saying those things were part of his investigation. All of my detailed knowledge is classified and you know I can't speak to any of your questions beyond what I have told you. There is definitely a 'need to know' limitation. Only the top brass know what he had found out. Not even I know the details of how close he was. Only the rumors have survived."

I continued my talk with Jerry as we watched the ball game and drank some more beer until around four when I had to leave to meet Tiama. "Jerry, I need to leave to meet with Tiama. Again, I'm sorry about your friend and wish you safe passage in your investigative travels. I still have a curiosity about what may have gotten into our country. I think I'll check with my contact at the State department to see what he can tell me. In the mean time be careful and we'll talk soon I'm sure."

"I'm going to leave too and head to the airport; I'll walk with you to the door".

CHAPTER TWELVE

Towards the end of October the initial strike on the terrorists in Afghanistan had begun and people were returning to a somewhat normal life. Spring of 2002 came and the economy was still faltering and the government had to authorize a special bill to loan the airlines money. Travel was off more than fifty percent and billions were being lost in the airline and travel industry. The stock market had lost almost fifty percent of its value and people who had invested their future in the market were devastated. The consensus was it could take ten years to fully recover the losses. More than one and a half million jobs had disappeared and of course unemployment was rising. Tiama was still with the Filipino Center and I was getting fed up with the United Nations. On the one hand they acknowledged the need to fight terrorism and on the other they gave no support to our government or President Cush. What hypocrites! I wanted out.

As the months passed the President and the government advisors reviewing the operations of the various security agencies recommended the centralization of all of the intelligence and enforcement community into the newly created Office of Homeland Security to improve the country's internal security and more effectively protect the country against terrorists. The new Office of Homeland Security under the executive department had been established on October 8th 2001 and was finally funded in March, 2002. The governor of Pennsylvania, the honorable Tom Rodgges, had been named to head up the department giving him the responsibility of correcting all of the operational problems existing in the FBI, CIA, and NSA and then to bring those and other departments into OHS with the intent of making all security operations more efficient. Each was blamed for not having been able to uncover the plot which unfolded on September the 11th, 2001. The analysis of their operations showed that each was an independent agency and never shared intelligence information. Everyone knew that it had taken a long time to have planned the surreptitious mission carried out by the nineteen terrorist, quite possibly years in the planning. And everyone suspected bin Laden was the mastermind and financial backer of the operation. What nobody knew was why the intelligence community failed to uncover such a monumental project carried out by our enemies. Failure of cooperation!

By Fall the seeking and eliminating of the terrorist elements in Afghanistan was a grand success while at home the investigation and even the arrest of some of the nineteen terrorist who were responsible for the 9-11 attack was going ahead full steam with the combined efforts of all of the agencies. President Cush announced that our country was on the right track and that all of the security improvements at home were working while the number of changes to our every day lives were somewhat of an inconvenience; but they were all necessary.

Tiama and I spent all of our time together while I was in New York and I found every reason to have to work in The City rather than in Seattle. The year passed by with the country slowly accepting all of the infringements on our rights that were being imposed by the OHS. And for a second time we both spent the Christmas holidays with my family in Westchester. On New Years Eve we went to the Hamptons on Long Island for a more quiet celebration. It was the off season however our favorite hotel 'The Shores of Hampton' was providing a magnificent week end from December the 28th through January the 2nd with ice skating on their small lake and romantic sleigh rides every night in the soft freshly fallen snow. The eastern seaboard was overcastted with a storm that seemed to be trapped right over the state like a moth in a cobweb; so every night as the temperature fell to around thirty degrees a gentle snowfall would blanket all of Long Island leaving the trees and roof tops a picture of white glistening wonder. This was a fabulous way to spend the New Years weekend; winter weather, an elegant hotel with delightful rooms and food as delectable as one would ever want. We were pampered and we loved it.

Coming back from the last sleigh ride on New Years Eve Tiama and I sat on the porch to enjoy the brisk cold air, some hot buttered rum, and look out over the frozen lake. "This has been a fabulous week end my love. Different than last New Years Eve sitting at home and watching the ball come down at Times Square on TV. What with all of the inhumane things going on in the World and the carnage of 9-11, enjoying this night with you seems like we are on a different life plane or at the least a different world. Looking at the lights shimmering off of the snow covered trees and smelling the fresh crisp winter air gives me a sense of great peace and comfort. This tranquility makes it so easy to forget about the events of this past year. All, except one major event."

Tiama set her cup down and twisted in my arms to look up at my face. With a real quizzical look she asked, "What major event was that?"

"My falling in love with you again. Not just 'in' love but so deeply in love that I don't want to ever lose you."

"I feel the same Hank. I want to thank you for coming back to me. I was always there for you and in every day of our future I will always be there for you. My heart throbs for you each day I am awake and at night my dreams are of you and my prayers are for us."

Hank set his cup down next to hers and turned Tiama completely around facing him with her long black hair draped over his hand. He reached in to his inside jacket pocket and took out the little white box he had been carrying the entire week end. As he opened the small lid exposing a two carrot pear shaped diamond his words came slow and softly. "I want to have you as my life long companion and my eternal wife, will you marry me?"

She looked straight into Hank's eyes and crossed her hands together, then answered. "Oh thank you God, yes my darling I will be your wife and be bound to you for eternity." There were still clouds in the sky and little wisps of snow flakes were floating in the air but from somewhere there was a sort of brightness surrounding them. They were in love, they had found love, and so the very nature around them was shinning.

As almost a year and half had passed since 9-11 there seemed to be a more positive atmosphere prevailing in the country. In March Jerry called me to let me know that ACE International which had been funded by the CIA no longer existed because it was folded into OHS.

He said he was now with NSA and was given a position with better pay and a government retirement program. As the section head of one of the counter intelligence units CI-4 he also coordinated logistics with TIU, the Terrorist Intelligence Unit. Due to his prior experience he had the freedom to work out some of his own missions with the counter signature of the director who had been his boss at ACE International and he sat on the counterterrorist review committee. He left a message on my cell phone that he wanted to talk to me about the opportunities that had opened up especially after I had told him a number of times I was fed up at the UN.

Finally on March 20, 2003 we invaded Iraq under the operation 'Shock and Awe' after Congress had spent months debating on whether to authorize the President to go forward and after President Cush gave Saddam a final chance to leave Iraq. All of us at the UN knew that it was a hollow offer and odds were that the administration thought it to be 'a fat chance' but the offer was politically necessary. With our knowledge of both the coming events and the military power of the United States that was to be thrown at the Iraqi army it was also the consensus of those in the UN that the surrender of Hussein would come quickly. I called my friend Jerry to hear what he had to say about Cush's decision and get his feeling on the length of the war. "Hello this is Jerry Ness, can I help you?"

I started out in a provocative way, "Well the President has done it now. What's going to happen now in the Middle East? Or better yet how long will we be in this situation?"

"Oh it's you Hank. The Middle East, I don't think anyone can know that at this time, but it is explosive. Was this necessary and will it be short and sweet as Chaney says? We all believe so. All of us in CI-4 and those in the TIU section have opened up a pool to bet on how long it would take us to wipe up the Iraqi forces and declare victory. It is from 4 weeks to 12 weeks, do you want in? We have to have a little fun in this high stress environment."

"Hey thanks for offering but I don't want to take your money. But I do want to take some of your time pretty soon and get some inside information. I'll call you in a few days, Okay?"

"Sure Hank, anytime. I'll wait for your call."

As the end of March rolled around I called Jerry after discussing with

Dad my uneasiness at the UN. Dad's advice was simple. 'Follow your gut not your emotions'. I dialed the number Jerry had left and the phone was answered directly by Jerry.

"Hello guy this is Hank." By now we recognized each others voices. I was interested in his previous discussion so I asked, "Jerry, where are your OHS offices at exactly? I want to come by and talk about leaving the United Nations and looking into the possibilities with the new OHS intelligence department, TIU."

"Sure anytime. We are in Alexandria. Let me know what day you will come down. Things are extremely lively here with a very high energy level at this moment. We have been reviewing the lap top computers captured in Afghanistan from some of the blown out Taliban/ al Qaeda fortifications and they are quite revealing with a lot of very interesting operational information about bin Laden's lieutenants in Europe and here in the states. Just as I have been saying, they are here and with this information we plan to be all over them like white on rice. This information has revealed that the operatives here have been casing many, many potential targets in various areas in the states for the past 15 years. We believe that these sites are being pinpointed for terrorist destruction and also we found information that gives us proof that al Qaeda started the plan to take out the Twin Towers in 1996. The chickens are coming home to roost and although I have been correct on my assessment of our enemy we only want all the upper commanders and the political leaders to wake up. It looks like the battle will start with us in the intelligence departments by alerting the public and our government leaders. Well as I said things are popping, I guess you still have your top secret clearance, right?"

Hank thought for a minute, "I believe so sense I spend a few days every quarter at the State Department's inner sanctum. But I will call tomorrow to my contact Jake Olmsted and make sure I have the proper credentials to get in."

That evening I picked up Tiama for diner at around 7:30. We strolled a short distance to a quaint 'mom and pop' pizza n hamburger joint around the corner from her apartment. I let Tiama know my plans. The burgers were the old fashion style hamburgers, mixed sirloin and round for the patty, aged cheddar cheese, grilled onions, kosher pickles and light mustard topping. The flavors always lasted for a couple of hours and the onions lasted all night. A little pleasure and a lot of pain! That's the way life is. With the hamburger over and coffee and desert on the table I made the announcement, "Honey I am thinking about leaving the UN and going back into government."

"Hank, honey, you know what ever you do is fine with me. Where will you be working?"

"I'm fairly sure out of DC but nothing is certain; I only started looking into it today. Let's set a new date for our marriage so we can make future plans about work as a married couple not two single people. I know we said New Years Eve 2003 and sometimes things change. What do you think?"

I could see the wheels turning and the 'I'm not sure look' as she mulled over my news about possible job change and my suggestion for changing of our wedding date. Her answer of course was very practical as always. "Let's see if the government thing works out and then work on the wedding date."

"Perfect", was my reply with a sigh of relief?

CHAPTER THIRTEEN

It was a gorgeous day in April when Abu arrived from his trip. He had first gone to London, picked up his foreign passport and then on to four other countries. After six months of travel to Riyadh, Manama in Bahrain, and then to Yemen where much of the banking for the al-Qaeda network was done, he had gone to Tehran, and then Gwadar on the Arabian Sea, a safe and convenient place to meet with other terrorist leaders. Abu would complete a final review of the preparations and readiness for the Ji'had. The meeting in Gwadar was attended by Dr Ayman al-Zawahiri, the right hand man of Osama bin Laden and one of the major planners of the 9-11 attack; Ahmed Yassin, a great Hamas leader with ties to Arafat; Khalifa Ali Abu Bakr, a renowned fundamentalist cleric backing al-Qaeda; Abdulla Azzam, the major recruiter and trainer for al-Qaeda; Zubayr al-Rimi, the military leader for the training camps in Afghanistan; Mustafa Mohammad Fadhil, the communications specialist who set up the web sites and established the procedure for communications between leaders; and Ibrahim al-Mughassil, al-Qaeda's relations officer for diplomacy between other Muslim nations. Returning back to London Abu changed passports and prepared for his trip from London to Brazil where he met with Jonathan then arrived in New York from Brazil thus completing his American passport tour which always kept his passport clean.

Musab picked Abu up from the JFK airport and after lunch at an out of the way restaurant where they spent a number of hours briefing each other they headed to East Orange for prayer in the new Mosque. The international company in London financed by Suddam Hussein that was putting money into building Mosques for Muslim believers had built a bigger and more beautiful Mosque in Newark. Located at 215 N. Oraton Parkway, it would hold five hundred for prayer and had a few small meeting rooms. Evening prayer could last for a long time; however twenty cell leaders who had been summoned to New Jersey left the rotunda after a short time and gathered in a room with no windows. Abu began with a, Praise to allah, "Praise allah! WE ARE READY! I met with our brothers in the East and then with Jonathan in Brazil and Musab here in Newark. Here is the report. According to Saja, Yassir, and Brada, the leaders of the eighty cells with all of our brothers who are in sympathy with the movement report that each of them is ready. They have been trained. They have been taught. They have studied the 'Military Manual' and accepted all orders, they will all be armed and fortified with ammunition and knifes when we are called on to begin the Ji'had. They have all pledged their lives to allah and are ready to kill and die for our god allah. Jonathan has brought in all of the special boats and Musab's people have brought in all of the required ATV's. We have available two hundred thousand kilos of plastic explosives and the targets have all been mapped and the attack plan is being detailed for each location. We have the battle plan ready and soon the plan will be divided into twenty geographic areas and loaded into our communication system to be sent to the cell leaders when allah has told our leaders that the time is right."

Musab rose to add, "Our most glorious leaders for many years have planned the destruction of the USA 'The Snake', and we have all been patient. As for the annihilation of the Icon of the west; remember, the initial plan to attack The Twin Towers and the killing of thousands of Americans took more than nine years to develop with the last three years maintaining a very low profile, almost undercover existence requiring exact planning, training and coordinating of the operation. It was successful and with the blessings of allah we will succeed again. Only our leaders know the complete plan of destruction and they will pass that plan on to each leader only at the chosen time and only the piece of the plan that effects each leader's individual operation. You and all of the leaders will be notified by a call to your cell phones to get the instructions, maps, diagrams and pictures of targets, and procedures for everyone's individual assignment. The calls will come from our people in Yemen with the address of a special web site that will not be up and running until four days before we strike. Each leader will get an ID and password at that time and those ID's will be coded to the pages they are to study. They can not make copies of the site's pages nor view all of the pages, only theirs. Our cache of explosives, weapons, and ammunition is stored across the states ready for use on attack day. The storage areas were set up in the areas where the equipment will be needed and by brothers that left the country after everything was stashed. They passed on the location and means of access to our separate cell leaders who are maintaining the locations and their security. So that information will be available to all of our brothers at the same time as the plans are posted. We are told it could be two or three years but we know it will be a time in conjunction with some event or activity that is of great importance to the Americans; like elections, holidays, or celebrations".

Abu finished the meeting. "The war Cush started in Afghanistan against our Taliban brothers has killed many and destroyed much of their infrastructure. Our leaders are safe but will need to disappear for a year or so. We here must stay low profile, quite, and patient, very patient. Our time will come. The security being set up internally by the government here and the investigation into any suspected Muslim requires us to be above suspicion. We have heard that the FBI has implemented a program to trap all international phone calls and e-mail activity based on preset word parameters such as bomb, blast, guns, weapons, fight, martyr, allah and so on; you get the picture! The name of their program is Carnivore. It can trap you only if they have a predetermined notion to look into your activity; however all of the calls and e-mails are archived. Use your computer for only normal internet functions like searching common web sites, going on line to our educational Muslim sites, buying things and etc, etc. If you have other needs to go on line always go to an internet café, the public libraries, or Kinko's and never use the same computer twice. This is a command. Again study and live by the manual. We have been instructed that if any one of the leaders here are suspected of any connection to terrorist groups or activity and picked up by authorities you are to take you poison pill and sacrifice your life. By orders of allah, Mohammed, and bin Laden. The Homeland Security alert here has us at a level of orange right now. Be careful traveling. Stay on your jobs, and stay with your family and do nothing to attract attention. Now go and return to prayer and then leave quietly."

I took the job with the Office of Homeland Security in June and was required to spend my first two weeks in training at Fort Bragg in North Carolina and then two weeks of orientation in the office at NSA. I told Tiama about the one month of initial training so we planned to spend the coming Fourth of July holiday in DC enjoying our countries celebration of our freedom and the sacrifices made some 230 years ago. I needed to get on track with any new governmental procedural changes that had taken place from when I had been at the State Department. Then there were the new PPP manuals of purpose, policy, and procedures for the new department of OHS. While I had a vast amount of experience in assimilating information and boiling down the guts of the refined data to a concise intelligence report, I also had some of the most extensive background of anyone in recognizing and interrupting information as opposed to disinformation that came from foreign sources. I was casting my future to the wind when I put in to be a foreign counterintelligence agent but I wanted that rush of adventure that I had not felt from my past work. I had knowledge and I knew I would be good; I only had to show the agency of my abilities and then convince Tiama there was no danger in that position. I went through two weeks of very rigorous testing both physical and mental back at Fort Bragg. The agency needed personnel so I was accepted and was ordered to go for one month of training at 'The Farm' in Virginia which was to start after the fourth of July week end.

In two days once again the nation would be celebrating the Forth and the recovery from 9-11 in a dynamic way. And again many Hollywood stars and singers were planning patriotic concerts and major American landmarks were gearing up to display the strength and resiliency of our country. This year in Philadelphia at Independence Hall, Houston at The Alamo, Washington DC on the Mall at Liberty Memorial, New York around the Statue of Liberty, Williamsburg, Virginia at the restoration of the old colony, and in San Francisco around the Golden Gate bridge, and in many other places the local authorities and numerous organizations were planning extraordinary fireworks displays.

The holidays were over and so was my tour at 'The Farm'; I had completed my intelligence and CIA basic training. I was now officially working at NSA headquarters and placed in unit CI-4 with Jerry. He had told me he would get me into his section. It was my second week at OHS when I bumped into Jerry as he was going to the cafeteria for lunch with under secretary of NSA, George Meeker. "Hey Jerry; oh and hello there George; can I grab a bite with you guys, I need help on knowing what is really good to eat here?"

"Sure, I guess George doesn't mind sitting with a newbie, a plebe, a trainee…….. OK just kidding."

As we walked along towards the cafeteria George open the conversation. "Hank after reading you dossier I am impressed with your vast knowledge about the inner sanctum of so many foreign countries' intelligence operations. After you get back from orientation on the up dated procedures for your job functions we'll have a meeting with the staff at CI-4 to advise them of your capabilities and what an asset you will be to that department."

"Well George I'm going to try and be a genuine asset to unit 4 and I do thank you for your acknowledgement. Hopefully with the training I've gotten and my experience with the assimilation of intelligence I will get some field assignments."

"Oh yes, your training, how does your wife feel about your taking covert assignments?"

Jerry piped up, "I can speak first hand on that. Tiama has personally said to me that she is behind Hank in everything he does. She is very glad he is out of the UN and with the government."

I wondered why Jerry spoke up but I added, "She is a great wife I am very happy to have her blessing on this new position with OHS." George gave a kind of Hummm sound and I could see he thought I was answering as diplomatically as I could. Most wives are uncertain exactly what their husbands work really is and that of course is the best way to have it.

A few weeks later, while reviewing reports on the travel patterns of Arabic nationals living in the states on visas that allowed multiple re-entries, Jerry came across a Brada al-Abaji. He read the name again… and again….and it seemed to ring a bell although not too loudly, he could not get the image focused on where he had heard that name. As Jerry glanced up from his work, Hank was about to knock on his door. "Hank, come on in. I see you are back, learn anything?"

"I learned that this is a crazy business compared to where I came from, but I am excited." "Good; look I have been pondering over a name for the past few minutes and I wonder ifffff……, that's it. It just now came to me while I was looking at you. You had a friend named Brada."

I paused, "Well, not a friend just and old classmate from NYU."

"That's right, I remember now. You wondered about his fundamentalist views about Islam." Again I paused, "Why do you ask?"

"I'm reviewing the reports we are now getting from our immigration section on frequent travelers in and out of the country during the past ten years that have Arabic names. The report has almost three thousand names on it in alpha order and also in the order of the number of trips made during that period with the exit and entry dates all listed. This Brada al-Abaji has more than forty exits and then reentries over the past ten years. I'm going to interview him. Do you have any input?"

"Not really, he runs a Journal on Hydro Electric power and as I understand it he does consulting with third world countries that have an urgent need for new sources of electrical power. I talked to him last summer about his Muslim back ground and he said it was as normal as any other person's religion."

"Okay we'll see. What do you need?"

"Just stopped by to say hello and let you know that I have my office down stairs now and I am settling in. I'll leave you alone, see you later."

It was already August and the CI-4 department was still establishing its operational guidelines and weekly work policies. Jerry kind of shook his head and thought to himself how slow things move in the government sector. What a crime!

Jerry made it to the train on time on Monday morning and boarded at the club car so he could have a cup of coffee and some breakfast. He wondered if Tiama was on his train since she had stayed over in DC while Hank was in training but unknown to him Tiama had gone back to 'The City' Sunday night. It was the early train which left at 5:30 am and arrived at Grand Central around 7:30. Jerry wanted to be first at Brada's office and meet with him before any other business affairs or clients would distract him from the interview which he had been anxiously awaiting. He looked for the address over the doors of the building. 3945, 3937, here it is 3923 Avenue of the Americas. The building was in the garment district and very old. He looked on the directory for World Wide Journal for Hydro Electric Power. No such name. Looking again he saw WWJHEP # 2308. Jerry looked around the corner for the elevators. There were only two elevators and all of the old buildings in New York had too few elevators. Finally he heard the bell and saw the up arrow. On the 23rd floor he found suite 2308 and the full name World Wide Journal for Hydro Electric Power printed on the door. Jerry walked into a rather moderate office with many pictures on the walls showing dams, power plants, nuclear, coal, and geothermal, and a strange underwater system with a submerged turbine. "Hello, may I help you?"

"Why yes, I am Jerry Ness from the Office of Homeland Security and I would like to talk to Brada al-Abaji."

"Just a moment, please have a seat."

A minute or so later Brada came down the hall and introduced himself as Jerry noticed a look of puzzlement on Brada's face. "I am Brada."

"Yes sir, I am Jerry Ness with the Offic......"

Cut short Brada said, "Yes the man at the desk told me, what can I do for you?"

"I am doing some follow up work here in New York on an investigation and would like to have a few minutes of your time."

"Of course, please come to my office."

This was a small office area and Brada's office had a light table or what looked like a light table, a large desk, and what looked like an 'Office Depot special' work table against the wall. One guest chair so I sat down pulling the chair up to his desk. I wanted to be as close to him as I could get and look straight at him as I began my questioning. First showing him my badge and picture ID I opened with, "Just exactly what is it that you do Mr. Brada?"

Brada countered, "Before we begin what is your investigation about and what do I have to do with it?"

Jerry unbuttoned his jacket just enough for the pistol grip of his gun to peek out from under the front edge of his jacket to add a bit of tension to the atmosphere. "Since 9-11 and the creation of Homeland Security, the department is conducting routine interviews with foreigners who are non-permanent residents and that do a considerable amount of international traveling. You fit that description and you have been assigned to me as the investigator, mind you this is just routine."

Brada smiled slightly and said, "Fine, go ahead."

"Mr. al-Abaji, where were you born?" - In Iran.

"What is your birth date?" - November 7th, 1965.

"Do you have family in the States?" - Immediate, No but two cousins, Yes.

"Why did you enter the United States?" - To go to college.

"Where did you attend college or did you?" - Yes at New York University.

"What do you do for a living?" - I own this publication.

"Are you the only owner?" - Yes

"What do you publish or what is the meat of the publication?" - News on the Hydro Electric Industry. Discussions about building facilities. Information on countries looking at new projects, advertising announcements on bids for construction, maintenance contracts open for bids, and help wanted, all on an international level. New or improved design ideas, etc.

"We have noticed you travel a lot to the Middle East, why?" "First to promote the journal, second to secure articles for the body of the publication including the section on bidding, and last to work with some countries on a consultant basis. This has been my studies and profession for over twenty years."

"Who are some of your clients?"

"A few are my country of Iran then there is Sudan, Pakistan, and Nigeria as examples."

"Are you affiliated with any International Organizations?"

"Only the United Nations committee on 'The World Environment, Energy Conservation, and Natural Resource Preservation Group'. And of course the World Bank's committee that publishes the 'Third World Financing Budgets for Future Energy Conservation' which is produced annually. Also I work closely with the Department Of Energy in Washington to influence other nations to look at Hydro Electric power as a necessity for their future energy needs knowing that there is a limited supply of fossil fuel available world wide. DOE is highly concerned about energy for the future just as we at WWUHEP are."

"You are Arabic, are you a Muslim?" - Yes.

"Do you attend a Mosque and if so which one?" - Yes, the one at 12 Warren Street.

"Do you belong to any terrorist groups or anti-American groups?" - No, of course not.

"Do you know any one who is a threat to this country?" - No.

"Our records also show a Yassir al-Jazziri at this address who has traveled many times over the past ten years, May I see him please?"

"Yassir was our foreign affairs officer who handled the interaction between us and our foreign clients. He does not work here now."

"Can you please tell me where he is now or where I can find him?"

"He has gone to the Middle East to study and I do not know exactly where. But he does call on occasions and I will be glad to ask him where he is and let you know."

"That will be fine; here is my card and my direct line. As soon as you hear from him let me know! How many employees do you have and can I get a list of their names?"

"Five here in this country and sure I'll give you a list on the way out."

As I was questioning Brada I made an analysis of his office. There seemed to be a lot of photos of different dams and power plants. There were photos of different kinds or transmission towers and what looked like a crisscrossing of black lines and small squares all over the state of California with a title of 'Example of Interconnecting Power Grid'. There was a bin of at lease forty or sixty rolled up plans or what looked like plans to me. Sketch boards leaning against the wall and a large stack of papers on the worktable. "I'm curious about all of you pictures. I think I recognize Hoover dam and The Grand Coulee Dam and then that funny layout on the map of California. What are these exactly and why the pictures?"

Brada's face was now completely relaxed as he explained, "Yes, the DOE has provided a lot of technical information for our journal and I have had these pictures for years and I show them to the internal affairs officers from my client countries so they can see some magnificent dams. Those two over there are in China and Egypt. I use the map of California to show examples of a massive transmission system and the major substations and transformer blocks needed to handle a country that size. It is an excellent example. Makes some of my work in preliminary conceptual meetings easier and many have not seen a system this detailed. Anything else I can help you with?"

"No, that is fine and I thank you." I left with mixed feelings about who he really was and for now any suspicions I may have had had generally subsided; Brada was informed and he had placated me on the operation of the journal.

I had nothing else to do in the city so I hailed a cab and went back to Grand Central. The next train to DC was not for an hour. The train is really faster than an airplane considering the time it takes for you to get to the airport, then go to the gate, and now in this environment arrive sixty minutes ahead of time, then the flight and finally the taxi ride back to headquarters in Alexandria. In this case it would be about the same time either way but I got an hour to relax with some coffee and a far better seat then those on airplanes. A train ride is like something out of the old days, like a vision of the west and wide open spaces plus I am always guaranteed a more relaxing ride on the train; I'm like coach Madden I'll take the train every time when ever I can.

Jerry had a couple of details about Brada he wanted to talk to Hank about so he called his cell phone. The phone rang in Tiama's apartment Friday afternoon and it was Jerry. Hank had set his cell phone to call forward to Tiama's phone for the evening. Tiama answered, "Hello."

"Yes I'm sorry I must have the wrong number I was calling my friend's cell phone."

Tiama recognized Jerry's loud voice so she played him on the phone for a while. "Well you can call me your friend, I won't mind." She was into a syrupy sexy voice as she went on, "What is your name darlin?"

Caught by surprise Jerry was trapped. "It's Jerry I was calling a friend, but you sound nicer. What's your name"

She had him. "Well it's 'come on over if you have the time', I want new friends."

"Where am I calling? I wanted a cell phone."

"I live here in New York."

Bang the joke was over. Putting two and two together with her voice and New York, Jerry knew he had been punked. "I think I had better just talk to Hank, this is really Jerry."

"I know, here he is."

"Hank you left a couple of days early, I wanted to tell you about my interview with Brada. Do you have some time now or should I call you on Saturday?"

"No, neither one, I've got a better idea; I have invited Dad and my sister and some New York friends to join Tiama and me for a very special dinner here in the City tomorrow night. It's on us. Come on up, bring Anna and stay till Monday morning."

"I was just there on Monday, what's the occasion?"

"It will be special but I can not tell you right now, it is a surprise. You will definitely enjoy the time off."

"Time off and the parties on you, that's great; I'm sure it will be okay with Anna, we'll call you when we get there."

The last Saturday in August and Hank's Grandmama and Caroline had come in from the farm late Friday night. Hank called Tom and asked him and Caroline to walk to the park and have a coffee and bagel at the Café in the Park. Coming in late Friday night, Caroline was still asleep and Tom suggested that they let her sleep and he would come by himself. Hank responded with a, "Sure, I'll see her later. Meet you at the Café."

Sitting down for the coffee Hank said with a feeling of excitement, "Dad, Tiama and I are going to get married before this coming New Years Eve, actually we are going to tell everyone tonight at dinner that we're going to be married Sunday and then next month we are going to move to Arlington, Virginia. I'm telling you now because I will need a bit of outside help to finish off all of the arrangements."

With a big grin Dad replied, "I kind of felt that you would be planning something like this. I think it is great and it's the right move for both of you with your job change and all. I have gotten to know her and the family thinks she is just perfect for you. And I guess it is about time, you're not getting any younger. This is really short notice so what can I do to help you?" I went over a few things that I knew he would be good at doing and we left after an hour or so.

Dad finished the dinner arrangements and picked up my tux while I went to the church to put the finishing touches on the ceremony and talk to the pastor. The wedding would be Sunday afternoon when the pastor had finished all of the church services. Tiama had left everything up to me except the flowers and of course the dresses for her and her bridesmaid. We had planned the announcement dinner at the Four Seasons and Dad and Caroline left together for the restaurant at 8:00 o'clock at the same time I left to pick up Tiama. Getting off the elevator I reminded myself how different this relationship was compared to ten years ago when we drifted apart, knowing that this was the real thing and knowing I was very lucky to have a second chance. I guess my finger was stuck on the doorbell while I was in such deep thought as the door opened, "Honey what are you doing? I hear the bell!"

Startled, I took my finger away from the button and then I got a look at the most scrumptious vision I had ever seen, my wife to be Tiama, "Does God know how beautiful you are tonight? I think he may even tell the angels in heaven to take notice." I had to surround her with my arms and give her a thank you kiss, a soul mate kiss and a kiss of spiritual commitment. "You are the one and you are forever. Let's go have dinner and tell everyone about our future." "I'm ready Hon, let's go." Tiama reminded me about Jerry and Anna. "Jerry called a couple of hours ago and is here so I told him to call your Dad and get instructions for the dinner time and location. Then I called Dad and ask him to meet them and have a drink with them till everyone arrived."

Dad made sure the dinner came off with out a glitch. There were Dad, Caroline, Grandma Mimi, three of my friends and their companions from the UN and Jerry and his wife Anna, two of Tiama's friends and her bridesmaid with her husband which made up the dinner list and probably tomorrow's guest list. A small wedding but we planned it that way. After a most unusual dinner of mixed entrees from foods of India, Thailand, Philippines, and Argentina, Tiama and I rose to make our announcement. Speaking alternately first me then Tiama. I started, "We both together.....want to tell all of you.....that tomorrow we are", and Tiama finished ",......going to be married!"

We heard 'congratulations' and 'all right' as Caroline rose with her glass of champagne to give us a very warm toast, "I will have to say that I am not surprised, instead I must say I am glad for both my brother Hank and Tiama and I'm glad for our father, Grandmama, and myself because we are getting a simply incredible addition to our family. From the first time I met Tiama I was attracted to how pleasant and giving a person she is. Hank you struck gold." "I totally agree; Grandmama, excuse us while I take my future bride to the dance floor." I wanted to take in the whole of the ambiance and pleasantness of the evening so I danced with my fiancée for almost an hour without stopping.

Having worn off the high from the champagne I made a suggestion, "Let's sit down for a while and enjoy our guests."

Her head nodded yes and we walked over to the table by the window. "We're back, why didn't you all come and dance?" No answer.

As soon as she sat down Tiama started to talk to her friends and I turned to my buddies from the UN asking if they were enjoying the evening when Jerry pulled up a chair and asked if he could join us. "Sure you may, remember these guys from the Saturday we spent watching football at O'Shaughnessy's a while back? Let me introduce you to Mike's wife Gloria and these two dazzling friends of Al and Sam; Sandi and Karen."

"Hello, nice to meet all of you. I've known Hank for almost three years and now we work together at OHS". Jerry bent over to whisper in my ear that maybe we could talk about Brada next week. As I nodded yes he continued, "What do you think about this getting hitch thing he's cooked up?"

"For Hank this is his shinning hour. He needed this settling period in his life. A beautiful wife, a government job, a house in the burbs, and two kids and two dogs, Right Hank?" Mike was a friend and was trying to be a little bit humorous.

"Number one right, number two right, number three right and we'll try real hard to get number four right; But for number five Mike, we'll let you take care of that with two pure white Samoyed pups from your bitch's next litter. Okay?"

Everyone applauded and Mike was kind of in a spot. His little joke bit him in the butt at $1,650 each for Samoyed pups. "Sure okay, but the kids come first."

A little more champagne and a little more dancing and talking and it was almost midnight. "Tiama come on we have to go, we have some work to do now; I mean we have some premarital procreating to do."

"Hank, cool down we've waited this long, one more night will not blow your cork!"

"Your right Hon!" We both turned to say goodbye to our guest. "Thank you all for coming and we'll see you at the church tomorrow. Do not forget Mike, I'm holding you to those puppies."

Sunday morning and Caroline picked up the bride and whisked her off to the church about an hour before the wedding and Dad waited for me to finish fitting into the standard arraignment for the 'submission to bondage' ceremony. Most men seem to enjoy strapping themselves into the uniform associated with everlasting servitude, 'The Wedding Tux'.

"Dad let's go. I'm all set." There is something very special about knowing you are planning a permanent relationship with a person you really know so little about and with whom you will be spending the rest of your life to get to know as intimately as you know the front and back of your hand. It will take a life time, but that venture of getting to know each other can make life sweeter than a bowl full of freshly sliced, vine ripened white Georgia peaches. And living every day with Tiama will be as delicious as each bite of that bowl of peaches. "I'm Ready, Ready, Ready Dad, where is the taxi?"

We left the church hand in hand heading for Atlantic City. "Hon, I didn't tell you or any one about our honeymoon plans and where we are going. That's our limo and we are off to Atlantic City for two days of gambling and making babies."

"We can try but remember we agreed, no children for the first three years. Hank darling you were wonderful, the wedding service was as I had dreamed and the whole thing has made me feel like the world stopped and that I am floating in this gigantic bubble of pure ecstasy. We are married and I love you! I will make you happy the rest of your life; that is a promise!"

I mused, a wonderful dinner, an emotional and beautiful wedding and a relaxing fun filled honeymoon and then back to the City and my or actually our apartment to enjoy the union 'Hank/Tiama and Tiama/ Hank'. We are happy

We got back from Atlantic City on Tuesday evening and went straight to my apartment. This would be where we would live until we moved to DC. Tiama had given up her apartment and needed to be out by the end of the month. Unlocking the door we heard from inside a loud "Who is there?"

At first we were taken back in shock to hear a voice and then almost instantaneously I recognized Dad's voice and we remembered that he and Caroline were staying in the city for a few days and of course they were still staying in my apartment. "Hello, we are back, it's just the newly weds."

Caroline was first to the door, "Well come on it and relax. Set your bags down, let me get you a drink and we want you to enjoy our simple abode."

"Ha-Ha, how long have you lived here and where did you pick up the old guy on the couch? Times Square?"

"Now look here you young whipper-snapper, I'm the one who lives here and this here girl has been in my keep for many years now."

Hank was laughing now as he asked, "Any important messages come in while we enjoyed the break and romanced each other the past two days? And did you leave us anything to eat?"

Looking at Tom Caroline continued, "What do you think Tom, can we share our grub with them? We got Chinese, Chinese and Chinese. Which do you want?"

"We want the Chinese want – tom and want - som."

"Okay funny guy, everything is in the kitchen."

My apartment had two bedrooms, a sleeper sofa in the living room, and a small bathroom and of course the kitchen. The closet bedroom as I called it, was about as big as a motorcycle garage; seven feet by eight feet. There was a bed, a small chest and a chair. Dad slept there and Caroline took the sofa bed. Tom of course had his own one bedroom apartment but chose to stay at my place before, during, and after the wedding. We came back a day early so Dad and Caroline were still at my apartment. Now with the food gone and drinks slowly melting away we said, "Good night", and we put our bodies to bed. My bed, now our bed was just perfect for both of us and tonight we initiated it after almost two years. It was about time.

Dad was up at 5:00am leaving for work early but on the way out checking to see if I was available for dinner Thursday night. Tiama had a Pilipino charity thing to attend so I said you bet. Friday would be my last day in The City for almost a month then Tiama and I would be doing our moving thing making it necessary for me to handle a lot of little chores between now and Friday. Caroline planned to stay in town until Friday and helped Tiama move her things to our apartment before catching a train home. Thursday evening seemed to appear out of no where and I was on the way to meet with Dad for dinner. We met across the street from UBC headquarters at the up scale Moran's restaurant specializing in fabulous corn fed steaks and fresh Maine lobster; One of my most favorite foods.

CHAPTER FOURTEEN

Boca Raton, Florida - Thursday 4:24am September 7, 2003

"Captain Jacobs of the Coast Guard has given us the go, so hit the power." The Lieutenant who skippered one of the patrol group was on board the number 4509 boat dispatched out of the coast guard station on the Keys and had just issued the last order to his three drug smuggling chaser boats to take down a pair of high speed power crafts from St Thomas that were identified by the surveillance satellite as carrying drugs. The lieutenant and his armada were about forty miles out from the Keys on a standard east southeast to south southwest sweep looking for any illicit activity and guided by both radar and satellite when the alert occurred. "Sir", the petty officer in charge of communications reviewed the target with his skipper, "the transmission is showing an erratic movement by the boats we are after! They are splitting from each other and then doing a Z shaped path on a heading of three hundred forty eight degrees north northwest at a speed of more than eighty knots."

The commander barked out his order, "All boats lower their wings and steer up on the waves. Tell 4520 to head towards the target directly on their path and we will go with 4501 after the southern most boat."

The Coast Guard had followed the procurement selection of the DEA and acquired their special built high speed boats from Florida Flash Boats in Biscayne Bay. The dealer had modified each of the V hull boats with three wing type extensions that could be extended while running at higher speeds to raise the boat up partially out of the water to cut down on the resistance of the waves and produce a smoother and faster ride. The chief petty officer at the helm answered, "Yes sir, we are at eighty five knots and based upon theirs and our combined speeds we should spot them in fifteen minutes."

"Sir they have each changed course headed towards each other and their Zig Zags are now putting them on their own collision course. It is still dark out there and they may hit each other unless they change their course."

"Helmsman, head directly to the point where their boats will meet."

"Sir we will not be there by the time they come together. We will be four minutes behind that event."

"Continue on course for intercept and give the same orders to 4520."

"Yes Sir." The communication petty officer in a frantic voice hollered, "Sir, it has been six minutes and they have just disappeared. My radar does not show any boats not even CC4520." He paused, "Okay wait a minute I've got a blip showing a boat approximately four miles off of our port side. Can any body spot any lights?"

The skipper instructed the helmsman, "I see lights twelve degrees off port, let's get there." "Skipper its CC4520!" "Pull along side so I can talk to the senior chief."

The CC4509 boat inched in along side CC4520 and the Lieutenant asked the chief what was going on and why had they stopped? "Look on the other side Sir. They dropped a decoy buoy with a radar jamming transmitter. It caused our radar screen to register a blank as if they had vaporized. We contacted base and told them what happened and they are right this minute getting satellite coordinates. They should come through in thirty seconds or so." "Great job chief lets go get these slim balls!"

"Lieutenant, here are the coordinates, 39° 10' by 79° 24', twenty miles ahead of us and based on their direction now they are going around the Keys. Shall I call in for an intercept?" "Hell no, these jerks are our catch. All boats full throttle and spread out a half mile port and starboard; we should be right on their ass in twenty minutes."

"Yesss Sirr!"

Twenty minutes later and the Lieutenant asked, "What do you think chief, its breaking daylight and we should be on them?"

The communications officer caught the eye of the Lieutenant and pointed, "They are dead ahead of us Sir."

"Everyone stand ready to board after I make the announcement and prepare for fire. Closer, Okay now along side, you on the boat, this is the United States Coast Guard, stop your engines and prepare for us to board you boats. Do Not and I repeat Do Not reach for any weapons. We have a fifty caliber machine gun pointed directly at all personnel on board your boat."

"Chief, tell CC4501 and CC4520 to board the boats and start a search for drugs."

With in less than twenty minutes the boarding crews returned to the decks, "Lieutenant, you can contact base and tell the Captain we have found more than five hundred kilos of pure brown heroin on each boat. Looks like there could be over one hundred million dollars in street value here."

It took an hour for the Coast guard cutter to arrive to clean up the bust, whereupon the three chase boats returned to the base on the Keys to complete the report and file the necessary paperwork. All three crews were met by the Captain to bolster their egos with a 'job well done'. "Gentlemen, this is a huge bust and I am proud to have you under my command. You are however ordered to keep silent on the event until we have completed our investigation. The DEA believes it already has the big fish on this one in their scopes, so no media. Your lips are sealed until further notice. That is all."

Dad was in the bar when I arrived after having finished the last of my errands for the day including hashing over the plans with the moving company for next months move. I hate moving. I heard a famous doctor on TV, I can't remember for sure but think it was Dr Phil, once say that the two greatest stresses in a person's life are divorce and moving and that moving was the number one stress related event that people do! I believe it. There were always some people from the media in Morton's Lounge either from CBS, NBC, Fox including Viacom and The Times. These were Dad's peers and I could tell that his mingling and bumping shoulders with them was a far greater pleasure for him than being in the press room at the White House. He was in his element and he was good. "Excuse me Dan, excuse me Morey, hey Peter, can I scoot pass here? Thanks." Looking two stools down the bar was Dad so I called out as I slid past another news anchor person, "Dad the place is sure crowded, what is happening tonight?"

"We've been told that al-Jazeera will be sending a message from Osama exclusively to CNN for broadcasting at 8:00pm at the same time releasing it to Europe and the Middle-East nations. Rumor has it he will show that he can not be captured and he will personally call for an uprising by all Muslims against the Jews and the United States declaring that other terrorist attacks are 'on the way'. Hank can you get clear to find the waiter to seat us at our table that I asked the Madre Dee to hold for us? This is becoming way too crowded, so I'll feel better sitting where we can sit in peace and talk."

"Sure, keep your eyes on me and come when I wave my hands."

"Boy this place really rocks after 7:00. I imagine you can find rumors, gossip, opinions, private news flashes, the latest buzzing and what have you passing from person to person or group to group almost any night of the week."

"Son, more than just news and future editorials are being generated; here are the untold stories about the media people and their personal happenings. The untold stories about lives, jobs, families, etc and I think this is my most favorite place to hang out after a long day's work. Well enough about this place, four days married and how are you doing?" "Actually five days if you count Sunday and we both are very happy. A little anxiety exists about this move and then my future at the new Department of Homeland Security since I haven't told Tiama the full ramifications of the job or I should say my actual position."

Tom had a quizzical look, "Position? I thought that you were an information's officer GS15 doing coordination between CIA, FBI, DOD, NSA and the liaison person at the White House! Has your position changed?"

"No Dad I made a technical change on my own. I joined the CI-4 section with Jerry and finished up my training about a month ago at Langley."

"Oh my lord son! Counter-Intelligence, so what does that mean? Are you going to become an undercover agent and if so where? Here inside our borders or overseas? What exactly is Homeland security doing with trained spies? That is what you trained for correct?"

"Dad, do not panic. First, I am not spying I am working in the TIU section which is the Terrorist Intelligence Unit and second I chose this because I want to be in that arena and I feel like I have a wealth of knowledge about the internal affairs of many, many nations and their covert dealings with terrorists and their activities in backing many of them. They may use me at home or I may have missions abroad. What ever comes my way. But most important to me is that after 9-11 I know I want to serve my country and like most Americans I have a raging hatred for the terrorist. They have a bulls-eye on our country and we are at war. As I now see it, a war that is not only on the hollowed ground of my birthplace but also a war against an enemy that is clandestinely occupying our land and damn it Dad, they must be routed out."

Tom choked a little and then put his hand on my shoulder as he said, "I am of course proud of your position and will always be behind you in what ever you do. The real question is how does Tiama feel about your new career change?"

Hank kind of looked side ways and with a slight wrinkle in his face he let Dad know. "She is very happy and excited about my leaving the UN and our moving to Washington and my joining the OHS department. I have held back a little about the details of the job, but in time I'll keep telling her about my work, a little bit more at a time and slowly a little bit more about my new responsibilities."

"Well," Dad's wisdom came out, "I suggest you do it sooner than later! And I really mean that. Before you head out for DC this weekend I have something I want to discuss with you. We have that person in accounting that was a classmate of yours at NYU, Ghassem Mahomeini, you remember him, right?"

"Sure he went to work for UBC almost right out of the university."

"Yes he has been a loyal employee for more than fifteen years as I am told. He is being promoted to head up our financial evaluation and planning division directly under our CFO. They started moving his office to the executive floor in the financial section and some of his papers have ended up on my desk. What happened was, they were in a box that must not have made it to his new office and one of the clerks in his old area that hadn't assisted in the move came across the box; so in trying to find out who the box belonged to and after looking at some of the papers in the box thought management should see them."

"What were the papers?"

Dad's expression was very serious as he when on, "Very strange because we are not sure if they are notes from some various news programs or his personal notes. Items like 'new covert immigration operations – have they started.' And then a scribbled 'Why'. Another note in blue pen, 'Information distribution? but how?' One that is most curious, 'those plans for attack..... no' and below that is 'Islam is peaceable'. We will talk to him about these notes tomorrow and now what I want to ask you is, who do you think he is?"

As Hank was going to answer, a major anchor from FOX TV passed by and saw Tom so he paused a moment. "Tom, nice to see you old buddy, are you here for the great food or for the yackety yak after CNN airs the bin Laden news clip? I'll sit for a second if its okay." He shook Dad's hand and asked, "Is this that son you've talked about? Hi, I'm Joe Scarbourgh."

"Yes this is Hank my son. Hank I know you've seen Joe on 'Scarbourgh Country' on Fox TV". "Sure have, Hi Joe, a pleasure to meet you."

"Well Tom back to the bin Laden thing; but first did you catch the news out of Florida on the huge bust the DEA made of two thousand pounds of pure heroine? Some insider with the Florida Drug Enforcement office was overheard telling the FBI about how a Brazilian boat manufacturer who has been supplying high speed chase boats to the DEA passed on some invaluable information that lead to the capture of two boats loaded with heroin. Street value when cut for street sales was estimated at over two hundred million dollars. The agency is really tooting its horn on this one, especially with the security on our borders and coastline always coming into question."

Tom interrupted, "I think the news from CNN showing the al-Jazeera film clip is beginning. Yes, there is the CNN anchor Bret Hummer announcing their coup with the exclusive presentation of Osama bin Laden's most current interview."

"Tonight we at CNN want all of our American countrymen to see a recorded interview al-Jazeera TV had with Osama bin Laden in a mountain camp somewhere in Afghanistan this past Sunday."

Recorded 09-01-2003

"I have a message for the Americans around the world. We will find those that are the infidels and you must know we will kill you every chance we have, we will kill your women and we will kill your children until Islam has triumphed through out the world. Our god allah will use our youths to carry out the battle and bring more attacks against the United States even more successful then our brothers on September the Eleventh. We are blessed and we praise the name of allah and the suicide bombers that fight for allah and punish those that give sanctuary to the enemy and protect the evil six pointed star. The world can see that we are well and still fighting for Islam. Muslims around the world must unite rising against the people that support the agents of America and against those that allow them to enter the holy lands of the Muslims and establish military footholds. I will die a martyr in the fight to rid their colonialist advances into the Middle East. The British and Americans came to steal our oil and destroy our culture and we must rise up and slay them. Listen, all of my brother Muslims world wide, the fight is every where and we must support each other with our lives. Again I say to you that we will bring destruction with suicide bombers to all of the countries that support Cush and the American aggression. Cush and his cronies now want to take over Iraq by attacking the innocent people of Iraq. The Americans attacked us and now we bring the war to their door step. We will attack within and we will attack outside and we will win. They will pay for the harm and treatment of the prisoners they are holding. The Russians tried to steal our lands and we defeated them and so we will triumph over the serpent of the west. Cush will see what we have for him and his followers. In the name of allah, the beneficent, the merciful."

Bret appeared on the screen, "Well 'there you have it', as my friend Dan Rathen would say. We all have known that Bin Laden is against the war we are waging in Afghanistan and now the new war we are waging in Iraq; he wants us out of the Middle East. He has said nothing really new but his threats are more severe and reflect the continued terrorist attacks we have seen world wide. This should give the Tom Rodgges group a lot to think about and put all of our citizens on an even greater alert. Their own personal 'We Had Better Watch Out' alert. Good night."

I left Dad with his cronies and hurried home to my wife. She had waited up for me not only to be up when I came in but to ask me if I had watched CNN News. We talked about the video of bin Ladin and I pushed pass any apprehension Tiama had by telling her 'all is under control'.

By Mid-September Tiama and I had moved to Alexandria into a small place just south of the main business district, a place not at all upscale but in line with the money we had saved and with my government pay. Tiama was waiting to hear from the Pilipino Embassy about any opening they might have in the coming months. We would wait on children for a few years if possible. The cost of a nice home in the outer areas of DC was ridiculous so until we could buy a nice home and had the space, babies would only appear as little smiley marks on our 2006 calendar. We had finished our unpacking and Tiama had done a marvelous job of decorating, sort of a collage of her well thought out second hand purchases and my mixture of Levitz and Penny's. She made the place an oasis in the midst of the most stressful city in the world. But more than oasis, what I really loved was to come home, relax and eat like a potentate; Malabon, Adobo, Tinola, Bopis, and Escabeche. It was on the last Tuesday of September in the evening as we sat around the coffee table after another delicious Pilipino meal, drinking some Merlot that I told Tiama a bit more about my job designation. "I want to let you know that as my responsibilities grow at work I may be coming and going day and night."

In a newlywed way Tiama assured me, "Honey, don't worry, I understand and I understood when I married you."

Hank with a rather serious look on his face had to tell her something he had postponed for some time. "I know you understand and I love you for your understanding. There is something I have to explain to you about my duties. I am in the same counterterrorist department as Jerry and will be given assignments that will take me on missions out of the country too."

Tiama gripped my hand in wide eyed surprise as she asked, "Hank why didn't you tell me about this? Are the assignments dangerous? Are you going to be a spy? What does this all mean? I want to know."

Dad's advice was to tell her and I did, but he mentioned nothing about scaring her and I was not going to put any fear in her heart about my future safety, "Normally just basic investigation work using my knowledge about the different countries I investigated while I was at the UN. And you know I can't discuss anything about the nature of my travels or where." "Of course, and you know I will always be worried and praying while you are gone." Pouring some more wine I kissed her on the ear and whispered, "I will always return, remember we have a commitment to make some babies."

October ushered in Hank's graduation and completion of his indoctrination to the world of national security. He soon found that the governmental red tape was frustrating and even though he had only been in the CI-4 section for a little over two months he thought that he was not productive in his position. Going into Jerry's office Hank asked if he had a few minutes. "Sure, grab a chair. What's on your mind?"

"You know Jerry I don't want to go to George but I feel like I am not contributing very much to our unit. I've been here for a few months all I do is assimilate incoming data for TIU and the other agencies. I was looking forward to some action of some kind. Any action at all would be Okay."

"Everything you are doing is not only helping to uncover persons of interest for the FBI to investigate but our department is making the states more secure by uncovering terrorist operatives."

"Yeah, I know, I just feel like I'm doing what I did at the UN and that's all."

"Look at me, I have been locked to my desk for a number of months and the only movement I get is to aid in the individual investigations on people who have suspicious travel history. Just like my meeting with Brada. I interviewed him a while back and all I could put in my report was that he appeared to have too much of an in road into our Department of Energy and data about our energy sources and supply; but I could not put my finger on any real suspicion. I did however put him on the OHS watch list which went to the FBI and CIA plus I had his name inputted into Carnivore. So right now any action if you can call it that is in the hands of the FBI and DOD."

On October 3rd Abu summoned Brada, Yassir, Saja, and Musab to meet at the barber shop on Eighth Ave. Taking a short time to greet each other they waited for Abu to finish his hair cut and then disappeared in to the back room. Abu opened with a question to Brada. "We want to know about the interview you had with a CIA agent a few weeks ago and what was his name?"

"His name is Jerry Ness and Yassir, Saja and I discussed the conversation I had with him. Saja was in the next office at the time and was able to record the entire conversation. I can provide you with a copy of the tape but basically this is what it was all about. He is with OHS, not the CIA and they are gathering the traveling data on all persons with Arabic names to see who has been moving in and out of the country an unusual number of times over the past few years. I explained my business and my need to travel from my New York office to many third world countries. I also added that the DOE was a provider of a lot of my technical information needed to plan Hydro Electric projects with the developing countries. I believe he was satisfied with the legitimacy of the Journal and my travels when he left."

Abu turned to Saja as he asked, "Do you feel the same? We can not have the authorities interrogating any of us! I want that tape when we leave here."

Saja responded, "I listened to the meeting and again to the tape and I truly believe this was one of their routine checks on our brother and the journal."

"Then I wonder why no one has come to question me on all of my trips in and out of the country?"

Brada answered the most logical answer there was, "You are a US citizen and you will never be under surveillance. You have been traveling for you business for many years and they can see that from the records."

"I hope you are correct but we must be extra cautious or disband if we are suspected of anything at all; which brings me to the next problem. There are rumors that Ghassem has been elevated in his position at UBC but something has arisen in his past or at the job that may cause an investigation of his living habits or even his associates. If for any reason his company goes to the government and they start a thorough investigation of his life back to days at the university too many may also be interrogated. We can not have an investigation into his associates because that will ultimately come back to you and each of you is too valuable to our plans. I have arranged for Ghassem to have dinner and go dancing with a lady operative of ours and tonight he will have an unfortunate hit and run car accident. Alcohol will be believed as the cause. This must be done for our protection! Each of us can be sacrificed! My brothers patience and peace in the name of allah. Good night."

It was Saturday when Dad called to ask how we were doing and how my new job at NSA was going. "Hello Tiama this is Tom is Hank around?"

"Yes, just a minute and I'll take him the phone."

"Tiama, Tiama can you hear me, I wanted to ask how you guys are doing and how is your work at the Pilipino embassy?"

"My work so far has been enjoyable and not at all tiring and Hank and I are great. I am hoping we can all get together this Thanksgiving again so let us know if that would be okay, well here's Hank I'll talk to you later."

"Good morning son, Tiama says that things are going great. Have you been assigned any missions yet or is that off the table for you?"

"No Dad, I am riding a desk for right now but there is a lot of information passing through our hands about what is happening in the hot spots. Most of it is classified information about how intense this war on terrorism is and how dangerous the world is becoming what with the invasion of Iraq, Iran working on a nuclear bomb and ending up on Cush's dart board, the nut in North Korea rattling his WMD at us and suicide bombings happening all around the world. Of course your news department gets all of the information that is allowed to be released."

Tom cut in, "Besides wanting to see how you guys were I have a strange thing to tell you about Ghassem. Remember we talked about some peculiar writings we found in his personal papers. When we talked to him about those notes he said that he had been watching al-Jazarre television and written down some of the things that bothered him. We accepted that since he had been with us for so long and then when I got to work on Monday we were informed that he was killed in a hit and run accident Sunday night. Appears from the police statement to our personnel department he was quite drunk and walked into the front of a large SUV and was drug about a block before ending up next to the curb as the SUV turned the corner and drove away. For some reason I kind of find the timing coincidental, especially when the SUV did not stop and the police are charging the death to the hit and run driver. You never got a chance to tell me what you thought about him. Do you have any thoughts about it or am I being a little paranoid about the coincidence?"

"I don't know Dad but I can run him through my computer at work to see if any thing comes up on Carnivore."

"Okay just thought it was a little strange. Glad to hear things are going well and tell Tiama I will have Caroline call her about Thanksgiving."

After hanging up the phone I turned to Tiama to tell her about our old university colleague. "Hon, Dad said that Caroline will give you a call to talk about Thanksgiving, but do you remember Ghassem from NYU? He had worked at UBC since we graduated. Well Dad told me that he was run over last Sunday and died. We didn't know him that well but it is sad. I never like hearing that some body has died."

"I agree. Where did it happen?"

"Dad didn't say, I guess somewhere in the city."

I ran Ghassem Mahomeini's name through the Carnivore data base for

Dad and nothing came up so I surmised that what had happened was a just an accident. Poor Ghassem. I gave Dad a call.

"Hello UBC, Number One in Worldwide News, how may I help you?"

"Would you please connect me with Tom Brayden's private line, this is his son Hank." Yes Sir of course, on moment please."

"Tom Brayden here."

"Hey Dad, I ran Ghassem's name through the data base and found nothing. Hope that helps."

"Sure thanks son."

Very strange but all of sudden I felt like the time at my job was really dragging along while I was just intercepting information that had first been filtered by all of the other agencies that were looking at the activity of those that were on the list of persons of interest. Then make a decision if a Field investigation needed to be issued. I knew the security of the country was the prime business of OHS and the work at NSA was to make the final decision before placing individuals or specific groups on the watch list, but I was getting bored and needed some action.

However, our intelligence gathering was reaping benefits as we were able to uncover much about the personal backgrounds and the connections the 9-11 hijackers had with al-Qaeda. Most importantly, using all of our hi-tech communication and eves dropping systems we provided Special Forces with locations of where lieutenants of bin Laden were hiding in Afghanistan and Pakistan which helped us captured some of the targets but in most instances we eliminated them and destroyed their physical locations. Two of our biggest successes were the location and capture of Khalid Sheikh Mohammed who was one of the main masterminds of the 9-11 attack and the capture of Hambali, the operations chief for Jamaah Islamiyah group who helped plan the 9-11 attack. Hambali was captured in Thailand after a plot to crash an Air India plane en-route to Los Angeles into the U S Bank tower in LA was foiled using intelligence information from on of our CI units. Our section was instrumental in using Carnivore to expose the plot.

It was more than year since I had joined the government when George came into our section to announce that a mission was set up for Jerry. "Jerry is leaving for South America on assignment tomorrow to find out about the soundings we have been getting suggesting the smuggling of arms by what are possible al-Qaeda operatives believed to be based somewhere in Brazil. As you know our department has uncovered some information coming out of Argentina which appears reliable and Jerry has taken the assignment. Everyone will be doing rotating shifts in the department's communications room while he is gone to provide him with Satellite visual and voice communication." I called Tiama to tell her I would be on call at odd hours at the office to back up Jerry while he was gone on assignment. Our CI unit would be on alert 24/7 to assist Jerry and I was to run point. Still no action for me.

CHAPTER FIFTEEN

September 10th Jerry arrived in Buenos Ares, Argentina to try to make connections with anyone that could give him leads on the sale of explosives to Middle Eastern buyers during the past five years. The sketchy reports indicated that there were illicit sales coming from underground plants in South American and that the buyers were dealing with sellers in Argentina. Jerry contacted each of the companies that were arms manufactures on the confidential list from the DOD and using his new government credentials he spoke with more than just the owners and managers. His broad travels with ACE for the past twelve years gave him a working knowledge of several languages and Spanish was one of his more fluent languages. He made it a point to ask for a tour of each plant by offering to prepare a reasonable report back to the undersecretary of procurement for the DOD to help the company qualify for possible future bids on contracts for military equipment. Jerry needed to observe the management and supervisory personnel in each plant to try and deduce who could be suspected of stealing and selling military material and specifically C4 from their manufacturing plants. He visited each of the four plants on his list spending a whole day as he toured the facility. Complete exposure to the plants gave him the opportunity to make careful observation of people who were in a position to have access to military materials that could be stolen. He would also have the ability to talk to them and use his gut feelings to key in on ones he would want to pursue further. His logic told him they would be the production or shipping managers but his senses said to look for money, in the eyes and on the body.

Plant by plant he waited for those individuals he selected to leave their work and follow them noting where they lived. Jerry felt that even if these people did not provide any direct leads they might be able to confirm some of his suspicions or they may know if there was a secret underground plant making contraband explosives. He was on a high level investigation and all avenues had to be scrutinized. Either way he was going to use his own method of getting information and that included a direct confrontation one by one with those he suspected. Their line of work was most probably one where everyone knew everyone else. Jerry was counting on it.

After identifying all of the persons he had surveyed from the four active arms facilities, Jerry very privately approached them one at a time and at a place where he could not be noticed by any one. Jerry suggested to them that he represented an anonymous buyer of plastic explosives. As each one refused to be a party to any clandestine activity, he read their body language and made a precise interpretation of their conversations. One person, Armondo from Groupo Equiptas Militaris, passed on a name of a co-owner who seemed to fit with other pieces of information Jerry was able to get as a person running a maverick operation of sales of contraband arms. Jerry contacted his liaison at CI-4 to run the name Raul Varges through the NSA data base. With Jerry's observations and the response back from Hank at everything pointed to this particular person Raul Varges. The DOD had his name as an associate of Kashsoggi a wealthy arms dealer from Saudi Arabia with an international reputation who worked the circuit in the eighties. He ran surveillance on him for two days as a matter of procedure, and then on the evening of the second day he confronted Mr. Varges out side a small Poperia in an up scale neighborhood and he showed him his persuader telling him to get into his car. "Raul, I am a buyer of C4 and I have been watching you and know that you have diverted materials and arms from your facility and sold the contraband on the black market. That is not important to me, what is important is that I believe you know people or have associates that operate an underground arms and munitions supply chain to third world countries. I only want names from you so that I can contact them personally, there is nothing in it for you; and I want those names now." I could tell he was not certain if I was really a buyer, a foreign agent or a killer so I pointed my 38 persuader at his belly and repeated my request again. I wanted him rattled and it worked. He gave me two names and said that he no longer dealt in contraband and had not worked with either of them for more than three years and could not tell me where they were. "Give me the last address you have or a contact person that may help me find them." He knew I was serious and in a split second he gave me the contacts he said could help me and he told me where he thought they could be contacted and then I drove back to within a block of the Poperia and let him out. It was dark and the street was still damp from the earlier drizzle. Only the light from the Poperia could be seen and I was sure I heard a sigh of relief as he walked passed the small building and away into the shadows.

He had said that Fernando Munoz who lived in the city of Avellaneda in Argentina was the most active and he was the last person he had contact with. Since he said that Munoz was his most active contact I started there. He said that he always talked to him at a phone in the office of his cousin's beer factory. He thought that he had a relationship with a small chemical company in Avellaneda that he believed was on the south side of town where product was stored as the shipments made their way to the buyers. He thought that Munoz was on the south side of Avellaneda too. So I followed the lead on Fernando Munoz went to the port city of Avellaneda and had a taxi drive me to the south side of town and with the help of the driver and some searching around we found a small chemical distributor near the town's beer plant. The small distributor was in a building that looked like the fumes from the chemicals had slowly deteriorated it to a point that it could fall down any minute. Most of the wood was etched and grayed and the windows were fogged up beyond recognition. I paid the taxi and entered to find a girl going over papers on an old table and two workers stacking some large bottles into cartons. A swarthy looking guy wearing a short sleeved shirt and gold hanging all over him came through a door that looked like it lead to the back warehouse. I approached him with certainty that he was the proprietor and asked him for a minute of his time in my best Spanish. "Who are you and what do you want?"

I quietly told him I had a friend with me, showing the 38 I had gripped in my hands and I wanted to talk privately to him. I had purposely caught him head on while his back was to his two workers. He knew I meant business looking at the redness of my knuckles wrapped around the pistol grip and there was no way for him to look at his workers. He nodded to a door behind the girl at the table and we both went straight in. I closed the door with my foot, then with no hesitation I put the gun at his forehead and said simply, "I don't care in the slightest who you are and if you are dead or alive; I know you trade in illicit high explosives, guns and other munitions and I want Fernando Munoz now."

He started to stutter an answer, "I don......"

I cocked a shell into the chamber and, "Stop, no bull shit! And understand this I will kill you right here right now and then your two workers and the girl unless you give me Munoz. I guarantee it." An immediate sweat came on his forehead and I knew I had hit pay dirt. "No phone calls, you will take me to him now! Open the door only a few inches slowly and tell the guys you want some boxes from the back storage area. Then ask your girl to come in here.

As he opened the door he immediately barked the command "Jose and Manuel go to the storage area and bring me two boxes of nitrates. Lidia, come in for a minute."

When she came to the door I pushed Mr. gold chains out of the door beside her and told them to move outside and get in his car. "Lidia you drive and you sit back here with me. Take your belt off." I looped the belt around her neck and tied his hands together behind her neck. "Now tell her where to go."

We drove south on the 'auto-pista' to a dirt road about eight kilometers out of the small port town and turned inland. After a few kilometers there were no more houses and then we came to a sharp turn into a rugged driveway that wound through some trees and then up to a neat adobe style house and with a wall around it about six feet high. I took some old rags from the trunk of his car and tied Lidia's hands to the steering wheel. "Stay right here, I know you won't try to get away or I'll shoot you. There is nobody around and I'm taking the distributor cap so you won't be able to drive if you tried. If all goes well we'll drive back to town and you'll never see me again. Munoz had better be here." I checked out the wall and it was typical Spanish architecture. The wall was about a foot thick and the top had tons of broken glass cemented in to protect against wall climbers. Back at the car I took my passengers pants off and after finding a stretch of wall that looked the most obscure I threw them over the glass and used them to protect my knees and hands. The property was meticulously landscaped and on the side of the house where two cars were parked I could see a gorgeous pool area. The front had a veranda and massive double doors. No question this Mr. Munoz had money. I went to the side of the house first. Unlike the large picture windows in the front the windows here were many and small and high off of the ground; meant only for light and not access. I could knock and wait for an answer. That would be dumb.

I needed a diversion. Back to the side of the house where the cars were I went up to the new white Mercedes and my luck was with me, the windows were down. Remembering my days as a kid and the Halloween pranks we used to play on our neighbors I pinned his horn. It immediately started honking and I quickly hid on the side of the car opposite from the house and waited. In only a few moments the illustrious Fernando Munoz came out with a shoot gun and walked towards the car looking in every direction with a very puzzled look. I felt he had never heard of the prank and would think it was a mechanical malfunction. I was right; he put his gun on top of the car and looked inside at the steering wheel. Just two seconds, but enough time for me to rise up, move around the car and stick my gun in his neck telling him to stand up. "Stand perfectly still. You are not in any danger yet and I want to keep it that way. Is there anyone in the house with you?" He shook his head sideways. "Careful, all I want is information. My very reliable sources have told me that you are an arms dealer and deal in explosives, more explicatively in C4 and I am chasing it maybe a lot of it. Give me the name, address and serial number of your repeat customers over the past ten years or I'll shoot you were you stand. Any phony names you make up and I will be back to kill you. You are quite visible."

"Name address and serial number, what are you talking about?"

"It's a joke to break the ice, are we all comfortable now? Good, I want the names of your repeat customers and how you contact them? In other words I want contact locations." Fernando kind of looked like Castro, but shorter. He gave me a look first of doubt and 'go to hell' all in one. Again I had to use my friend Glock and shoved it in his ear; either you heard me or you'll hear this as it spreads your brains all over your Mercedes. He gulped and started talking as fast as he could.

"Over the past ten years I have only had two repeat buyers and they are both form the Middle East, one from the Sudan and one from Jordan. The name"......

"Hey slow down we got time."

.... "of the buyer from Sudan is.... Abdul Aziz Rantisi and the other is.... Ahmad al-Masri. Rantisi always arranged for his own shipping so I don't have any addresses and al-Masri had me ship the product he bought to Brazil using a different address each time."

"How much did each one bought?"

"Rantisi bought up to twenty thousand plus kilos a year in shipments of five hundred kilos. And Masri has stopped buying from me."

"Stopped buying? Why and how much was he buying?" Jerry felt he had opened a big paper bag and soon he was going to unload tons of groceries.

"He told me that he had acquired all that his leader was going to need and that if he needed to buy again he would contact me. I have no contact to give you for him."

Jerry pushed the gun deeper into his ear, "How much did ai-Masri buy and when did he stop?"

"In the ten or eleven years he bought around two hundred fifty thousand kilos and he has not been here since October 2000. I heard a rumor that he actually had a place across the bay in Montevideo, Uruguay. I never knew for sure, it was a rumor."

"How did you get paid and do you have any idea where the shipments went in Brazil."

"He paid me by a wire into my account on the Falcon Islands. I have a list of the locations in Brazil for the years 98, 99, and 2000 someplace in the house but they were just drop offs on the docks with pier and building number and no permanent locations. Mainly some small port towns north of Sao Luis near the gulf Baja de Marajo ."

"Okay I believe you, give me the names an I'll be on my way!"

"Acaran and Fortalez and Sao Luis and Belem I think."

"You think; I want the exact locations. We're going to get your list from the house. And no mistakes and you had better be alone or you won't have a future and you won't be able to enjoy any of your opulence. Who drives the second car?"

"Okay, Okay. They're both mine and I let my friends use it if they need it." Munoz opened the door and went to a cabinet next to the sofa. "Here is the book where I kept my notes and list of delivery locations."

"Good, I'm taking it with me. Where is your telephone?"

"We don't have any telephones out here, just cell phones."

"Okay, where is it? I need it."

"Right here."

"You won't need it any more. Now I am going to take your car and drive back into town. I will leave it at your friend's the place, the chemical supplier who is sitting outside of your gate in his car with no pants on and his hands tied to the neck of his office girl. Toss me your car keys and open that gate. Oh! And here is your buddies broken distributor cap."

Jerry drove to town, dropped of the car and left for Montevideo immediately. He didn't have a clue where to find Ahmad al-Masri or if he even really was to be found in Montevideo. But C-4 shipped to Brazil seemed to be the best possibility for any movements on to the States. He took a taxi to Buenos Aires and caught the ferry to Colenia, Uruguay. Outside of the dock area was a place to rent a car for the long drive to Montevideo. It had grown late when Jerry arrived in Montevideo so checking into the Plaza Fuerte he took some time to rest and make some kind of plan to find this al-Masri person. He went to his room and took a hot relaxing shower. Jerry thought to himself how important it is to wash away the dirt and sweat of a day like today so one could get a good sleep. He was definitely hungry and went out into the street to find some good food. "Pardon senor", as he stopped a passerby, "Me puedes desir donde puedo encontrar un restaurante bueno?" Pointing towards the Mercado del Puerto the passerby told Jerry to go three hundred meters to a place called Las Margaritas. The suggestion was excellent. Jerry found fabulous margaritas and Carnitas Verde with the best rice cooked with tomatoes and peppers he had ever eaten. It was after ten when he started on his fourth margarita and as his waiter passed by his table he struck up a conversation with him. "Would you know if there is a Muslim Mosque in Montevideo?" The town was a thriving metropolis with modern high rises and a European influence yet still with a cultural beauty that was purely Uruguay. The French had been a major influence since they had become a part of the population over two hundred years ago. The waiter was French and had provided great service like the waiters in New York. Jerry thought about the similarity as he got the answer from his waiter in Spanish with a heavy French accent.

"Messier, I am aware of un Mosque east of here bout five kilometers on Calle Vidaurreta n 1063 La Teja."

"Thank you; I'll have one more margarita and the check please." As Jerry finished his drink he made plans for the next day, left a nice tip for the waiter and went out into the night air.

The next day Jerry went to the U S consulate and called in to Hank to hook him up with the foreign project task force at NSA for help to find an operative in the area that spoke Arabic. He needed to keep his identity secret and was sure that neither Munoz nor the chemical supplier had tried to contact al-Masri. Hank was available and started the wheels turning. Jerry took out Munoz's note book and read the list to Hank. "Hank, I have a list of cities where Munoz says he shipment contraband to his buyer al-Masri. I'm here in Montevideo to find this guy and track the C4 to see if the ultimate destination was the States. Here is the list. Fortaleza, Recife, Abaetetuba, Salinoplis, Belem, Acaran, Salo Luis, and Camocim. Let's run them through Carnivore to see if we get some hits. Let me know what you find."

Three hours later, a heavily bearded man entered the room at the consulate where Jerry was having some coffee and talking to a civilian consulate employee from Uruguay. She politely excused herself and the man introduced himself to Jerry as Sean Unger. He was his go between to make inquiries at the Mosque. Sean had work as an Arabic translator and agent in Pakistan for five years in the nineties. "Hi, I believe your name is Jerry Ness and I was told that you are on a hunt for an Arab speaking individual that may provide you with important information on terrorist activities here in Uruguay."

"Actually I am looking for an arms dealer whose operations may have deep implications for the States."

"Okay, tell me what you can about the person and as much as you can about your mission." Jerry looked Sean up and down and could have sworn he was talking to a Muslim if one could identify a Muslim directly from looks.

"I am on the trail of suppliers of C4 and armament and we have Intel that indicates that both could have entered the States in large quantities and is now in the hands of Muslim terrorist but we have no idea of who, where or even if the info is true."

"Interesting, do you have details, names, address or any solid facts to pursue?"

"Only a name of the person who was described as the middle man; the buyer and then the seller." Jerry went on, "Sean do you have a way to communicate with the Arab community to find a Ahmad al-Masri. He is the one we believe is the supplier to a terrorist operation in Brazil. From there the trail is cold and I need to find him now!"

"Give me till six o'clock and we will meet at where ever you are staying."

"I'm at the Plaza Fuerte in room number 311."

"I'll either call you at seven or come to your room."

"I'll be waiting for your call. Ask for 'jacked up' so I'll know it is you."

I was thinking about my friend Jack from the CIA when the phone rang in my room. "Hello, who Is calling?"

"It is Sean looking for 'jacked up' and I have positive information for him."

"It's Jerry, go ahead."

"Please meet me in front of your hotel and we'll take a short walk."

"Right now?"

"Yes, right now."

As I exited the hotel Sean walk over to me and motioned me to walk with him towards the Parque Central. "I found out your al-Masri character is living here and attends prayers at the Mosque on Calle Vidaurreta. Do you have any idea of what he looks like; do you? Any known features at all?"

"No!"

"Okay then we will have to trust my source for an ID when the men leave the Mosque. We will need to be careful and not approach him till he is alone. I will use his name and if he responds you can approach. We will then escort him to a location where you can do some initial questioning. If you feel you have your guy and interrogation is necessary then I have set up a car to pick us all up and a private house that we can use so as to not implicate our country."

At Eight thirty pm the prayers were over. "Look they are starting to leave. We will get a signal from my informant by him stopping to ask your man for a light for his cigarette. That should be your al-Masri" We waited while more than thirty or so men filed out of the door on to Calle Vidaurreta and only a few stopped to light up cigarettes but each lit their own. "In the dark, over there see the small flame and it's my man getting a light for his cigarette. There we need to follow that one turning down Avenida Vente." Sean and I walked rather quickly towards the street where the figure had turn down. He was about twenty meters in front of us but we were able to quietly move in on him at the corner. I laid back as Sean called out his name in Arabic. He paused and said something to Sean. It must have been correct because I saw Sean pull his gun and told him to be very quite. As I approached, Sean said that he had answered to his name and I could see fear begin to come over al-Marsi's face.

"Tell him all I want is some information and everything will be alright." Sean spoke to him in Arabic again.

"Ask him if he knows Fernando Munoz? And has he ever bought any of Mr. Munoz's products?"

After a short inter change of what sounded like two people mad at each other and coughing at the same time Sean said, "No he has no idea what you are talking about."

"Just a minute tell him this"; as I put my Glock to his neck, "I am ready to leave Uruguay tonight and if I kill him right now I could care less. Does he know Fernando Munoz?" With his eyes flashing back and forth between Sean and I he stumbled with his guttural sounding words and then I could see from Sean that he had said yes. "Let's go to where I can get some answers and tell him all I want is information from him and he won't get hurt."

Sean assured him that I was only wanting information as we walked about sixty meters East from the Mosque where Sean then motioned us into a small alcove that had a door leading to an open garden area in front of a broken down pueblo house. It looked like it was deserted. As we waited for the car to pull up to us I began my questions and Sean translated. "Where had you met Fernando?"

"In Argentina!"

"What did he supply you with and what did you do with it?"

"He was my supplier of explosives and guns which I delivered to my brothers and sold to rebels in Africa."

"Did you also work with an Abdul al-Rantisi? Was he part of your organization for supplying armament to terrorists? And as to your brothers, do you mean other Muslims?"

"Yes, we all worked together."

"Where did most of the explosives go and was it all C4?"

"I had it shipped to different addresses in BRAZ....." BANG – BANG – BANG- shots rang out from the roof of the house next to the garden and al-Masri was down on his knees. Sean was firing back but at what, there was no target, then from over head and behind more shots and Sean hollered I'm hit and then al-Masri fell forward motionless. Sean hollered to me to run into the alcove but I was not leaving him there. I emptied my gun at the direction of the last shots as I grab Sean and pulled him along to the alcove with me. He was hit in the shoulder about one inch from his neck but the bullet had gone clean through. "You're lucky," I said. "How do we get out of here?" I reloaded waiting for his answer; and heard foot steps running away from us. "What is going on here? The assassins seem to be running away."

"Listen, your right they were only after al-Masri to shut him up. Not us. We had better get to the car right now! There will be police here in minutes. I can walk just fine. Rip off my shirt sleeve and stuff it under my jacket to catch the blood. Let's go."

We were driven to a house about two kilometers from the encounter and left to spend an hour or so waiting for different transportation to get us back to the consulate where Sean could be taken care of but no one showed up. While we waited I asked Sean what he thought al-Marsi was about to say.

"I think he was saying that they had shipments going to places in Brazil. It's anybody's guess as to why Brazil." We were on our own so we left the house on foot and slowly jockeyed our way back to the consulate and Sean took us in the back entrance which was guarded all night by a Marine guard. After getting Sean patched up I contacted Washington to send my report to the communications officer on duty at TIU section for CI-4 but hated the fact that I was reporting that my mission took me to a dead end somewhere in Brazil. I knew that the C4 had gone to Brazil but I needed specific locations of deliveries and names and addresses or what ever Ahmed could have given me. I wasn't certain that the contraband had even gone to the States. But even the most remote possibility is frightening so I identified my report as high priority.

CHAPTER SIXTEEN

Jerry arrived back in Washington on the twentieth of September and the next day at NSA headquarters he was preparing to go over his mission in depth with the review staff which was SOP after a mission like the one he had been on when George called him into his office to notify him that he would do his debriefing with the CI oversight committee that afternoon.

The following day at work Jerry took some time to get orientated and learned that Hank had been given an assignment and had gone on his first mission to Hong Kong on the eighteenth to make contact with a person that had called the embassy in Hong Kong and said that he could shed more light on the killing of Jack Madden and what he had been after in Indonesia when he was disposed of by an al-Qaeda hit squad.

The information in the CIA's file indicated that the ambush on Jack had occurred about eight thirty just after Jack left a dinner with a long time associate from Interpol and was driving to some unknown location. A car with four Arab looking men drove up along side of him on a street in Jakarta and blasted more than one hundred bullets into his car. Jack had been running solo and no one knew what exactly he was pursuing except his prey and they had shut him down. Witnesses at the scene had said that there was no identifying the car or occupants. Now there is just a number on the wall at the CIA.

The Embassy in Hong Kong had said that a Mr. Gutung would call for the representative from the OHS on September twenty second and

Jerry's section chief at CI-4 had sent Hank Brayden the unit's most available agent with knowledge of the intelligence operations in the Hong Kong area to be that representative. The call came through and Hank was waiting. It was Mr. Gutung. "Hello, this is Hank Brayden with the OHS, you want to talk to me?"

"Yes, I know someone who talked to a person from your government over a year ago about terrorist activities that threatened your country and was paid $50,000 U S. I understand that the information was considered bogus and that your agent had been hunting him down until he was killed in Indonesia. I have information to verify that not only was the information correct but I know what happened to the container he was searching for at the port here in Hong Kong and I have further information on all of the shipments that went to the States. Meet me in the central area at the Royal Plaza hotel inside their restaurant Ye Shanghais.. Say at ten am tomorrow." Then click and the phone went dead.

Hank knew that with this being his first foreign assignment he needed to be careful and extremely alert as his actual experience with an adversary was no greater than his training at the 'Farm'. He felt comfortable in the Hong Kong environment having traveled to this area many times with the UN but mentally he was quite tense. As he settled in to his hotel room that evening the phone rang and it was Jerry. "Hello buddy, I understand that you are meeting with some informant who has information about Mr. Taug; the informant that sent Jack on his search to Indonesia and that caused him to loose his life! I don't know why the chief sent you but I tell you to be on guard. These people are not to be trusted at all and are dangerous with a capital D."

"I know Jerry, I read the whole file. No one was able to prove that any container with contraband ever existed. According to the file Mr. Taug took $50,000 and we got nothing which is why Jack kept going on his mission. I was told that Jack was one who would never give up until he had the truth and some felt that he needed to save face over the lost $50,000; well you know about that as well as anyone. In his last report from the field just before he was exterminated in Jakarta he stated that he had found the location where the shipments Mr. Taug referred to had originated. Then the staff in Jack's section at the CIA reviewed all of the reports and the data and concluded that Mr. Taug may have been correct and the fact that Jack was taken out is substantial prove that Jack was very close to uncovering real evidence and establishing the truth, but there were no leads on where to go or where to look state side. Everything that was left was just a dead end. Maybe this meeting will give us some new facts to start the investigation anew."

"Well we need solid information so good luck but again be careful."

"My mission is to just interview this person and report back to you guys at TUI. I'll be fine." "Hank, here is an added comment. I just returned from my mission to South America and I hit a dead end. Either the soundings we are getting are false and meant to mislead our intelligence or somehow the enemy has delivered C4 inside of our borders and we have no clue. The same thing happened to Jack and I on our mission to Hong Kong in January last year, a dead end. There was no contraband in the container. Just be careful and contact me if you need help. The whole team is here for you."

I was at the Royal Plaza Hotel by ten as Gutung had requested and entered the Ye Shanghais restaurant wondering how I would know him. He had given me no way to identify him since he hung up too soon. Immediately I understood why he did not need to tell me how to find him since the restaurant was empty except for some employees setting up for lunch. The restaurant was officially not open so as I looked around an Indian looking person stood up from a booth to my left behind a large fern and motioned to me to come over. "Are you Hank? I am the one you want to talk to. We can go to the rear patio and have some tea. It is now open and private."

I agreed as I looked around the restaurant and the patio, then I started the conversation, "What do you know about our agent who was here last year and how would you know anything? And if it is money you want I came unauthorized to pay for any information."

"Just like Americans, no ice breaking but instead right up the gullet. Take a moment and enjoy the tea. The blend is excellent and I am not here for money."

Taking a small sip I asked, "Well then why!"

"First you must be told that I am Mr. Taug the person your two agents met on the floating restaurant that day in January and everything I told them was correct. I was watching a small boat coming towards us while I was talking to them and I could feel that I had been detected so I had to be quick. I don't know how the associates of al-Qaeda found me out but they are the ones that blew up my San-Pan after it left the restaurant. I dropped down from the deck and grabbed on to a beam under the deck just as the driver pulled away and then I grab a piling and stayed there for a few minutes. I saw everything as your people circled the site looking for me. Then they headed off towards the freighter carrying the containers I had showed them."

"I still do not know why I am here. I read the file on the events you just discussed and nothing is new except you are alive and have a different name."

"Would you care for some bread with your tea?"

"No, go on."

"I changed my name and appearance to stay alive. After all I had been a freelance arms dealer and all of sudden I was a target for any loose gun in Hong Kong. I took up a new profession so now I deliver high grade Heroin to the highest bidder. There is an ever hungry market and it is extremely lucrative; besides the chance for eradication is very low."

"So what do you have for me?"

"You need to listen to me very carefully. I want to protect my market so I don't want anything to happen to your country. I made eight hundred thousand dollars from my dealings with west coast clients and this year is going to be better. The guns and ammunition I sold to the Arabs from Indonesia along with the last two thousand kilos of C-4 went to the states, I am absolutely sure even though your people did not find the shipment."

"How do you know that with such confidence?"

"That is easy, this was their last shipment and the terrorist agents in Hong Kong must have learned that I was not dead and was in Hong Kong. They were pursuing me and they saw me talking to your agents. That is why they tried again to kill me so I am certain that as a result they changed the labeling on the container with the contraband. There were at least four containers of ATV's, Motorcycles, parts and other items on that freighter and the one I identified was the one that I helped load and that one had what your people wanted. So all they had to do was paint a different one to match and changing the identifying marking became very simple."

"The report in our file says that your San Pan was blown up, how did you survive?" "I am extremely cautious and they had tried to kill me once so I took extra precaution and as I said I hide in the pilings under the restaurant and waited a long time before I left. I slipped in to the restaurant and then through a door that lead to a short stair to the super structure under the building."

"What evidence do you have that that happened and that there was all of the other shipments; I read in the file you claimed there had been many shipments to the States."

"No evidence at all, but look at me, why would I be here telling you this and at the same time taking a risk that my new identity may be exposed."

With total doubt I said, "I DO NOT KNOW!"

"Okay, here is why. Again, listen to me, I supplied or was the middle man for many arms packages to both militant and terrorist groups for over twenty years. I supplied thousands of kilos of C4 and guns to those that I believe were al-Qaeda terrorist who I think were part of a group called Al Gama'at al Islamiyya who I was told was based in Los Angeles. They had been shipping this stuff into the States in containers a little at a time for the past eight to ten years and stopped in January of 2001. Everyone knew that there was no security check on overseas containers and who knows what else your enemies have sent into your country. As I told your people when we met at the floating restaurant, the container I pointed out held the shipment that was my last sale to them and then they tried to dispose of me. Believe me this is true! After the world saw 9-11 I would guess anything is possible and I really do not want to see any major disruption in my drug market. Hard core and selfish, but that is the bottom line. Your agent in Indonesia was able to get to a Pakistani who had been in on the shipments that started sometime around 1992. He got him to tell him how to find one of the leaders in Jakarta with the radical Hamas group, Islamiyya and their location. This was coerced information at the time but the information he had uncovered must have been real. That is all I know."

"WOW! What a spin on reasons and causes. I believe you are serious up to a point, of course you are right, our ports have really been porous for all of these past years. Anything is possible. I will have our people look into this yarn and see what shakes out. I am sure we will do our due diligence but discovery of facts is imperative to buy this story a second time. What is it you want from me or more accurately my government?"

Gutung or Taug which ever he was answered immediately, "Nothing, absolutely nothing. Just follow the containers. Okay then, the tea is on me and my cousin who is the waiter over there, you see, the one with the gun in his lap just in case. Have a safe trip back to the states. And remember; protect my market."

My mission lasted two days and I was back in DC on the twenty-sixth of September. I went straight home to be with my Tiama not only to give her relief but to quietly meditate on this crazy story and how I was going to present my report to George at NSA or much worst a debriefing team. He trusted me to get all of the facts I could on Jack's discoveries from this informant and the truth on the original operation. Jack had been pursuing what was unsubstantiated information and this guy loves the U S drug market. That's my report. My, oh my, my first mission! An eye witness and a declared arms dealer who now says that he is a drug dealer claims that potential terrorist have shipped tons of C4 and guns into the United States through our west coast ports.

It was the first week in October before Jerry and I saw each other when we both entered the parking garage at the same time at TIU's end of our building. After I parked my car there was Jerry. "Hey Hank" I heard his trumpeted voice over the sound of the other arriving cars and the giant blowers used to change the air in the underground garage.
  "Wait up and I'll buy you a coffee." I wanted to exchange stories with him but I've been so busy trying to get some kind of Intel out of the guys at the agency that I couldn't get by his office. "Did you finish your debriefing and how did it go?"
  He caught the door to the elevator as he continued, "Actually wait till I get you that coffee. My whole mission was really exciting, you know guns, dead people, and blood; that kind of thing, but no brass ring."

In the cafeteria I grabbed a black coffee and two donuts and Jerry asked for some hot chocolate. Unusual! We sat on a couple of easy chairs in the reading area. "Okay Hank what happened to my friend Jack that I don't already know and the fifty thousand dollars; or better yet the shipping container?"
  I was finishing my first donut as I told him the same thing as I had told the review group, "In a nut shell I believe that shipments of armament and explosives have entered the states through our ports which were wide open before OHS and it looks like they still appear to be wide open for smuggling. This guy Gutung who is really Taug, the

169

guy you and Jack talked to, is now working the drug trade business and claims that his information was accurate and he kept the money and changed his identity. He never did get into the San Pan but slipped into the restaurant and through a door that lead to the super structure under the building. He wants us to believe him because the States is his biggest drug market."

"No! You are serious!"

"That's the reaction I got from everyone else when I went through debriefing. But my feelings tell me that it is all true. Jerry I want you to tell me how to get my gut feelings communicated to the right sections here at NSA so that we can get OHS to begin investigations into the terrorists shipping in materials to attack our country."

"What do you mean, just like that without some kind of evidence? To begin a massive inspection of all of the incoming containers at all of our ports on what we have and your gut feelings, the system needs hard evidence." He wrinkled his face as he said, "Listen to this, I feel like you do. As you know I went from Buenos Ares, Argentina to a small port town called Avellaneda where the dealer I located sent me to Montevideo, Uruguay. That's where you lost me when George pulled you off to get ready for your mission. Well, I found the Arabic buyer Ahmad al Masri that supposedly was the go between of Fernando in Avellaneda and the contact in Brazil. One of our agents stationed at that location spoke Arabic and was able to pin point his whereabouts so we could contact him and I could question him to get some needed information to help me move on with my investigation. Our approach was in the evening after prayer at the mosque and it was perfect, he was totally surprised. We escorted him down a rather narrow street and into a doorway where Sean began interrogating him in Arabic and then within just a couple of minutes from overhead on a roof top someone shot him. I fired back but at nothing. From a different direction we were fired on again and Ahmad was dead and Sean took a bullet to the shoulder. We had to leave him there and hightail it where a car was supposed to be waiting for us to take us to a safe house, but we became temporarily stranded. After a while, as we weaved through some narrow side streets to dodge any police we were able to get back to the consulate and Sean got medical help. I waited till morning to get out of town, but here is the irony. I was close to what I thought was the final destination on both armament and explosives and just that quick I had no leads on contraband or any certainty that anything had gone pass the borders of Brazil and entered the States. BUT, and I say but, like you my gut feelings tell me that there is something there. And like you I want further investigation. We need to press George to see what is happening with the reviewing of our mission reports at OHS and the intelligence you and I brought home."

By November George had not given Jerry or me any response to our request to raise the level on our intelligence reports pass IDR (Internal Data Review) to PFI (Priority Field Investigation) or at least WUAI (Warranted Unit Analysis & Investigation). Most all of the resources and energies were being concentrated on the war in Iraq and Intel from Pakistan and Afghanistan. Things were beginning to unravel in Iraq even though our military had swept through to Baghdad and defeated the Iraqis in less than 3 months we were under attack from small but mobile groups of Saddum loyalist. They were continually inflicting damage and causalities on a daily basis. Most of the agencies daily efforts in the directives that were coming from the highest level, were centered on accumulating data from the satellites, flyovers and undercover agents on the ground to find the terrorist operating in hot zones and get that Intel to the field for offensive action. Still we were suffering too many casualties and rouge groups of terrorist seemed to be unstoppable as they appeared, did damage and then faded into the various neighborhoods unnoticed like a pebble in the gutter.

Our Generals kept telling the defense department that we were suffering from a growing insurgency maybe even an uprising of the Iraqis due to our occupation of their country and they felt they needed more troops to handle the hit and run tactics being used through out most of the cities. Our section was not privy to the DOD's highly classified reporting to the President or the Defense secretary however those of us that intercepted Intel and analyzed it for DOD all knew that the Generals were on course but that we went in to Iraq misguided with no long term plan and unprepared for an insurgency that would operate from one neighborhood to another protected by the Iraqi people.

Jerry called me to meet him outside of George's office to see what was happening to our request. We both entered and Jerry took the lead. "Excuse us George but do you have a minute that Hank and I could talk to you?"

"Sure, I'm open till 3:00 o'clock. What is on your minds besides all of the bad news we are getting from Iraq, Afghanistan, Tom Rodgges,

Tenant at the CIA and bin Laden? What more can we do to help stop the increased insurgency in Iraq?" He paused, "Well, at least we are getting a hold on the situation at home but the machinery inside of OHS is still not functioning well and it may take a few years yet."

Jerry had a response as usual, "YEARS! Is that what Tom Rodgges is confidently telling the President and the oversight committee? We would all love to get our two cents in on that one. After all, this humongous government can not even get out of its own way and we can thank the stupid representatives we have had over the past 40 years for building an uncontrollable and unchangeable globule of humanity that operates like millions of molecules in a single cell; a lot of continuous action and no direction! And meanwhile there is festering a germ that is getting ready to destroy the dumb molecule forever, May God Help us."

"You nailed it! They have built a giant blob of hundreds of thousands of human bodies that are filling hundreds of government buildings and accomplishing little or nothing. Sorry, just some of my personal rhetoric. Again what can I help you guys with or to be more exact, what do you need?"

I decided it was my turn, "Sir both Jerry and I had missions that gave us Intel that we thought; well I will let Jerry speak for himself but I for one believe the data in my report needs further follow up and we have not heard a peep from anyone about the review. I haven't, have you Jerry?"

"No, and George I know that my mission was a dead end but send me to Brazil and let me dig into what ever leads we can get from Carnivore! There has to be something we haven't been told about contraband moving in and out of Brazil. After all there is a big flow of military goods coming out of Brazil" I chimed in again, "Sir; I truly believe that Gutung or Taug was not inventing his story. He has no righteous reason to break his cover to us unless he means what he told me. And based on that, we could have allowed shipment after shipment of terrorist weapons into our country over the past ten years or so through our open ports not only on the West Coast but on the East Coast. We just were never smart enough in the those great whiskey and cigar smoking clutches in the congressional meeting rooms conducted by our almighty representatives nor in those high powered Washington Think Tanks operated by the supposed intellectual elite to imagine that we really had enemies and that they may have brains enough to destroy us. God forbid another disaster will occur inside of our borders but listen, Jerry's leads and information and mine are identical in indicating we probably have clandestine operatives in our country who may have massive amounts of weapons. We need statesmen that will stand up against adversity and are interested in the good of our country and especially the welfare of our citizens; not these pompous beaurocrats who think they are invincible so they foolishly believe no harm could ever come to the USA."

"Okay, enough of the soap boxing. We can all agree that we are and have been openly venerable. But you called it when you said that the monster was in control and we can't move it. I am waiting for upper level response and until we get that we are in the 'GOGLG' state." Jerry was curious when he said, "What is that, it's a new one to me?"

George clarified the anonym, "You know, 'Good Ole Government Limbo Game'. Jerry, you and Hank know that the agencies have had many soundings about terrorists here in the States and hundreds of our agents are out there verifying leads and gathering information for us here at the CI units which you know in turn precipitated reports for the command section at OHS to issue either a CFI or NSR directive. A PFI is less restrictive but we follow protocol and that is what I have been doing. Nothing right now has been elevated to a Critical Field Investigation or a National Security Response so I am asking for a PFI on your Intel Hank. Jerry I can't guarantee anything on more man power for the Argentina/Brazil investigation. We are going straight into the holidays and I'm not sure I'll have anything before the end of the year."

We sucked it all in and Jerry and I left George's office with governmental protocol and foolish politics stuck in our bellies. I went to my office to call Tiama and Jerry said goodnight as he headed towards the elevator to go to the garage.

"Hello Brayden residence, if you are calling about my husband, he is not here right now but I love him very much and expect him home very soon."

"Hey sweetheart why did you answer the phone lik……. Oh I get it I forgot you saw my cell phone number on the display. I love you too and yes, I am heading home. See ya shortly. Kisses."

I dialed Dad at his office to see about the holidays. George made it clear that things would be status quo till the New Year. "Hi Dad, just heading home for the week end and I was wondering if the girls had made any holiday plans yet?"

"Son I don't know but I'll ask Caroline to call Tiama tomorrow, OK? How's every thing?"

"Kind of slow but alright, we can talk tomorrow, see you then, Goodnight."

Tiama and I spent the Thanksgiving holidays with my family in Connecticut eating lobster instead of turkey and for Christmas the two of us took off a week from work and went to Jamaica to breath some salt air and enjoy some relaxing beaches where we could just run our toes through the white sand leaving all of the stress for the waves to wash away. We swan, sunbathed, danced, slept, read, and walked on the beach at night. Made love by the moonlight and planned our future family. Tiama said that she wanted to invite her mother from the Philippines to stay through the spring and let her enjoy some time with her only daughter and of course her new son-in-law. Sounded fine to me and I agreed that we should have her come on the first of March.

March arrived and so did Tiama's mom, Maryta. It brought more activity for both me at my work and for Tiama around the house with her mom trying to help us plan for our own house by searching the newspaper and the Homes for Sale magazines she got at the supermarket.

Jerry had been given an assignment to review the DOD's additional Intel given to the TIU section on terrorist buying military supplies from Brazil armament manufactures. As usual my job was to assimilate all of the data into a report that would substantiate his request for a CFI so he could go back to South America. He had been waiting for the opportunity to go back to what he called his 'original mission' so he decided to push this assignment in a personal way. The Intel did not actually specify anyone as terrorist operatives and no photos of persons of interest were listed in the report. All Jerry had to go on would be personal briefings from agents working for Spain in that region. Spain was one of the major countries aiding us in Iraq by providing troops as were England, Norway, Denmark, Netherlands, New Zealand, Australia and others. Being a part of Interpol they had excellent contacts and were as interested as most of the world was to find and disable terrorist. George had finally been able to get OHS to issue a PFI authorization for the FBI to start their probe into the possibility that terrorist were using the free access to shipping ports for smuggling in military items from guns and explosives to WMD which was the very volatile subject that precipitated the Iraqi war. Since I had been assigned point on Jerry's previous mission and now I was to run technical for Jerry where ever he would be on this mission. That desk assignment suited Tiama just fine. Although I could not tell her what I was doing, just my staying in town while some of our friends had been sent on special operations was okay with her.

It was a rather cool Thursday morning in March and Tiama had the small TV in the kitchen on when I sat down to a cup of my favorite Costa Rican coffee and English muffins before leaving for work. Fox news channel was on which was our favorite and I was on the second and my last cup of coffee when the headlines of the morning came up showing train cars damaged and scattered around the tracks at a train station as the news anchor began his report. "Suicide bombers have struck the commuter trains at a station in Madrid, Spain during the morning rush hour and there maybe as many as 190 dead and more than 1,200 people injured. And this comes only three days before the presidential elections. It is apparent that this attack on Spain is meant to intimidate the people of Spain and influence the coming elections since bin Laden has told Spain to remove their troops from Iraq. I am told that in Madrid and other areas through out Spain the people are traumatized and no wonder, this is a massive attack on their country."

I sat stunned as I looked at Tiama. "Oh my lord, this is getting more unbelievable and according to what we have heard from al-Zarqawi the worst is yet to come. In-bread into these terrorist is the tenant that 'Islam grows on the blood of martyrs'. That Martyrdom is one of the highest achievements a Muslim can attain!"

Tiama was still looking at the TV as Hank went on. "We are not even telling our citizens of the emanate danger that exits here in side of our country much less taking action to rout out potential terrorist here. You know Honey, since I moved from the UN to OHS I have seen the massive amount of information on the activity worldwide by all of the many terrorist groups and we are operating like an ostrich; full body exposed and our head in a hole hidden from the facts. This idiotic politically correct idea that we can not profile people to ferret out those that are anxiously waiting to destroy us comes from escapees of the asylum or more accurately left wing liberals bent on the complete restructuring of the world politics and religions."

"Well my love what can we do? Move to the Philippines or to the mountains?"

"What?"

Tiama cracked a smile, "Sorry I was jesting a little bit but where is this all going?"

"I really do not know; I really don't. I do know this, let's you and I catch a movie tonight." And with that I planted a nice one on her tulips and was out the door. I knew I had left her with unanswered questions and as I drove to work I pondered the fact that there are unanswered questions right up from our CI units to the bureau chief at the CIA to the head of NSA to the secretary of OHS to Defense Secretary Rummey to Secretary Rice to the President. Who is going to really stop them or more importantly what is going to stop them?

CHAPTER SEVENTEEN

A reign of terror prevailed in Iraq over the next few weeks and not only were the road side bombs (IED's) planted by the insurgents taking multiple lives of both our troops and the Iraqis but this al-Zarqawi person had unleashed a barrage of both suicide bombing attacks on Iraqi leaders and groups of Iraqi police trainees and his followers were killing and kidnapping workers employed by foreign contractors.

Time passed quickly from the events in Spain to the deterioration of the war in Iraq. It was now the second week-end in April. The weatherman had announced an approaching storm with heavy rains and wind gusts up to thirty miles per hour so knowing that, Tiama and I planned to stay at home for the weekend. I took the report # 03-911 produced by the '9-11 Commission' home to read since the weather was going to be so nasty. Actually not the whole 600 plus page report but the synopsis. Sitting down in my easy chair with a tall scotch I was very curious to see how close to the facts the report was and so I began breezing past the section on who, how and where and I went straight to analysis and conclusions; 'Many foreigners of all extractions have entered the United States and we find that many of them who are from the Middle East and Pacific Rim own cash type businesses such as liquor stores, gasoline stations, convenience stores, car repair centers, carwashes, check cashing centers, used car lots, barber and beauty shops, real estate sales offices, mortgage offices, etc. For the most part the businesses are legitimate operations and we leave the problems on taxes to the Treasury Department but we believe that there are many owned by individuals who are members of sleeper cells and who are financing the cell operations and aiding the members.

Others are operating phony charities for the purpose of funding terrorist activities in other countries. The FBI with information from the National Counter Terrorist Center is trying to investigate these organizations and the individuals involved at this current time but have been stopped due to laws of privacy and the sheer numbers of potential suspects. Records from the IRS, State Sales Tax departments, and multiple upon multiple county business licensing departments are needed to do meticulous investigations but some of the records are only available under subpoena 'With Cause'.

Homeland security knows that many, many cells exist but they can not identify them with any real accuracy. They are too fluid and too deep. Most have been organized for a decade or more but each organization is quite loose. The members are extremely secret and yet quite informal. The irony is that so many came from various Muslim nations and they were allowed entrance with 'political asylum visa's' even though they actually present a threat to the security of the United states.

It was no surprise to read that the commission found that many illegals who maybe potential terrorists have come in from Canada where people like David Haryis a Canadian Intelligence Official reported that the Canadian Immigration Department has continually allowed members of Hamas, Hezabola, and Habanist to enter their country with no restrictions and through any of their many points of entry; airports, seaports, and private docks. No documentation is ever required because their government's position is that everyone has their right to privacy. 'YOU CAN NOT PROFILE BECAUSE THAT IS DISCRIMINATION'.

The authorities at the OHS have reported to the commission that; 'To protect our ports, our trains, our water supply, and most importantly our nuclear facilities will be a monumental task and take tens if not hundreds of billion of dollars and more than ten years. We are basically unprotected at this moment in time. And at the same time those that need to be under the microscope have taken jobs in industry and commerce besides owning their own businesses. They are also employed in government, at public utilities, at power stations, railroads, trucking companies, airports, communications facilities, and we believe at many other critical positions and they have blended in to the fabric of our nation with none showing their true agenda; they are like a ticking time bomb but the ticking is completely muffled. Of course a few of the extreme radicals have taken action under the direction of bin Ladin but the majority of the radical extremists are invisible and are just waiting. Those that are devoted Islamic radicals are smart and patient just waiting to carry out their ambitions and their goals as instructed by Mohammed's prophetic writings demanding to eliminate all infidels.

Countries like Syria who openly supports and promotes terrorism has added to the danger that exist in our country today and others like Iran and their president Mahmood Ahmadi-Najad are quite open about their ideology and their mission to exterminate all infidels everywhere and without a doubt all Jews.

The wrap on the report stated that the commission believed unequivocally that, 'Many Muslims in the States are not radicals or affiliated with al-Qaeda or Hezbollah or Hamas operatives or even potential terrorist and instead they are liberal in their thinking due to many years of living here in the American culture with their families and enjoying the freedom and the luxury of the Western economy.'

I had no more than finished reading the 9-11 synopsis report than the next morning as Tiama and I read the Sunday edition of the Washington post, Dad called and asked if we had the TV on.
"Why Dad, what's happening?"
"Just turn on UBC and look at the report out of Iraq showing one of our countries citizens who was working around Bagdad with a civilian contractor and was kidnapped two weeks ago. We have the original news clip from al-Jazeera. Do not let Tiama see this report! Do it now."
"Okay", and I hung up and told Tiama I was going upstairs to look for some papers for Dad. Upstairs I hurriedly turned on the TV with low volume and clicked over to UBC. Immediately I saw the picture of the kidnapped man down on his knees with four masked gun totting individuals standing along side him. They spoke some kind of gibberish and then the fifth man started to cut the throat and then the head off of the kidnapped American. It was grisly, it was ghastly, it was gruesome, and it was barbaric!
"Honey, what are you doing up there?"
"I'll tell you when I come back down stairs." Tiama was at the bottom of the stairs as I came down with some papers in my hand I had taken from my briefcase so I embraced her and walked her to the kitchen. Hon, "I took a few minutes to turn on the TV while I was getting those papers just so I could see a report Dad said was on UBC about the ter-

rorist kidnapping in Iraq. These kidnappings are more frequent now and meant to undermine our resolve to complete the military operation in Iraq just like the resolve of Spain was destroyed with the train bombings in Spain. The terrorist insurgency does not understand the fortitude of the American people and our power to win when we have set our determination to rid the world of these barbaric terrorist. Well honey they did just what they had threaten to do, they decapitated the head of Nick Berg yesterday."

Tiama looked at me through eyes that were both shocked and full of tears. Yet at the same time her face took on an expression of holiness. "Hank I want to go to church today if it is not too late! I have been thinking about the need for some type of spiritually in our lives and the more I read about happenings in the world and what you talk about from time to time the more I feel we are lost in a world that is coming unglued. That's the woman in me coming out and my perception of the decline of the morals around the world and more importantly in our country."

"Okay, but I don't know where. Our family never was religious so I couldn't even think where we could go."

"Don't worry, one of the girls at the Pilipino consulate told me about a church called Calvary Chapel on West 32nd Street NE and we can take a cab there, it's not that far. I guess they primarily believe in Jesus Christ which goes with my Catholic up bringing as I was growing up. Is that okay?"

"Sure, I'll change my shirt and you call a cab."

It was May and the DC area had shown a fantastic display of the beauty of the Eastern States during spring. As Spring flowed into Summer, Tiama and I spent the weekends outdoors walking by the Potomac enjoying the Cherry blossoms, or picnicking in the parks and now of course going to church. I felt church to be very soothing so I imagined that my spirit was getting refreshed for the next work week and I liked that. I felt it really important to clean out the past week's garbage and be empowered for the stress of the coming week.

Being in the information center for all of the CI units just seemed to fill me with too much stress and I had no way to personally act on the Intel. For some reason I felt some kind of anxiety and I could not pin point the cause. Jerry had returned from his mission to Brazil and had not yet given us his final report. As his liaison person in operations I had followed his progress and knew there had to have been movement of armament into some point of entry in Florida but he had not been able to get any lead as to where. I was going to suggest that we look at the shipping docks when we reviewed the report.

When Jerry arrived at his office on Monday of the week after his return he asked me to join him in George's office and bring the Intel we had from our department so he could present his report and recommend a plan for investigation in Florida. I arrived first, "Good morning George, I brought all of the printouts on Jerry's trip and he said..........", Just then Jerry came in. "Hi George, I asked Hank to bring in all of the data gathered from the satellite surveillance and from our people we had watching all of the associates of al-Masri. We were guided to two associates of al-Masri in Brazil who headed up extremist Islamic cells. As my reports show I was able to corner one of the two, Amer el-Matti and induce him in to telling me what he knew about C-4 sold to al-Masri by Munoz and his participation in the movement of the purchases. It took four days of confinement in a safe house in Rio to finally get answers and names of other conspirators associated with al-Masri and a last known location for them. I fed that information to Hank here at CI who gave it to the TIU section and we put two of our people on the ones Hank found in the Sudan. It appears that they were all working with Abdul Aziz-Rantisi one of the Hamas leaders in Palestine where C4 is the explosive of choice for the suicide bombers and we have surveillance confirming close association with lieutenants in bin Ladin's group. Off the record, it cost Amer four fingers from his left hand but he confirmed that they had delivered more that half of the C-4 bought from Munoz to a ship company who then sent it to the U.S. by boat but he had no more details than that. He said that as far as he knew al-Masri was in charge of the smuggling into the States so if we can find his Brazilian accomplices who he thought were now in Sudan he said we could learn more about al-Masri's operation and you know I really believed him; I call that four finger truth."

"Your right, it is off the record and forgotten, right Hank"."

"Yes sir."

Jerry looking into George's face and with a very forceful voice asked, "Can we get a CFR on this situation immediately George?"

"I'll call and see if I can get a meeting with Tom Rodgges to review this right away. Can we add anything else to the request? Like Intel from the agents in The Sudan." Hank handed the file to George, "Its all here George."

"Okay, good work lets see what we can do."

As Jerry left George's office he read a memo given to him by George issued by OHS undersecretary John Poles notifying the head's of the Critical Intelligence Review departments at the FBI, CIA, DOD and the chiefs from sections CI-1 to CI-6 at NSA of a joint classified meeting, 'Integrated Operations' scheduled for Monday June 26th at JOCC (Joint Operations Command Center). The memo read 'A joint meeting is set for June Twenty-sixth with an Agenda consisting of three items. Number one; What is the progress of the information sharing protocols for all of the government agencies under the supervision of OHS and various authorized enforcement agencies. Number two; What is the strength and scheme of major international terrorist groups. And last: What is the progress of our efforts for penetration by our undercover agents into known terrorist groups operating within the borders of the U S and Canada'. Jerry somehow convinced George that due to my UN background and current security clearance I should be invited to attend stating that I still had a wealth of knowledge on international terrorist groups.

John Poles opened the meeting -

"Ladies and Gentlemen, I want to start off this joint meeting with two short statements; One from one of our Washington Think Tanks, 'Kislenger/Bresheimer and the other one is the most current announcement from bin Laden. First statements from the Think Tank, "As we look at and analyze the terrorist plague that has infected so many of the countries around the globe one must look deep inside what is motivating the different factions that propagate this infection. Truly the plague is really a war. A war that is against the very basic foundation of society as it now exists; a foundation that provides for people to live side by side and yet to have different philosophies, doctrine, and opinions without the interference into each others lives. They are waging a war and their battle is a battle of Ideologies. The politicians say that the terrorist are not fighting because of religion, only that they are thugs and henchmen that are nothing more than criminals. This includes the news media, the pundits, the political corrects, and the liberals who are completely out of touch with reality, oh what fools they are. Criminals the terrorist they may be because of their atrocities, but they themselves say it is 'All about religion, the fight of their Good against our Evil'. And now the second statement from bin Laden just a few days ago; "Al-Qaeda is moving and growing and the Muslim invasion is worldwide, Spain, Germany, Indonesia, England, Russia, and soon to other nations. You can not stop us. I am alive and well and our movement is alive like an octopus. The fighting has just begun, we will destroy you. Get out of our lands and take you evil ways with you. Turn to Islam."

"Let's all stand and say the Pledge Allegiance to our flag and country before we continue." The JOCC was a typical government meeting room with a long table in front and microphones for the department heads and two groups of chairs right and left for the attendees. Of course behind the front table were the American flag on the left and the DOJ and DOD flag on the right. With a slight choking in his throat John continued, "Despite the threats from the enemy in specific terrorist strongholds in some fifteen different Muslim countries we have not extracted any definitive soundings supporting future attacks on our homeland. It is the consensus that our agencies are all working together and sharing information in a most timely manner. We have been on multiple missions from Pakistan, to Indonesian to the Sudan, to Syria to Brazil to Hong Kong and other places and have no evidence yet that al-Qaeda, Hamas, Hezbollah or any other group is planning another attack on our country. On the one hand we have no evidence, only our unsupported suspicions that there are plans for more attacks on our country and on the other hand we have the continued threats from bin Laden himself and other Islamic clerics. Missions are on going to infiltrate the enemy's camps or break down any one of their captured leaders. All reporting has been going through the assigned protocol at the NSA. So far so good."

Undersecretary John Poles of OHS continued, "Well now, as we digest those two statements it is imperative that we at OHS understand the enemy even if many politicians do not. All of us are entrusted in making our country secure for our families, our brothers and sisters, our fellow citizens, our friends, and yes even the politicians and the media that just does not get it. We have made great progress on the information sharing of intelligence generated by DOD's intelligence section DIA, the CIA, the FBI and NCTC. All of our accumulated information is being routed to NSA and then combined with law enforcement information from all over the nation to be scrubbed and assimilated for accuracy and compliance before being transmitted on a shared basis to all intelligence departments within OHS. We have been able to reduce the time table for this shared information from our previously unacceptable time of four weeks down to three days. Of course this is on the Intel we have listed as HC (highly critical) and the balance of information which is considered lower lever Intel is reported to an area in CI-1 where it is analyzed within four days to one week based on considered importance. This has been a giant step in efficiency of information management that could only have been achieved with the new OHS protocols."

One of the CIA chiefs, Betty Albright, an authority on international terrorism took the floor next and read off pages of data and statistics engulfing the over 2,000 terrorist attacks during this current year alone but she added that none had been directed towards the United States and that most were rather incidental while acknowledging that the attack in Spain in March was not one that was incidental but it had a specific purpose and of course it was quite unfortunate. She continued saying that the agency had complied completely with information protocols and their new information sharing section was one hundred percent operational. The international terrorist situation shows that the Taliban is coming back in Afghanistan possibly stronger that before and the Insurgents in Iraq are growing in numbers and stronger every moment. They are being supplied and inspired by Syria, the Mujahideen in Saudi Arabia and actively on a daily basis by Iran.

I thought to myself nothing new here.

FBI assistant to the head of Internal Intelligence in the terrorist activity section, Robert Dire opened his report keynoting the success the agency was having identifying with the help of Carnivore the many individuals that had been either detained or arrested as persons suspected of terrorist activities. He further reported on how Carnivore even with the tremendous amount of information being accumulated and processed had sorted out and identified all detainees who were under suspicion of terrorist activities i.e. 'the bad guys' from others who were cleared and just processed and released. This allowed the TIU at NSA to work on further data matching to provide a complete dossier on each of the suspects who were charged with terrorist activities and incarcerated Those that were tagged as potential terrorist were fingerprinted, captured in the electronic image generator and their information passed on to both the CIA and NSA for further dissemination to other law enforcement agencies. They were released and put under continuing scrutiny and added to Carnivore's WOA 'web of associates' data base where investigations into their past, their associates and their living habits was appended to their file. The WOA data base continues building it's own list of persons of interest as each suspect's communication is monitored and added to their files along with information gathered from intermittent surveillance. And then the same process is automatically begun by Carnivore on each of their associates and then the same process on each that individual's associates then on all of their associates and so on. We will be building an invaluable catalog of potential suspects.

There had been no plots uncovered involving future terrorist attacks on our nation that we have not discovered and thwarted. We have consistently received outside information from SIGINT, IMINT, and HUMINT. HUMINT that comes from many different sources, some from the public, some from foreign governments, and even from internal operations. This information comes in as rumor based and receives no classification until it is run through the computers at Fort Meade looking for any shred of accuracy. If the information meets the criteria for continued investigation then it is classified as either live Intel where it is systematically labeled and coded so a report can go on to one of the CI units at NSA or it enters the miscellaneous 'trash bin' where it is filed by its primary subject matter. Thank God for the capacity of the huge storage facility at Fort Meade. The Carnivore system is how we uncovered the threat on the LA International Airport and the Financial Buildings in Los Angeles and so on. Rumors from HUMINT that are proven to be just rumors are discovered almost immediately and removed from the data investigation systems and stored as I said.

Betty from the CIA presented a question to Robert before he left the microphone. "Robert, just for clarification and to put it in the record, can you tell us how many suspected terrorist in the States are now in our jails or in our data bases with a full dossier?"

"I do not have exact numbers but as to those in jail at this time it is under 200 and I have been informed that NSA now has over 1300 active suspects that we are continuing to keep under surveillance."

The CIA person pressed the point, "We have passed on to NSA, Intel that comes from our field operatives that there maybe as many as five hundred Muslim cells in the States and that al-Qaeda claims as many as nine thousand Muslims living in our country that are true to bin Laden."

Robert was quick to answer, "As I said we have over one thousand three hundred active suspects that have been identified and are under continual surveillance, but we know there are many more that are buried in the populace. That is why Carnivore and the other operations of the Treasury Department are so important and I might add they are providing a great amount of Intel for our CI units at NSA. We are fully aware that there is a big Islamic network here in our country located mostly in our population centers such as Boston, New York, Detroit, Cleveland, Chicago, Dallas, Denver, Seattle, San Francisco, Los Angeles, San Diego where we are continually monitoring their activity. This network is made up mainly of al-Qaeda, Hamas, Islamic Jihad, Hezbollah, and the Muslim Brotherhood to name the larger ones. You can refer to the map inserted in the agenda papers. That is why operation 'Black World' is so important to our internal information gathering. Using Carnivore in the 'Black World' operation and combining it with 'SWIFT' in Belgium and 'FINCEN' inside the Treasury Department we are gaining on our enemies and infiltrating their cells."

Betty continued, "We at the CIA have been following the investigations being supervised by the CI units at NSA and we get the reports that they have yet unsubstantiated Intel that both guns and explosives have been transported into the States. Can you tell us what the FBI has done with this HUMINT? And whether this is some of the 'trash bin' information you spoke of? The people at NSA have authorized a number of missions to investigate what seem to be rumors based on various reports we have seen."

I rose to my feet and asked for the floor quite surprised with the languid manner and direction this meeting was going. "My name is Hank Brayden of CI-4 at NSA and I am here by special invitation of the head of our section George Meeker and accompanied by Jerry Ness whom I believe many of you know. I believe that Jerry's reliability and dedication to his work speaks for itself when it comes to looking into possible terrorism in our country. So from leads provided by just one of our eavesdropping systems and not even taking into the equation the other streams of intelligence, but most importantly realizing Jerry has a sixth sense on the accuracy of Intel; if Jerry says there is a high probability of massive armament existing inside our borders ready for the terrorists that maybe at this very moment waiting for their orders to attack us; then I suggest that we had better believe it. Sorry, but this is a little off of the agenda of this meeting but I need to express my thoughts about the need to get action on all of our Intel, the data that you have elaborated on and the Intel we get from field operatives. Much of the field Intel has gone to our headquarters through the proper protocols but I personally fear that the reports on the possibility of terrorist inside of our borders having access to armament and explosives has gone the way of your data 'trash bin' system. While we at CI-4 and the other CI units uncover suspicious information that on the surface has no factual data to back it up, we believe that the underlying possibilities should be sufficient to require an investigation. I know that such investigations on hearsay intelligence especially only backed up with gut feelings are not in the manuals and outside of protocol and are to be considered equal to pursuing a needle in a haystack. But I contend that if the haystack is much smaller then an average haystack and there are only a few haystacks instead of hundreds than based on just the science of statistics we should follow up on unsubstantiated Intel where it is about the possibility that terrorist within our borders have a large cache of weapons and explosives. At this time I am referring to three missions undertaken by our CI-4 section head, Jerry Ness. One where he and Jack Madden who is now deceased received information that arms and explosives had entered the States through West coast shipping ports. A second report also came from Jerry that there may have been shipments of armament that entered into the Florida from Argentina or possibly Brazil. And there are solid reports on other missions made by your agents from the CIA which started out as just fishing trips which have given us specific reports that operatives in Pakistan have confirmed that some sleeper cells in the States are well armed and these reports have been forwarded to each of the appropriate departments as per our protocol. Jerry and I have been on follow up investigations on the two original missions and as our reports state there is some measure of reliability to all of the Intel. And we have asked for at least a PFI if not a CFR"

John Poles interrupted to ask, "If what you are saying is true then why haven't we been apprised of these reports so that a PFI could be authorized to look into those allegations and if proven accurate possibly go to a CFR?"

Again Hank took a hold of the conversation, "Sir I do not mean to take over this meeting and I hope I am not out of line but I have asked the same question of George Meeker who was finally able to get a PFI for the hundreds of thousands of overseas containers received at all of our maritime docks each year. What we believe is more important is the need for an authorization of the release of the funds which have already been allocated that are required to carry out the PFI on all these past shipments over the past ten years and which he has also been trying to get for a number of months, actually many months. Now he has just requested a CFR on Intel out of the Sudan. I believe that just like the needle in a hay stack, if there is just a thousand to one chance that our Intel has some measure of reliability then that one chance should merit an immediate CFR authorization for a third mission to Brazil to go non stop until verification one way or the other is confirmed that thousands of pounds of C-4 have been shipped into the States. As to your awareness to my statements I would like to offer the suggestion that the protocols for information sharing be reviewed and the command section that establishes the investigation priorities consider my needle in a haystack theory. We all know that if the information is discovered to be true then we have an internal disaster in the boiling stages, just waiting to explode!"

After my bombshell the meeting continued with the CIA representative reviewing the unrest in Pakistan and making a case for the Taliban being helped by sympathizers crossing the borders. Also she reported that fundamentalist Muslim youths in Saudi Arabia were pressuring the royal families for internal reform of its policies towards the West, further she provided confirmed reports that Syria was supplying the insurgents in Iraq with money and armament plus helping to recruit more militant activist to enter into Iraq.

The officer from the DOD presented his departments report on the progress Iran was making on their attempt to build a nuclear device thus putting Israel in eminent danger and how increasingly dangerous the threat has become from Korea with its Nuclear proliferation. For the next hour a number of questions were raised by various participants followed by departmental commentary and recommendations.

Robert Drier concluded the agenda to present the status of the different agencies and the military's ability to infiltrate the enemies operations. He presented the problem that each of the different entities had a manpower shortage of persons that could speak Arabic fluently enough to penetrate the many different groups that are believed to be or are known to be terrorist factions.

At the end I was asked to meet with John, Robert, George, and Jerry in an ante room next to the director's office. After thirty minutes Secretary of OHS Tom Rodgges entered and took a chair next to his office's entry door. "Gentlemen, I have reviewed the minutes of your 'Integrated Operations' meeting and with the briefing from John I am in full agreement with Hank here. I will get the paperwork started tomorrow to set in motion a special task force to do the internal investigation and to commence additional missions to where ever they may lead concentrating on the pursuit of foreign contraband entering our country. I have named this 'Operation Open Sesame' and I am personally issuing a NSD for the implementation of the operation along with my request that a NSR be sent to the FBI, CIA, and you George at the CI unit headquarters at NSA. Further I am personally going to get the appropriations committee to release funds immediately to finance these requests. George, keep me posted and see to it that reports are properly distributed. I will personally deliver all reports to the President and advise him that we have placed a National Security Response in the NSD directive on this matter. However, as of now we are going on hearsay and I will not alert anyone until we get reliable facts. This authority stays between your CI sections and my office period. Thank your for your work and devotion to our country and carry on. John, can you come into my office for a few minutes?"

As we all left the door to the Secretaries office was quickly shut and Tom turned to John. "What has happened to our information sharing and why hasn't a NSR been issued on this before now?"

"Sir, those request are highly classified and must go through our review department and then to the congressional oversight committee to guarantee that the rights of all those to be investigated at this level are protected."

"That is just 'BS', I'm going to see Stephen Haddle, the President's National Security Advisor. We can not operate with these kinds of hurdles. Carry on with my request for a National Security Response on this matter."

"Yes Sir."

The next day I met Jerry in his office and all he could say was, "Well you are one of us now. I could not have said it better or more diplomatically. George told me yesterday that he appreciated your guts to let them know what we all were thinking. There is going to be some major investigation work done and special agents assigned to us here at CI. I hope you will stay in operations to assist in the coordination of the missions as they progress. It will take real time correct analyst and integration of the daily inflow of information into our artificial intelligent programs to produce terrorist impending plans of any clandestine assault against us and I know you are highly experienced at that from your work at the UN. Me personally, I'm asking to be assigned as a freelance operative going into the middle of any hot investigation to guide the strategic part of uncovering the facts. I will count on you to control the ops section to handle 'SIGINT' (communication), 'IMGINT' (imagery surveillance), and 'HUMINT' (human observation)."

I was torn between my desire to see action again and to stay at home as I nodded to him, "Jerry, I'll be at the center of the CONOPT section and you know that you can count on our full support."

CHAPTER EIGHTEEN

It was Monday following the Fourth of July week end and I was going to be working in the sequencer section all week since we still needed to bring every work station on line with the decryption simulator. On Wednesday morning as I checked to see if my people could complete sequencing the decryption satellite input modules by that afternoon, one of my communications officers came into the section to tell that there had been a problem in London. I went to the briefing room to find three other section chiefs viewing incoming news from London on the big screen TV showing buses having been blown up by suicide bombers and suggesting that there may be subways in jeopardy. Another attack by Islamic terrorists. We would now be receiving a massive amount of Intel from our agents assigned to England as their investigations and interviews began. It went on and on and our department catalogued everything.

It was almost three weeks later when Tiama called me at work to remind me that Dad's birthday was tomorrow the thirty first of July and she had invited him down to celebrate becoming part of the ever increasing senior citizen numbers and being well positioned to look towards retirement. I was pleasant but somewhat concerned when I replied, "You didn't tell him that did you? Even though he is 65 now he looks at himself as just entering the middle of his life and career. I really think he may make the century mark so I encourage him to press on in his work, especially since Mom is gone and Caroline is there to keep him young."

"Of course I didn't say that to him. I only said that to you. I respect your Dad a lot and after all he was responsible for you. I kind of think

191

that was an okay achievement. But really, he is coming and you should buy him something because I know you forgot about this birthday and to celebrate it I will make him a special desert. Would it be alright to take him to Morton's Steak House? I would like to have their lobster dinner and Mom would be impressed with the restaurant, plus she has never had Maine lobster."

"Sure Honey and I'll stop at the Grand Mall to get him something before I go to the station to pick him up."

As usual the dinner was fantastic and even though we were all stuffed after we had finished we all had room for some coffee and Baileys Irish Cream. Dad started the conversation and after some pleasantries about our families he asked me if I was going be doing any traveling soon.
"No, I've been stationed in our operations section to assist some of our agents in their missions. We are concentrating on any enemy attack plans directed towards the states and that is currently the primary effort of all of my unit's staff. Of course I can't go into any details but I am here stateside for a while."

"Suits me just fine", Tiama smiled as she looked at her Mom and then Dad.

Kind of smiling Hank changed the subject as he eyed everyone at the table, "You know how I hate politics but what about this rhetoric coming from Kerry? The presidential race is becoming a circus with the world looking at the clowns in the arena and our ring master trying to organize the show to let the audience know there is still intelligence somewhere in the 'Big Top'. Cush says that we must stay the course and do what ever it takes to rid the world of potential disasters from the terrorists. Mister's Kerry and Edwards say they will be strong on terrorism by putting together a strong coalition, how? With magical Kerry dust. And then he suggests that we just sit down with them and negotiate a peace. He really can not be for real. Naivety must reign in the area where he lives. The only peace that would come from a sit down with Muslim terrorists would be a piece of his throat as they cut his head off. He seems to be a clone of old Chappaquiddick Kennedy but not at all as soused looking; it would appear that they are both cut from the same cloth, a bolt of naïve liberalism. He is 'Flipper' in disguise and another typical democrat flip-flopper. A card carrying Dove in the Vietnam War, then a Hawk at 9-11, and now a Dove on the Iraqi War after supporting it in Congress. He is all politics and would reduce the personal safety of our citizens for his own personal ambitions."

"Well son you don't hold back any horses when you have an opinion. As I am able to review the scene must of the politicians are positioning themselves for the elections, I think you are correct in your thinking about a Kerry/Edwards ticket. Who wants Cush for president? Strong Americans, that's who. Who wants Kerry, etal for president? Al Qaeda. They would be a real disaster for our country and I think the entire nation knows it. We must not ever forget that the enemy of our country wants us all eradicated. And speaking about the enemy of our country how is the enemy of the enemy, Jerry Ness? Is he still in your section?"

"Well yes and no, he is in charge of a special OPTs unit and at this moment may even be on a mission. Even though we are technically under Homeland Security a few of our missions do require some personnel for covert assignments."

Tom was anxious to add a bit of extra news highlights since he liked to feel his news department was number one and ahead of competition, "Before we finish this last Bailey"s and coffee here is some information straight from the Russian playbook. We've been told by one of our interpreters in our news department that Al-Qaeda is releasing rumors and disinformation to cause additional stress for us here at home and to totally misguide our efforts in Afghanistan and even Iraq. We believe that because as we receive the communications in our bureau the interpretation is quite often not considered correct. And yet misinformation can keep the American people on a yo-yo. Sometimes we go to yellow then orange then back. Their language is subject to so many dialects the proper readings of what is said are many times not possible. While at the same time our language is transparent and that makes us sometimes quite vulnerable."

"You're right Dad; we deal with this information and misinformation daily. That is what my unit has been dealing with constantly. Thank god we have a strong organization at NSA and people devoted to determining what is good intelligence and foul intelligence".

"Hey guys," Tiama cut in, "we are all interested in the country but don't the two of you get enough of the heavy side of life at work. Its Dad's birthday and Mom and I are wishing you many more; let's raise our cups, Happy Birthday Dad. Now I have a special treat at home, Hank pay up and let's go."

When we got home Tiama surprised us with a totally typical American desert of strawberries and shortcake with real whipped cream. Dad's eyes beamed since Mom had always made this desert for us during the summer months and now Caroline usually buys the store made deserts for Dad instead of going to the trouble of doing personal fixin's.

"Son, Tiama, and Maryta, Thank you for a very nice evening and for the absolutely handsome pipe and imported tobacco. You know that since I gave up cigarettes a fine bowl full of tobacco is one of my quiet pleasures. Maybe I'll break it in tonight as I watch our late news. Thanks again I'll just hail a cab on the street to go to Grand Central. My next train is at 9:10. Good night"

Tiama and I both said Good night.

Then Maryta, "Good Night Tom."

The November chill was setting in around the DC area and a light jacket was needed as Tiama and I stepped out of our front door to walk to get breakfast at Watkins grill about a mile from our apartment. The traffic on the streets was usually light on Saturday mornings making the air a little fresher and there was the aroma of logs burning in some people's fireplace which added to the enjoyment of our walk to the restaurant. We arrived early enough that there wasn't any waiting for a booth which was where I wanted to sit. Tiama and I enjoyed sitting next to each other when we were out.

After the waitress brought us some coffee I took my wife's hand and we gave our devotion to the Lord for our work and our food. It was now a common thing for us. I added, "Lord I see coming disasters to our world and our lives so I pray for our personal protection, our re-elected president, our nation and our military who are taking the brunt of this war on terrorism, Amen."

Tiama held on to my hand and said, "Thank you Hon for those thoughts. I feel like sometimes you have deep worries that you don't share with me and they must come from the inner sanctum of your work at OHS."

"I guess it does show now and the….." The waitress arrived to serve us our order, my bagel with lox and cream cheese and Tiama's chicken and spinach omelet, so I cut my words short. "Could you please bring us some more coffee?"

"You are right sweetheart. I bring the affairs of my work home. With

Cush winning the election over Kerry which was no surprise to the Washington insiders and the Republicans in control of the Congress, you would think the country would be in for sweet times but we at the office see it quite differently. We are fighting a war that is, for those who have all of the facts, a responsible action yet embroiled in many miscalculations and it appears that terrorism world wide has not been stymied in the least."

Tiama intervened, "Seems like we watch TV and we talk about this and we go out and so often our conversation is about this. Will we get some peace soon?"

"I'm sorry my love, but you did ask me why I seem worried when my thoughts go to the World's state of affairs. I have an idea, let's get far away from here and go to the mountains next weekend and spend some time enjoying nature and some fresh air laced with the aroma of pines trees!" I had to take this opportunity to explain the new mission I would be going on. "But for just a moment back to our discussion, I want to let you know that I will be sent out again probably right after the New Year on a mission that will not be defined until this next month."

"Wait, Hon is this going to be a dangerous mission? You have been with OHS for almost two and a half years and as far as I know you have not been at risk, I always want to know!"

It was once again time to offer up security for her, "First my love look at me, I have always been on information gathering missions and that will probably not change. We have other agents that go after the bad guys; you know kind of like Jerry. But secondly, my thoughts that cause me to look worried at times are these; and I want you to know what the world environment is like so that you really understand what a good job the President is doing and what an important job we have at OHS. No matter what their cause or where they strike terrorists are this planets greatest menace and terrorism is worldwide and must be stopped. Just remember this year's events and the latest happenings just a couple of months past. Terrorist blew up two Russian jetliners and then they invaded a Russian school and blew up little children. At our last briefing we compiled all of the announcements and video tapes on bin Laden and we could see a pattern of the threats against us and the call for an uprising of all of his Muslim brothers for the complete destruction of the West. John Ashcroft has confirmed that the war on terrorism is not only still raging but it is expanding. Al-Zawahri is screaming at the world that the battle has not even begun. The young fundamentalist Muslims in Saudi Arabia are rebelling against the royal family and demanding that the U.S. bases be kicked out of their country and that their cultural and political reform take place under strict cleric discipline. Syria is continuing to stir the pot and help insurgents enter into Iraq supplied with military supplies purchased from Russia. Iran is threatening to build nuclear weapons to use them against all of their enemies and our highly trusted friend Israel is in the middle of real estate that is in the most dangerous place on earth. Prime Minister of Israel Benjamin Natanyahu has stated that what is at stake today is the survival of our civilization. The French are battling Muslim threats inside of their borders as the march of Islam is taking over their country while at the same time they resist supporting Cush or the United States. And then we have warnings coming from Hamas and Mujahedin to all Muslims living in Europe and America to leave before it is too late or protect themselves because they, that is their 'Movement' will soon commence a battle in a form that this era has never before witnessed! All of this going on while we are trying to live a normal life. The world has changed and it is hard to know who to trust or where it will end up."

"Hank, I am proud of you for changing jobs and wanting to service our country by going with the OHS, but are we truly safe here? I read that the fact that our borders are not under control there are potential terrorist entering our country every week both from Mexico and very easily from across Canada. Also I read that just a month ago two groups of radical Arabic males who had penetrated the Mexican border were discovered in Wilcox, Arizona and then over twenty two thousand non-Mexican immigrants from where ever in the world, who had been detained for some time were released from detention into the populace pending some kind of hearing. What kind of security is that?"

"I know, we all know we have a border problem but Congress has to settle that. It is out of our hands at the OHS. Law makers such as Kennedy and Pelosi, and Feinstein and the rest of the liberals don't care about our country they only look at their political future. It is criminal and they should be accused of subversion against the people of the United States by not administering the people's wishes, if not maybe even treason! Most of us feel the pain of the mistakes these fools make."

"Well okay my love, pay the check so we can leave. Let's go to the health club and start those tennis lessons again."

"A wonderful idea and then we can do some laps in the pool, I can use some stress relief and more practice with my incredible serve."

The last words are always said by the wife, "Serve yes but incredible, well that's a good way to describe it. Race you to the corner."

December sixteenth and instead of a NSR, a CFR came through from OHS, due to the continual persistence of John Poles, authorizing a full scale investigation into the possibility that military weapons, explosives, and even WMD could have entered the United States. George read the CFR which authorized two separate critical investigations. The key points were based on all of CI's Intel on military contraband coming into the states through Florida and West coast ports of entry. It stated, 'Some of the intelligence suggests that this could have happened over the past seven to ten years'. The first order 'authorizes a small team of agents to start in Sudan, Argentina and Brazil and work the smallest bit of information that could provide any authenticity to the reports from agent Jerry Ness. Their mission is to follow each and every rumor or lead verifying the source and the reliability'. The second CFR order 'authorizes stepped up efforts for the investigation of the contents of containers received at all ports since 1996 and asks congress to move swiftly with funding of the National Port Security measure'. Additionally 'the documentation on all shipments during the past ten years are to be reviewed by a task force from NSA and should any of the shipments appear to be suspicious then those shipments are to be tagged as PFI and given to FBI agents to investigate thoroughly; tracking the movement of each tagged shipment from its point of origination to the final recipient'.

Task forces of two hundred clerical oriented agents for each of two locations, one at Long Beach and one at Norfolk were put in place to begin the shipping documentation reviews. With millions of containers arriving annually at all of the various ports on both coasts over the past ten years and with the task forces having four hundred people to review all of the sets of packets of shipping documents besides having to discern what should be tagged as a PFI file; George looked at the requirements of the overall task and conjectured that it would probably take at least two years to complete the review with no possible estimate on how many would be tagged for further investigation. He looked at the order through the eyes of a well trained and very experienced investigating agent and thought to himself that it was good that the CFR came through but it should have been a NSR and how ridiculous to not have enough staff to complete the review of the previous ten years of shipping documentation in a timely manner. That is our government at work by committee not by individual authority. What could happen to us in the mean time?

George called all of the heads of the CI units for a meeting on Friday and went over the key points of the CFR. Two of the unit heads along with Jerry voiced their opinion about the time frame for completing the documentation reviews elaborating on the need to find any kind of a trail to help the field investigations currently under way. Even though George agreed with their thinking he quickly added, "There is no other way to do this but with a hands on personal review of the documentation and all I have been given is a staff of four hundred. We must follow the orders as presented. I will ask for more people but who knows when I might get additional manpower or even if I get any at all."

"We get it George; we live with this bureaucracy every day too. I want to head up the investigating team going to Brazil." Jerry could not stay in the office. As he always says, 'I'm getting cabin fever!'

I was in my office when the phone rang with a very familiar ring, it was Tiama and how did I always know it was her. We had such a close relationship spiritually that I would be thinking about her or a glimpse of her would flash before me just before the phone would ring and I knew it was her. "Hello Honey, how are you?"

"How do you always know it is me?"

I hear her voice and I want to be next to her, how great is that, I love her and our coming child. "I just get that feeling as the phone rings. What's up?"

"Here it is the Christmas season already and I want us to relax and maybe take a trip somewhere and spend the Christmas weekend in the mountains. You know, like the Adirondacks or Lake Placed, kind of away from all of this Washington stuff and national security. Can we take mom and ask your family to join us on a trip for the holidays. I'm beginning to feel some sort of anxiety."

"I'll check to see if I can take a week of vacation time and you call Dad and Caroline, but your anxiety is more than likely the baby. I've heard that the first three months can do that to a woman. But what do I know. Ask your mom. I'll be home around 6:00, I don't want to miss my TV program."

"What program?"

You know '24', it's getting good. Majuah has fooled them again."

"Honey don't you get enough of that at work?"

"I don't get any intrigue here, I'm an information analysis specialist among other things. No action in my job. Well I'll be there around 6:00. Bye Hon."

When I talked to George he said things were fairly quite and that since the inauguration preparedness was not till mid January a week off was no problem. We left DC on Tuesday before Christmas weekend and stopped at the farm to pick up Dad, Caroline, and Grandma before heading north to Lake Placid. With Tiama, me and her mom our car was not going to make for a comfortable drive so we switched cars to Dad's Navigator to make room for six and our luggage plus to make a more relaxing trip to the mountains. "Hey Dad can we leave the Christmas gifts here at the house? I was thinking we might want to drive back Christmas day and open them in the evening when we return. How does everyone feel about that?"

"Ay, ay chief, sounds fine." "I agree." "Okay by me." "Sure that way we can have Christmas and a couple of days to relax before going back to our routines".

The trip up to the lake was stunning after we hit the higher elevations. There was snow in the mountains and the higher we went the more there was on the pine trees. What a site to see the bright white snow against the dark green needles of the pines and the afternoon sun coming in between trees to make the snow glisten like shattered glass fragments. It was about 30 degrees outside and as I rolled the window halfway down on my side. Grandma at first quietly asked me to close the window because of the chill but when she smelled the fresh mountain air she just wrapped her sweater around herself tighter and said to leave it alone. That got a unanimous vote of yes.

About four hours after leaving the farm we reached the lake and Dad stopped at a gas station for fuel and sodas. Inside he made a call to one of his media friends and came out smiling as he got back into the car. "I called one of my counter parts at NBC, Brent Hummer and asked him if he was up here for the holidays. He said no and offered us his winter place for the week. He has a caretaker close by who has the key so we can all enjoy a warm rustic log cabin on the lake for the week instead of the Motelodge. Even though the lodge is beautiful and very comfortable, I kind of prefer my privacy."

Maryta thought that was great of Mr. Hummer and privacy sounded good to her. They stopped to buy groceries and then to pick up the key from the caretaker. As Tom stopped in the driveway of the caretaker's house he was already on his porch waiting to greet the guest. "Mr. Hummer said that you would be here for the key shortly, what was your name again?"

"I'm Tom Brayden form New York with UBC."

"Oh right, I think I have seen you on TV before. Not very often, just once in a while."

"Well, thank you for the key and thanks for watching UBC. How do we get to Brent's cabin?" "It's easy, go right then left a ways, then left again and then right for a block or so and then right and then right again."

"WHAT?"

"Just kidding I'll go in front of you and you just follow. I was over there fifteen minutes ago and put a fire in the fire place for you. It should be just right by now."

Upon arrival at the cabin, we thanked him and hauled the bags and groceries in before hauling in more logs. It was rustic but very big with two floors and a deck around part of the second floor looking out to the lake and covering what appeared to be a sun room below it. The sun room was all glass looking out over a picturesque scene of fifty and seventy foot dark and light green pine trees, snow covered landscape and a frozen lake with three kids ice skating. "Oh honey I want to try and ice skate. It looks like great fun. And this is my first time to see a big frozen lake."

"I noticed some skates and skis in the foyer as we came in. We can try to see if any that are there will fit us."

Tiama was acting like a little child with a big grin on her face and almost frolicking around the sunroom as she said it. "I want to try to see if some will fit, how do I know?"

"You try a pair on while I see who has KP for the evening then I'll come back to show you how to lace them up and how to walk on them. Who is volunteering to fix a little diner?" I got a few shoulder shrugs as I said it so, "Everyone for them selves then. I'll open a can of potato soup for now so don't ask for some later, but I can do two cans if you speak up now. Hey Tiama, take off the skates and we'll eat some soup and crackers and then I'll help you try on the ice skates."

Tiama's seem to fit fairly well but mine were a bit tight. Outside on the lake some more people were skating on the ice inside of a cove near the cabin and they had a fire going in a rock fire pit so we joined them thinking the ice must be better where they were skating. We didn't know anything about skating or ice. Out we went, I fell down and then Tiama fell on her rear end, up again then down I went. "Hey sweetheart, let's hold on to each other as we try. I'll help you and you can help me." That seemed to work okay although we looked like a couple of straw figures as we pushed our skates along, first Tiama was fairly straight upon her skates and I was all wiggly and then I would gain some control and she would slip sideways on one skate almost pulling me down. We looked ridiculous I am sure but nobody was really watching us. There have been other clowns out here before so we were not the first act on the stage.

As we were about to go in a couple came over to us and asked if we would like some suggestions to help us stay more stable. "We could sure use some only first I would like to get warmed up by the fire."

"Let us know when you want to try again. We will be on the ice." We watched them as they turned in circles and then held each other going around and around the cove; they seemed to just float on top of the ice and their moves were as polished as any Olympic skater. We tried to learn from their instructions until Tiama said she was tired so she and I said thanks and went back to the cabin.

Back at the cabin everyone was getting ready for the night and Tiama asked them if they saw us skating. "Yes, and you did pretty good." Maryta was being kind. Nobody else made a comment but Caroline had a grin on her face as she headed up stairs for bed.

"Honey, let's get our suitcase and get ready for bed."

"I'll be up stairs in a minute; I want to fix a hot chocolate. Do you want one?"

"That would taste great, thanks hon."

"Me too, I'll take a cup."

"Fix one for me too," Grandma said from the sun room where see was gazing out on the moon lit lake.

"Me too," was a Tom's voice coming from the sofa.

"Five cups of hot chocolate coming up. Where is the box of Swiss Miss packets?"

Friday evening and Tom had prepared a rib roast in the oven with spices and garlic and cloves. Caroline fixed old fashion green bean casserole with mushroom soup and fried onion rings with a thin amount of melted Swiss cheese on top. I had put my favorite vegetable in the oven to start baking about forty five minutes before Dad's roast was to come out, baked spuds. As we all sat down to a delicious holiday dinner Dad and Grandma took a moment to asked us to bow our heads to give thanks for our family, our lives, our country, and especially for our military in Iraq who where so far away from the special feelings of Christmas and their loved ones. Dad added a special moment of prayer for the world to overcome the monster of terrorism and the terrorists who were invading so many countries. "Lord we pray for all humanity to come to its senses and we look to you to effect a change in the direction the world is going. We ask that you bring your wrath down on those who are violating your commandments to love their neighbor as their selves and to live in peace. AMEN!"

The dinner was over and with full stomachs Dad and I offered to clean up but Tiama and Grandma said no, they would do it for our pre Christmas present. Dad went to the sun room to look out over the lake and read some of his magazines he had brought on the trip. Caroline and I sat by the fireplace and talked about family things. I wondered if Dad had talked to her about retiring so I asked her.

She said no and added, "You know he loves the station and since mother has been gone he has taken his work on as his second bride." She changed the subject immediately and I felt it was because mom's passing was still a touchy subject for her. "How is your work going and have you guys gotten a house yet. Or I guess first will you be staying in Washington and then about the house? And what about the baby? When is he due?"

Tiama could hear Caroline's question so she helped Hank with the answer, "Oh, I guess Hank has been so wrapped up in his work he has totally forgotten to tell anyone about our good fortune. Hey Dad and Grandma, I want to be the first to pass on our good news. Hank and I with mom's help have found a house in the Prince George area that Hank thinks is perfect for us and we made an offer last week, but the owner is on a skiing vacation in Austria and will not return until the first week in January so it is kind of up in the air till then. Since the baby is going to join us around mid June we thought that we should move now during the slow winter months and because Hank has committed to a minimum of five more years at his government job, buying right now makes good sense to us. There honey I broke the news." Everyone clapped for the house and raised their cups to cheer for the coming baby.

CHAPTER NINETEEN

January 14th at the Razor Cuts barber shop.

Brada entered the barber shop on Eight Avenue early Friday morning to beat the crowd. Friday after 10am and all day Saturday were the busiest times to get hair cuts in New York. And why not with Friday night's being the prowling night and Saturday being the date night. All the want-a-be Romeos in New York got hair cuts, manicures, and new shirts for the week end. Brada had been traveling and needed a hair cut while he waited to keep a prearranged meeting with Musab, Yassir, and Saja. The small shop was run by a brother from Jordan who had excellent skills at cutting hair for the Arabic community. With mainly Arabic patrons the shop made a great front to house a meeting with almost one hundred per cent assured privacy. Brada greeted Ali the owner, "Good morning, allah shines on you my brother."

Ali looked up from his first customer of the day and nodded, "Brada, its good to see you, some friends want to see you today."

"I am glad to see you Ali. Did they say when?"

"Yes in about one hour."

"Okay, I'll just sit over here and watch the early morning news."

CNN was on the TV showing more roadside IED bombings in Iraq as Brada settle in to see what the Headline News might be. Brent Hummer came on to comment on an earlier interview with both John Ashcroft and Dick Chaney. "As we announced earlier the Department of Homeland Security has elevated the security alert level to Yellow before the inauguration with the possibility of Orange if the intelligence sources tell them that there is a need for an increase. As we heard from Secretary Ashcroft, 'OHS is working twenty four - seven to defuse any efforts made by terrorists to carry out another major attack on our country', which he added 'most everyone believes is inevitable, including our top intelligence gurus at NSA'. In the same interview Dick Chaney added that 'the question raised about another major attack was a mute question', he continued with, 'the important question is not if but when'. Hummer added a straight quote from Chaney, "We need to roust, infiltrate, and capture the al-Qaeda operatives in the States and prevent another 9-11, and we owe that to the citizens of our country!"

Brada turned his head towards Ali with a smirk on his lips as he said in a low voice, "If they only knew." As he said that, he saw Musab opening the door so he got up and headed to the back room. Musab followed and went through the door at the rear of the shop and entered into the meeting room that had been used many times by important visitors from the East and leaders from other cells and those stationed in New York. As soon as Yassir and Saja joined the meeting Musab addressed the gathering, "Greeting from allah and the prophets who have led us to this point in our struggles against the Infidels, allah is good allah is great! Abu has brought us words from Dr Zawahiri. We are all anxious to start the Jihad against the United States, but it will have nothing to do with the coming Presidential inauguration. The Americans are fools, as of today they have raised the alert level to Yellow and we all know there is no alert needed. Here is what is important! During the next six months we are each of us to travel by car to visit the leaders of our eighty cells making the trips to appear as if we are on vacation. The cities will be assigned to us by cell phone communication and the trips organized so that we can see all of our brothers by July. In each city we are to buy a throw away cell phone and then dial up the computer in Yemen from a public phone with a phone card and leave the throw away cell phone number so the computer can call each of us back. In a short time we will get a call with the directions for the cell leader to follow to get the plans and responsibilities that have been assigned to that cell. Dr Zawahiri and other well trained planners of bin Laden have spent months putting together the logistics needed to win the battle and bring the 'serpent' to it's knees. Our cell leaders have all been well trained and now they must be informed which part of that training they will need to pass on to their members. We must tell them the wait may be over in a year or two but they will be able to taste battle against the infidels only when bin Laden gives the order. But no one can become over zealous and act any differently or break our code of silence. After all of the individual cell leaders have been visited and given their orders they must be patient and go over their role in the coming battle in their mind again and again and again so their command of their brothers will be spontaneous without a single flaw. During that period all of our brothers are to add to their daily prayers the "Giving of thanks to allah for allowing each of us to be a part of the greatest Jihad ever waged and to ask allah for strength to carry out their individual orders, the wisdom to be accurate and decisive, and the courage to go all of the way to martyrdom if necessary for the success and glory of allah. All of their efforts and investigations will be of no avail so, we give thanks now and every day to allah for his blessings."

Finally in February the review operations were under way in Long Beach and Norfolk and George had exceeded has limits on investigative teams to carry out the CFR. George sent Jerry to Brazil as he had requested to meet a local CIA person stationed in Brasilia, Brazil. Plus he sent a two man team to Argentina to get more detailed information from Jerry's original contacts and from any of their personal associates. And a top black agent Melvin Norris from CI-1 went to Sudan to find Abdul Aziz Rantisi. Jerry had been told by Munoz that Rantisi and al-Masri had been very close associates and had trained together in the Afghan Training camps plus Amer al-Matti had verified it. Rantisi had to be an excellent link to get facts on all of the chatter about the explosive C-4 entering the States. The Intel from our people in the Gaza strip had prompted NSA to put satellite surveillance on three suspected areas where Rantisi might be found. Out of the three Port Sudan in the Sudan on the Black Sea was CI's first choice to start Norris's undercover operation. George's orders to Melvin were to find this Hamas operative were ever he was and take any means necessary to get at the truth about possible shipments into the States of explosives and/or guns. Further he instructed him that if it becomes necessary he must subdue him at his location then extract him in order to break him and George added, we will provide the tactical assistance you will need.

Arriving in Egypt at the end of February Melvin was driven from Egypt to Wadi Halfa just inside of Sudan across the Egyptian border. He made his connection with Nastigie, who had been on assignment in Northeastern African for five years, and was driven to the port town of Port Sudan. Nastigie gave him a local cell phone and his number if he needed to make contact. Nastigie told him where an Internet Café was since that was going to be his method of contacting his tactical team at CI. "Don't worry about the phone or the Internet here. They have no Carnivore here or any means of eves-dropping on you! The International Muslim terrorist organizations love the Coastal countries like Somalia and Sudan to hibernate so to speak because of the total privacy and ability to disappear into the many nondescript neighborhoods. Especially Port Sudan were they can charter a boat and be gone in hours. Looking for someone here is going to be like looking for one particular fish in the Red Sea. I was told that you speak Arabic so if you have your cover planned, just be sure to watch your dialect. The Arabic in this area is based on Afro-Asiatic roots; I am very serious about this." Melvin nodded his head slowly in agreement and let Nastigie know that he was assuming his standard Arabic name Ibrahim which he always used in the Middle-East when operating undercover. "I am taking the position as a possible buyer of Marble from the many quarries in Sudan for export to Germany and Austria."

Nastigie nodded his head.

Melvin said good-by to Nastigie, found a taxi and asked for the Hilton Port Sudan but first he wanted to know where the docks were so he asked the driver to show him the location of the Major shipping docks. The driver headed east for short time and then took a sudden left on a narrow street between some moderate commercial buildings to expose the water of the Red Sea, a few small boats floating between a dingy warehouse and a large freighter loaded with Gypsum and then a long row of commercial piers. He asked him to go on to the Hotel and tried to memorize the way to the hotel and some of the more noticeable land marks. Melvin knew he was in an uncharted area and had to not only become familiar with the where but also the how and the why of the daily routine of the most common Sudanese on the street. "I'll get my bag, how much is the fare?"

"Five and a half pounds."

"Here is a five hundred dinar note" I took the change and entered the hotel. Nice but with its own aromas drifting into the lobby. I recognized this one smell as warm fuul, the native and always available food. Smashed beans cooked with garlic, olive oil, onions and sometimes tomatoes. No drinking in this Muslim country but you can always get a cup of tea and I could see the small area inside the veranda where the fuul was being prepared and served with some baked Kisra and if requested a cup of tea.

I turned back as the desk clerk tapped the key to my room on the counter, "Mr. Norris, here is your key to room 234 up the stairs and to your left and we will keep your credit card for payment."

"Oh no, just a minute I will need my card back, how much is the room and I will pay in dinars."

"That will be fifty five thousand dinars per night and we will want a minimum of two nights so if you leave after only one night you can get a refund."

"Alright", but under my breath I cursed the system. I went to my room and found it quite comfortable, dropped my bag and took the package Nastigie gave me to hide under the sink in the bathroom, and went downstairs to have some tea and go for a walk.

After thirty days I had to report that attending the Mosques for any loose information and trying to penetrate the Muslim community where our surveillance had pin pointed Rantisi's location was slow and not as fruitful as we had expected. This investigation needed additional help from our alliances with the agencies in England, Spain, Italy, Germany and Israel. Each of our allies had Intelligence agents operating in Middle-Eastern countries and we needed more information on Rantisi.

On a Saturday afternoon in April after the rain had cleared I was out for some fresh air and was not far from the front of the hotel when two medium built pedestrians with dark beards walking towards me stopped and asked for my passport. I quickly flashed on thieves, then on private police checking legitimate documents and then on possible kidnappers; but who would want to kidnap me? I was reluctant to do anything until I saw an official looking badge on one of my assailants belt and the observation of a small caliber gun in a small belt holster. I took my passport from my rear pocket and realized I would now have to convince the authorities that I was legitimately here on business and not an American spy. "Mr. Norris, if you would please let us escort you to the small benches over there on the other side of the street. We will need to talk." Okay I thought, maybe this is just a shake down of another foreign businessman and that will be just fine so long as we have no commotion. I quickly asked how much they wanted to return my passport. That did not work. "Melvin Norris, that is your name right, Melvin Norris. Be careful, you are too easily restrained here in this country. We are with Shin-Bet and have been asked to help you while you are here in any way we can and before we have finished our own business. Your team in the States under the command of Hank Brayden picked up on our mission here and had a satellite communiqué sent to us through our headquarters in Tel Aviv. We were sent here to locate one of the major supply routes of C-4 to the Palestinians and to destroy it. If you need any of our Intel we can collaborate since we understand that you are on a similar mission."

"Well......Thank you, Hank". Shaking their hands he acknowledged their notoriety, "Agents from Israel's top secret service department, I am impressed that you would take a chance to open up to me and place yourselves in some degree of exposure. I am here to find an upper level operative of Hezbollah; Abdul Aziz Rantisi who we believe can confirm facts about any shipments of guns or explosives into our country. I have been sent solo since I blend in with the populace and I speak Arabic fluently. We know he has been a prime link with C-4 manufactured in Argentina and with shipments to Sudan but we believe that through his relationship with a suspected arms dealer Ahmad al-Masri who was shot and killed in Uruguay he can confirm our suspicions that terrorist in the States have been supplied with both guns and explosives and maybe even WMDs."

"Don't concern yourself about us. We carry Iranian passports and unquestionable documentation and have gotten within striking distance of our target. Our orders are to systematically eliminate everyone in the supply chain all within a twenty four hour period and then leave. That event is coming soon so if we can help you it will be in the next few days. Our intelligence people know Rantisi is the buyer in Argentina for Hamas and Hezbollah but they have not said he is in Sudan, however if he is here he will be part of our target."

I broke in, "He is my total mission so if our intelligence is correct and he can be found don't eliminate him but turn him over to me. We are on the same team."

"Not quite, similar but not the same team. We suffer daily from the attacks of Hezbollah. Our job and our orders are to eliminate the supply chain that brings death and destruction to our people every day from the Islamic suicide bombers who are supplied explosives from countries sympathetic to the Palestinians or more accurately the Hamas and Hezbollah cause."

Knowing the reputation of the professionalism and dedication of the Shin-Bet agents, Melvin had to be diplomatic with these guys. "Alright, I understand so should Rantisi appear in your cross hairs will you give me a chance to come with you so that I can get some answers critical to this investigation before he is eliminated?"

"Our Commander said to help you with any Intel we may have so let us contact him to present your request. We are fighting the same enemy. We'll contact you the same way again by tomorrow."

"Hey what are your names?"

"I am known as Hymen and this is Abdullah. Will you still be checked in at this hotel?"

"Yes, until I hear from you."

It was rather late as I entered the Internet café and the proprietor greeted me, "Melvin, would you like a cup of tea? Where have you been?"

"Yes, a cup of tea would be fine. I have been going to the Quarries and I am doing well thank you." There were only three people in the café so I went to the corner cubical and opened up the e-mail service. Typing in the address to get to CI required me to go through a server in Germany and then start an encryption program that was sent to me from the server in Germany that would take the e-mail I was typing and send it in a scrambled format to NSA headquarters in Washington. I started out the message to: 'Hank, you got me connected. I now have some help to make the purchase. I hope I can complete the transaction soon. My negotiations have taken too long here. On what shipping line will you want the order to go out? The help you got me will finish their part in just a few days. They want to take a shipment too."

I closed the e-mail window and got up to pay when three policemen came through the front door and told me to stand still. They took my arms and one grabbed my neck from behind pushing me back out the door. "That's alright Melvin you don't have to pay this time. They have already taken care of me." I realized that somehow the proprietor of the café had been looking at or getting in to my encrypted e-mails and because of his curiosity he had reported me to the authorities for money. I stumbled as they pushed me and falling to my knees I took the pistol that Nastigie had provide me from my ankle strap and shot two of them before they saw what was happening. Jumping up I smashed the head of the third policeman and dragged him back into the café. He was out and not moving. The proprietor was making a phone call so I went over to him and put a bullet in his forehead. There was only one person left on the computer in the café and he was a young boy who had been writing in his school books. I looked at him and he looked back scared from top to bottom with a yellow liquid running down his pants leg. I put my finger to my lips and went shhh, "don't be afraid." Then I went outside and pulled the bodies of the other two policemen in side and shoot the third one in the head. Leave no one behind alive. I left.

The hotel was about three hundred kilometers from the café and I walked a zig-zag path back to the hotel. I entered my room and took stock of my circumstances. Well my mission is finished here and I need to get out of Sudan. The question was how soon. The Israeli agents were getting back to me tomorrow but there was no Rantisi in sight and how intense would the investigation of the killing of three policemen be. Stupid me, very intense. Here are the facts; No witnesses except a young boy who was scared to death and would have a tough time trying to describe me. I mix in with the rest of the people very well. I can check out tomorrow leaving forwarding information to the El Obeid area where the quarries are. If there was a follow up on all hotel guests who checked out I should be able to gain two or three days by using that as a forwarding location. For tonight I will stay put and check out tomorrow and look for the Israelis.

I checked out very early and left the hotel with my bag slung over my shoulder and walked about one hundred meters to the east to wait for the Israeli agents to show. Sunday morning and with businesses opening soon the streets will be filled with pedestrians and trucks with deliveries. There did not seem to be any more police in the area so I was partly relieved as I waited for the Abdullah and Hymen to show. After about an hour I was beginning to attract attention so I called Nastigie and asked him to come and pick me up. To just ride around in a car or park temporarily in various spots made more sense as the time went by. Nastigie arrived in about fifteen minutes with a nondescript truck providing a measure of cover for me as I waited for the agents. "Nastigie, I don't want to jeopardize you so you need to know that I was about to be arrested last night when I wasted three police officers and a shop owner. I may have two to three days at the most to continue my mission here so when you leave me I will disappear into East Town and I want a boat to pick me up at the pier next to the old Gypsum warehouse by Wednesday. Pass on my message." I looked out the window towards the Hilton and saw the two agents walking towards the park area in front of the hotel so I asked Nastigie to pass down Gamdiles Ave. I looked out of the side window as we passed by them before they got to the park and caught their attention with a slight wave and a motion of my hand towards the bench where we talked yesterday. "Okay Nastigie, I can get out here and thanks for all you have done, good-by and if I don't see you again good luck."

I had my bag in hand when the Israeli agents came up to the bench. Hyman with out a word motioned me to follow as they headed to a white car park about fifty meters around the corner from the little park. Hyman drove and Abdullah told me to get in. "We are astonished, either you are have lost it or you are desperate! It had to be you that was in the Internet cafe last night. Only an agent would have completed the execution of four people and leave a young boy alive. It is on the news this morning but no comments on who the police are looking for."

"What about the boy; I felt he was to frighten to be able to recall very much."

"There was nothing, only a boy reported he saw killings."

"I hope he left before anyone arrived to investigate the place."

Abdullah continued, "Rantisi has been here but he left for a meeting with Hezbollah brothers in Somalia. Our people have had that group in Somalia under surveillance as part of the supply chain coming from the south into Gaza and they are part of our elimination program. You are in luck because he is returning to Sudan on the same ship that has a shipment of rockets on board and we believe that another C-4 shipment will be loaded here at Port Sudan before the final route to Gaza. Our intelligence indicates that after he completes his missions he usually goes to the Emirates then to Iran. We will be eradicating their people in Brazil, Somalia, Sudan, and destroying the ship tomorrow night after they have completed loading. Everything is timed for the same hour, 10:30. Four more of my associates will arrive by 4:00 in the afternoon and we will leave when the task is completed the same way they came in. If you want him you must make your contact with him before 10:30 or it will be too late!"

"I won't somehow tip your hand if I corner him and interrogate him? That is not going to be good for your mission."

Hyman turned down a street where he could momentarily park and turned in his seat. "Now we know you have lost it, interrogate him? We are not handing him over to you to take him away, find out what you need to know and kill him. We are on an eradication trip not a communication tour! If that does not suit you then don't come with us and we will kill him just before the boat blows up. We have already put the plans in to action to blow up the boat after everyone is disposed of. YOU KILL HIM OR WE KILL HIM! Which way is it?"

Hyman turned back around as Melvin sat working a plan in his mind. "I'll go with you; it would be my honor to go on an OPT with a team from Shin-Bet."

Once again Hyman responded, "Off the record you do not exist in case something happens to you, there is no Melvin."

"Understood, do you have a better weapon I can have then this stub nose 38. This will be no good in a confrontation."

"No problem, we'll pick you up at the tea shop on the south corner from the Hilton. Where are you staying tonight? I notice you have your bag?"

"I've got a safe house in East Town, see you tomorrow. What time?"

"Seven o'clock."

I had to call Nastigie to take me to a place to get some food then off to East Town. I ate the best Fuul I had ever eaten and what I think was chicken but I was not to sure since chicken is not so common.

Monday morning and D-day for the Shin Bet. I decided to leave my bag and go for a walk. It was safe to walk in East Town since this was the area that most of the families of middle class stature in Sudan lived, if there is such a thing as middle class here. More like shelter, average food, minimal clothes, mainly bicycle transportation or fifteen to twenty year old cars and dirt streets. But the children were everywhere and playing in the streets with old bats, tires, and balls that they used for street soccer. Yes, it was devoid of any major crime but a bit depressing to me. The world is not an equal place and it is full of leaders that need to be put to rest six feet under, Oh well I'm here with blinders on. Just to do my thing and then go home. Back at the safe house I watch the government controlled TV and pass my time. Five o'clock and I used the cell to call Nastigie again. "Come get me." I was out front for about six minutes and the truck pulled up. I jumped in with my bag and he took me to a tea shop near the docks. I did not really want to eat so after he parked the truck we sat out in front enjoying some tea and the accompanying basket of Kisra. "If the boat is set for me on Wednesday I think I am going to need to change it to tomorrow. Can that be done?"

"Sure, but I will need another six hundred thousand Dinars. Changes are expensive."

"Right, I'll give it to you at the dock when I get on the boat. Let's say at six am. My mission is finished here and so am I."

"It will be ready. My tea is gone and so am I; I'll see you tomorrow."

"Wait a minute, my bag is in your car and I'm going to be busy tonight so could you keep my bag and bring it with you to the dock in the morning?"

"Sure."

I could feel a slight breeze coming in from the sea so I ordered another cup of tea and gazed up at the stars in the clear sky. Being south of the equator, night had settled in before seven o'clock and since pollution was nonexistent here the clarity of a thick cluster of stars just above the city made them look like diamonds hanging on invisible strings in the black sky. It was shortly after seven when Hyman sat down at a small table at the edge of the outside railing of the shop. Looking past me he moved his lips to say with no sound, "Follow me in five minutes."

I slowly nodded as I glanced his way. He walked in a direction away from the docks and towards the main commercial district. I followed. He then turned in to a narrow parking lot and there was Abdullah waiting in their car. Hyman got in to the back seat and I slipped into the front seat. "Okay my friend" Hyman spoke with a totally serious tone, "look under your seat. You have a Jericho 941 automatic with two extra belt clips and a MP-A5 with four 30 round clips. We are headed to the ship now. Rantisi is yours if you are ready. We and two other agents have just finished the elimination of seven Hamas operatives that have been part of this supply group and now we believe from our Intel that there are six more members along with Rantisi on board doing a little celebration before they take off for Gaza. We also believe that they have around thirty five thousand kilos of C4 on board and four to five hundred Russian AK-47 rifles. Our other two associates will meet us before we get to the ship. We will leave the car and all go together to board the ship. You will notice that all of our weapons have silencers. As you know the click of the hammer on a MP5 is louder than the discharge of the bullet from the mussel. Our plan is to be quick and stealth with a window of time of thirty minutes after the last of our targets is dead and the explosive activator is set to detonate the C4 shipment. We have our escape plans set; do you have any problems going on with us?"

"No I'm good. Get me Rantisi."

"Let's go."

It was pitch black as we walked in the shadows of the commercial buildings leading to the docks. Even though the stars were bright like little dots of a million pin lights they did not add any light to our path to the docks. After we passed the last building and about a hundred and fifty meters from the ship or I should say a small old vintage freighter, the other two Shin Bet agents joined us. "This is agent Melvin from the States who we told you about. Watch out for him because this is not his fight and he only wants Rantisi. If you spot him hold him, and gag him, and cuff him for Melvin. Let's do this in less than three minutes and meet back at the bridge. Whoever enters the bridge first kills the lights and turns on the red cabin lights. Okay, Let's go."

I was last to board the boat. Each of the Israeli agents went one at a time in ten second sequences and then in different directions. Only one person was on the bridge and he was shot immediately when the door was opened. That agent shut the lights off. I saw Abdullah go to the rear of the ship and disappear down some stairs. Hyman took the stairs in front of the bridge and the other agent went to the front of the boat. I passed by the bridge and went down the front stairs thinking Rantisi would be somewhere below celebrating with his comrades, having no thought about what was soon to be his fate. At the bottom of the stairs I heard some voices in garbled Arabic and puff, puff, and puff, puff, puff and then silence. Behind me I heard a cocking of a pistol and a 'don't move' in Arabic followed by another puff, puff-puff-puff sound. The Shin Bat agent that had gone to the front of the boat seeing no one on the front deck had turned back to go down the stairs when one of the Hamas members appeared from a door just in front of the stairs and pointed his gun at my head from about twelve feet away. He dropped like a hundred pound sack of rice. His head was all over the wall to my right and some even hit my neck. I shivered.

I turned around to say thanks and he just nodded as he put his finger to his lips. We both listened. Nothing! And then there was struggling on the upper deck. We turned and went back up the stairs and then to the bridge. One dead Muslim on the floor bleeding profusely and one Rantisi bound and gagged. Hyman looked at his watch and said to Abdullah, "Not good, my watch says four minutes and eleven seconds. You guys are going back into training next month."

Abdullah responded, "Wait a minute there were three with this guy when I entered the galley, what have you been you doing?"

Hyman broke a neat little smile. "Just a joke guys." Then he turned to me and whispered in my ear, "You have thirty minutes after I place the explosive device. Then it is curtains. I would get on with your job now. We'll do our thing and you close the door."

I laid him down on the floor straddling his legs so with his hands bound behind him he could not move. Pulling him up by his shirt collar I spoke in Arabic as I started my interrogation. "You have been supplying Hamas in Gaza with guns and explosives." No comment. "I am from the States and we know that you have a steady supply of C4 coming out of Argentina or Uruguay or possibly Brazil or even all of them. I do not care about you or your operation; I want to know what you know about your friend Ahmad al-Masri."

"He is dead."

"We know that but what was his mission. He also trafficked in C4 but where did it go? Who did he have connections with?"

Rantisi broke with a smile from ear to ear, "You already know or you would not be here and associated with these Israeli pigs."

I took a hand full of his hair and pulled him half off of the floor, "No I don't; you tell me. Our Intel tells us that you and he were like brothers. Basically, he and you are exactly the same kind of terrorist; just that both of you stay out of the line of fire. Now tell me where did his contraband go?"

And again with a smile he taunted me with his answer, "To our Islamic brothers inside of your country for the coming Jihad. They have a great present for the United States, we call it Jihad candy, but you will call it great pain and destruction."

I pulled him back up off of the floor, "How many organizations did he sell to and how much C-4 do they have?"

"You go ask him! Oh, that's right he is dead so nobody knows. You'll find out when the time is right. Yes, repent before it is too late, before we destroy the serpent."

Hyman came back, "Melvin, finish up now, it's been eighteen minutes. Shoot him, we have to go."

"Throw me that tape and take your guns, I won't need them now." I am upset that now I had him but they wanted him dead and I still had nothing concrete. No not upset; I am mad. I taped off his mouth and then took his arms and taped them to the round post holding the captains chair. Around and around I wrapped the tape, he was not going anywhere. The Shin Bet said he had to die and I had to leave him.

As I went out the door I looked back and said, "You fool, you go to Hell." We left five minutes before the timers were going to set off the fireworks. The Israeli agents were quick and professional as we got off the boat and they said good-by in the same stoic manner; walking north while I disappeared into the shadows of the buildings running along side all of the docks. I knew exactly where I could stay for the night but I only got about five hundred meters or so before the freighter blew up. Even at that distance I was still knocked to the ground and a fire ball rose about two thousand feet in the air above the place where the freighter and all of its contents were now only a vapor cloud. Jumping up I ran straight ahead passing warehouses and a lean-too and old vacant flat roof buildings one after another until I reached the location of a deserted fishing boat that for a long time had been on dry dock blocks. I had seen it when I first arrived in Port Sudan and had passed by the docks on my way to the hotel. I knew it would be a perfect place for my refuge until Nastigie arrived in the morning.

I was up before five and walked about three hundred meters along the road that was used for ingress to this dock area. No one else was around at this time in the morning. From this vantage point I was able to look at the old warehouse and the freighter that had been docked for a number of months. It was where my contact was to arrive with transportation out of here and bringing this mission to a finale. Just as I was daydreaming about getting back to the States, a truck that I believed was Nastigie's truck was coming towards me. I edged back against the wall of the building to make the smallest silhouette and make sure it was Nastigie. "Melvin, get in, this has to be quick because there are patrols about everywhere since some ship blew up last night about two kilometers from here. There was a lot of destruction and according to the authorities on the TV there is not much left of the ship that blew up. You said that you were going to be busy last night. Did you have anything to do with that devastation? Don't answer, of course you did.

Your boat is here and I want to get out of here now. You are too hot. Give me the other six hundred thousand dinars."

Trusting and not trusting him I said, "Right, give me my bag and get on the boat. That was our deal."

"On the boat? Do you have the money or not? I will tell them to leave if not."

"You doubt me? Just what I suspected, no matter, I have the money inside of my bag that you had all of the time. Here, see the money is in the inside zipper pouch with my shorts now let's go to the boat together." After we stepped from the dock on to what was a semi- converted fishing boat with some nets and boom for trawling I walked from stem to stern and below to make sure this ride was going to be safe. Returning top side I gave Nastigie the money and gave him my hand in thanks. I knew he was not a Muslim but not knowing his religious background I added, "And may God be with you for all you have done." He turned and hopped on to the dock as the motor turned over a number of times prior to starting and the boat slowly inched away from the dock. I had finished and soon would be back with friends and family. The boat went south on the Red Sea and took me to Dijbouti south of Ekitkea where the agency had a private plane to take me to Germany to catch an Air Force transport filled with marines from Iraq returning to the States. On the flight out of Germany I was anxious to tell my wife Roselind I was headed home and to find out how she was feeling with our second child due shortly. I ask the pilot to get me an open line into the States so I could call my wife. "Hello darling its me your husband and I'm on my way home; how are you doing? What, What was that? Alright! Alright!..... Alright!...... Alright;" I let everyone know I was a father of a beautiful baby girl. Beautiful because Roselind told me so and mothers always know. HOO-RAH HOO-RAH HOO-RAH, all the Marines gave me a mission complete on this one.

Melvin return just after the forth of July with one more mission under his belt. He spent the weekend of the eighth and ninth with his family before returning to work. On Monday he entered the NSA building and passed by the cafeteria for a real cappuccino before heading to the debriefing section. It was the practice of all the people on the third floor to place a large placard in the cafeteria announcing the births of new babies of fellow employees so as he was paying for his drink he saw the poster of his new baby girl. And beside his baby girl's placard was the poster of Hank's baby boy. He thought to himself how wonderful new life was and how blessed he was. He had just been on a mission where death was the number one event. On his way he passed through the CI departments to say hello to his associates who had read the internal mission reports on NSA's secure e-mail pages and they were all handing out high fives for a successful mission.

It was about a month after Melvin had returned from Sudan and only a week since Jerry reappeared from his mission in South America. Jerry had gone dark in June after reporting in that he was going to all of the ports on Munoz's list looking for any evidence of the shipping of C4 to the States from Brazil and would not be able to stay in touch with central control in Hank's section at CI-4 so he came under Langley control. Hank had handed him off to the CIA control on orders from George when Jerry demanded that he go dark. The missions authorized by John Poles under the NSD issued some months before brought more direct confirmation that Hezbollah and Hamas cells had been able to get arms and explosives into the States but there was no Intel to provide any locations where the contraband might have come from or where it might be.

John Poles was heading to his office and eyeing the sky brightly lit with the early morning sun. Is it going rain today? August in Washington sucks, it is hard to tell what the weather is going to be. And the forecasts are either very hot and steamy or just plain hot or cloudy with rain storms and flooding proving the weatherman are from DC; just like the politicians there is no accuracy in their reporting. Oh well, the global weather was changing with no way of truly providing a preview of the coming climate near the Atlantic coastal region. He thought to himself hot or rainy. By afternoon probably both making the climate very steamy; not only on the streets of DC but in the OHS oversight committee meeting with Chairman Peter Wing who was a stickler for unadulterated reports laden with only facts and no fluff. There isn't anything fluffy about worldwide terrorism or about how deep terrorists may have embedded themselves into the United States.

As he drove he continued to review the meat of his report to the committee. The problem with these committee meetings is that NSA always has a lot of Intel to provide to the members of congress and reviews of the NSD directives but just like the investigations on the PFI's most of the investigations have either led to a kind of spider web to other sources to be investigated or to hearsay and therefore unsubstantiated information. The probability of weapons and explosives and WMD being in the States is over seventy five percent based on all of the data from the investigative missions the CI units have undertaken over the past six to eight months. He continued his mental salvo with himself sometimes moving his lips so that words actually came out. Granted we can provide a joint report from the FBI, CIA, and DIA with explicit details of our over two hundred arrests of accused fanatical Islamist and the number of plots we have derailed that were designed to destroy buildings and blow up tunnels, but as to the other more scary possibility concerning cells equipped with guns and massive amounts of explosives we still have not documented any solid facts and therefore I must go before the committee with a certain amount of fluff.

Entering the congressional building through the left wing I passed a busy array of reporters standing by the largest meeting room in this wing where the Armed Services committee was again rehashing the status of the Iraqi war and the immediate need for appropriations from congress for the next quarter. This has been and still is off budget. I couldn't help but muse to my self about what is the most important war; Iraq or World Terrorism! If we lose either one, we will lose them both. I arrived at the door to the meeting room where two Marine guards stood to keep unauthorized persons from entering the OHS oversight committee hearing. All information and records of these meetings are labeled with the highest classified rating and marked Top Secret.

"Mr. Chairman, honorable members of congress, and invited guest, our monthly report has been presented to each of you for perusal and you will note that NSA has in this report contributed additional details on the operation of known sleeper cells inside our borders and our invaluable information coming from Carnivore. As you know the President has been taking it on the chin both from the media and some in Congress on this program which has given us so much intelligence on the enemies within our borders and on SWIFT which has helped uncover the movement of money from both Hezbollah and Al-Qaeda sympathizers to money centers in Yemen, Abu Dhabi, Qatar, etc. I have with me our section chiefs from CI one through six and their updates on those groups activity here in the States and specifically identifying sympathizers who are at this very moment under surveillance, all of which you will find is well documented. They are prepared to answer any questions you deem appropriate and when they have finished and your questioning is over I would like to present a closing statement."

The hearing took a little over three hours which put us at eleven forty. "Mr. Chairman, we thank you for your astute questions, your input to our on going efforts to protect the citizens of our country and to the committee's acknowledgement that more must be done by OHS to shut down any detrimental operations of Hezbollah and al-Qaeda operatives inside the States and especially to provide security at our ports, the public transportation facilities, utilities such as water and power, and the list goes on. All of these items are on the table to be expedited by OHS; however, we can not wait and we need the immediate release of funds already allocated in the budget for these tasks because even though we have been given NSD directives to act on some of these fronts, we do not have the personnel or the facilities at this time. And this brings me to three current issues which I have saved for last."

'One, we have what we believe is reliable intelligence that arms and explosives have been smuggled into the States both on the West coast and the East Coast but we can not get enough manpower to go external to get reliable evidence for verification of this Intel or convince the FBI that they should start an immediate one on one investigation of all of the individuals we have in the Carnivore files that fit a profile of suspects as defined by Memo 03/02-IP1392. The problem for our sister agency is that first, they operate under a veil of condemnation of 'illegal profiling' and second, the data base has some four thousand seven hundred names of possible Muslim fanatics and because the agency is suffering from a shortage of manpower its ability to perform investigations which are needed now is considerably curtailed. Besides in many of their previous investigative efforts they have found that the high profile individuals they are looking for are always on the move with no permanent residence. That is why the numbers that has been arrested and are in jail is so small. And as you all know there are a far greater number, more probably tens of thousands of potential radicals in the States according to data brought to the 9-11 commission's attention, even though that number was not codified in the report.

Two, we have asked that congress authorizes an emergency

funding of port security from coast to coast since our ports are a sieve and they are the most likely opening for the entry of contraband into the States. Our borders may need to be closed to stop unwanted people from entering our country but our ports must be closed to the potential importing of contraband that can be used for damage and destruction to our country.

And third, we have received enough Intel from the missions authorized in the last NSA directive to warrant the complete review of all past incoming shipments through our ports for the last ten years, but with the limited personnel budgeted to this task it could take us through 2007 to complete the job. However if our Intel is accurate as I believe it is and can be confirmed by expediting the investigations on individuals that are both selected by Carnivore as outlined in my first point and then cross referenced with names on the receiving end of shipments specifically from Hong Kong and Brazil; then we will probably find the trail of one or more of these shipments and we can trace the final destination so that we can capture the perpetrators and uncover and capture their contraband. The theory here is that finding one strand of the web will lead us to the spiders nest'.

Now, as I continue; in June of last year a NSD was approved by the then Secretary Tom Rodgges and in December the CFR for a critical investigation of essentially the same three issues I just outlined came through to NSA for execution. Bureaucracy red tape or just plain other priorities, I do not know which has held up our funding and we feel that time is running out. What I do know is this. In fulfilling our duties and responsibilities, the direction my department must take on our fight against terrorism in our country is based on the following premise. A premise that I believe the congress should embrace and give credence to so that we are operating in unity; and that premise which I know is not in contention, is the fact that we are confronted by Islamic fascists who are hell bent on the destruction of the United States of America and most other free democratic societies. We need funding now! May I close by saying that you have an awesome responsibility to our nation and that I look forward to your response to this briefing on the status of funding from OHS and the urgency as viewed by the CI departments at NSA and my personal input as undersecretary, may God be with you all."

'Mr. Poles and fellow participants, we thank you for the reports, the insight into the need for more security and the candid breakdown you presented of our need to allocate the funding more rapidly plus your evaluation and summation on the real enemy within. You will receive our review and response in five days."

By September the committee chairman, Peter Wing signed and had delivered to the President and undersecretary Poles a finished twenty two page report form the August meeting in which Congressman Wing implored the President to immediately authorize additional money from the OHS budget to go to both NSA to expand its investigative staff and to the FBI to increase the number of field agents available to perform a PFI on all persons of interest in the Carnivore data base. He further requested the President call on the available National Guard members to be assigned to duty with the FBI in the Long Beach and Norfolk stations to speed up the investigation of the shipping documents from 1996 to present. Congress was currently working on legislation to give proper authority and funding to lock down the ports. The proposed bill would give OHS the ability to know what is in every incoming container even if the authorities needed to hold ships off shore to be certain of their contents. The legislation had extensive authority for the OHS to be allowed placement of customs agents in the ports of foreign countries if these countries were going to be allowed to trade with the States.

"Good morning Mr. President", a standard greeting by the staff, which was waiting to accompany George Cush in to the Cabinet Room where many of the daily briefings took place. "Here Mr. President is today's PDB and there are copies on the table for Chaney, Rice, Blumenthal, Berger, Stein, Smith, Podesta, and Stern and the other participants who will be attending." With a look of consternation Cush opened his folder and began, "Folks, we have a disturbing situation in Iraq today revolving around the media's statements that civil war is emanate and Col. Frank's reports that the insurgents have latched on to that postulate espoused by the liberal press to wage a propaganda barrage for recruitment of more foreign radicals to join the terrorist groups in Iraq. Further he states that they have more than tripled their attacks in Baghdad and Fallujah. I am asking for correct information on exactly what the status is as of today and a press release prepared to counter the media's deliberate effort to undermine this administration with counter productive news articles that only stimulate distressing feelings both for our troops and the Iraqi officials. John you run with this one. Any comments on this please meet with John to help smooth out public option. Next I want some camouflage brought in on this issue about the personal intrusion into the assumed privacy of suspected terrorists who are communicating overseas by using international phone calls, e-mails, wires transfers, and so on. If we did not maintain this type of surveillance on our potential enemies there is no telling what they maybe planning next. We must always be one step ahead of these bastards. This negative democratic rhetoric must be gotten under control. Todd I want you to go to congress and meet with Pete on the House Permanent Select Committee on Terrorism to help us clear this up and go on record for the media that everything is operating according to protocol. I have the authority under the War Powers act to eavesdrop on suspected enemies of the State and I want to keep them informed. Now, a side from the other items on the agenda I must go over the report from the Chairman of the OHS on a briefing that took place last week which has some disturbing information attached to it regarding existing sleeper cells which we have know about for some time but as the Intel suggests have been supplied with both arms and possibly explosives. The FBI has not reported any valid information on these accusations to the Whitehouse but the report quite correctly requests additional funding from the OHS budget to immediately implement three stages of investigation into the when, how, and where of all of this. Further the report is asking for congress to complete their legislation to put into operation a blanket of security around our ports of entry to prevent any kind of military implements of destruction from entering into our country. I agree with the Chairman's report and I want action taken on it immediately. Deliver copies of my confirmation of the request and copies of this report with all attached reviews to the appropriate department heads at the FBI, CIA, DIA, and JOCC."

"Mr. President, you are wanted for a moment in the Oval office."

"Please excuse me for thirty minutes; we will adjourn until ten thirty."

Dick Chaney announced that the President was unable to return and he finished the briefing instructing the aids to carry out the Presidents wishes.

Back at our section at NSA George called the top agents from CI units four, five and six to meet to review the details on some special assignments to begin the first week in October authorized by the NSD. George summarized the directive he had gotten from John Poles which had a Whitehouse stamp of approval under John's signature. Jerry and I were among the group of ten George had selected and four of the ten were our colleagues from unit six who had convincing Arabic appearances, slightly darker skin, black hair, and somewhat bigger proboscis.

I did not consider my self an experienced top counter intelligence agent so I privately queried George, "Why have you brought me into this group? How can I possibly add to any mission being planned with as little operational experience as I have compared to the others you have selected?"

"I will go over that in this meeting. Lady and Gentlemen"; George asked Ana to be part of the group because she was fluent in Spanish and had been an operative in a number of South American countries.

At the academy I watched some training films with her defending herself from two of the martial arts trainers and I thought at the time I would not want to come up against her in a confrontation. She had the speed and the moves of a banshee. I would partner with her any time.

George continued, "Our orders are indirectly from the President himself and the first assignment is to infiltrate certain pre-selected groups of Muslim organizations and operations which Carnivore identified as dangerous and of course our agents from unit six are getting this assignment." George passed each of those agents his sealed packet. "Our second assignment is to find out how weapons that maybe in the hands of sleeper cells of al-Qaeda and/or Hezbollah entered the country. Jerry here has been in South America returning a short time ago after uncovering more information on the when and how shipments have come into the States and will be the head of the group going to Florida. His undercover Intel causes us to believe that many shipments have come in by boat to Florida and just before the death of Rantisi, a close associate of al-Masri, Melvin who was in Sudan said that Rantisi virtually confirmed the Intel. Jerry will lead his team of three agents from CI-5 which includes Ana who will add the addition of her various language skills to the mission and their investigation will target every port and every dock in Florida." Pointing to Jerry's team George went on, "Somewhere, if there is evidence of weapons and explosives coming into Florida you are to talk to anyone and everyone that has the most minuscule lead to follow and then you will get hot on the trail of that lead. You have Carte Blanche and unlimited funds for this mission and carnivore should be a big help. You can use bribery, payoffs, and even force to complete you assignment."

George turned to Hank as he pointed to him and the last four agents. "Hank has been picked to go to the West Coast with the three of you from CI-4 and we are aware that he has less experience than you guys but we have our reasons for making him the lead person on this team. He was in Hong Kong to meet Mr. Gutung or aka Mr. Taug; who was the CIA's first point of contact by agent Jack Madden who as I believe you all know was a friend of Jerry and Hank and who was later killed on one of his missions trying to get more information on the alleged massive shipments of contraband to Long Beach. The first contact came from an unsolicited and anonymous phone call to our U S Embassy in Hong Kong from a Mr. Taug at which time he was paid $50,000 for information about container shipments to the States of automatic rifles, ammunition, and C-4. A clandestine investigation in Hong Kong of one container identified by Taug revealed absolutely nothing after completely unloading the container. All of this and the continuing investigations by Jack and the follow up by Hank here is available for you in your packet. Hank is convinced that Mr. Gutung's effort to have a second meeting with us and his insistent statements that shipments have come in to the West Coast ports was instrumental in influencing the OHS Oversight Committee to authorize this investigation.

CHAPTER TWENTY

Tartus, Syria November 11, 2005

"Is the yacht ready for our trip today"? Approaching the young boy who was standing next to the sixty foot Aristocraft as if he was guarding it from leaving the dock, Khalifa Abu Bakr asked the question again. "Is our ship ready to leave and is any one on board?"

A man with a skipper's cap on his head appeared from out of the door on the bridge yelling at the boy in Arabic to leave the dock area, and then he looked at the cleric and answered both questions. "If you are Abu Bakr then YES and YES. Please come up the steps and go into the salon. We are ready to leave for the port of Nicosta in Cypress where we will pick up the rest of your friends."

Somewhere off of the coast of Lebanon in the deep blue waters of the Mediterranean the Yacht 'Miraj' idled down to three knots per hour, just enough for the skipper to maintain control and the prestigious gathering to began their prayers to allah. It was noon and they had finished their greetings and their morning tea. Dr. Zawahiri arranged for the meeting of Brada, Abu, Musab, Jonathan, Yassir, Raed Hijazi, Mustafa Fadhil, Cleric Hassan Nasrallah, and Khalifa Bakr.

After prayers a setting of various fine foods was arranged on the dining table and a variety of fruit juices and sodas were available for lunch. As everyone was seated and Dr Zawahiri had thanked allah for the safe trip, the food and the attending brothers, he opened a computer to view his notes. "My brothers, allah is in control of our destiny and the world political atmosphere is perfect, the timing could never be better and the plan is now complete. The Cush war is destroying the morale of the American people and the insurgents are winning in every part of Iraq thanks to Syria and our faithful leader in Iran. As you have seen he has confronted the 'Snake' and they do not know what to do. Under direction of Cush the West will not talk to President Ahmadinejad and they do not dare to attack Iran. Many world leaders have condemned Cush and their country's military power wanes too thin with their troops entangled in Iraq. Iran will increase the insurgents in Iraq and they will continue to provide massive numbers of IED's which are destroying the American military in every area of the country and creating Iraqi disdain for the Americans because the IED's are also killing average Iraqi citizens. We must consider these unfortunate deaths that make these blessed citizens Shaheeds. Now let me go to the details of why we are gathered here at this time. We believe that the time has arrived to outline our leaders Miraj and to be briefed on the general plan for the destruction of the United States and ultimately the rest of the western world. They will not be able to stand. Brother Khalifa Ali Abu Bakr is here from bin Laden's camp to give us the basic outline and Raed Hijazi will fill in as much detail as can be offered at this time. First here is Abu Hindi."

"In the name of allah and with the al-Salawaat of the great prophet I greet you with this report. We have been able to finance the operations known as 'Ball Buster' and 'Over-ground Death' in the United States in preparation for the final judgment against the Infidels. We have been able to buy all of the required vehicles, guns and ammunition and explosives and Brada and Musab have reported that everything and everyone is in place. They will explain later. We have provided enough money for all of our people and their families so they can leave when the country falls. We provided off shore accounts for our cell leaders in the States and along with the operation of our insurance company, our Florida boat dealership, and our Land n Sea dealers we have made enough money to help finance our internal operation and provide money to the 2,300 cell members who are trained and ready. Here is Brada, Yassir and Musab."

Brada opened with his report spot lighting the cell leaders and the devoted members. "Musab will describe how we have been able to protect our brother's identity and still be able to arm them. Yassir along with Saja, who could not be here, have visited the cell leaders from coast to coast and Yassir has the follow assessment of our readiness." Yassir turned in his chair so he could look directly at Dr. Zawahiri. "I bring what I believe is the most important report of all. As Saja and I traveled to meet our cell leaders we were able to also meet with many of our brothers in the different cells who are committed to our cause. I am reporting that we have a complete unity of the faithful to allah, a al-Tauhid. Less than half have families to get ready for evacuation if required. Here is Musab." "My report is short but important. I believe everyone knows that the last boat with C4 arrived from our plant in Brazil and the plant has been closed down. Everything that was there has been removed and destroyed and last month it was burned down. Jonathan will discuss more on this. All of my ATV dealers have received their last shipment and we have taken great care to distribute the explosives and guns to the 20 cell distribution centers in a proportional amount for each area that will be needed for the attack. Many of these storage areas are very small buildings that we have bought under American names. Buying with no financing, allowed us to not need social security identification and so we could use any name we selected. Only our cell leaders know about the locations. We have also placed a small amount of C4 and a few guns in rented storage units in about 10 major cities as a diversion in case any OHS investigation concluded that a terrorist group under their microscope was planning sabotage or suicide bombings and they knew that a place to store materials would be needed. So we provided these storage areas as a distraction."

Brada concluded the report on the cells by adding, "As you have heard, the cells are ready, the leaders are ready, and our dedicated Muslim brothers have been patient and are ready. The announcement to all of them that the battle is on the horizon will be great news to all. We have gone to great efforts to guide them and have them stay hidden from the investigative eyes of the OHS. The protocol for the use of cell phones has been our best tool for our protection. And as all of us have learned the U.S. government administration has been eavesdropping on every method of telecommunications for a number of years. Even though the authorities in the States have interrogated a few of our brothers; I have a count of fifty four, they were all released. As the operational orders required; each of them left the country so as to not provide any clues of our operation and any links to other brothers. Beware of their implementation of the new program 'Black World' with a super search engine called Echelon which traps everything. Raed will bring all us up to date on all future communications to each cell leader. Jonathan has something to say."

"My brothers, I salute you on the organization and achievement that has been made on the plans of our leaders through the inspiration of bin Laden and the organization of Hezbollah. To add a few details at this time not only was the plant in Brazil destroyed but I closed the Florida Fast Boat dealership three months ago and destroyed all records of the boats imported to Miami. Only the boats in the hands of the DEA are accounted for. There of course are other boats that were sold to people in the Eastern part of the States but no records exist. The other boats needed for the attack are in a safe place at the locations of our targets and the rest have been disassembled for the C4 packed in the hulls. All of that was completed sometime ago and the C4 delivered to the storage centers, as Musab explained. We have left no trace of the boats or who has them."

Dr. Zawahiri motioned towards Raed. As Raed got up he asked if anyone wanted a drink while he poured himself a cool glass of pomegranate juice. As each responded he fixed a drink for them before outlining as much of the operation as was necessary at this meeting. "As we can all see the vision of Hezbollah and al-Qaeda is soon to be realized. We have the Mu'min, the fighters for the battle against satan. We have the equipment and supplies. We have a plan which can not fail. And we have the cause of allah our prophet. I have orchestrated the plan and reviewed all of the selected targets which when destroyed will bring the United States to its knees; leaving the people begging for help, for food, for water and forgiveness. Each of the cell leaders will be given their targets two days before the attack and the number of individual fighters needed to destroy each target to carry out their mission. The vehicles, the guns, and the C4 will be distributed the day before the attack with each attack beginning the next day at five am on the East coast and one hour earlier in each of the remaining three time zones. The successful test run of 9-11 shows us the inability for the monstrous size of the Cush government to anticipate our attack, to make conclusive decisions, or to respond to a crisis. They are flawed and that is our added weapon. During the coming months the cell leaders are to never communicate concerning our mission or our operation on cell phones. Make sure all conversations on telephones either in English or Arabic are trivial. You are to instruct all of our people to buy phone cards and call the computer in Yemen from public phones or phones belonging to someone they do not know. At the time appointed you will be told the web site to go to get your final instructions. As our manual has instructed, the leaders are to use a computer in a library, school, Internet café or Kinko's in the final days. The plans and targets for each group will be sent on the web site. Hassan wants to encourage our coming fight with news about the battle in our homelands. Please Hassan take my chair so you can be more comfortable."

Hassan started very slow in Arabic with a deep throated inflection. "We fight the Infidels everywhere, we fight the Zionists with suicide bombers who are dedicated to allah, and we even fight unbelievers in our midst. Hezbollah with the help of money from Iran and rockets and weapons is soon going to go to battle the Jews from the south of Lebanon. The great Mahmond Ahmadinejad knows the Jews must be eliminated before the East has peace and the land that is ours is returned to the Arab nations. We have sent many good brothers to your cause in the States over the past ten years and they too are well trained and anxious to start the fight. As we cause ciaos in the East and other countries you will have less critical eyes on what you are preparing. We have disasters planned for many areas around the world until the word is given to strike. I have seen the plans and you will not fail. Before Dr. Zawahiri speaks to you again I would like to offer to all of our brothers this prayer. 'allah blesses the Shia, allah blesses the Wahhabis, allah blesses the Jihad, allah wants a Fatah, Innaa Lillaahiwa Innaa Ilayhi Raajioon!' Go in peace as we will all part tomorrow."

Zawahiri stood up and first bowed slightly to his brothers and then kissed each four times before his last affirmation. "I leave you with my commander bin Laden's words, 'we have won because this is a fight not of politics, not of economics, but of ideology; the good against the evil. And allah has prophesied that our good will win! Let us now take prayer and then eat."

Tiama and Hank were enjoying the baby Tank trying to crawl on the floor in the small family room as the fire in the fireplace provided a charming ambience to off set the chill of the December evening. "Honey let's not go anywhere this Christmas and instead invite a few friends in for Christmas eve and have a nice eggnog and buffet diner; and of course ask Dad and Caroline with Grandma to come here to

Washington to spend the holidays. We have enough room with the sleeper here in the family room."

"Can Tank come too? Just kidding. Sure. I really do not feel like traveling. I'll call Dad tomorrow from the office. We have not swapped stories for a while like the Media's prospective on Cush, the War and who is ahead politically; especially their misinformation on the growth of terrorism."

"Oh stop it and come over here next to me and the warm fire. You want to try for a playmate for Tank? You know maybe he will need a sister to sooth the Tank if he gets hurt in battle."

I crawled next to her and gently rested her head on the pillow we kept by the fireplace and began to stroke her hair. Kissing her on the ear I whispered loving words to her as I stroked her beautiful full length hair. Her hair shined and glistened in the light of the fire as I moved the strands back and forth. Stroking and stroking her ever so gently. Tank had fallen asleep and so I stroked, and stroked and stroked most of the night.

Thursday morning I called Dad from the office around 9:00 am and the station operator said that he was busy but I could talk to his secretary. "Sure, put me through to her. Hello Maria it is Hank, can you have Dad call me when he gets a chance?"

"I will let him know when he gets off of this call to the Whitehouse. How are you and the family, and that human milking machine, Tank?"

"We are all fine, thank you for asking. Tell Dad I will be in the office until noon."

Ten minutes later Dad called, "What's up son?"

"Well Tiama is thinking that with baby Tank still a hand full and since traveling is not his best talent at this time; she feels that we should stay low and keep the holidays here in DC. She is planning a Christmas Eve gathering and wanted me to make sure and ask you and Caroline and of course Grandma to joint us for a few days. How does that sound?"

"Are you kidding? I would not miss my Grandson's first Christmas for all the TV ratings or Emmys in the world. I think we can come down on Thursday the 22nd but I'll call next week to let you know or better yet I need to be in Washington tomorrow for a few hours for a press briefing with Rummey at the DOD on the crisis developing in Iraq, so maybe I can call after that and firm up the day with you then."

USA: THE SERPENT IS CRUSHED!

Two PM Friday, December Fifteenth - Press Room in the Pentagon.

"Ladies and Gentlemen of the Press, here is Secretary Rummey."

"Good afternoon. The President has asked me to request this news conference to go over the latest on the situation in Iraq and the insurgency. We have been making headway on routing out those that are determined to undermine the elected government of Iraq and take away those good citizen's efforts there to become a free people. As you have been told by President Cush it is his hope that the world community will embrace the struggle taking place in Iraq and come to the aid of the Iraqi people's sacrifice to secure their own destiny and have the freedom deserving of all human beings. However, as many of you have been predicting in your news reporting that a civil war is imminent between the Sunnis and the Shia, it is in the opinion of our intelligence department here at the DOD that all you are doing is enticing the terrorist insurgents and therefore aiding and abiding the enemies of our country and our citizens. First I must ask you to look at this fuel you are thro on the fire and reconsider your own politically driven propaganda to see the effects you are having on our people, our troops, and the enemy. If you are uncertain about the facts then go to Iraq and see what the people there are doing to secure their own future and their individual efforts to build a free country. Different than ours YES; but none the less a country free of an oppressive dictatorship.

Now whether it has been your left activism in the press or just the encouragement you have bestowed on Iran to step up its efforts to create a civil war in Iraq, I must say that we are possibly on the verge of a crisis there. We know where the increase in numbers of insurgent fighters are coming from and where they are getting their backing and IED's and other military armament but what is important, do you know where the real problems effecting the success in Iraq are coming from? IF YOU DO THEN REPORT IT and back our country and our loyal military personal. But if you don't know the real facts then first, get over there and find out the truth so that you don't pervert the news any more. Let me tell all of you reporters one thing about the truth; IT IS AS STAIGHT AS AN ARROW AND AS SHARP AND CUTTING AS A SUSI CHEFS KNIFE! WHILE ON THE OTHER HAND THE TWISTED WORDS OF THE SPIN MASTERS IS LIKE A WET NOODLE HANGING IN THE WIND. And second, you need to know this; 'Where there is no justice, where poverty is a common way of life, where people are denied any education, and when a down trodden class of people believe that the society they live in is designed to oppress and degrade them then no one is safe; not the moderates, not the religious, not the down trodden, not the liberators and not even the radicals.' The terrorist fascists know this and are using this common logic against our efforts in Iraq. And now last as you undermine our efforts in Iraq you are strengthening the terrorists that are hidden and are undercover here in our country. YES, we know they are here and you are energizing them with your rhetoric and bull shit. But here is what you do not know or I guess just do not remember; they are careful planners and can organize as well as any General or CEO. Their missions are well planned and the participants may only know what is their own personal task and any failure by one will not effect the success of another, Now this is the kicker, remember they are not military people but they are terrorists and terror is their game. We have exposed plans to blow up bridges, airport facilities, buildings, tunnels, and even individual suicide attacks in shopping malls; so where do all of you stand? Have you forgotten 9-11? Cush is not your enemy; the enemy is your enemy. Recognize who they are and be straight with the citizens with whom you live. Al-Qaeda and Hezbollah want all of us destroyed, even you. Better that we fight them over there than over here! Good afternoon and we ask you for honest and true journalism." Some clapped but most walked out calling the secretary a demagogue.

Tom called Hank after the news conference to go over the holiday plans and invite Tiama, Hank and Tank to have diner before he headed back to New York. "Hello Tiama, its Tom and I just finished my business here in DC, did Hank tell you I was going to be in town?"

"No, but he will be home soon, He is picking up some diapers for me."

"Well, That's always important. I have an idea, why don't you guys meet me for diner at Morrison House and I'll just stay over and go back to New York in the morning. I'm about ready to send my report back to my director so he can make the six o'clock news and when I am finished I'll call back and see if my offer is OK with my grandson, Tank."

"I'm sure it will be just fine with him and by then Hank should be home."

"Great."

This cell phone always has problems inside the Pentagon. Ring. Ring. Ring. "Hello this is the United Broadcasting production department, my I help you?"

"Yes, this is Tom Brayden, who is scheduled to be in the news production department for the evening news?" One minute Mr. Brayden I am not sure since it is almost time for the five o'clock news and the production staff has finish that production and stepped out for a bite. Or I mean they went to the cafeteria but I will connect you to Miner who is setting up for the six o'clock news."

"Okay, I can talk to Miner."

"Hello Miner speaking can I hel......."

"Hello Miner this is Tom Brayden."

"Oh good evening Sir, how can I help you?"

"I am going to send over on my Blackberry the review of the news conference Rummey held this afternoon at the Pentagon so it can go on the six o'clock news. Please take it to who is charge of the production for the Six O'clock news and see to it that it gets first or second headlining."

"Yes Sir."

"Hello Hank, its Dad. How are you?"

"A little tired Dad, how are you?"

"The same but I could stand a little dinner, a shot of scotch and a visit with Tank."

"I'm with you on that and Tiama did say something about dinner, I guess it is alright but I think Tank has gone to sleep on us. Still want to visit him."

"Absolutely, I called Morrison House and got us a reservation for four. Can you be there in thirty minutes?"

"Sure we are on our way, but I think you mean reservations for three and half?"

Hank drove into the hotel parking lot and asked the valet to park the car. Tiama had dressed little Tank in warm clothes and she had a baby blanket to protect him from the winter winds, but Hank wanted to be right at the front door so the cold December air could not give his son his first winter sniffles. The walk from the parking lot was too far to take the chance and from day one Hank had been over protective. As the Valet was parking the car they went into the lobby and then to the restaurant looking for Tom.

"Sir, may I help you? Do you have reservations?"

"Yes you can, we are looking for my father, Tom Brayden and he said that he had made reservation for us, are we early?"

The maître d' could not have looked more the part of the head of a fine East coast restaurant; black tux, white gloves, and elegance only found today in the places of the gathering of the rich and famous. "Messier Brayden has not arrived yet but his company called and secured the reservations. May I take you to his table while you wait?"

"Of course." Immediately after seating us a waiter came to ask if we would care for something to drink and if we would be having wine to go with our diner then appropriately he open the folded napkins and gently placed them on our laps. Tank had already gone back to sleep and did not need has napkin.

I nodded yes on the wine question and then asked Tiama what she wanted. "Bailey's and coffee, I'm cold."

"And for you sir?"

I glanced around to look at the other tables as if that would help me decide on a drink. Stammering a bit I finally came up with a brain storm, "You know just bring me a plain Dewar's and soda tall."

Tiama reached over and poked me in the side, "Great monumental decision, just kidding. I think the maitre d' is directing Dad to our table. Yes, it is him."

Tom was smiling as he usually did when he saw his new grandson. Nodding to the maitre d' Tom said thank you and then looked into the bassinette, "Hello Tank, and how are my daughter and son doing? Are you taking care of them?"

"I can answer that, we are doing fine except now the wind chill has dropped to around ten degrees or so and with flue season here we have to watch out for colds. I thought that I noticed some snow flurries as we came in. Is it snowing yet?"

"My news room says yes on Long Island and the first major storm is heading inland and to the South, so I think it will be a white weekend in DC."

"Dad, Tiama and I were thinking, this is a very expensive place to eat and kind of out of our budget. Can we just have a drink or two and an appetizer?"

"Nonsense, this one is on me and I wanted you to see some of the places our royal family of government representatives spend our tax dollars. Right, wrong, or who cares; it is important to get a complete perspective of the workings of this monster you now work for."

"I have never been here before and I doubt that ninety nine percent of our people at OHS have frequented this or any other ultra expensive restaurant in the DC area!"

The waiter approached and as he deposited our drinks on the table he asked Dad for his choice of beverage. "I'll take a Chavez on the rocks with a splash."

"Yes Sir."

Son, you didn't order for me, I'm surprised. Oh well back to our DC aristocracy. How many work at OHS with all of its sections? Forty thousand or so and one percent or 400 enjoy the good life paid for by the public and most of them are in DC. Take the other vast number of government departments and agencies; or no, that number will boggle the mind, let's take the over seven hundred representatives to congress and their top aids. They have all of the people's money they need to enjoy this good life. Sorry you are on the proletariats side of life."

"Dad, I'm kind of astonished by your comments; what has gotten into you tonight? Why so hard on the Washington establishment? After all you are here footing the bill and have actually spent the last twenty years of your life as part of the upper crust. It doesn't seem like you Dad, something has triggered this."

"Hank honey, maybe Dad is a little tired and wants to just unload a bit; after all it is Friday night."

Tiama, always the cool head. "You're right, I am sorry Dad just seemed to me that these comments are not normal for you."

Tom broke a smile and motioned to the waiter, "Hey let's eat and talk about the coming holidays and my grandson Tank. Maybe after dinner possibly over a brandy I'll explain."

Tiama was first to ask for an after dinner drink. "Hank can I have a small Galliano?"

"Sure and I'll take a coffee black and a snifter of Courvoisier. Dad, are you having anything else and can you tell us what caused the chastising of our government leaders?"

"Well I think I'll pass on another drink and just stay here at the hotel for the night. It's too late to head back to New York. This afternoon I attended a news conference requested by the President which included Secretary Rummey and listened to him blast our news media for hijacking the real truth in their reporting and misguiding the citizens of our country with their left influence on most all political subjects, on all of the current foreign affairs operations and on the Whitehouse's policies in dealing with the war in Iraq, the Iranians, the continual attacks on Israel, and the Koreans. He had to remind the attending reporters that as they kept spinning and twisting the news to fit their own agenda they were in effect giving strength to our enemies all over the world and especially to those that are inside of our country. He told them to go to Iraq and to go into the cities and talk to the thousands and thousands of people who are happy that they are no longer under bondage even though their life is not back to normal: then report the truth. Take pictures of the good that is happening which overwhelms the trouble spots. And of course I am certain that we at UBC have tried to be honest in our reporting. I was one that stood up and clapped for his effort to bring truthful reporting to the airways. My blame is on some of our government officials and representatives for their pandering to the press and the politicizing of their personal agendas in complete disregard of the will and desires of the citizens of this country. The liberal press takes their side in every instance and the public gets only one side. That kind of control of people's thinking is more than dangerous it will be the destruction of our country and our sovereignty. And therefore I call them the DC nobility or better than that the aristocracy who with total arrogance taught themselves to believe that they, out of three hundred million Americans, are the only ones with wisdom. They come to Washington and spend the people's money and live lavish lives and look in the mirror admiring how great they are as they burn the very foundation that is the underpinning our nation. They believe they are the upper crust"

Tom took a moment to look at Tank, and Tiama and then Hank, "Sorry but I had to admire Rummey on this one even though there have been many mistakes made in the past four years by his group, those that criticize would have made many mistakes too. I could win every past game by looking at the Monday morning replays. As you look around there are those that enjoy this lifestyle because they have worked hard and they have earned it and they deserve it. I believe that if you work hard and produce admirable things for society you deserve excellent rewards. Most in here probably fall into that category. That's all; I'm off of my soapbox."

"Off of you're what?" Tiama was puzzled.

"Honey, that is just a euphemism. It means that he will stop preaching."

"Dad there is a lot I am not allowed to talk about but I can say that we need powerful supporters of finding and fighting the terrorists where ever they are and who ever they may be. As to Rummey saying that the press has on many occasions electrified the radical Islamist is true based on all of our intelligence. We feel like those that are in our country are a powder keg waiting to explode with the fuse already lit. There are some intense investigations going on now and authorizations to step up all phases of internal investigations from coast to coast before it is too late. There will be news coming out soon from the President about these internal terrorist problems and we believe that within six months we will be on Red Alert for many months. I can't say more than that but as the weeks go by UBC can help keep the flag waving, patriotic bent incorporated into the news on our war on terrorism. We will need it."

"OK, enough. Let's see what the Christmas plans are. Hank said that you guys would love to come down for a few days from the twenty second on so if that is firm I will get the house all ready for you, Caroline and Grandma. We have plenty of room and I want to take Tank's first Christmas pictures with family around. Hank told me that he will be gone most of January on assignment on the West coast so to have some company over the holidays will help take the lonesomeness away that's coming in January."

Hank looked at Tom as he edged next to Tiama, "Dad do you think Caroline would like to stay through January and keep Tank and Tiama company? I'm sure she would like the help with the baby and the shopping and what ever else might come up."

"I'll bet she would, give her a call tomorrow and see. The check is paid and I'm ready for some sleep. Let me say good night to Tank and I'll walk you guys to the front."

"Goodnight Dad and thanks for the great meal, we'll see you all on the Twenty Second, say around one or so in the afternoon."

Out the front door Hank wrapped Tank tightly in his little baby blanket and headed to the car. The Valet parked it as close as he could to the door but with the wind gusting Tiama had to grab his arm to keep from sliding on the thin layer of snow that had fallen while they were having dinner. In the car Tiama clutched her little boy in her arms as she turned to Hank. "Thank you for inviting Caroline to stay with me while you will be on assignment. I was worried that I would be a little frightened and even full of anxiety with you being gone."

"Don't worry Hon I will be doing routine work with our people on the West Coast."

CHAPTER TWENTY ONE

December 20, 2005

Jerry and one of his assigned CIA partner Jeff Howell were in the briefing room opening the mission file containing all of the HUMINT compiled on the assignment to Brazil when George came in with a supervisor from the IMGINT section and carrying a classified memo from the Agencia Brazilian de Intelligencia in Brazil.

"Jerry and Jeff, we have an extremely important bit of Intel from our counterpart in the Brazilian government and some of our satellite imagery confirming their report. It appears that a few months ago a boat manufacturing plant in the port city of Belem was burned to the ground'.

"Belem! George, that was one of the cities on Munoz's list where he said that he had shipped C-4 for al-Masri."

"Well hold that thought, this gets better. The report shows pictures of the remains which are nothing but ashes. And the satellite photos show the entire event as the plant was destroyed. Our experts have scrutinized each still photo and identified observers that are clearly there to see that nothing was left. You can see that, when the firefighters left, those images that are about fifty meters to the southwest stay for three more hours looking at the ruins with what looks like binoculars. Now of course this would not really be so unusual had the observers been the owners or even concerned employees. But the Belem fire investigators made the following report and then gave it to the police. It has been translated for us and the report is in both English and Spanish"

George prompted them to take note of the statement in the second paragraph. 'Upon investigation the Agencia de Investigasion de Fuego has determined that the fire at the Grupo Rizzo boat manufacturing plant was purposely set. The owner one Jonathan al-Aziz can not be found and Brazilian immigration has no record of him leaving the country.'

"Please read on to see why this has far reaching consequences." 'After our AIF agency's request to find key personnel from the plant; the police were successful in locating and interrogating three persons who were able to shed some light on the reason the plant was destroyed. One person was the accountant and is an immigrant from Pakistan who handled all of the buying of supplies and payroll and said that the owner al-Aziz maintained complete security on the plant and that no one else had access. Further the accountant told police that on many occasions al-Aziz would work in the plant all night with a special crew over the weekends just before they would complete the interior finishing of certain select boats. The owner told the accountant that these were special order boats for the DEA in Florida. While he thought it a little strange he passed it off as trivial and besides he was being paid twice what he could earn with any other company. But after the plant stopped making boats he stopped by on a Friday and al-Aziz was alone in the plant. All of the past employees were gone. He says that this guy al-Aziz was destroying all of the records from the office and everything was piled in the center of the plant, frames, tables, tools, etc. According to the interrogation he told the police that al-Aziz was polite to him but quickly escorted him from the plant saying that the U.S. DEA had told him to destroy everything. That night the plant burned to the ground.'

"Okay you guys, now keep reading; this is where it gets really intriguing." 'The investigators took the names of two of the supervisors the accountant named and with the police department's help brought them back to Belem and after continued interrogation they learned that al-Aziz paid a lot of money to them on the day before the fire to dismantle the plant and pile everything in the center of the plant with all of the chemicals stacked at the bottom. He told them he had to burn the plant to the ground. There could not be any evidence of the boat factory left standing. They also said that because al-Aziz was always doing something in the plant in secret maybe involving drugs they didn't think twice about his request to take the plant apart. They said that they did not care and they just were not concerned.'

"They still have the three in jail awaiting further investigation for conspiracy to commit arson. So who is this Jonathan al-Aziz and why did he say the DEA wanted special boats and then they wanted him to destroy his boat plant? And why did the two detainees in jail in Brazil say they thought al-Aziz might be into drugs. Where this goes you will have to find out but if it is drugs and not contraband then turn that part over to the DEA to work with their own agents. Listen both of you, your mission has changed and the two of you will go to Brazil and Ana and her partner will handle the Florida mission. You will be working with the ABI agents in Brazil to find out the answers to these questions and whether there is any tying together the boats in Brazil with the shipping of armament to the states. This investigation is operating under a NSD authorization, so go deep into this with answers back as soon as possible. You are scheduled to leave the day after New Years."

"George this must be it! It ties together! We don't need to go to anywhere in Brazil but Belem. It is boats delivered to the U.S, this coincides with Melvin's report from Rantisi, but the DEA, what is that all about?"

Hank had to spent the first week of January in the office setting up the new procedures for the review of all of the previously stored 'incoming shipping packets' that were stored at the customs office in San Diego attached to the Navy supply depot building on Harbor Drive. Going over to Jerry's office he passed by Melvin's office.

"Hi Hank, how is the Tank 'Varooom' doing?" Melvin kidded him about using a mixture of the kid's Grandfather's name and his own to get T-ank, but he kind of thought that it was rather cool. "Did you get a look at the Intel Jerry and George went over on that burned down boat manufacturing plant in Brazil? He's all over this Intel like a kid in Toys-R-Us after the employees have all gone home. I think he and some one from the CIA is leaving this week for Brazil. If you pass over to his section I'm sure you'll get the buzz and his excitement. He thinks he has found the way the terrorist have been bringing in explosives which totally confirms his past missions and puts credibility on what I felt when talking to Rantisi just before the ship blew up."
"No, but I'll stop by now."

"Hey Jerry, I missed the satellite Intel on the boat plant in Brazil, but I hear you may be on to something that can give our CI units real evidence on terrorist armed with guns and explosives to take to the boss, Mertoff. You're leaving tomorrow, right?"

"No, today," as Jerry gave me the report to look at.

"Man I think this is awesome. My gut tells me that you are on the fringes of breaking all of the past rumors wide open so we are all with you and your new partner. Verifying this Intel with names and places and you'll have what you need to get to the contraband before it's too late. I'd love to be around while you're in Brazil but I'll be on the West coast. Oh, I didn't tell you, pick up on this, I was rehashing that mission that Jack was on to Jakarta when he got killed. First, you know I'm conducting the detail review or I mean I am supervising the detail review of the archived documents pertaining to all incoming container shipments over the past ten years which unfortunately is moving like a snail in a lake of molasses."

"I believe you; you need to have more people and fewer papers to look at. You'll be there till, I don't know Christmas after next Christmas."

"Well, I was going over the files of your first mission with Jack to Hong Kong, then the file on Jack's second trip which includes his report from the field and the investigation of his killing, or at least what there was of that investigation. And then it hit me like a Monster Truck Rally at a field of Toure de France bicycle riders. It was right there all of the time and I missed it."

"Missed what? What? I was on the first mission with Jack and we could not make anything verify anything else!"

"No, you don't get it. It is right there. I do not need to have all of the archived shipping packets reviewed with a 'fine tooth comb' as it were. I am setting a new procedure and by next week we will be going at warp speed through those packets."

"Okay, great, so what is this new procedure?"

"Easy, all my people need to do is open the packets and look for one thing. SIND/POLB with a Blue strip."

"What the heck is SIND/POLB and why a Blue str.... OH MY GOD. Sumatra-Indonesia and Port of Long Beach, the container with the Blue strip, I forgot. Of course, the identifying markings on the container Taug said had the guns and explosives. Just locate that packet and run a delivery tracer and you have found what Taug said was a container with contraband for the terrorists in the States."

"And don't forget that when I went to Hong Kong to meet him as Mr. Gutung he did not change his story one iota. He said that his information was as accurate as any we have ever received and that some how we made a mistake."

"Well, all along Jack thought that there had to have been a second container at the docks in Hong Kong with the same makings as the one Taug pointed out since the terrorist knew that Taug was an informant and as we now know they tried to kill him. He must have been right and they quickly used a dummy set up that was ready for just such an investigation. Fully loaded with ATV's and motorcycles just waiting to be used as a decoy! Now my guts tell me you are one hundred per cent correct and have you told George yet?"

"No, I'm going to wait till I am ready next week with the procedures in place and all proper protocols ready so that we can get these bad guys now. I think we are both as close to finding the Islamic Fascists as Cush calls them as we could ever hope for. And don't forget I now have a very short time line to work with; January, 2001 when you and Jack went to Hong Kong through September 11, 2001 when the attack on the Towers took place. I think the shipment would have arrived before 9-11 and after that no more shipments."

"Buddy, you've got it and we got them. Go get this done. I will get my target by the end of January if not sooner and we will both celebrate by taking our wives to, well where ever they want to go and Tank too. We are going to bust this "Operation Open Sesame' wide open."

"So 'good hunting' to you and Jeff. I'm going to be in San Diego next week. I'll check in with CI information section to see how you are doing and if you get a chance you do the same from Brazil. See you at the end of the month and God speed buddy."

"Thanks and the same to ya!"

Jerry and Jeff landed in Belem on a Brazilin helicopter belonging to ABI and were driven to the police department which was fairly close to the docks and only about six kilometers from the Groupo Rizzo boat plant or actually the remaining ashes of the plant. Once inside the building they were met by the day watch commander, Bastian Hernandez who escorted them to a small office next to the chief's office. Commander Hernandez offered each of them a bottle of water and then explained that the chief had an appointment with his wife to take their daughter to a school play and was sorry he could not be present to give you the unfortunate information.

"Unfortunate information! What information? Do you have some kind of bad news?" Jerry asked.

Bastian was a little hesitant to answer since he could see the strained look on face of the investigator from the CIA.

Jerry continued, "What has happened? Did they kill them selves? Did they escape? What is going on?"

"Well no senior, they are not here. We kept them as long as we could but with no direct evidence their lawyer got them a release from the court. It works like that here. We could not stop it."

This had Jerry fairly up tight, "Where are they? Have you kept surveillance on them?"

"Yes, with certainty the ABI has them, how do you say 'locked in their sites'. We tracked them to Rio de Janeiro and the Rio ABI picked them up just after their arrival there to answer a few questions according to the bilateral 'Terrorist Memorandum under article 1145 of the United Nations' but they did release them just as we had to. They are currently living on a boat in one of the harbors in Guanabara Bay. But we are told that they are not sure that they are still on the boat. According to our contact at ABI there has been no movement for the past two days."

That did it, Jerry let lose on Bastian, "Then why the Hell did your agents from ABI bring us all the way to Belem when the people that I want to interrogate are in Rio?"

"Because they felt that you may want to investigate the scene and ask around the area for people who may have some information for you even though it might be vague."

"People in the area, vague information, didn't you do any direct interviews with witnesses or locals to find out what was going on at Groupo Rizzo?"

"Yes of course we did but our investigation was into arson and not what you are asserting. We had no evidence along those lines so we confined our questions and interviews towards the idea of arson."

"Can you get us to Rio muy pronto? And give us exact locations of the harbor, the place where the boat is now, any dock or berthing identification numbers, the name of the boat or registration number and the agent in Rio who is in charge of the case?"

"Yes, I will let you look at what ever we have in their files and then ask the ABI to have the helicopter take you to Rio tomorrow if they are still available. But you know it is a long trip."

"Still available nothing; I want confirmation on all of this now including the chopper!"

San Diego provided the excellent weather for Hank that it was known for. January and no clouds with a slight breeze coming across Harbor Drive and a chilling seventy four degrees; my kind of town he thought as he parked his government car in the security lot next to the customs building. On the elevator to the forth floor a shapely dressed female Navy Officer kept looking at him and he had to say Hi, but he mainly just looked at his leather folder embossed with OHS and the OHS government insignia so as to not gaze at this super pretty and stunning woman in her Navy uniform.

Getting off of the elevator he filled his mind with a vision of Tiama and his son in her arms so that he could absolve himself for looking at the female officer but he did take a last glance at her. There is nothing wrong in admiring beauty when you see it he thought; provided it is not accompanied with lust. What kind of mind trip am I on, only gone from home for twelve hours? My wife is beautiful and I love her, I love my son and I love my work. This is a wonderful day and a wonderful country; I'm here to do all I can to protect everything about our life in the United States so 'get to work Hank'!

As I knocked on the door marked Customs – Secure Records Room a clerk I had never seen before opened the door and asked to see my badge. I showed her my OHS badge and ID card where upon she said, "Oh, hello Mr. Brayden. Jocelyn has been waiting for you. She is in the back of our storage area setting up to reorganize the review process per the orders she received yesterday from your CI unit at NSA."

Walking down the isle of ten foot high storage racks I came to the work area set up to implement my special packet review system. "Hello Jocelyn, how have you been?"

"Actually, very well Hank."

"I think the tedious chore of going through ten years of documentation on shipping containers received at our West coast ports is about to draw to a close. Please take a few minutes and sit with me while I expand on the orders you received for the new procedures to complete our review task.'

"Would you like a drink or some water?"

"Yes, how about a Pepsi?"

Motioning to a clerk sitting at one of the tables waiting for instructions on what the work routine was going to be, she asked, "Darlene could you please get Hank and I a Pepsi from the cooler? Thank You."

"Okay Jocelyn, you got the instructions to set out all of the boxes of documents on incoming containers to the Long Beach piers from January 1, 2001 to September 11, 2001."

Hank looked up just as Darlene arrived with the Pepsis, "Thanks Darlene," then turning back to Jocelyn, "will we be able to start tomorrow?"

"Yes."

"All I want your people to do is open each folder in a systematic manner keeping them in perfect chronological order and look at the container ID on the shipping manifest. Just as we were doing in the past but now we do not need to analysis every piece of documentation to try and determine if something is out of the ordinary thus requiring a secondary review of the documents. The secondary review is no longer needed. As a matter of fact all we will need is to find one folder out of all of these with the following container ID. Hundi will be the shipping company and 'SIND/POLB' will be the identifying making with a blue strip around the container that came from the Port of Hong Kong. When this packet is found I want you to contact me immediately. I will then need to take time to go to the corresponding daily security tape for the exit gates and view the container that has that ID on it. If I am right our job will at least for a while go into abeyance. When we have our first container tracked and success in finding the contraband then we will go back and find the other containers Gutung claimed his Muslim clients had shipped to the states."

"Sounds good to me; I'll give out the instructions and where will you be when we find what you are looking for?"

"I'm going to our offices in the Federal building. When I am in San Diego I will be working out of there. Otherwise I will be back at my NSA office in Washington." Hank knew he would find exactly what he was looking for so after settling in to an office kept for visiting agents he began to compile the plan he would need to follow to track the movement of the subject container. It has been around five years by his calculations since the container would have arrived at the Port of Long Beach.

At the Federal building on Front Street, a big over grown brick monument to the waste of tax payer's money, Hank located the OHS section and moved into a visitor's office space. He was so use to using his cell phone to place his government calls that he didn't even notice that the office had no telephone. Looking around as he waited for his call to go through he observed a small leather couch, two side chairs, rather nice pictures of mountain scenes on the walls, of course a typical government desk and high back chair, a printer/fax machine and the miscellaneous desk accessories; but no telephone, strange. "Hello, George? I have the team working on the project here in San Diego again and I have come up with a major change in the procedures we are following to complete the orders given us in the CFR. I am sure you will okay this change as I unfold my reasoning on this. First, we are moving the dates on the packets we are reviewing up to January of 2001 and through September 2001."

"Why have you jumped from 1996 which is where we were in the last report I received before the holidays?"

"Look George, this is not a whim. I was reviewing the files on Jerry's and Jack's missions to Hong Kong, and the one on Jack's death plus remembering my interview with Taug or rather Gutung when it hit me. They had information on a container that Gutung swears entered the United States along with visual ID markings. Jack and Jerry were after a Hundi container with the shipping ID of SIND/POLB and a Blue strip. All I need to do to find that suspected container is to find the shipping packet that has an incoming Hundi container with those ID markings and we can identify the recipient and trace the delivery route from the port."

"Yes Hank, but don't you remember, Jack had that container completely unloaded and found nothing. Just ATVs and motorcycles which is what the manifest indicated were in the container."

"Right and now remember my meeting with Gutung last year. I looked at him straight in the eye and I could tell that he was one hundred percent certain that the container that he had brokered to al-Qaeda had the armament inside and that it was the container that Jerry and Jack saw. SIND/POLD with a Blue stripe."

"I don't get it."

"Neither did I until it hit me! They had a dummy container in Hong Kong set up just in case they were investigated and that was the one Jack had unloaded. The other one with the guns, ammunition, and C-4 went on its way to Long Beach and was unloaded on to the docks and delivered to the predetermined recipient. All I need is that specific packet and using my new parameters for our investigation it will not take more than a few weeks to find it. Then we'll have a path right to the ones who have the contraband or for sure we will know where it was delivered."

"Sounds like a plan to me; carry on and call me when you have the information."

Jerry and Jeff contacted their mission coordinator at the CIA communications center and requested a plane to pick them up to fly them the fifteen hundred miles from Belem to Rio. Bastian was a little short in his card deck if he thought that two special opts guys were going to fly in an old slow Bell helicopter for ten to twelve hours to Rio de Janeiro. The ABI agent Enrique Escobar did meet them at the airport and provided them with the investigation files to review while they were on the way to a hotel near the docks which had been pre-selected by the agent. The file contained the picture of the two of the three that had been released, a shallow historical on them with names---countries of citizenship---date of entry into Brazil---known contacts---etc, copies of agent Escobar's interrogations and the location of the boat they were using, dock space number, and the boat's name. As he explained, it was in the area of first class hotels where many luxury boats were docked including the one under surveillance so they could use a nearby hotel as an operating base in case the targets were not found immediately.

The agent left them at around four in the afternoon in front of a moderate hotel stating that someone would contact them from his office in the morning. "Great, so we'll be right here." Jerry nudged Jeff, "Let's go to the bar and get a drink while we plan this caper we have been handed by these fools here in Brazil."

The only bar was half outside and half inside set up with small hard wood tables and flat ass chairs. Sitting down Jeff wanted Jerry to know his thoughts before they started looking at what options were available to get their two targets. "I'm here with Carte Blanc operating instructions directly from Tenant's office that got them from Rodgges's office. We need to intercept these two now before the local yahoos fumble this completely."

"I'm with you on that. What are your thoughts?"

"Probably just exactly what yours are; we are here on a mission, we are well trained for operations in foreign lands and I personally am not leaving Brazil with out these guys. So I'll check in under an alias and let's stow our gear in our room, head to the docks and snoop around the boat. That file said that the boat's name is Mi Fiesta."

"Perfect, can you take my bag and I'll take another rum and coke for you? And bring me two more clips for my gun and my night scope."

"Sure, no problem Jerry......., and don't choke on my rum and coke!"

We wondered around the area as if we were tourist going past the restaurants and then down to the docks where we walked casually up and down them looking at some of the bigger yachts. All of the time we took turns at observing the one named 'Mi Fiesta'. No activity just like Bastian had told us, but it was still light out and activity from people on the run will usually be at night. "Jeff as we have been moving about and looking around I have not seen any surveillance by any one, have you?"

"No, that's why we are here, right!"

"Obviously. They don't have the same urgency on this as we do. Let's locate a spot where we can see but not be seen as night approaches. Actually two spots, one for you and one for me, which will give us a better range of view and chance to identify some one getting on the boat."

Jerry and Jeff had been keeping watch on the yacht for four days and no suspicious people had been coming or going on the dock where the boat was tied down much less any one getting on of off of the boat except the Brazilian playboy owner of the boat and his female guest who came and went occasionally. Frustration was causing stress so Jerry felt it was time to go to ABI offices in Rio and swap information. Their agent contact had not come back to see them or contact them at the hotel during that time so it was time to find out why.

They entered the one story building on a short street off of the rotunda next to the main calle in front of the supreme courts. At the front counter behind a glass cage was the receptionist so Jerry approached and asked, "We are looking for the department that handles investigations of possible foreign terrorist activities. Could you help us?"

"What! May I ask who you are?"

"Sure, we are with the United States government and I believe we want to talk to Enrique Escobar."

"One moment please. Have a seat over there, I'll check with my supervisor."

We took a seat on a bench covered in government green plastic. Every government building from one country to another that I have ever been in has green plastic covered benches somewhere in their offices. There is some company that got the contracts to sell hundreds of thousands of unwanted green plastic bench covering material to most of the governments around the world; 'Great salesmanship'.

Mrs. 'I'll ask my supervisor' returned, "I am sorry but Enrique is on assignment and we can not disclose where."

Jerry in a rather disgusted manner asked for the Commander. "And by the way what is the name of your Commander?"

"I am not sure if he is available, I'll see."

"No, no, before you go what is his name?" "Please."

"Senor Castillanos, excuse me."

"While you do that I am going outside to call our Ambassador and I will be calling the head of our agency in the States that is equal to your ABI here in Brazil. Tell that to your Commander Castillanos. We are here on an urgent matter. Oh, and our names are Jeff Howell and Jerry Ness. And we are tired of your agencies inefficiencies."

While we waited a new lady came to take over the desk behind the glass partition. The original woman returned after about thirty minutes to confirm that Senor 'Important person' would see us shortly.

More than two hours went by with Jerry and Jeff dusting off the ugly green benches with their butts and pushing the already short supply of the personal commodity called patience to its limit.

Finally the receptionist opened a door next to her area and motioned for them to enter. Inside she introduced us to a man with a rather kind looking smile on his face as he apologized to us, "Forgive me for the delay in meeting with you but it was unexpected and there are so many urgent matters on my agenda that I had to clear up first. Please follow me to a small meeting area. Is your business involving a situation I am aware of?"

As we entered and sat down Jerry started the conversation, "You may or may not be aware of our mission here in Brazil but one of your agents, one Enrique Escobar is fully aware and has now disappeared. We have been tracking people who could be terrorists and may have shipped illegal items into the United States from your port in Belem. But when we arrived we were told by the police chief in Belem, Bastian Hernandez that the two suspected conspirators had been released and we were given the police file on them to review. In the police file their report indicated that there was no evidence against them concerning arson and that they were released and then that they had traveled to Rio. Follow them here we met your agent here who took us to the location where they were believed to be staying, a boat docked in a small harbor in your Guanabara Bay. After leaving us agent Escobar said that he would return the next day but he never returned with any more information for us; however just now we were told that he has been sent on an extended assignment. We have been on surveillance of the boat for four days with no success. We were hoping to talk to Senor Escobar and review any information he may have gathered. That is it, can you help us."

"On moment and let me see what I can find out." Turning to the door he called out for his assistant, "Luz, please come in!"

"Yes Commander."

"Luz, I want the file that agent Escobar has on ...., what are the names of these people you are hunting?"

"In the police file they were listed as Moran Vegas and Allan Glutez."

"Okay, Luz please locate any files or what ever Agent Escobar has on them and anything we have in our data base and bring all of it to me." Motioning to Jeff and I, Castillanos pointed to more green benches. "In the meantime if you would not mind resting here, I have some things I need to attend to. I'll have tea brought in for you."

Returning Commander Castillanos was sugary polite, "Gentlemen, Gentlemen, I am finish for the afternoon so I can be available to help in any way I can. Here are two small files and Luz also printed up our information from our date base on your two suspects. There is not much in the files but I did notice that a couple of days after agent Escobar left you he reported that both of the individuals, Vegas and Glutez used their passports and flew to Québec in Canada."

"Whoa, hold on a minute!" Jerry had that tomato red face again. "Are you telling us that we have been on surveillance at the docks where that boat is for four days for absolutely no reason and have wasted all of that time while our suspects had already fled the country? What the HELL is going on here!!! Why didn't you tell us?"

"Temprano Senor! Your investigation is not our investigation and after they left Brazil we had no more interest in them. Remember they were suspects in an arson case and even though we did some interrogation into terrorist activities we really had no evidence to hold them any longer, and besides agent Escobar was dispatched to assist in a small tribal uprising in the southern rain forest over deforestation so he was not available to notify you and I was not aware of your, how do you say 'stake-out'. But we have what maybe more important information in both of their statements taken here before they were released. In them they deny any involvement in burning down the plant and in fact they provided alibis covering the night of the fire. But they both under separate interrogations told the police interrogators at our station where they were detained that on numerous weekend's the owner, al-Aziz would meet someone at the plant and then bring a truck inside of the plant with a load of perfectly wrapped packages and have the workers mold them into the body of the boat putting extra resin around the packages. As they said he paid them extra money so they turned a 'blind eye' as it were, to what was going on. They thought that he was in the drug trafficking business and shipping drugs to Florida. The money was good and the jobs in Belem were not easy to come by. Later they stated that the packages did not have the aroma of pure cocaine. They both thought that the packages were some other kind of illegal drugs. The police report was not any more informative on that subject but with the plant burned to the ground and no Mr. al-Aziz we had no crime to charge them with, I am sorry. That is all we have. Oh, one minute there are some scribbled notes here made by the investigator that one of the supervisors thought that the name of the person who came to the plant on the week-end's with the trucks was al Masri and they thought he could have been a supplier of the packages. Yes, It looks like the name is al-Masri."

"al-Masri; are you sure it is al-Masri? This is it! Oh my god! This is my connection. Why didn't we get that report with the other information? That is important and no one gave that to us WHY!"

"Sorry Senor, I just found it myself."

"Are you sure that they said the boats were shipped to Florida and this part is very important can we verify that they said al-Masri? NO, no, wait a minute it has to be accurate, they would not know that name from any other way. Senor Castillanos they may or may not be terrorist but they worked with one. Jeff, this is our guy and we have confirmation. There is no doubt in my mind but that C-4 has been shipped to Florida not in ships to shipping docks but inside of small boats. Senor Castillanos, this I believe has been the base from which a terrorist conspiracy has been fueled with armament and explosives for many years and we will need your agency's full cooperation."

"But of course, we will not tolerate terrorists in our country, how can we help?"

"We will need complete copies of all of your files and the Belem police files including copies of all of the interrogations with each of the three suspects and any accompanying notes and any photographs etc. I will contact a special forensic team to immediately come in to sift through every inch of that site. Please provide for us security around the entire area today. Also if you can provide us with the suspect's departure information from your immigration department and subsequent embarkation information in Canada; it is vital to our investigation. I believe the police report referred to the boat manufacturer as 'Groupo Rizzo' and the owner as Jonathan al-Aziz. Jeff let's get to the consulate and inform our ambassador so he can get in to play on this. We will need permission and cooperation from the Brazilian authorities asap."

"Senor Ness, I will get our commandant at ABI to implement your request and to contact your embassy in Brasilia to set up the logistics for your investigating team."

"We need to contact our people in the states and get to our consulate right away; do you have someone that could drive us there?"

"Absolutely. Luz, please have one of our agents secure a vehicle and take Senor Ness and Howell to the United States consulate. Then get the commandant on the telephone for me. I will take care of my end and good luck on your operation."

Back in San Diego

By mid March Hank and his team had finished all of the shipping packets and he and Jocelyn met with Darlene to confer on the completed project and the disappointment of the search outcome. "Jocelyn, we need to go over and over and over our procedure to see what could have gone wrong. I know that that container came in during the time segment that I selected and something is wrong. Let's all of us go over to K C Bar-B-Que and get something to eat while we hash this out. Hey Darlene come and join us for lunch."

It was one thirty in the afternoon before we could get to the restaurant and it was not packed like normal but we went out the back door to a table on the side area next to the trolley tracks so that we could have some privacy.

"Okay Darlene I guess we will have to let you iterate to us the step by step routine used and kind of tell us what you think may have gone wrong with our procedures in reviewing each of the shipping packets and Jocelyn and I, as we listen will see if we can determine where the packet we are looking for could have been missed. I know the container in question came into the States."

The long time waitress Betty came out the back door to get our order. "What would you like for lunch today and we are out of ribs."

After Betty brought our food Darlene went over her review procedures with us. "Jocelyn, I did just as we had discussed. I wrote out the instructions for each of our team to follow in opening the packets and organizing the documents for accurate analysis."

I had to interrupt, "Let me understand exactly what that was. Go over the step by step routine with me so I can follow the flow."

"Okay Hank, well, all packets were kept in sequential order and distributed down one side of the line up of tables and up the other side so as to not get them out of chronological order. Then each team member would make sure that all documents were in the packet and that they were in chronological order as to the date on the document. They would then take the container identification form out of the group and place it on top of the sack, stapling the complete set together. They then looked for the identifying marks for that container and highlight the description with a yellow marker. The next step was to look at the highlighted markings to see if they matched the typed description you gave us to use for locating the container in question. Last they would past the packet from their right to their left and that person would open the packet and review once again the descriptive markings listed on the container identification form."

"Jocelyn, what do you think? We did not find the container. But why?"

"Hank, you are so certain. This procedure was flawless and yet no container with your specified identifying marks arrived at Long Beach during your time frame. It's like it just disappeared or it went somewhere else."

Darlene added, "You know Jocelyn; we found many containers with the Hundi label on them and even some with SIND/POLB and yellow stripes and even one with two yellow strips and a blue stripe. But of course there was none with just a blue stripe."

Hank finished his ham sandwich and then asked Darlene, "Give that to me again, you said that there were many containers with Hundi on them and of course their identifying yellow stripes."

"Yes."

"And how many from Indonesia or I mean how many with SIND/POLB markings?"

"We did keep track of that since that was part of the identifying markings you were looking for. The list is back there at the customs building but I believe it was one thousand three hundred and fifty something."

"And after double checking none had a single blue strip around the container?"

"That is correct and there was one that had two yellow stripes and a blue stripe but none had a single blue stripe marking."

"I didn't know that, did you Jocelyn? What if they changed the markings before it left Hong Kong? Let's get back to the customs building now. I want to see that file. Can you find it quickly?"

"Sure we kept a chronological record of the Hundi shipments."

Hank took the file and went off to a private office. "Hello George, I have one file here with delivery confirmation by a Coastal Express trucking company to an Awai dealer in Las Vegas Nevada by the name of 'Desert Sports and Tour Company' out on West Sahara Blvd. Can we get an investigative team out there today? The only difference on this container is that it has two yellow strips and the blue identifying strip, but the yellow strips could have been added back in Hong Kong before the shipment headed to the States."

"Okay Hank I'll put a priority on this and call you back. It's four fifty here so it may take an hour to get it into operation. I'll put a CFR on the order."

Hank added, "I'll fax you the land carrier information and delivery address and you will have to get confirmation of the delivery address with our Vegas people."

"I'll get back to you in less than an hour."

"Okay and the Vegas team will need to track down the disposition of the container and the contents."

Hank waited around for a few hours after telling Jocelyn and Darlene to go home along with their people and return tomorrow for the outcome of the investigation. He didn't hear from George so he headed to his room at the Marriott next to the convention center and called it a day.

It was six am when Hank dialed George's number at NSA. "Hello George what did we find out?"

"I was waiting to call you in an hour. I don't know why Hank, but it's a bust. Our team met with the owners of Desert Sports. They are a man and wife who are in their late fifties and have owned the business for twenty nine years. They first started out offering tours of the dam and the Las Vegas strip. Then they produced some desert tours on ATV's for gold hunters who thought that they could find old mines in the mountain like hills to the East of the city and then they decided to start selling the vehicles to tourists and locals. They have been selling Awai four wheelers and motorcycles ever since and have no idea what our people are talking about. They definitely have no recollection of any particular container that has come and gone over the past five years. And their sons who now help in the business are not suspects either. One went to fight in the gulf war and the other was a jock at ULV; just an all American family with a perfect background."

"Okay George then its back to the drawing board. Any suggestions?"

"No, we will run this problem through our simulator system inputting all of the data we have along with your hypotheses to see what probabilities and/or alternative postulates can be derived from the information we have. I will get back with you when we have something. In the meantime stay there and see what you may have missed."

I went back to the Marriott and sat out by the pool sipping on a delicious margarita and looked out at the bay. I wondered, what could have happened? Gutung was so convincing, he was so sure!

The next day Hank went to the customs office to wait for Jocelyn and Darlene. Jocelyn was already in the room assigned for the review processing when Hank arrived. "Hi there, did we get some good answers yesterday?"

"No, not at all, it is back to the drawing board."

Just then Darlene entered with some Jelly rolls and coffee. "Well good morning and I guess we can all go back to our previous assignments?"

"Nope, as I just told Jocelyn. The lead we had was a false trail. Nothing at the end of that trail but good old solid Americans. Not a terrorist in sight according to the investigating team and as reported by my boss at NSA. Let's enjoy your Jelly rolls and coffee and talk about what could have happened. Both of you have seen the file I put together going over the facts that we had from Jerry, Jack, and my interview with Mr. Gutung."

Darlene thought about Jocelyn's comment over lunch at K C Bar-B-Que. "As Jocelyn said, the shipment you are looking for Hank just seems to have disappeared or 'gone up in smoke' as the saying goes."

"Disappeared? Yeah, disappeared, like at sea, I don't think so! Disappeared to somewhere else maybe? Like Ensenada, Mexico, or Panama, or Hawaii."

Jocelyn sat her coffee down and pointed her finger right at Hank, "No, No, but to Oakland, or Seattle or Montreal? Maybe it was diverted."

Hank stood up, "That's not possible; we tracked the container to Las Vegas. And besides it's not possible to divert a shipment pass customs to a port other than the one on the manifest is it? Is it possible to divert a shipment that is scheduled to go to one port and instead it is delivered to a different location or I mean port?"

"I am not sure, but I don't see why not! Anything is possible with enough grease to the right people. So what is there to be diverted? The container in question that you thought had the changed markings went to Las Vegas."

Hank had a gleam in his eye as if a light bulb had gone off. "Did it, did it really? Jocelyn, if that was to be done then is there any special authorization needed or what would be the requirement for the shipping line to off load a container to a port that was not on the manifest?"

"I am not sure. This question has never come up so I'll call a customs officer downstairs and ask. Oops, my phone slipped too much Jelly roll on my fingers. I will run down stairs and get our answer."

Darlene and I finished our coffee while Jocelyn went to find a customs officer. A few minutes later she came off of the elevator with the news that this customs office had no idea so they would call Washington.

"Jocelyn, let's assume that if it did not come through Long Beach then where would it have gone? I'm just looking for your woman's tuition."

"Again what are you talking about?"

"Hey forgive me my thoughts were way ahead of my explanation, I was thinking that if there was a container in Hong Kong that was used as a diversion when Jerry and Jack had a container unloaded then maybe they used it as a secondary diversion here and the one we want to find went someplace other than Long Beach!"

The rest of the crew came in just then and Hank motioned to Jocelyn to move over by the windows.

"I imagine that if you are correct and we are looking for a container of expl........" Hank put his finger to his lips, "Shuuu." Then he quietly asked Jocelyn "Is everyone in here with a secret clearance or better?"

"Of course, as I was saying; if it is a container full of guns and explosives then to make the distribution a little easier I would probably go up higher on the coast then Long Beach. I would try Oakland or Vallejo."

"You know I would agree. Let's move our team to Vallejo tomorrow and get started up there."

"Hold on cowboy, put them six shooters away. We don't need to go anywhere. All of the customs shipping records are here. We just have to ask them to put Long Beach back into storage and have them bring us Vallejo. I'll do that this afternoon and it may take a few days for them to handle it. You know government protocol. Do you still want me to find out about the diverting of a shipment to another port?"

"You bet. I want all of the facts I can accumulate before reporting in to my unit at OHS."

Rio de Janeiro

Jerry reported to George at NSA from the consulate in Rio and laid out the information as he and Jeff had uncovered it. "George, we are sending our detailed report over secure lines but here is what we know. A person by the name of Jonathan al-Aziz owned a boat manufacturing plant in Belem Brazil and shipped his boats to his own boat dealership in Ft Lauderdale Florida. He burned down his own plant explaining to two of his supervisors that the United States Drug Enforcement Agency made him do it and they believed him. We are told that he claimed to have a relationship with the DEA in Florida and sold them low profile fast boats for their drug chasing fleet. The important information is that employees that worked at the plant claim that al-Aziz packed the inside of the hulls of some of the boats with resin covered packages that they thought was cocaine or some other hard drug. I am positive that it was really C-4 and here is why. One of the supervisors said that the name of one person that brought the small packages to the plant was one al-Masri. So listen, there is no way that this employee would know that name except it is our supplier from Argentina. That is all of the connection we need to prove that the terrorist organization in Ft Lauderdale has in fact received hundreds of pounds of C-4, but as of now we do not know exactly how much and over what period of time. We need to get a team to that dealership and over to the chief of the Florida DEA department to see what if anything they know about this person or what involvement they may have had in this dealership and al-Aziz. Jeff and I will be back tomorrow and see what you have found out about the dealership and from the DEA. Any questions on our end?"

"No, great work. Tell Jeff that also. I'll see you guys in the office tomorrow"

San Diego

It was not until Tuesday the twenty first of March that the files for all of the shipping ports in the Bay area were available to Hank and his team. Meeting in the same area as before Jocelyn started her crew on the same procedures to review the new batch of shipping records as before.

"Hank! Any special instructions before we get started?"

"No, I am just anxious to get an answer to the puzzle. I hope it is in this batch of records from the Bay area ports. I desperately want a positive answer not only for the sake of our investigation but to confirm what Mr. Gutung told me and what has been my hunch all along. We need to get answers for the security of our country! And I want to eulogize a great CIA agent, Jack Madden"

"Well using the previous efforts as a measuring stick we maybe working for two months on these records. Will you be going back to Washington?"

"Yes, but as I said before, contact me when you have found the container."

CHAPTER TWENTY TWO

The phone rang at Hank's home and Tiama answered while holding Tank. "Hello Tiama is Hank there?"

It was almost nine o'clock at night so she was a little surprised about the call. "No Jerry, he is still on the West coast, but he told me yesterday he might be back home on Wednesday or Thursday. Haven't you talked to him?"

"Not since I went to Brazil. My trip was extended until Jeff and I finished our mission. We just got back a few days ago and I wanted to talk to him about our mission and find out how he was doing. I guess I will know tomorrow when I get in the office."

"Okay I can't tell you anything except he is fine and he keeps telling me he is protecting me and Tank."

"Well, we all are, so I'll see you soon I am sure. Good night and say good night to Tank."

The phone ring again as Tiama came from Tank's bedroom. "Hello, this is Tiama Brayden."

"Hi honey. I just came from the customs offices here in San Diego and we are still working on my mission here. I'll be back around noon tomorrow, but I will have to go into the office before I come home. I love you kisses for you and Tank."

"I love you too and I just put him to bed so I'll go give him your kisses. Oh, and Jerry is back and he just called wondering how you were doing and of course I didn't know so you will probably see him tomorrow. Good night love."

"Good night honey I will see you tomorrow."

More than two months had gone by since Hank and Jerry had seen each other. Jerry had been home for a couple of days when they both met in George's office on a Thursday morning.

"Jerry, you old fox, you look just as disheveled as ever. But I do believe you have lost some weight since January. Those corduroys are beginning to sag on you. Were the Latino girls too much for you down there? It's okay; my lips will be sealed forever."

"Ha ha ha, this trip was not at all exciting even though there are a lot of beautiful girls in Brazil. You should be so lucky to have had our scenery. I heard that you were partnered with Jocelyn, your grandmother's high school friend."

"Jocelyn doesn't know my Grandmother and she is not that old but she is good at organization. My mission has been extended and we have not located the mystery container. You and Jack were tricked with two containers. It would appear that after you guys left Hong Kong both containers were sent to the states. We believe one came into Long Beach but we think a second one was shipped to the Bay area. So now we start on the custom's records from the Bay area ports. How, did your lead on the boat factory end up? I was so busy I never talked to communications to get briefed on your operation."

"We struck pay dirt! Everything tied in together from the supplier of the C-4 who was killed in Sudan to the method that the terrorists transported the explosives into Florida. The owner of the boat factory also owned the boat dealership in Ft Lauderdale where the boats entered the country. His name is Jonathan al-Aziz. I'll give you more on that after I finish my report. By the way, George asked us to put together our reports for review and inclusion in the President's PDB for the first week of April."

George finished his telephone call as Hank said good morning. "Jerry here was telling me that we need to get our reports ready for you so that the agency can add them to the Presidents briefings. As you know George I don't have anything positive to report. I understand that Jerry's investigation may have us a lot closer to finding that 'needle in the hay stack'."

"You guys take the next week off. Jerry you need a rest and some time to get ready for your debriefing and Hank I know it was disappointing for us to find a dead end in Vegas but the idea of a second container coming in covertly has some logic to it. I didn't tell you yet but we set up for the Intel department to program a query for the simulator using 'Artificial Intelligence' to run all of the information we have from 2001 to present on the hypothesis that terrorist have used overseas containers to smuggle military goods into the states. Our project will be ready to run on next Monday and we should have the out come on Tuesday. Jerry, I have asked Poles to assign a couple of Florida field agents to investigate the boat dealership in Ft Lauderdale and contact the DEA to get all of their information on Jonathan al-Aziz. We can expect a report back by the middle of next week. I have asked that all of our work and investigations be covered with the CFR."

Hank was in early on Tuesday to go to the Intel department and see what the output from the program George had authorized on Hanks investigation. George was already there going over all of the computer's postulates with the programmer. "Hank, come on over and have a look at this, we have a number of suggestions for avenues of investigations but the most logical is the simplest." George kind of moved his head back and forth and back and forth as if to say how dumb we are at the same time as Jerry came in.

"Hey George what's wrong? The electronic brain fail us?" Jerry was all old school and had always been skeptical that asking computers to think was going to help field investigators. "What are you doing here? You have the week to recharge the battery."

"I wanted to see how an electric brain could stand up to a human brain."

"Here is the primary action it recommended; 'find, investigate, and interrogate all Awai dealers in the western eleven states'."

Jerry hollered, "Oh my Hank, of course, where were we when all of the time we knew Gutung had said the terrorist had hidden the contraband in containers with Awai motorcycles and ATV's."

"Hank it's your mission. Get on the phone to Dryer at the FBI and I'll contact Poles to call Director Mules to authorize an immediate memorandum of action for a CFR to locate and interview all Awai dealers as the simulator recommended."

"I'm headed to my office right now and consider it done. And I am going to call Jocelyn to tighten the parameters on our shipping packet reviews to add only shipping containers with motorcycles and ATV"s. I must have been totally brain dead to have not seen that as a limiting factor."

Jerry left for the cafeteria, but not before he told George, "If this works like it looks like it is going to I may just bow to the computers."

"Jerry, the report from the Florida agents will not be available to us until Friday. Come in after lunch on Friday so we can review it before you prepare for the debriefing next week."

The next day Jocelyn called Hank at his office to give him the good news. "Hank, we cut a lot of time off of our search and in February of 2001 a Hundi container from Hong Kong was diverted from Long Beach to Oakland and the markings were exactly like the one that went to the Awai dealer in Vegas."

"Oh my Jocelyn, looks like you have found it."

"We think so. It was picked up by Pacific-Mountain Transport company showing a destination of Salt Lake City. There are no addresses in the file, just the dealer name. Land-N-Sea Sports."

"Fantastic Jocelyn. I need to get this information to the commander at the FBI here so he can locate the dealer's address and get some agents there immediately. Send me a copy of the complete packet so I can include it in my information to the FBI commander in charge and put it in my report."

Hank called George as soon as he hung up with Jocelyn. "George, I have called the commander under Poles who is in charge of the Awai dealership investigations to let him know we have found the other container. Jocelyn just called me to let me know they located a duplicate Hundi container with the markings like the one that went to Vegas and it was picked up by Pacific-Mountain Transport company who took it to Salt Lake City for delivery to Land N Sea Sports. Can you follow up on the agent's progress through Poles?"

"Absolutely, this is great work. We'll congratulate everyone after we find the container and the contents. I'll keep everyone up to date."

On Friday Jerry was back at his office to review the FBI agent's investigation of the boat dealership and finish up some details on his report when he heard Melvin talking to one of the Intel guys. "Did I hear you say that Hank has found the missing container?"

"He thinks so and he is waiting for the FBI's report now."

"Where is Hank? I didn't see him in his office."

"I think he and George are in the briefing room by the elevator."

When Jerry entered they were listening to the commander's report on the telecom screen. "Our agents discovered that the dealership was sold almost three years ago and that the owner was a Mr. Al Sober. After extensive interviews with neighbors at both his previous business location and his home and then with the local business people, the Rotary Club where he was a member, his banker, restaurants in his area, etc, etc, etc, they all had nothing negative to say about him and we could not prove he was even closely tied to a terrorist operation. That is all we have. No evidence, no container, and no indication of terrorist activities. Sorry George, I'll forward you a copy of the report."

By Monday April third Jerry and Hank were waiting for George in the Cafeteria. "Here comes George with someone important. He must really be someone; he has his personal entourage with him." Hank ended the comment to stand and greet George and the other people.

"Good morning Hank, Good morning Jerry. Where is Jeff?"

"Sorry George but he had a previous meeting with the Imagery department to set up the visual documentation we need to augment our report. I believe I can handle the debriefing on this myself."

"Good, Hank are you all set to go over your report? And before you answer let me formally introduce you to Mr. Stephen Haddle, who as you know is the National Security Advisor to the President, and his aid Jon Hinson and his secretary Betty Moran. We have a meeting room reserved on the eighth floor where we can view all of the satellite visuals to go along with Jerry's report. On the way up ask someone in the cafeteria and to have some coffee, cream and sugar brought up. I think we may be there for some time."

Hank looked a little overwhelmed as he answered George, "Right, it is all here. Give me a moment and I'll get the cafeteria to have a number of different drinks brought up and I'll also request some sandwiches for lunch."

Returning from the cafeteria, Hank, still in awe, slowed down heading to the elevator and whispered to Jerry. "I never thought I would be briefing the President's National Security Advisor on one of my missions; well not quite a mission but an investigation. What we have found out is one thing but what I believe is yet another thing and is still unproven. I don't want to send the President any false alarms."

"Don't worry with what the two of us have it does not have to be set in stone yet. The investigation is on going and this afternoon when we are finished I will be going to Ft Lauderdale to try to find out where my missing suspect Jonathan has disappeared to and I understand your guy Al Sober in Salt Lake City also has disappeared. We are both close to verifying the truth about our missions. We just can't lose faith about where we are! I feel certain that we are very close to putting an important 'notch in our gun', that's my Texas talk for getting the bad guy, well, you know what I mean."

The elevator seemed to take an hour to go four floors. Hank still felt he was on thin ice without the confirmation of finding the container's contraband. Jerry proceeded before everyone else to the specially equipped meeting room which was used only for what are called strategic debriefings or in this case briefings and special tactical analysis of the classified missions carried out by NSA operatives.

George sat in front of the large vie screen with a half dozen smaller monitors on each side which were used to present multiple views and different scenes covering the same subject matter. The room was wired into the communications section in the basement which was also connected to the major data center at Langley. There was also a representative of NSA's legal department present to witness the entire mission reports from Jerry and Hank even though everything was being taped from the second the door open until the last person left. In this case the witness was a lawyer transferred to NSA from the defense department after the crash into the pentagon on that infamous day in September and she had never been reassigned.

"'First we welcome Stephen and his people to this debriefing and to hear the reports of agent Hank Brayden and Jerry Ness. Before they individually begin to cover their missions I will bring you up to speed on the reason I invited you Stephen to be a part of what is covered here today. I am fully aware the President does not get any unsubstantiated information in his PDB's but Tenant has told us that the President listens to information that comes from his advisors and today we are going to fill you up with information. Now both Jerry and Hank have been tracking the shipments of explosives and armament into our country by terrorist. Today you will hear their reports and see the visual backup from the archives of our satellite tracking systems."

"Excuse me George but where is the difference between your information and the Intel which we are aware of that we have been receiving from the customs and immigration departments?"

"Completely on a different scale; as you will see this is on a massive scale so big that you will or I believe you should 'Quake in your boots' as it were. Going forward, briefly, Jerry has been tracking C-4 being shipped to a boat dealer in Ft Lauderdale Florida and Hank has been tracking a container filled with guns, ammunition and C-4 from Indonesia that entered one of our ports on the West coast. In Florida, we sent a team from the FBI to go to the boat dealership in Ft Lauderdale and to find the owner of the boat dealership Mr. Jonathan al-Aziz. That's bad news for us, because the boat dealership has now become a used car dealership run by two Italian brothers who have been in the used car business for fifteen years. And they check out. They are not terrorists. The other business owners around there said that the Mr. al-Aziz shut the place down four or five months before the used car dealership opened. They searched the property and there is no trace of anything. And your Mr. al-Aziz has totally disappeared. The FBI also went to the DEA offices in Miami and spoke to the commander in charge about the DEA buying boats for their chase fleet from Mr. al-Aziz and everything was on the up and up. They tested his product against other competitors and his boats were far superior in speed and maneuverability. They never suspected him of any smuggling, as a matter of fact they reported that they took apart some of his first shipments during the first two years of importing. After that they kind of gave the green light to customs to let his boats pass through when ever his shipments came in. They would replace their fast boats every two years or so and he was not under suspicion. The report did say that he was able to get the opportunity to present his boats for testing against the rival manufactures with the help of someone in the state department. One thing that they did find out that ties him directly to some terrorist connection in the states is he is friends with Khalid Misha'al in Oklahoma. Mr. Khalid is a radical Islamist and has been preaching the death of Christians and Jews and the destruction of the West for a number of years and he openly recruits young people from college campuses to join Islam and become a Muslim, a Muslim full of hate! Mr. Khalid claims there are thousands of Muslims here that are going to demand the conversion of all Infidels to Islam or die!"

Turning towards Hank he went on, "Oh, and Hank's Mr. Sober can not be found as of now either."

"George,. are you telling me that you brought us here to hear unconfirmed stories about possible armament and explosives, no not just some but you said a massive amount of guns and C-4 in the hands of terrorist but now the suspected culprit's that are at the center of your investigation have just disappeared and so has the contraband? First there is nothing here for me if it is all based on just supposition and

second how is it possible for two suspects that you claim are two pur-
portedly dangerous terrorist to just disappear?"

"I am sure you have heard this before. When they want to leave after
any dirty work they go north through the sieve known as the Canadian
border and blend into no where. They are simply gone."

Then George went to the credenza and poured out some coffee,
added a little sugar and then sat down. "Stephen this is not a wild
goose chase. Take a cup of coffee and listen to our reports and watch
the big screen."

Almost two hours passed with Jerry going into great detail on his mission and explaining how the visuals tied into his investigation. He
started back when he made his first trip to Argentina looking for suppliers of illicit explosives and when he watched as his best potential informant was assassinated outside a Mosque in Montevideo. Detailing
agent Norris's special opt to Sudan to find a terrorist named al-Rantisi who al-Masri claimed worked with him on buying and delivering
thousands of kilos of C-4 to terrorists around the world. Further agent
Norris learned from al-Rantisi before the Shin-Bet eliminated him that
the boat manufacturer Jonathan al-Aziz was one of al-Masri buyers of
C-4. With the continued investigation of the boat manufacturing plant
fire in Belem Brazil and the interrogation of the suspects involved the
pieces began to fall into place. Al-Aziz the boat manufacturer is also
the Ft. Lauderdale boat dealer where we believe all of the boats from
Brazil were shipped. And now the prime suspect has closed shop and
run. The IMGINT helped to back up the scenario as Jerry laid out step
by step why he was one hundred per cent convinced that Jonathan al-
Aziz had brought thousands of pounds of explosives into the States
and distributed it to where ever. Locations totally unknown.

Hank proceeded to present his case in almost the exact same manner
along with some very convincing IMGINT. Hank began with the file on
the first mission Jerry and the former Jack Madden took to Hong Kong
together and their first association with Mr. Taug in Hong Kong. An
arms dealer turned informant. The lost container and then the unloading of what turned out to be a bogus container which in reality was a
duplicate of the one containing contraband. Hank opened the file on
Jack's assassination in Indonesia by those that thought he was to close
to the truth on what had gone on with the container. Hank elaborated
on his trip to Hong Kong where he met Mr. Gutung, who was formerly

known as Mr. Taug and who reiterated the facts of the original container having guns, ammunition, and explosives packed in with the Awai ATVs and Awai motorcycles. His original claim was that he was the go between for the supplier and the Muslims in Indonesia and that he had worked with them for over ten years. Archived images showed trucks taking containers from the docks in Long Beach and Oakland to locations that ultimately ended in dead ends. Most convincing however were the satellite images of those same containers having been in Hong Kong and then placed on freighters that took them to the ports identified in his completed review of the custom's files on incoming containers. It was the three different missions that Jerry, Jack and he had carried out that brought him to the final conclusion that everyone had been tricked with two identical containers. And last Hank detailed how he was able to uncover the proof that both containers actually arrived in the States and that they were delivered to their assigned destinations. Even though it appeared that the one delivered to Salt Lake City was the hot container.

"Stephen, we don't have our hands on the contraband but the evidence is overwhelming. Terrorist cells in the United Sates have their hands on weapons, ammunition, and the highly destructive C-4 explosive. What quantity of weapons and C-4 we do not know yet but our statistical guys will let me know this afternoon? They are projecting some time lines which we hope will give us the approximate dates the terrorists began their undertaking, possible entry intervals, and when they terminated their operations which we think will be fairly accurate based on all of our latest Intel. We will then be able to develop some numbers, but I can tell you now that at first estimates we are talking about ten thousand automatic rifles and who knows how much ammunition but worst than that possibly three to four hundred thousand pounds of C-4."

Stephen shouted, "What the Hell are you saying! That is enough to start a small war!"

"That is why you are here. As soon as I get a final report drawn up and the actual statistics confirmed by our guys I will be sending you a copy and giving a copy of it to Mr. Mertoff, Mr. Tenant, Mr. Dire at the FBI, and Senator Peter Wing, Chairman of the OHS oversight committee. This morning I asked for a NSR from Mr. Mertoff on the basis that our report would be convincing. You can help us get the investigative response authorized immediately. We believe that any lost time could be catastrophic for our country."

"OH MY GOD, what have we here? I can not put this in the President's PDB. I will have to meet with him privately and go over your report with him one on one. He is going to want some real facts because you do not have a 'habeas corpus'. He will not be able to take any action on your report without discovery of some of the contraband. George, you need the NSR now and NSA must move fast and precise; it is vital and I will ask the President to call Michael to have him put all the resources he can on this investigation. Where will they look? The stuff could be spread from Maine to San Diego and wherever. They have had enough time to disperse all of the weapons and explosives into small caches from coast to coast."

George stood up to stretch and take deep breath. "Tell the President that we have a vast data base on suspected cell members of al-Qaeda, Hamas, and Hezbollah. We must be able to target them and implement all of our surveillance tools to get the intelligence we need to find out exactly who is involved and what their plans are and more importantly where the contraband is. We must infiltrate their organizations and tell the congress and all of the liberal bastards that they can take their political correctness and shove it up their back side. We will do profiling and in a massive way. There are millions of Muslims in our country and consequently there are thousands of terrorist ready to attack us.. Since we at NSA are one hundred per cent convinced that this is all completely true then any delay or precious loss of time is NUTS and will bring us closer to Armageddon and their attack on 9-11 will have been just child's play!"

Stephen appeared to have a sweat bead or two on his brow when he responded, "Yes, I agree but the President will more than likely say that they are not all radicals who have a bent towards terrorism."

"Tell him in a very diplomatic way, TO WAKE UP and stop the politicking. Our citizens are at jeopardy, Damn it."

Jerry went over to the credenza for a Pepsi. "If I may Sir, I have studied the numbers on this since I was with ACE International and the estimate at this time is that there are approximately five million six hundred thousand Muslims in this country and according to the statistics regarding all of the Muslims in the world ten per cent of them or five hundred sixty thousand are radical believers in the death and destruction of all Jews and Christians and here is the kicker, of those radicals, twenty to twenty five percent of them can become terrorists on any given day. That would be somewhere around one hundred twelve thousand, at a minimum, potential Fascist Islamist here ready to take down the United States. They are openly preaching an 'American Jihad' in their Mosques, on the Internet, in their meetings, and in their families and they have posters in their little communities and fliers they give out to their brothers and sisters and to their children; advocating a Jihad and death to the Infidels! I have been telling everyone that for almost six years now that they are getting ready for a blood bath; so not only with their ability to buy weapons almost anywhere in the country, they may now have thousands of automatic weapons and hundreds of thousands of pounds of high explosives. That constitutes the makings of an army and our leaders had better act and act now!"

"George, Hank, Jerry; I have the picture. Get me your reports and the rest of the data and visuals to back up Jerry's claims over to my office forthwith. Thank you guys, I will see the President, but he is not going to like it and Norm you are in charge of the record keeping of this meeting so label all of this as a Top Secret meeting. We are out of here."

There were starch and expressionless looks on each of the attendee's faces as they filed out of the meeting room. George hesitated at the door and asked Jerry to meet him downstairs in the communications department and then shook Hank's hand. "Good job to both of you, we will finally get some attention after this meeting. Have a rest-full weekend and I'll see you Monday to see where your investigation goes. Jerry and I need to go over some visuals on al-Aziz's boat dealership."
"Yes Sir, see you all Monday."

Once inside George ushered Jerry to a glassed-in viewing room while a tech brought up visuals on six different screens.

"Jerry, I have asked Melvin to meet you in Miami and start with the FBI team in their search for where all of these boats al-Aziz brought in disappeared to. Go with the FBI team to talk to the DEA chief there in Miami and see if they have even the slightest clue to follow up on and get the agents investigating the sales tax records, the vehicle licensing department, and all delivery companies that can handle the transporting of those large high speed 'Fast Boats'. Someone knows something.

I will set you up with an open subpoena to any records your team believes it needs to find these bastards. You will be granted search warrants for any business, home, or shrine. Find them and don't contact me again until you can give us some 'heads on the platter' so to speak! Now get out of here and take your wife somewhere on this weekend before you leave next week. You need to clear your head and relax; this assignment is going to be stressful."

CHAPTER TWENTY THREE

Hank took Tiama and Tank to New York to see Grandpapa 'Tom' and take in a play. He and Tiama had not spent any enjoyable time together for a while and Dad had no problem baby sitting with his grandson. "Hey Dad, we thought we would come up to the City and have dinner and go to a play for the weekend, okay with you?"

"You bet son, it will be good to see you and Tiama and The Tank. When will you be here and do you want to stay in my new place in the Towers?"

"We are actually getting on the train now and should be at Grand Central at 9:15. How about meeting us in China Town for some Egg Rolls and Sizzling Duck?"

"Great, I'll pick you up at the station and we'll go to my favorite restaurant from there."

"Welcome again to Lo Choy's Mr. Brayden. How many are you?"

"Three and a half tonight. Can we get a booth with a highchair?"

We were escorted to a corner booth by the window which gave us a view of the Bowery. People scurrying everywhere.

"It's been a while kids. I don't need to ask how Tank is, he looks great. Give him a fried egg noodle and he is as happy as a pig in a mud hole. How are you two doing?"

"I've been gone a lot since the holidays but thaaa…"

"Tom I am glad we have a chance to get together. I need to ask a favor, since Hank is gone a lot and I am not working at the Pilipino Embassy I am hoping you can get me on at UBC in Washington doing anything, just anything. I need to get out. I am going a little coo- coo. Sorry my love to cut you off but I have been a little lonesome."

"Well, I'll see what I can find out next week and you know I will call you. Sorry son I missed what you were saying."

"That this duck is very tasty. No, I am kidding what I was about to say was that I am finished with any travels for awhile since my mission is officially over except some coordination from my office with the FBI's investigative teams that will be running with my Intel."

Kissing Tiama on the cheek Hank whispered in her ear, "I know it has been lonesome for you and as I pledged to you earlier, even though I will be home for a while I think it would be fine for you to get a job if it could be less than eight hours a day or even just a couple or three days a week. You know Tank needs his Mama. And have you looked for a nanny?"

"We'll see Hon, it has just been on my mind. Excuse me I think Tank is ready for a diaper change. I'll take him to the rest room."

"What's the latest on the political front with the coming 2006 elections and the effects of how the war is still beating the President's rating down? It's a crime how the editors at the Post and Times can spin the truth into the 'so called news' they feed everyone daily. Their one sided control and biased reporting is so hard to accept. Sometimes I wish there was a way to change the reporters and news staff every four years like we do with politicians."

"Point well taken son. The President and Rummey are losing ground to the antiwar crowd every week. It's almost like the entire country has forgotten about 9-11 and the President can't make a case for a terrorist threat anymore. Too much in the media and on TV showing the beginnings of chaos in Iraq and too many pictures of dead and badly wounded young men and women coming back home. You know son we try to present fair and unbiased news coverage at UBC. And it breaks my heart to see the ages of these young people dying over there while I feel like the Iraqis don't care about their own future. The people seem to let the insurgents operate freely within their own communities and our guys get killed daily trying to bring them security and freedom. I think the President will be speaking next week on the 10th about the war and urging us to stand strong against the terrorist, but I just don't know!"

"Oh my god Dad, If I could only tell you what we now know; you wouldn't say those things. Jerry was on your program almost four years ago with some basic facts about the terrorist threat and it seems like the media has lulled the public to sleep since then. They are still a threat, a very big threat and they are here in our country planning an 'American Jihad'! I can not go into any detail but they have the makings of a small army right here in the United States. The next attack will be beyond our imagination and our leaders must do something Dad."

"What do you mean a small army? It sounds freaky and very clandestine. Does the NSA have information on an inevitable attack just around the corner?"

"It is freaky and I can not say more. But just have your investigative reporters start snooping around some of the Mosques in some of our medium size cities and the Midwest. They can feed you info I can'......." Tiama came back with Tank. Tom reached out his arms, "How is he? Looks like he wants the bottle and some sleep?"

"I have one ready for him. What were you guys talking about?"

"Nothing really."

"Nothing really always means something deep that I am not supposed to hear."

"Hon, you know my clearance and anything I can tell Dad I can tell you. I was only saying that while the war in Iraq is on everyone's mind the terrorist threats around the world are getting worst. That's all and we don't want to get into all this political stuff tonight. Let's call it a night. Tank needs his beauty sleep."

"Oh, I almost forgot about the tickets for the play tomorrow night. I was able to get center orchestra seats for 'Mamma Mia' or row eleven almost center for 'Legally Blonde'. Let me know tomorrow before I get into work and I will have them at the reserved ticket window for which ever one you decide on."

Stepping out of the door of Lo Choy's I said, "Thanks Dad, that's great. I'll get us both a cab."

As we stepped off of the train in DC on Sunday afternoon we were caught in a gusty April wind swirling about on the platform blowing dust and papers all about. "Cover his eyes Hon; I just got a mouthful of dust. This is nasty. Let's hurry over to the cabs and get home. My hair is full of dust and grit and I feel dirty."

Tiama protected her two boys in the most motherly way. Sunday night would be unpacking, baths for everyone and errands for Hank. Diapers, milk, and some Mexican food to go.

Mondays always started off with the cafeteria offering a delicious main course so it was very crowded compared to other days of the week and Jerry and Melvin had to wait for a table. The specialty this day was fresh Eastern sea bass with rice pilaf, creamed peas and key lime pie for desert. A perfect spring time meal, light but very tasty, "You know Melvin I think fish may just be my favorite meat as I get older. Being from Texas steak has always been a staple for me and now I find it a little too heavy for my stomach especially for lunch. Look, catch that table over there and I'll bring your Pepsi on my tray. Hank is coming in I'll wave at him so we will need three chairs. Hank! Hank, get some lunch and join us over there, see Melvin?"

Hank waved back and ordered the special and chose apple pie with cheddar cheese instead of key lime pie. Setting his plates down, he asked Melvin about the new assignment. "Hey Melvin when do you and Jerry head to Florida?"

"We are waiting for the FBI team to complete the review of our reports and get up to date on everything including the computer lists of all parties of interest identified in NSA's data base. George requested a subpoena for the records that customs has for the Groupo Aziz boat imports and for the Florida Board of Equalization sales tax receipts and the Department of Vehicle registration records from 1992 to 2001. When all of the records have been inputted into our computer at Langley and each list cross referenced for matching names we can put together a systematic investigation of every boat imported beginning back when the Florida Fast Boat dealership started up. Then the fun begins. We will find these boats and get these bastards! What about you?"

"I guess I am going to be here while we put a plan of action together on how we can most efficiently identify and then find the delivery locations of containers with contraband. I am also going to have Al Sober run through Carnivore to find all of his contacts and have them interrogated. We'll get something!"

It was finally Friday and CU-4 had new information from the FBI on the possible location of Al Sober or better known by his Arabic name of Akria Sorubra. The Canadians had allowed the entrance of a business man by the name of Al Sober into the country and reported that to the FBI after the FBI sent them his name on its weekly STAL list, (Suspected Terrorist At Large). But after the name was run through their immigration department ID computer an aka was listed as Akria Sorubra who had been traveling through Canada to London and Hong Kong many times over the past fifteen years. There were also some close contacts of Al Sober generated by carnivore that were given to Hank.

Hank knew the importance of getting this guy and bringing him back to the states for interrogation. He was a key in this investigation and Hank wanted him. Going to George he discussed the need to immediately get Sober and bring him back to the U.S. for questioning.

"George, look I have brought this all the way to this point and I want to head up the Opt to get him." With that request Hank broke his pledge to Tiama but he was emphatic about leading the team into Canada to get Sober. Tiama will understand.

"You're right, I can understand your passion on this one, no problem. You've got the assignment but in partners with Melvin; no Melvin is going to Florida with Jerry. Let me get Jeff to go on this as your partner. He is seasoned and he grew up in Minnesota so he has a sort of Canuck twang to his speech. I have to make this clear, you know you will be on your own up there and you can not make this an international incident with our neighbor, Canada. This must be smooth and it is totally unauthorized. We will have an unregistered and non-descript SUV available and four CIA agents in Canada to help you complete the extraction. We will keep you under surveillance the second that you notify us the extraction has begun and you must stay on the air with us until you are across the border. Where ever you finally get him head directly to the nearest crossing and we will keep immigration notified. This will be operation 'Pluck a Canuck'."

As I entered the front door and smelled the aroma of spaghetti cooking for dinner I dreaded telling Tiama I would be gone again for a short assignment. It was Friday the twenty first of April and President Cush was going to talk to the country. We sat down in front of the TV to watch the President's speech on the situation of the war in Iraq as we ate dinner. "What is he going to say, Hank?"

"What can he say; things are going the wrong way. Here is the announcer."

"The President of the United States"
"Good Evening my fellow Americans, Tonight I want to up date everyone on the progress of the war on terrorism and the Iraqi conflict-

USA: THE SERPENT IS CRUSHED!

We are facing the most serious threat to our existence and to our personal peace and freedom that we have ever faced in our country's short existence and I believe in good conscience a threat that is greater than the Civil War, World War 1, or World War 2. It is the worldwide war on terrorism and the ancillary war in Afghanistan and Iraq. A confrontation that is propagated by those that have no allegiance to any country but their alliance is to an ideology. And what is explosively serious is that there are some of my colleagues in congress and I believe many of our patriotic citizens around the country who believe that we will lose this war. It is my firm belief that there are very few who understand what losing may really mean to us and the world.

I think most citizens would tell you that the war on terrorism started on September 11, 2001 but we know from looking back on history it started during the Carter administration more than twenty seven years ago. First with the Iranian take over of our embassy in Tehran, the bombing of our Embassy and our Marine barracks in Lebanon, the hijacking of TWA flight #847, the blowing up of PAN-AM flight # 103 over Scotland, the 1993 attack on the World Trade Center, the bombing of our Marine barracks at Kho'dor Towers, the bombing of our two Embassies in Kenya and Tanzania, the bombing of the USS Cole in Yemen waters, 9-11 attack on New York, the bombing of a commuter train in Spain, the bombing of buses in London, and all of the other hundreds of terrorist attacks around the world. If you add up all of the worldwide major terrorist's attacks from 1979 to today there have been over two thousand involving radical Muslims, more specifically 'Fascist Islamist'. All of these terrorist operations happened during the watch of Carter, Regan, my father George H W, Clinton and myself. Neither Democrats nor Republicans can be blamed. But who can be blamed for these provocations and who is it that is supporting and assisting all the terrorist groups?

Who are all of these different factions that have carried out the attacks on the United States Government, the American Citizens, and our interest around the world? These horrific acts were all carried out by Muslims. Not Jews or Christians or Buddhist or Hindus or any other sectarian group. There are approximately one billion two hundred million Muslims in the world or twenty percent of the population.

Many people ask aren't the Muslims really peaceful? Isn't this worldwide religion peaceful? There are radicals and fundamentalist in every religion. Most are led by individuals who carry some banner of authenticity but they always act alone as despots. Nero, Gangues Kahn, Napoleon, the Czar, Mussolini, Hitler all were radicals. Probably as many Christians were killed during World War two as Jews. And today there is not one single individual operating as an appointed leader of the terrorists that who are ordering the annihilation of multiple groups of people in many areas of the world but theirs is a disjointed movement of radical Muslim suicide bombers and would be martyrs who are directing their attacks against Jews and others and fascist Islamist that are carrying out genocide of Christians around the world. I understand that the actual count could be five million over the past thirty years. However, we realize that at the time of Hitler's power there were many peaceful people in Germany, Poland, Italy, Yugoslavia, just as there are peaceful people in Syria, Iraq, Iran, Indonesia, Sudan, and other Muslim countries.

So even the existence of peaceful Muslims does not stop the radical Muslim terrorists who have sworn to destroy and eliminate the Jew and the Christian, who they claim to be 'infidels'. It is easy to see that in the case of Iraq there are complacent Muslims who will not take a stand against the radicals in their midst or who are under the threat of retaliation if they did.

So now we must understand that we are at war and we must declare explicitly who is our enemy. If I, the congress, and all of our patriotic citizens do not face up to the fact that 'WE ARE AT WAR', not against a nation or any one individual but against an ideology and if we do not recognize that this ideology is what is driving our enemies then we will lose the war and we will lose our country and our peace and freedom forever!

Many of my fellow citizens too are complacent and do not know what losing in Iraq would mean. Some think just like Vietnam we should retreat, bring our fighting men and women home and be ashamed in the eyes of the world. This is the farthest thing from the truth. Here is the truth!

ONE-   We would become a humiliated country that would be labeled a cut and run secondary power. Both China and Russia would thrive on that allegory.

TWO-   Other countries would shun us in fear of internal terrorists reprisals as happened in Spain.

THREE-   Terrorism would flourish worldwide and attacks would increase ridding on the banner of the failure of the great United States in Iraq. The Taliban would be reconstituted with the help of Iran and al Qaeda would rapidly expand.

FOUR-   Nation after nation would fall to Islamic terrorism as the Muslims march across Europe and Africa defeating country after country just as Hitler did and slaughtering millions in their glory of victory.

FIVE-   Our international trade with those fallen nations would cease and a true oil embargo would follow. Our economy would be devastated and we would be on the verge of becoming a third world country. The only choice would be to give in to the Fascist Islamist or wither and die.

This great nation of ours can not and will not give in to the narrow mindedness of those liberal thinkers, those touters of political correctness that believe we are out of bounds in our fight against the terrorists; that we must leave Iraq to its own internal destruction and come home.

These same 'girly boy' types want us to be tolerant of everyone, believing that those who are amongst us that are possibly dangerous to our security should not have their rights infringed on. Even with suspicious actions, these liberals would say that those persons can not be investigated without their permission and that profiling to uncover the enemy within our neighborhoods, in our schools and universities, in our businesses and even in our government is a process that leads to an SS squad.

My fellow Americans this is WAR and we must be aware and alert. I ask you, is it politically correct or is it just foolishness to condemn the imprisonment of those identified terrorists who are consider prisoners of war and that maintain their loyalty to those who destroyed the twin towers, who have murdered their own fellow citizens and advocate the cutting off of people's hands, and tongues? Is it politically correct or foolishness to degrade and cast criminal accusations towards those who caused embarrassment and humiliation of a few Muslim prisoners while their Islamist brothers were burning victims alive, dragging dead Americans behind their cars, and cheering for the most horrific act of all, the beheading of Americans?

Read the news from around the world; the Fascists Islamist have plans to conquer the world and eliminate all other ideologies. I ask you each and everyone to get behind us, the congress, myself, and our fighting heroes who are dying for our security and freedom. So that we are all on the same page, Stand up to Win and Protect America, this great country God gave to us so we could live and prosper as free people! God bless America and my fellow citizens."
"Good night"

"'Oh my honey, maybe we should go to my home in the Philippines to live. I get the chills after I hear talk like that. How can we be safe?"
Hank looked at Tiama with compassion trying to comfort her feeling of fear. "We are all working on the protection of our country. I guess you know that the Philippines is not safe with the amount of Muslims living there. Just remember the bombings in your country over the past five years. These Islamic radicals are all over the world. We need to live our normal life and let the system work for us."
"Hold me Hank," as Tiama snuggled up to Hank, "I trust you and I know we are a strong country, hold me!"
As Hank reassured his wife the knowledge that there were terrorists all around that had access to guns and explosives raced through his mind. "Everything here will be alright", he told Tiama but he had to wonder when suicide bombers might start using the C-4 and where would they strike and could it be in Washington or maybe at the local shopping center and could Tiama and Tank be there at the exact moment! The thoughts caused his body to quake for a moment.
"What is it honey, what is wrong?"
"Oh nothing, just a muscle contraction. Let's turn on a movie and relax. You pick out one we haven't seen and I'll get us a couple of glasses of wine".
The night played on and Hank and Tiama played on after the movie was over. And the week-end came and went with Tank getting the most attention. Sunday evening while Tiama was feeding little Tank, Hank dropped a small bombshell, well not quite a bombshell just a small bang as he cleared Tank's Yogi Bear bowl and headed to the sink.

"I have to go to Canada for a couple of days this coming week". Then to drown out the sound of the bang he turned on the water and rinsed the bowl.

"Hank, did you say go to Canada? Oh, darling, I was counting on some real family time together this coming few weeks. What has happened?"

"George wants me to go pick up some classified package for the department. Nothing real big but I am the chosen one. Should only be gone a couple of days honey, not to worry, we'll have plenty of time together."

"I won't worry. I just wanted some extended and uninterrupted family time together, that's all. I love you. I know you have to go. Maybe when you come back we can take a vacation and go for a boating weekend on the Severin River?"

"I think that would be wonderful. It's a deal."

CHAPTER TWENTY FOUR

Jerry and Melvin caught a flight out to Ft Lauderdale Monday afternoon to meet the FBI team working the information the DEA and the local authorities had sent them. They had the list of probable suspects or acquaintances of al-Aziz with them and during the short trip they read the summation of each one's dossier so they could be on their game when they met with the FBI team.

"Melvin, did you check to see if the FBI received the cross referenced list of boat registrations and the sales tax payers from our Intel department? I hope they have done the necessary sorting to get the list reduced down to the Fast Boats imported by Groupo Aziz."

"Well if those records are correct we should find some of the same names on our computer lists as the FBI has on the two combined list."

We landed at Miami International Airport just after an all clear had been issued by the airport security involving a bomb scare. There was no one there to meet us so I called the FBI offices and talked to the officer on duty. "Hello, this is OHS agent Jerry Ness and my associate and I just arrived at the airport where we were to be met by agents from your office. Do you know anything about it and where are they waiting for us?"

"As you have seen there at the airport we had a situation which, as I am now told, is all clear and agents Melendez and Hopper are at the main security office. Ask one of the cart drivers to take you there."

"Right, thanks for your help."

I turned and Melvin was looking at all of the tourist as they file back into the building. "Hey Melvin, I checked and we are to grab one of those people carts and meet our guys at the main security office. There is one over there by the entrance doors, get that girl's attention."

"Hey miss, miss, over here we need a ride." Melvin showed her his badge and she swung the cart around and head right at us. "Please take us to your main security office."

Inside there was still a lot of commotion and a number of officers were questioning employees. Four private offices each had a number of people either going over airport layouts or talking to different persons on the airport management team. At the end of the small hallway standing next to an empty office were two guys in suits (one dark blue and the other black) with their hands folded just waiting. "What do you think Melvin are those our guys?"

"Do Monkeys live in trees?"

As we approached them the one in the black suit asked us if we were from CIA. "No fellows we are with OHS counter intelligence unit. This is Melvin and I am Jerry. Here are our ID's and you?"

"I am Juan Melendez and this is Gary Hopper. We can use this office temporarily or would you rather go to our offices."

"Here is fine. We can see what you have and what the assignment has produced so far."

Agent Melendez open his case and spread out three files. "We want you to know we have not had much time to work on this case. We did go to the site and verified that the boat dealership 'Florida Fast Boats' was no longer there and a used car agency was now the occupant. Here, our first list has the names of buyers who were charged sales taxes and filed for a vehicle registration on the boat they bought. From the years you gave us we went back one extra year and forward one extra year and over the twelve years we have records showing only sixty three boat buyers who were on the sales tax list and who also registered their boat for a water vehicle license. And none of these people appeared on your list of suspicious persons with possible terrorist ties. We also tried to review the Florida State Department of Commerce transportation records to look for any special hauling permits they may have issued to haul the boats to buyers in other states, but with no luck. They had no regulations that required special permits to haul that size boat. On a trailer the boats are about the size of a forty foot RV. And as a side note we asked the Board of Equalization who has the responsibility to collect the sales tax as to why only sixty three persons had paid taxes on boats sold by the dealership and their response made sense. They would have no way of being aware of any non reporting if inventory control was manipulated, but the prime factor they felt was that the boats were sold to out of state buyers which excludes the collection of any sales tax."

"What do you have Hopper?"

"We did interview the head of the department for the DEA and they bought about twenty five boats every two or three years after their first order. Seems they had a budget and had to use up the money or loose it so they sold the used boats and replaced them with new ones. With out checking the DEA's requisition records for twelve years he estimated that they acquired around one hundred thirty five boats from Florida Fast Boats. We did go to the U S customs office and had them pull up all of their records to sort out the number of boats that Groupo Rizo shipped in from Brazil. The total was nine hundred eighty six. The first boats were spot checked and completely dismantled according to their records. After the DEA started buying their chase boats from Florida Fast Boats they basically stopped looking at them. The records show that they would select five or six boats per year and just do a casual visual on them. So we can account for one hundred ninety eight boats of the total that were shipped from Brazil."

"Looks like that leaves about seven hundred eighty eight boats some where in the states and all or some with smuggled in C4. And the other file?"

Melendez took the file folder as he answered, "This is the list sent to us from the NCTC at NSA. We thought that list might have matching names on it with a couple of characters whose names we came across during our investigations. Oh, and I did not mention we asked the commander of the south Florida Coast Guard post to provided us with any information they might have on the dealership's use of the waters off of the coast for testing or demonstrating their boats. They had a number of items in their files. That is where we listed some names we wanted to cross check. One involved an accident with another competitor's boat during a manufacture's regatta. Another report was involving a breakdown of one of their boats about eight miles out from the coast and the Coast Guard had to assist in getting the boat back to the boat pier. The driver did not seem to know very much about skippering a boat that large. His name in the report indicated he was Arabic so we listed him as a person of interest. Still another incident happened with one of their boats running out of gas while traversing the south tip of the state headed to the Gulf of Mexico. When the guardsmen were helping with gas to get the boat back to shore the driver-owner seemed to be a little nervous so they checked the boat for drugs but it was clear. They did tell us that the dealership did ship a lot of their boats by water either up the coast all the way to Cape Cod and around the peninsula to the Mississippi River and to Texas from port Houston to Padre Island."

"Where are those names you have as persons of interest?"

"It is in this file and we have sent one on to the processing section in your TIU section routed through OHS and take note of this. There was one high profile individual who was in the boat that broke down; one Sami al-Fazi with some of his friends from the University of Southern Florida. We have found out that al-Fazi was later indicted on terrorists activities. The name of the owner of the boat that ran out of gas on the Gulf side was listed as Abraham Mastanian and there were two passengers listed; James Tasi and K. Abdul Misha'al. They do not know of any disposition of that boat and it did not have an ID number at that time."

Jerry's eyes lit up, "We are aware of the al-Fazi connection with some Jihadist organizations and W.I.S.E. which is a front for the solicitation of money specifically for Palestinian Judaist. But Misha'al is very important. When we ran Jonathan al-Aziz's name through our data base for cross referencing of associates both the name of al-Fazi and Khalid Misha'al came up along with others in Los Angeles and New York. We have some people from our department interviewing each of them right now for possible links to our investigation. Khalid is on the NSA watch list and has been for some time. He is a Muslim leader in Oklahoma who has been openly preaching death to all Christians and Jews. Seems it is okay to preach hate towards a religious group or specific ethnic group and nothing is done about it, but say one thing about queers and lesbians and a hate crime is charged against you in half a wink. The ignorant and arrogant ACLU and political leftist just don't get it. These fools advocate political correctness about not interfering with foreigner's right to express free speech while the Fascist Islamist laugh at the entire American culture. The ACLU, the liberal press, and the liberal politicians have put box cutters at the throats of the American People – all I can say is, WATCH OUT!"

Melendez was a bit edgy when Jerry finished. "Hey we all have our concerns but you can't take on the whole world – the press, the politicians, the ACLU. It's one little battle at a time. Let's get this one won, what is our next move."

"Sorry my friend but I have been doing this for twenty years and I know my enemy. We may be on the verge of an internal armed conflict with these Judaists and that is all we can say."

Melvin added, "Let me add this, it is not one little battle this time. Jerry and I will return to Washington and recommend that the FBI start investigations for boat deliveries or even sightings at all of the small ports with private boat docks all the way up the coast and along the entire Gulf coast line. We have to believe some one has seen these boats somewhere. But right now when you are back at your office please contact the bureau in Oklahoma City to begin an in depth investigation of where the boat that Misha'al was on is now. We will call our people to get the NSR order out tomorrow to all field offices. We must find all of these boats."

It was Wednesday the twenty sixth of April when Hank and Jeff stepped off of the plane in Calgary Canada and caught a cab to the American Consulate offices in an office complex near the airport. Inside of the front door were a desk and a solid glass wall with a secured door opening in to a hall. No one was at the desk or in the hallway but Jeff noticed a camera pointed directly at the front door and at them. A voice filled the room with a simple announcement, "We are sorry no one is available at the front desk but please state your name and your business."

"We are from the OHS department in Washington and we are here to see the vice-consulate on government business; our names are Hank Brayden and Jeff Howell."

"One moment please."

Hank turned to Jeff, "I hope we have everything in position to get this guy. I don't want to be spinning our wheels here while the advance team finishes the set up for our snatch and run. I want to get going!" Hank told himself to slow down because he knew he got a little bit of the jitters each time he starts on a mission since this was only his forth time in the field, or he thought for a second, was this the fifth?

Again the voice from the ceiling, "I'll click the door open for you and when you are in the hallway turn to your left and then down the corridor on your right. The vice-consulate office is next to the last door and she will meet you in the meeting room which will be the last door on your left."

We had each carried a small case with a change of clothes and our weapons. Inside we sat the cases on the table, sat down and waited for our hostess to enter. The door behind us opened and in came four fairly stout guys dressed in plain plaid shirts and jeans. "Hello, we are your team from the Seattle office. Which one of you is Hank and which is Jeff?"

We identified our selves and then showed them our ID's.

"The vice-consular will not be with us but she wants it made clear that this mission does not exist and neither do we. Our job is to provide you with the SUV's needed and to make the grab and get you to the border. We have located the target and are ready to complete the task tonight. When we get to the border we will take one vehicle and disappear and you take the other unit and your cargo to your assigned location. Our orders are to assist you and then leave. We have not been here and there is no record of you having been at the consulate. All cameras have been off. As we were all informed the Canadian authorities do not smile on espionage or kidnapping in their country. Ready, let's go out the back door, our SUV's are ready. And no names, this is a silent mission. If for any reason we have trouble or stopped by the Mounties we don't know each other. You are with driver team two and we are driver team one."

"Where are we going and at what time will you execute?"

"We are going to Edmonton and your driver will go over all of the details on the drive there."

It took around two hours to get to Edmonton after stopping for something to eat and drink at the Red Deer restaurant. Our driver went over the plan after we left Red Deer. "The grab will be at a favorite little espresso and smoking house frequented by our target where a number of the Muslims that live in Edmonton go after their evening prayer to cajole each other. Al Sober or aka Akria Sorubra as he is known here in Canada enjoys his Syrian culture and stops at the coffee house almost every evening that he is in town. He is the leader of two radical Islamic cells, one in Calgary and one in Edmonton so he is always on the road and hard to pin down. This night if he acts according to his routine we will wait for him to leave and bang, we have him. We have a spotter on assignment and if the target's routine changes we will be informed. Any movement will be under continuous surveillance"

Arriving in Edmonton the driver of team one made audio contact with the spotter and received a green light so the two SUV's moved into position at the designated location. Hank and Jeff's driver parked a short distance from the Espresso House and asked Jeff to take the wheel and to drive into position behind team one on their signal just before the snatch. The two agents left the SUV to move in next to vehicle number one. Team one was to wait for the spotter to make a visual ID of Akria as he exited the building and then on the signal that the Opt was on one of the agents from team two was to walk a short distance ahead of the target towards the parking lot.

The other agent lingered around the doorway of the shop three units away from the Espresso House while the driver in SUV one parked across the street waiting for Akria to exit and head to his car. They were told that his habit was to leave around nine thirty to ten in the evening and sometimes with a fellow Muslim. Everyone was ready. Hank was anxious; he wanted him so bad he was salivating. He was thinking that after all of this chasing of the contraband, the assertions of Mr. Taug, the death of Jack, and his encounter with Gutung; this guy can give us facts and verification that will break his investigation wide open.

"Is that him?"

Yes, that's him."

"Are you sure, we must be sure; command, what does your surveillance show? Double check the visual. We only have less than a minute. Bob, tighten up that view and get a clear frontal."

"It's him, we have a confirmed positive ID, but he has two companions with him!"

"That's okay, we are prepared for that. GO! GO! Go unit one and unit two move into position and hold."

The agent from the doorway had already started walking in the shadows of the building and came in from behind the three suspects when the go signal came. In the mean time the number one SUV had made a U turn and was moving into where there was open space next to the curb. As they arrived next to the curb and right in front of the three men walking towards the parking area the door of the SUV was opened just as the agent came from behind and knocked out the two companions walking with the target while the agent in front had stopped and turned around and shoved a gun in Akria's face. The agent who opened the door helped pick him up just as the one with the gun injected him with a heavy tranquilizer and they placed him in the SUV. Then all three loaded his two companions into the SUV and away they went; all in less than one minute.

"Great job team one, we are right behind you. We will stay in radio contact but follow behind at about thirty meters or so."

Hank grabbed the radio to say his piece. "It's Hank here and I am impressed; you have given us a real live major player in this conspiracy. This guy can be the witness we need to back up our case on how dangerous the threat is that we believe is awaiting our country and now most importantly he is our prisoner. Way to go guys, we can report on a perfect mission and an outstanding performance."

"Hey, hold on, we are not finished until you two and your package cross the border."

"Then let's get to the border. How many hours till we are in the States?"

"Obeying the speed laws about six hours so settle back and relax. They are giving an injection to the other two so that we don't get any disturbance as we drive south."

It was almost four am when the two SUV's approached the border crossing on Highway #4 which lead into the states. Then the team one car stopped and found a place to leave the unwanted two passengers. About a half mile before the immigration check point and across the street from a Shell gas station there was a covered cabaña type waiting area for a Grey-line bus. They could see that no one was around so they placed the two on the empty bench and left them in Canada. As they approached, the border patrol officer waved the two vehicles through without stopping them since the Seattle office had informed them to be on the look out for two black SUV's with specific license numbers. Across the border Hank wanted to stop for a chance to relieve himself and to get some coffee and maybe a roll. They stopped just on the outskirts of Sunburst and switched SUVs so the Seattle agents could be on their way. Hank had arranged to go to Helena and have a NSA plane waiting for them.

Hank and Jeff found a small diner attached to a truck stop that was open and pulled in. "I'll stay here while you get us something. I'd like coffee with cream and three sugars and maybe a donut or what have you."

Jeff nodded his head, "Okay, but I thought you needed a restroom?"

"Right, I'll go after you return."

Hank opened the door for Jeff as he returned, "Watch out the coffee is real hot and the roll is one day old. The fresh stuff hasn't arrived yet, too early."

"Right, I'll be right back."

Not more than a minute later Akria began to utter some sounds. Jeff turned to look at what the noise was and Akria who had been leaning against the rear window straightened up and looking very dazed asked, "Is that coffee I smell? Can I get some? My head feels terrible. Where am I and who are you?"

"I am an agent of the United States Government and you are inside our border and are our prisoner."

"Why have you done this and how can you take me out of Canada? I am a citizen of Syria. You have no right to kidnap me!"

"I'm afraid that we didn't take time to ask you about your rights or to talk to the Canadian authorities. We believe that you are a terrorist and part of a major conspiracy to do lethal damage to our country. We will be taking you back to our people at OHS and they are waiting to ask you a whole lot of questions about your activities while you lived in the States."

"This is absolutely insane. I am a business man in Canada. I used to have a business in Salt Lake City but I sold it and moved to Canada. You are making a big mistake. You, you can't do this."

"We'll see."

"Can you please ease up on the chains so I can stretch a bit and can I have some coffee?"

Hank returned and said, "Okay, let's roll", as he buckled his seat belt.

"Our passenger is awake. He asked for some coffee and wants his chains loosened a bit so he can stretch."

"Sure, why not. His chains are still attacked to the ring in the floor. I'll loosen them a bit so he can move his arms from side to side but he still will not be able to reach out to the backs of our seats. Now I'll get you a coffee. Now do you want it?"

"Just black please."

After Hank left to get Akria a coffee, he reached down to his shoe and pulled the tips off of each of his shoe laces and put them in his mouth and waited for his coffee. In a couple of minutes Hank returned, handed Akria his coffee and jumped into the front seat. "Let's go, I want to get him on the plane."

Akria was able to drink his coffee and swallow the ends of his shoe laces which contained a heart stopping drug that was a derivative of Conium Maculatum. He knew he was finished and now he could join his blessed allah.

When Hank and Jeff arrived at the airport in Helena their plane was waiting for them in the private air terminal area so Hank pulled along side of the stairs which were lowered so they could quickly board. Two agents form Helena were there to help them with the prisoner and they open the doors to get Akria out but he was limp and blue. "Hey you guys, you got a dead man here."

"Dead, what the hell are you talking about? We just bought him a coffee an hour or so ago." Hank moved the agents aside and reached in to look at Akria. "He can't be deeaa.... Jeff what happened?"

"I don't know; did he have a heart attack? Hey someone! Can we get an ambulance here immediately? And a doctor!"

Hank still stunned sat down on the tarmac just saying, "Oh my god, Oh my god, Oh my god." Again and again until Jeff was able to shake him out of it. Jeff got him to get up and sit in the front seat.

Hank just stared at Jeff, "There goes our witness and under our protection, what are we going to do?"

"Hank he just died, it's not our fault."

"How could he have just died? He was fine. He drank some coffee. Wait you loosened his hands so he could drink coffee, right. This can not be our fault. Was he able to cause his own death! Could he have choked himself with those chains or held his breath and caused an attack? Did he have anything to kill himself with?"

"Hank, you were with me in our SUV; we were together. I didn't search him; the other agents had control over each of the captives."

"Okay, Okay, this is a disaster. Is the ambulance here? Maybe they can do something. Sometimes people can be brought back, oh here it comes."

Two Medivac guys jump out and started to bring their bags. "No get a fibulator, hurry, we think this man's heart stopped. We are with counterintelligence and we must save this man's life!"

They worked on him for ten minutes giving him an adrenaline shot and continued to fire the charge on the fibulator but he did not respond. "He is gone."

"Gone? Gone?"

"We'll get him into a body bag and then what? Do you want us to put him on the plane?"

Jeff answered, "Yes."

Hank looking still shocked, "I'm calling George now!"

It was nine thirty when the call came in for George at the CI section at NSA and it took a few minutes for the operator in CI section to locate George before he came on the phone, "George Meeker here, who is this?"

"George this is Hank."

"Hank, I'm glad you called. I have set a meeting with John at OHS to review your report on what Sorubra had to say. We are ready to interrogate him and then John is going to get all of this into the hands of Peter Rodman and Stephen Hadl......."

Hank cut him off, "No George, don't do anything yet."

"What are you saying, why not?"

"Akria is dead."

"Dead, what are you saying? What happened? What went wrong? Did you kill him? Why? Your whole investigation hinged on him! Who fouled up? You, we, this entire mission depended on interrogating him. Hank, what in the world happened?" A long pause from George....... And then, "We have nothing!"

"George, we don't know what happened. He was alive when we crossed the border headed for Helena and when we arrived at the airport and opened the door to get him out he was dead; maybe a heart attack. We just do not know, damn it."

'Get that body back here and get an autopsy done. This leaves us where?"

"I don't know. I'll think of something on the flight back to DC."

Meanwhile in Washington, Jerry and Melvin had returned from their Florida mission.   George met with them in the debriefing room on the second floor. They reported to George that approximately seven hundred eighty eight of the boats that had been imported from Brazil were unaccounted for and were somewhere in the states. "It would appear that they had perfect plans on making sure these boats disappeared and that there would not be a trace of where they went."

"At least we know that much. I have already had a NSR order issued and I checked with Robert Dryer to find out how quickly he would have his field units respond to the order and I asked about how many agents they could put on the case. His best estimate was that all of the field offices around any water areas large enough to operate a Fast Boat would have their authorizations by Friday the thirty first and that the agency would reassign approximately eight hundred agents to the mission. When the reassignment would occur he could not say nor when they would actually be doing field interviews. In order to get the highest degree of effectiveness from our people we need a plan of action designed to give us expediency and no wasted operations; we need to find these boats. Everyone, that has been apprized of our investigation, from Mertoff to Gonzales to Dryer to Haddle is demanding some real proof to back up our allegations but what we need is to find just a few of these boats. They go hand in hand."

"George, any ideas on what can we do from here?"

"For now nothing I can think of until they actually have the agents in the field and we start getting some input from their field units. Just review everything we have on Jonathan from his entry into Brazil till he sold the boat dealership and use all of the archived Sat-tel visuals we have. Keep me posted Jerry. I want you to study the files we have on him and the investigative reports and if you get anything day or night, notify me. You guys have two weeks"

George closed the door as he left Jerry and Melvin and then turned to open the door back up as he offered the latest on Hank. "In my anxiety I almost forgot to let you know about Hank. He and Jeff were successful in capturing Akria in Canada but just before they were to board the plane in Helena, Akria died. Hank has no idea how, except for a possible heart attack. I got the impression that he is pretty down with this set back to all of his hard work to prove the theories Jack had and the confessions of Gutung. That event pretty much puts a stone wall in front of his case. He and Jeff are bringing the body back for an autopsy and will be here tonight; thought you would want to know."

"Yeah, I think I'll stick around to talk to him."

Jerry wanted to get home to Anna but he knew Hank would need some encouragement and they both had the same purpose in their missions. Find the terrorists who were planning an attack on the States and expose the plot before another evil and diabolical event like 9-11 was carried out.

Jerry called Anna to let her know that everything was okay, but that he was staying at the office to meet with Hank when he got in from Montana.

The plane from Montana landed around three thirty and Hank asked Jeff to escort the body to forensics at FBI. They have the best people around to do the autopsy.

He knew he would know by the next morning what had happened. When he arrived, security let him know that Jerry was waiting in the debriefing room by the elevator to see him. He took his small carrying case in his left hand as he open the door and spied Jerry in a chair looking at satellite views of Ft Lauderdale. "Hey Jerry, how was your trip to Florida?"

"Not much to report but I understand that you have bad news."

"I guess one dead terrorist is not really bad news but it is a complete bust for our trip to Canada. We do not understand what happened and when I look at the big picture I wonder why are there so many set backs on the investigations into this conspiracy? You have been at this longer than I so what does your wisdom tell you?"

"Just keep going. When you least expect it and many times out of the blue you get a clue, a bit of information fits into something you remember from some previous investigation or a report or an interview and bingo you are out of the tunnel and into the light. Or something like that."

"Okay so we keep on going and naturally I will. My impatience is showing, but we need to get some kind of communication to more government officials that are in a position to review what we know and understand what we believe. The obsession with the war in Iraq is smothering everything else that is happening not only here but in the rest of the world."

"You're right. And I agree so I think maybe we should draft a detailed report based on the information we have gathered from our missions that clarifies our assessment of what is actually happening inside the states regarding a probable widespread plot to start suicide bombings and more probably terrorists attacks on buildings or other targets and expose it to the Senate and the House and of course the President. I believe that Mertoff is in agreement with our suppositions and George and John and Robert at the FBI are in accord but you know everyone is walking on egg shells since the accusations that most all of the Intel used to attack Iraq was fabricated or at least carried a one sided spin on it. We just need some solid hard evidence but the wheels of the government grind too slow. George authorized a NSR which is a start but it could be from now until June or July before all of the agents are deployed and then three or four months before we get our first hard evidence."

"Jerry I am in the same boat right now. I will never get a NSR issued on what evidence we have on shipments coming from middle-east. I know there are guns and explosives smuggled into the States just like you know that there have been hundreds of boats used to bring in C4 from South America but we have no hard evidence. Maybe your idea is a correct step. I think with the uproar on the failed policies on the war and the concentration the candidates for Congress are placing on Iraq; these hypothesizes we have been presenting are not hitting home, they are just not being given credibility or alerting the right people; just like what happened before 9-11."

"Well we are thinking along the same lines. Let's go home and sleep on it and talk about what we could formulate in the way of a report that would not continue to be stacked in the 'I'll get to that later' reading material but something that can force immediate attention and not be political and more importantly not get us fired."

CHAPTER   TWENTY FIVE

Friday the twenty eighth and Tiama and Tank picked up Hank from the office early to have a picnic on the promenade. She had felt like Hank had been wound up tighter than a guitar string ever since he had learned the cause of the death of one of the agencies most significant terrorist captives was self inflicted by eating poison contained in the tips of his shoe laces. She was sure he needed some kind of special time away in a peaceful environment where she could talk to him. They had not been able to take the weekend trip to the river she had planned back in March so at least a picnic might bring some calm into his behavior. Tiama had picked a gorgeous day and the trees and landscaping were a dynamic contrast against the stark whiteness of the Capital. The movement of hundreds of tourist enjoying the monuments and statures added to Tiama's feeling of joy and pride to be an American. She handed the large quilt to Hank and helped to spread it under one of the trees along side the walk way. "Before we eat let's enjoy the beauty of the cherry blossoms and the fragrance in the air." Tiama went on, "This is God's beauty. I'll pray to thank God for you, for Tank, our family, our country and the all that He has given us."

Hank paused to look around and then, "Amen."

"Here Hon, can you get the food out of the basket as I set up some plates and arrange for Tank to sit between us."

"Of course, I'm not letting that fried chicken and baked beans stay in there a minute longer. It all smells too good. And I am really hungry. This is a wonderful idea; did Tank talk you into it?"

"Absolutely, here is a breast and a leg. I cooked plenty so enjoy."

Hank tore a small piece of white meat off of the breast and put it on

Tank's plate. Then smacking his lips he took a big bite of the crispy and juicy center and smiled at Tiama.

"Now that we have some relaxing quite time and you with some of your favorite food in you month I can ask you why you have been so somber lately. I see your expressions around the house and our friends and sometimes your attitude gets a little testy and it has kind of started to stress me out."

"Oh my! I had no idea I was doing that to you. I am sorry; I guess I need to take stock of what I bring home these days."

"Has work become so difficult that you haven't noticed your changes?"

"It is all my fault because there have been some developments in our department that has Jerry and Melvin and Jeff and well, a lot of us concerned about the things happening to our country."

"You mean like the war and the conflicts between the President and the Congress?"

Hank took a napkin to wipe the bean juice from his lips and bent over to kiss first Tank on the cheeks and then Tiama on the lips. "I am truly sorry. I love both of you so much that the state of the affairs of this world plagues my thoughts of what our future will be like, yours and mine and Tank's. I mean am I in the right place at the right time and are we where we should be for the coming next five to ten years?"

"Do you mean that you don't like your work or you don't want to live here in Washington?"

"Kind of. The exposure I get at work on all of the turmoil in the world gets to you after a while and I think about you in this city with everything being about politics and Tank growing up here and I remember the family farm and my childhood growing up in the country environment. It is a better life style, a more secure life, with far more pleasant surroundings then this place. That's all; I'm just looking into the future."

"Well I guess Tank and I kind of agree. It is lonesome here some times and not much for him to do in our little house. I see why you have been a little edgy lately so I'll try to add a lot more female comfort in the evenings to make that face of yours smile more, OK!"

Hank broke a wide smile, "You get an amen to that. So I guess a grumpy face can get you a little loving now and then, huh?"

With that Tiama punched him on the arm, "That's not fair!"

And then she crawled over Tank, jumped into Hank's lap and Frenched him for, well a long enough time that Hank said, "That's it we're cleaning up and going home. Come on Tank, it could be sister shopping time."

Saturday morning and Hank was still in bed when Tiama came in with coffee and a sweet roll. "Good morning my love, sweet rolls for my sweetheart and coffee just the way you like it. Sugar and cream, lots and lots of cream. Thank you for a dreamy night!"

"Come here you. I have some kisses for you and a personal question." Whispering in her ear Hank asked; "Was the timing right for Tank's 'sister' order?"

"We'll see, we'll see."

A couple of hours later Hank was on the phone to Tom.

"Hello Dad, I was just talking to Tiama about the good old times at the farm and was wondering how are things with Grandma and Caroline and how are things at the station?"

"Everybody is doing well and Caroline is going to spend the summer at the Cape. I'm making some long term plans for retirement and have started the search for my replacement."

"Really, do you think you can really give up the broadcast business after more than thirty years and leave the 'BIG APPLE'? I mean really give up!"

"As of now my plans are to leave after the two thousand and nine inauguration and build a hunting lodge in Montana. You know my love of the out doors and for hunting."

"I guess we think a lot alike because I was telling Tiama yesterday that I think we as a family would be better off some place other than DC and that raising our family should be in a different environment. She agreed so who knows we may follow you to your 'happy hunting grounds'. I see things building up to cause a lot of unrest here. At times she has even mentioned the Philippines."

"More unrest than we already have, with the President feuding with congressional candidates over troop increases for Iraq and threatening to cut off funding for the war? Then we have his approval rating in the dumper and we see that the Taliban is back and expanding in Afghanistan while Pakistan is allowing the northern tribes to control the area between their borders. And of course we have North Korea testing their first nuclear weapon and that idiot, Mahmoud Ahmadf-Inejad in Iran expanding their research at top speed so they can build a nuclear bomb while claiming Israel must be destroyed. So the President sends signals that Iran must stop their efforts to develop a nuclear weapon or the worst might happen. What more unrest can we possibly have?"

"Dad, off the record and with out divulging top secret information you know that there are Muslim cells in this country that are not friendly to our country or as they would say it, adverse to the President and his objectives in the Mid-east and to our basic western philosophy or more bluntly they are our enemies. And beyond that there are radical Islamist in numerous mosques here like the Imam Husham Al-Husainy and Imam Khalid Misha'al or that guy at the University of Southern Florida that are preaching death to the Americans and the violent indoctrination of Islam into the Western world. And then we have the fact that there is an escalation of Muslims in countries like France, England, and Germany and a tremendous increase of mosques in these countries. There are now more mosques in France and England then there are churches and we have over five thousand mosques in the States which provides a hot bed for covert teaching of the destruction of our country."

"Of course I have seen this information and the news investigative reports on most all of these things. And so has your OHS and the Congress as you know. All of this is on their watch list."

"Yes Dad on their watch list but not on a very active basis. But the OHS is just a little overwhelmed. I don't believe that the enemy here at home knows that yet but we just do not have the personnel to put all of the potentially destructive sleeper cells under the microscope. Now here is the shocker and it is to be kept under your hat so to speak. After I pose this hypothesis you of course can have your own media folks do some investigations and what ever you find of course is public information. There are over one hundred sleeper cells here as many people have surmised, and they are comprised of as many as eight to nine thousand committed terrorist who present a strong clandestine force that is armed, ready and possess what it takes to become suicide bombers."

"Son, verified or conjecture."

"Dad we need to get together for Tank's birthday. I would like us all to take some time and celebrate it at the farm. What do you think?"

"Well wait a minute, verified or conjec...... oh I see it's my call. I got you. Okay, we'll work on it. Maybe I'll get my hunting lodge started a little sooner. Say hi to Tiama and Tank and a birthday party at the farm will be great, love you guys. Goodbye."

"Here Hon, hold Tank for a little bit while I finish getting dressed. What did Dad have to say? And how are he and grandma and Caroline doing?"

"Everyone is fine. I asked Dad if having Tank's birthday celebration at the farm would work and he said it sounded great to him. Let's go to the mall and then if Tank gets sleepy enough we can take in a movie."

"That's my Hank, what are you waiting for? Grab the stroller and baby bag; I'll get the car keys."

May had come and turned into June and then it was July. Hank caught himself mulling over his associations with all of the Arabic students at NYU from his university days up to his latest encounters and he wondered, as he looked out his office window at the large elm and two oak trees that were between the north wing of NSA headquarters and the distant freeway, just who were these Muslims? Past buddies at school and past acquaintances at reunions and now possibly what? Are they all alike? Just then George knocked on the door and opened it all at the same time as he entered to ask Hank to meet with him, Jerry and Robert from the FBI in his office at eleven thirty. "Sure, I'll be there. What should I bring?"

"Nothing."

Robert was the last to arrive and presented a short update on the NSR regarding Jonathan al-Aziz. "I want to first let you guys know in case you have not heard that there has been a terrible bombing of a commuter train in Mumbai, India and an estimated two hundred were killed. No one has acknowledged responsibility for the bombing yet so we are monitoring the event closely. Now here is where we are on the al-Aziz investigation. Five hundred agents have been on assignment looking for any one that may have observed one of his boats. Yes I had hoped for at least eight hundred but we believe we can get the job done with the current number. We are using pictures of the DEA boats because we do not think the other boats sold at Jonathan's dealership would look any different. They started both along the Atlantic coast in Florida going north and going to any and all boat docks and the along the Gulf coast going west boat dock to boat dock. We have also sent a bulletin to all of the Eastern state's highway departments and patrol agencies to go back through their records for the past ten years for any possible violations that would have occurred involving a vehicle carrying an over sized boat that could have had a breakdown on the highway or a ticket for speeding or any other violation. So far no luck but we just started and the information from the various state highway departments will be slow in coming."

"Okay Robert, we are now on the mark for this critical investigation but we must keep this in mind. Based on the evidence backing our NSR the boats that may have contained smuggled C4 would have been disbursed over approximately an eight year period and they would have immediately been put in to hiding when delivered to their destination. I am suggesting that there will have been very little observation of these boats by anyone. It maybe a little like finding a feather in a hay stack in a Kansas wind storm. Your agent's interrogation must be intense. And even then if some boats were clean they will be just a decoy and waste of our time."

"On that we all agree and they know it too."

Hank nudged George as he said, "Ask him about the cargo shipments."

"Right Hank, I've been talking to Robert on that also. I am pressing for authorization to have a NSR issued to look into the use of containers for smuggling in the C-4, my problem is evidence. There are millions of containers coming in every year and to go back and follow up on the delivery and contents on all of them over a ten year period is a monumental undertaking. I have been shot down on my request. And I know Al Sober would have been a key person to provide us information but we don't have anything."

Like Jerry had predicted the FBI's investigations were just now getting under full steam and it could be a few more months before the agents developed anything tangible. And my concerns about the danger to our country are going no where. The impossibility of investigating hundreds of thousands of containers is a checkmate for the terrorist. We lose.

"Robert I know you will keep trying and some how we will find a way to get to the bottom of these allegations. Thank you for our up date." George then looked at Jerry and Hank as he made a request for a second meeting. "Jerry and Hank could you get Jeff and Melvin to meet us here around two this afternoon, I have some ideas. We'll take a lunch break and instead of here, let's all meet in the situation room."

"I think I'll skip lunch and do some work in my office. I'll see you and the other guys at two." Hank then headed to his office. Staring out of his window again he tried to figure out what he could do to stop the impending terror that was inevitable for the country. Looking past the top of the North wing of his building and off in a distance he could barely make out the top of the Capital building where the battle for the congressional seats in the house and the senate was centered; he thought to himself how ridiculous that these candidate's cross fighting was not only catching all of the headlines at this time but that accusations were being aimed at the very heart of the various candidate's patriotism. All of it fulminated because of the President's stance on the war and his terrible approval rating which was bumping against the twenties. Still very little concern by the Whitehouse or the Congress about terrorism anywhere except Iraq and especially not within the States and there had been no mention of bin Laden for months so it was as if a threat to the States was now on the back burner as the day of the elections approached.

The media obsessed with their criticism of Cush's war and continually lambasting the Republicans as the media claimed that the conservatives entire dialog was centered on their ability to protect against the terrorist and who warned that losing the war in Iraq would bring ship loads of terrorist to our shores the next day. In the minds of those in the inner sanctum at OHS and NSA, the boat loads had arrived a long time ago. On the other hand the threat from all of the Democrats was to stop the war at all cost, even shutting off funding to the troops or more accurately to the military so that Rummey would be forced to pull the soldiers out of Iraq. In espousing that position as their banner for election they were distancing themselves from very patriotic Americans and alienating most of the military and veterans. They however avoided tackling the terrorist problem almost as though it didn't exist; or surely not in our country. What naive pigs. I guess calling the Democrats pigs is alright since they are the originators of and the advocates of PORK! I kind of imagine they are the soft under belly of our democracy.

It was 2:00 pm and Hank couldn't help but wonder that George had something up his sleeve as he entered the situation room. Melvin and Jeff had rounded the corner at the end of the hall just as the door closed behind Hank and he walked over to where Jerry and George were sitting and discussing the wall video screen with a display of data from the carnivore system.

After Melvin and Jeff came in and grabbed a seat Jerry spoke without any air of doubt which was his usual approach, "I think you will like George's proposal which may get us closer to our goals of finding some bits and pieces of helpful information as he refers to it."

George pointed to the large video screen as he began, "Well here it is and this maybe a long shot, but I want you to supervise the cross referencing of our data in Carnivore with all key items or points of interest from your investigations. There is a high probability that in all of the data in our stored phone calls and/or e-mails on your persons of interest you will find some linkage and then you can have the program do 'spider searches' on each of the individual links. Jerry, you think about all you have learned about this al-Aziz, his associates, his places of residence, his travels, his origin before entering the States, and then cross reference all of those bits and pieces and expand the search to wherever the information leads you. We must know all about his activities here in this country from the first moment he ever set foot on our ground and I mean day by day."

"Makes good sense to me, I'll do it, maybe there is some loose clue he left behind. Or possibly something will trigger some information that will lead to a clue or an association that will lead us to some of those boats. "

"And Hank you do the same with Akria Sorubra. It looks like all you will have are phone numbers, but hopefully there will be more spider webs and even loops in your search."

'Well at least it can be a positive effort while we wait on the rest of the reports from the FBI."

It was July twelfth when Sayyed Nasrallah the Hezbollah leader in Lebanon left Damascus and went to Southern Lebanon where Hezbollah's planned incursion into Israel had begun with the firing of rockets into Hifa and other Northern Israeli areas. By Friday the fourteenth, hundreds of rockets had been fired on Israel and Israel declared war on Hezbollah sending troops into Lebanon to destroy their missile supply and wipe out their position at the Southern border. The department of Homeland Security raised the alert level to Orange.

The Intel section at NSA was monitoring the various television broadcasts from around the world on the thirty first of July when al-Jazeera broadcast a video from the bin Ladin camp with his claims that the United States will suffer greatly for it's aid to Israel and the backing of Israel against Hezbollah and for their occupation of Arabic lands. He pronounced that 'A force has been put into motion to destroy the Satan of the west and nothing can stop the path of the righteousness of allah'.

Later that day as they were still monitoring the broadcast from Israel and the various Arabic stations the President held a special news conference to discuss the situation in Lebanon. In President Cush's news conferences he made no mention of the bin Ladin video but he along with Tony Blair backed the Israeli attack as a defensive against the aggression of Muslim organized Hezbollah. The agents in the CI monitoring section and most of the public knew that both the President and Tony Blair had taken the safe ground and announced to their citizens and the world that Islam is a peaceful religion and that there are no Muslim terrorists, just plain terrorists.

Allen who was an old timer with the agency chuckled out loud as he quipped, "All of the Muslim attacks in the Sudan and in Bali and in Indonesia and in Spain, and in India and in Blair's own London by Muslims were just a bunch of coincidences. And it was only a coincidence that it was Muslims that orchestrated the two attacks on the world trade center and planned the blowing up of an airplane with a shoe bomb and the bringing in of explosives from Canada headed to the Los Angles airport and the planned attack on nine airplanes headed to the States and the twenty two other planned attacks that our guys in the agencies have thwarted." And he went on in a loud sarcastic tone acting like President Cush and Blair could hear him, "And Israel has really only been attacked by peaceful Islamic believers. No by golly Islam is a peaceful geopolitical organized religion; verifiable by the words of bin Ladin and the threats of the Imams and the teachings of the Muslim Clerics who say all Kuffers must die. And then there is of course the verification from the Qur'an itself which is full of hate and of commands for the elimination of all non-believers which is further amplified by the fact that nowhere in the Qur'an is there ever an expression of love of your fellow man or kindness towards all people. Again I say 'Islam must be a religion of peace', HA."

The rest of the crew at NSA watched as NBC, CBS, ABC, CNN news programs showed Clerics in England openly voicing in large public gatherings that the Muslim agenda is the destruction of the UK and the USA. They could see hundreds of Muslims in these crowds who continually yelled 'Bomb, Bomb the USA' and 'Death to America' and who carried placards that read 'behead those who insult Islam' and 'death to infidels' and 'Europe take some lessons from 9-11' and 'be prepared for the real holocaust!'. It was only FOX news that broadcast any substantial confirmation that the terrorist threat was global and headed to the western hemisphere. The crew had recorded different editorials and news reports as a matter of course for the archived terrorist data base. These editorials were replete with declarations by Islamic Fascists, as President Cush had named them, that they were destined to destroy those people who love freedom and they would make every effort to kill democracy. These insane radical terrorists groups go on to iterate that they are motivated by all of the many radical Qur'an thumping Islamic Shia clerics and that they are everywhere. It only takes as few as five terrorists to make up an organization and to create a viable cell.

The most recent venom spewed by the Clerics in France and the Imams in the States is their public verbal attack to 'Destroy the Jews, the Christians, the Hindus, and the Buddhist'. "We will rule the World, allah is the Greatest, he is the only god." 'allah akbar'

Everyone from the top down had been warned on many occasions that Hamas and al-Qaeda was embedded in the USA. It would appear that included everyone but the directors of the news departments and the commentators at the three major television networks. There was never any kind of news reporting from these networks about the potential Hamas and al-Qaeda threat from sleeper cells embedded in the States.

CHAPTER TWENTY SIX

First week in September and Hank stayed home with Tank so Tiama could have a day off and go out with her girl friends from the Pilipino Consulate. He knew that giving a wife a break from her routine was good for their intimate life and besides he had to get away from work so he could quietly read all of the reports produced by the team that was reviewing Carnivore's output. It was late in the afternoon, so while Tank napped Hank took a break and watched Judge Judy. Fun personality but this afternoon she was coming down on a liar; judges can not stand for in your face lying, so who can? At news break the announcer said that Cush was going to have a news conference about the continual railing of the Democrats who threaten to cut off funding for the war in Iraq.

Hank thought to himself that it's the President's umpteen news conference at a time when his approval ratings are at thirty three percent due mainly from his stance on the war in Iraq but also because of his position on the millions and millions of illegal aliens who had been allowed to enter across the Mexican border because our government is in cahoots with Fox of Mexico. The voice of seventy per cent of the American public was to harden our borders and stop the encroachment into our country now! Silly American public; why wouldn't Fox help move millions of his most desperate and poor people into the States. Mexico gets rid of their financial burden on Mexico's government. Then with eight to ten million workers here illegally who basically pay no taxes and who send half of their earnings back to their families in Mexico, he has surreptitiously added six to seven hundred dollars per month times say six million illegal's, which equates to more than four billion dollars a month, to his counties economy and all he had to do was export his unwanted people to the States.

The president lashed out at all of those against the war restating his position on stopping terrorism over there so we don't fight them over here. He used the latest message from Abu Ayyub al-Masri, who succeeded al-Zarqawi and who advocated the same exact threats as al-Zarqawi, urging all Muslims to attack Americans and to kidnap any Westerners they could find and to hold, kill, or exchange them for prisoners. In the same message Abu entreated that those that are experts in explosives, biological weapons and nuclear science to join his holy war against the West. The President made a declaration that he would destroy al-Qaeda. He spent some time to warn Iran to stop the proliferation of nuclear armament or the world community would take a firm stance. Silly girl, they ain't stopping! Seemed to me these were all just hollow threats made before election time.

With those comments being the main thrust of his talk Hank shook his head as he murmured under his breath, 'I would say that the rating on this latest news conference, if they were rated would score below twenty per cent that is, if they were rated. All he did was present mostly all the old rhetoric. No meat in his speech and no teeth in his words'.

The media's backing of the liberal's battle went on and on and it soon became apparent that the Republicans could very easily lose their foot hold on the congress.

October arrived with a chill of the coming Fall and blew through New York bring out people's winter coats. Brada, Musab, Saja, Yassir, Jonathan who had crossed back from Canada, and Abu al-Hindi met at the barber shop on Eighth Avenue for what would be the last time they would all be together in the States.

Abu greeted his brothers and began with a prepared statement from Zubaydah bin Ladin's lieutenant. "May allah be shining on you at this moment as we begin the final countdown to doomsday for the 'Great Serpent'. Cush has killed thousands of our brothers in Iraq and he continues the slaughter of innocent people even though the congress people are against the war. We will stop the aggression against our Muslim world. One by one we are taking over countries and one by one we are implanting our religious base until all nations will have seen the light and been converted. As allah has commanded, we are building the nation of Islam so now is the time to kill this mighty root of Christendom and Judaism, the United States."

Allah akbar, allah akbar, allah akbar!

"Our orders are for all you, our trusted leaders here in the States, and those that are in command of our mission. Begin to close your businesses, sell all that you have, move with your families and blend into a community away from where you have been living and working. Leave no trace of your existence. Pay all bills in full and close all utility company accounts, store accounts and credit card accounts except your ATM card on the Bank of Curraco. You will have all of the money you will need for you and your families but you are to live a frugal life style. Take any kind of a non-descript job and wait. These are immediate orders. The time will come after their mid term elections and then all of the people will see that Cush has caused much pain to our Muslim brothers. Each of you and the cell leaders in your section are to call the number in Yemen on a throw away cell phone to get the address for the Web site where the final instructions will be given. No one knows at this time where the server for the Web site is located so until we activate the site no one will be able to find it. When it has been activated a notice on one of your weekly calls will tell you the site address and the time to go on line during the day for the instructions for everyone's individual responsibility. All of our people are to find a place to go to get on line to pull up the site and the instructions will appear for one hour only, then we will shut it down so no one can find it. This will happen the day before the attack so tell all of our brothers that they can not fail. After each month until the operation begins everyone is to get a new phone and call in every Sunday. Most of you know that one of Musab's people, Akria Sorubra was taken from Canada by U.S. government agents and is now dead. We think that he was able to martyr himself before the people at Homeland Security got any information. And we have knowledge that their investigation of the boat factory in Brazil has given them reasons to be interrogating many, many people in boating communities from here to the West coast about odd activity or ownership of a Fast Boat. With the expansion of their investigations our leaders believe the time is right to begin the Jihad before they uncover any solid confirmation of our existence."

Musab stood up by Abu to confirm the message. "I agree with our leaders. Even though the fools are all caught up in their politics and their approval ratings of both the war and Cush, they are not showing any concern about terrorist activity; which each of us can see by the current low level of the security alert system. They are however on the trail of Jonathan's boat operation and the shipments from Indonesia. We are certain of that. We have destroyed every fragment of evidence of the boats except the ones sunk in the lakes and all shipments from the Middle-east have been repackaged and distributed and securely hidden. And once again we must get the word out to all of our people to be especially cautious and do nothing to create any kind of suspicion. We are safe for now, but the leaders are telling us the time is coming soon. Praise be to allah for the insight and the intelligence he has given to our leaders."

Abu offered a prayer to allah. "Innaa Lillaahiwa Innaa Ilayhi Raajioon. Let us say good-by for now and we will all see each other in our triumph here or in our paradise with allah."

They left the barber shop for the last time giving each other a kiss of brotherly attachment and the next day the shop was closed. Brada closed his office in Manhattan and Musab asked his manager to operate the agency while he and his family when to Lebanon to visit relatives. Saja moved to Detroit and went to work in a small liquor store in a heavily Arabic populated area.

The elections were over and the public had spoken. The republicans had shot themselves in the foot. It appeared that the Cush-Chaney-Rummey coalition had bankrupted the Republican Party's ability to get their candidates elected. It was their extremely unpopular dogmatic position on the war that had precipitated the victory the Democrats enjoyed. And it was becoming increasingly apparent that the war had been mismanaged and caused too many deaths of American soldiers and waste of billions of dollars. The shame of the whole thing is that almost any college political scholar could have mapped out a better plan of action after the defeat of Hussein. And any top notch CEO or COO of a fortune five hundred company could have put together a realistic organized initiative to stabilize and rebuild the broken Iraq caused by the war. All the B-C-R triad did was throw money, lots of money at the mismanagement and the saddest part they threw good young soldiers into the mismanagement. Hank's feelings were embraced by millions of Americans and even though he was patriotic to the bone he disliked the elitist that were in control at the highest levels of the government. They were all battling the right cause in completely the wrong way and the country was paying a very high price.

Hank sent Jerry, George, Robert and John Poles an e-mail on November the eighth highlighting the phenomenon that the raging battle over funding of the war and amnesty for the illegals was still the main focus of the media and the politicians, while the subject of terrorism was not even showing up on the back burner.

In response to Hank's e-mail Jerry called to voice his thoughts, "We can only hope that there is no attack on us before we can get our people to authorize and commence an all out Muslim interrogation person by person cell by cell and to hell with the politically incorrect idea of profiling. Did they even read our report?"

"Of course they did and I know that Peter Wing brought it before the committee where they issued a memo to Mertoff to keep them informed on the FBI's progress."

Jerry grimaced, "What progress? We have seen the FBI reports for the last three months and there are only a few witnesses that say they remember seeing a boat similar to the Fast Boats but they have no clues as to where any of them may have gone. After all of this time we are still no further along on finding even one boat and George made it clear that if the boats were what they were suspected to be then it would be logical that they have completely disappeared." Jerry cleared his throat so he could roll into his next comment, "But on a brighter side, look at your secure internal e-mails and print up the latest report. There is some good news coming out of the three months our Intel people have been perusing the data from Carnivore and cross tracing numbers and they may have some excellent loop backs on this latest report. There are no cell phone records for our two suspects after 2003 but the computer even though it has taken a bit longer than our people had imagined; has done the tracing and then cross tracing on all calls from other than cell phones and the spider has come up with many individuals that are under the FBI's microscope. A few of those that are in the data base who are currently under investigation were contacted by our own guys over the past four years; so then the spider reached out to the next three generations of contacts and some very interesting names appeared. They are for Jonathan al-Aziz, my friend Fernando Munoz in Argentina, one al-Masri, Khalifa Ali Abu Bakr in Afghanistan, and a Brada al-Abaji. And for you on your Al Sober they have one Mustafa Fadhil, Abdella Azzam, a Yassir al-Jaziri and a Musab Yasin in New Jersey. Isn't this Brada your college friend and the one I interviewed a few years ago?"

"I would think so. Did the report list locations for these people, I mean current addresses."

"I believe they have a full dossier on each of them and we will get them delivered by the thirteenth. I want to talk to George to let us go on the search to uncover these associates and do our own personal interviews. Are you up for some undercover work that may prove dangerous? "

"I'm more than ready now with suspects that may have the key to cracking our investigations wide open. And especially if some of those suspects turn out to be past acquaintances. When will we get the go ahead and will we have carte-blanc?"

"Let's both talk to George tomorrow and let him know that we want priority and unlimited freedom to pursue our objective and to ensure our success. I know he has enough confidence in us as long as he can cover his own tail on permitting a solo operation. We can't let him down."

A week before Thanksgiving and Jerry was in New York going to the office of Brada. He remembers his first visit like yesterday to a small office in an old building on the Avenue of the Americas on the twenty third floor. The Intel confirmed that the phone calls had come from this office under the name of WWJHEP showing a B. al-Abaji. On the directory there was no Brada listed or a WWJHEP. He remembered that this was the name he had looked up before. Getting off on the twenty third floor he was confronted with ladders, buckets, sheet rock, other materials strewn down the hallway and he could not remember which was the exact door to Brada's office. Catching the eye of a workman with a carpenter's bag on his waist he asked if he knew where the offices for WWJHEP were.

"Sorry buddy but most of the offices are vacant and going to be renovated and the names are gone from the doors but I can tell you that there are only two occupants on this floor and they are around the corner."

Jerry thought to himself that he didn't turn any corner the last time so he asked, "Is it okay to look into the offices here in this hallway?"

"Sure I don't care."

"How long have you been working here?"

'Going on a year. It has been a steady job and it pays above scale. I started on the fifteenth floor."

"No I mean on this floor. How long on this floor?"

"Oh, about two weeks."

"Thanks." Jerry began opening doors and looking around. The office contents varied and were mostly trash and some empty boxes, an occasional broken chair or beat up desk. In the sixth office he kind of recognized the lay out and he went down the hall to where he thought Brada's office had been. There was nothing of any real interest, just some old pins in the walls and some trash in a card board box. He grabbed the box and left headed to the elevator.

"Hey where are you going with that?"

"It's nothing, just a box of old papers." Just then the elevator opened and he has gone and headed to the main floor. Going through the papers he found nothing important except possibly a crumpled up check order form for a checking account. Sticking it in his pocket he rummaged through some of the other items. He finished inspecting everything for the slightest bit of valuable information; nothing! He called, what information there was on the check, into the agency data resources department to find out whose account it was and get their address. He couldn't find George so he left a message for him that Brada had vacated the offices in New York. Confirmation came in less than five minutes. Account holder Brada al-Jaziri, address 534 East 55th Street number 1011 and a disconnected phone number of 213-112-0199. Jerry took a cab to the address on 55th Street and got the Super. on the phone. "My name is Jerry Ness and I am with Homeland Security, are you the superintendent for 534 East 55th Street?"

"Yes I am and what was your name again?"

"Jerry Ness, can you tell me who your tenant in 1011 is? Oh and what is your name?"

"Huh, can I have some ID or something; I can't just give out information."

"ID sure I'm in the lobby. Come and look at it!" Jerry was not in his best mood after leaving Brada's previous office location.

"I'm not in that building and I can't come over there."

"What, you want to see my ID and you can't come over here. Look, I am with Homeland Security and either you come look at my ID or you tell me the name of the tenant in 1011 or listen to this, I'll find your location and come there and bust your balls. I hope that is very clear and what is your name Mr. Superintendent."

"Jason, Jason McGuiness and Mrs. Overstreet lives in 1011 and has for the past couple of months."

"Who was the previous tenant?"

"Brada al-Ab........

Jerry cut him short, "Brada al-Abaji, I know and did he leave a for-warding address or any contact name or number? Or did he possibly leave some belongings behind."

"NO Sir."

Another dead-end and Jerry hailed a taxi for Grand Central.

It was a few days after Thanksgiving when the phone rang in the office of John Poles at the FBI with a transferred in coming call from the cur-rent commander Castillanos with the ABI in Brazil.

"Hello, this is Undersecretary John Poles at the Office of Homeland Security with whom am I speaking?"

"This is commander Castillanos in Rio de Janeiro, Brazil with Agencia Brazilia Intelligencia. You had sent some agents to investigate the explosion of a boat factory in our city Belem in January of this year. We had one of our agents assist them while they were here. Is that cor-rect and do I have the right person in charge of that operation?"

"Mr. Castillanos I appreciate your call and I am only slightly aware of that matter. It was handled by our Counter Intelligence unit at our National Security Agency. Can you tell me the nature of your call and I will direct you to the person in charge of that operation."

John started to listen to the Commander explain what he wanted to pass on to the investigative team but after only two minutes he decided not to pass on the call and instead he held a twenty minute phone dis-sertation with Mr. Castillanos.

"Thank you very much for this information. You said that your in-vestigating people have documented this evidence and it is available to us, correct? This is vitally important to us and I will keep in touch. I am going to ask one of my assistants to get on the line and let you know how I would like to have you deliver the report. Once again thank you."

December 4, 2006

When George arrived at work on Monday his assistant handed him an urgent message to call John Poles at OHS before anything else.

"Hello John, this is George Meeker, what can I do for you?"

"George, Michael has asked me to request that you, Robert Dryer,

Stephen Haddle, and myself meet with him here at OHS building by Ten am, okay?"

"Sure, are there any files I need to bring?"

"He specifically asked for all of the files on the Fast Boat investigation from all section heads. Ask the secretary in his office which meeting room and she will direct you."

"Right."

Everyone was early. They felt that this meeting was spontaneous so it had to be of a high priority. Mertoff had the meeting room set with a large video screen and one of OHS's stenos record the meeting to keep a record of documentation presented in the meeting and be a witness for the security report.

Mertoff started by opening with an informal announcement to everyone. "Thank you for showing up on time. As all of us know we must report to our congressional oversight committee on the progress of all NSR's issued by OHS. We are all here to review the progress of the NSR issued to respond to the allegation that one suspected individual and possibly a Muslim cell have been importing boats aka Fast Boats into Florida from Brazil containing the explosive C4 hidden in the infrastructure of the boats. Each of you has brought the status of your sections investigations that have been authorized by the NSR. We will enter a summation into the report from each of your sections up dated security file as we go along."

John started the formal portion of the meeting.

"This meeting is initiated on the fourth day of December 2006 at Ten a.m. and is a joint meeting with the Secretary of the Department of Homeland Security, the FBI, and the Counter Intelligence section at the National Security Agency. In attendance is Secretary Michael Mertoff and Undersecretary John Poles of the Department of Homeland Security, Assistant to the Director of the FBI Robert Dryer, National Security Adviser to the President Stephen Haddle, and Director of Counter Intelligence at the National Security Agency George Meeker. The purpose of this meeting is to prepare a top secret report for the congressional oversight committee for OHS on the NSR that was issued to investigate the Intelligence reports gathered on a suspected conspiracy that Muslim factions were importing into the States the explosive material C4 inside of boats from Brazil."

Michael requested that both Robert and George read their summarized report to the steno and allowing all in attendance to hear and thereby save some time.

The reports were quite simple as they only described the number of agents that were working on the operation and the amount of time that had been spent to date. The investigations had yielded no positive information and no evidence had been collected that could verify the initial premise for the investigations.

Michael asked John to take over.

"We do not want this to be a meeting where someone's head must roll or where any department needs to feel abused about what I am about to reveal. The whole theory about combining all of the agencies under the umbrella of OHS was to gather intelligence and share it after confirmation. On November the twenty-eighth I received a call from a Commander Castillanos of ABI in Brazil with what could be referred to as their internal FBI. He presented over the phone information that his agents had secured in regards to the boat factory that burned down in Belem Brazil which was a big part of the basis of out issuing a NRS. It was believed that all roads for the exporting of C4 from Brazil lead to this boat factory operated by Groupo Rizo. It does turn out that they were exporting illegal contraband but it was Cocaine. And how can we be sure of that? Commander Castillanos sent me a copy of his agent's six month investigation and arrest of more than eight people who were involved in the process for almost ten years. Further in-depth investigation of the site of the destroyed factory ultimately turned up traces of cocaine."

"John," George interrupted, "this is refuting everything our people have found out about this conspiracy and the Groupo Rizo – Jonathan al Aziz connection. Their new investigation and the report needs to be scrutinized by my people. Most of the intelligence used by our CI unit was gathered by one of the best in the business, Jerry Ness. I trust his skills, his perception and most of all his experience."

"Yes I know and I am aware of agent Ness's ability. And I said this is not to discredit anyone, however I need to go on. We found one of the Florida Fast Boats in Detroit where it had been used as a fun boat for one of the more flamboyant drug dealers in that town. He had used it to both entertain some of his wealthier clients, but also to make runs up to Canada. The DEA had confiscated it about two years ago and it was still in an impound yard when we came across it. One of their agents happened to be going over one of the FBI's bulletins when he thought that the description listed was quite like the boat he and some other agents had confiscated from a dealer they had busted even though there had been some alterations to the original boat. Although the whole thing happen almost two years ago he still felt that he should notify us to investigate since our bulletin carried a high priority for any information. Sure enough when we finished reviewing their impounded boat and comparing it to the detail literature, specs, and pictures from the DEA and the Florida Coast Guard files we not only concluded that it was from the Groupo Rizi but that it had been used to import cocaine into the states. There was residue inside the hull when we took the boat apart. All evidence confirms that your Jonathan al-Azeri was a cocaine smuggler. There is no concrete evidence to cause us to believe that he was smuggling explosives into the States."

"Wait a minute you guys, Michael, Robert, Stephen, John let's look at Jerry and Melvin's investigations and study the reports on their missions. They found and traced C4 from Argentina to Brazil to the boat factory and got confirmation from the supplier when he was confronted in Sawakin, Sudan. He did not remain a live witness unfortunately."

"George, we all have reviewed the various reports but the facts stand. The Brazilian authorities confirm the residue of cocaine in the destroyed plant in Brazil, interviews with some past employees back up that fact with their statements that they knew Jonathan was into cocaine smuggling, the FBI has found a Fast Boat and after a meticulous inspection they confirmed that cocaine had been smuggled in the hull of the boat, and the FBI's four month investigation has turned up nothing to the contrary."
Michael knew he had to drop the bombshell, "To legitimism our report to Peter Wing and the committee my department has got to cancel the NSR authorization and state that our suppositions could not be proven. Too much expense on the agency's budget for the manpower Robert had authorized and at this point we must be accountable."

George closed his file, "Well that's it then, our entire unit is going to go ballistic. It's going to be a blow to their keenness and fervor for the job."

"George, you still have your own budget and your team can work on what you feel is justifiable. But really I know your people and they are professionals. There is no way this will affect them like that!"

"You are one hundred per cent correct; I am the one that is disappointed. I know how diligent they have all been."

Steven kind of smiled as he added to the comments. "We all are very proud of the job that the FBI and NSA is doing to protect the country and the scrutiny your people are applying in their investigations. They are to be complimented. I will give the President a short summary of this meeting and let the committees comments come in his PDB. If we are at an end I must get back to the White House."

"If you have pressing business go ahead, I only have one more subject to cover but it will not be of importance to you now since it will be in the committees report."

"Okay, thank you Michael and nice seeing you again John, and you Robert, and George tell your CU team they did good work."

John started to wrap up the meeting. "I have to finish with this last piece of negative news. The NSR is not going to happen for the investigation of the contents or distributed contents of hundreds of thousands of containers that have come into our ports. Even getting a program in place to scrutinize every incoming container at all of the ports of entry appears to be a monumental task that so far has been a failed effort. We are in the planning stages only and over one billion dollars will be needed to fund just the preliminary plans."

Michael stood to close the meeting. "Steno, off the record; I want to say that knowing what these terrorists are capable of doing, the protection of the country is the most overwhelming undertaking our investigative and enforcement sections of our government has ever encountered. Now steno we can go back on the record. This meeting is adjourned and the report is to be completed and distributed as a secret OHS report."

Michael said goodbye and John spent a couple of minutes with Robert and George before leaving.

Both of them walked out together, "Well Robert our work is cut out for us now. Our CI units are ninety nine per cent positive that we have potential suicide bombers here ready to commit mayhem."

"Let's pray to God we can get to them before they get to us. Under complete deniability I want you to know that I have asked all of my section heads to do what ever profiling their agents need to do to uncover any potential terrorist without it being obvious. As you know we have added a few thousand more radical Muslims to our 'suspect alert' list and stopped twenty nine planned objectives by Hamas extremist. If we were not investigating based on our hush-hush profiling features, we believe that ninety per cent of those planned missions would have taken place and the country would have experienced suffering at least equal to 9-11."

"Good for you, it takes guts to implement a policy like that even if it is under the radar and we both know our country's future is a stake. God bless you and your courage, I'll talk to you later."

CHAPTER TWENTY SEVEN

Hank and Jerry were informed about the OHS's position on the cancellation of the NSR issued for the Fast Boat project and its lack of desire to under take the problem of hundreds of thousands of un-inspected shipping containers having entered the States on the very same day the official secret report on the OHS meeting was released.

It happened to be two weeks before Christmas on that shocking Monday that put all of the six CI units under George's command into a fury over such a dogmatic bureaucracy that would allow budget restraints to prevent the FBI's involvement in such a critical matter as going after secreted terrorists being armed for an attack on the United States.

Around noon on Monday Jerry walked into George's office to confirm his request for some time off. "George I really believe I need to take a couple of weeks off and I just e-mailed HR requesting vacation time starting as soon as I get my work in order and until after Christmas or maybe even till the First of the year. I'm sure it is obvious to you that I am astonished over the decision by Mertoff. Oh, and by the way has anybody other than me wondered where a lot of the suspects that Carnivore listed in it's chain of association may have gone and why they don't show up in the immigration records as having left the country or maybe they just walk across the border into Mexico where there is no checking of the passage of anyone across the border and then they flew to a safe haven? You know across the border just like thousands of them got into the states. And I'll give you one more I have been thinking about; if they have disappeared or essentially gone underground how are they living and how are they getting any money? We have their names listed on the hot sheet with every bank in the states. So when I am gone that should give everyone something to chew on."

"Jerry it sounds like you're going to leave us lot of crap on the table for us to stress over. I'll throw those questions over to Melvin's unit. Maybe they can look at how to get some answers on them while you're gone."

"Was that a little sarcastic?"

"Kind of. I'll send my confirmation over to Human Resources tomorrow. You take Ana and go some place exotic for the holidays. You take those two weeks and have a good time and do some mental cleansing."

As Jerry open the door he turned to George, "Well then tell it to Mertoff who pulled the plug on our operation. Our country is at risk and all we get is rhetoric from the bureaucrats. I plan to come back and find the link of Jonathan and this Brada person and I will find those damn boats and the C-4, believe me!

Jerry went back to his office to clean up his paperwork for the week and get a few of his personal items and call Ana to let her know he was taking off on the eighteenth for a few weeks and that she should plan where she wanted to go for Christmas and maybe even New Years.

Hank stopped by George's office shortly after Jerry had left but his office was vacant, no George. Hank took off to the cafeteria for a beef dip sandwich and some mashed potatoes with au jus, his favorite lunch at the building's in house eatery. With his tray in hand he spied George at a table next to the Starbuck's coffee counter so he decided it was as good a time as any to talk to him especially since he was alone. "Hi George, okay if I join you?"

"Sure, if you aren't going to bend my ear over the OHS report everyone got today!"

Unbeknownst to Hank, Jerry had in a very backhanded way let George know how he felt about the decision from the secretary at OHS and was planning to take off for a few weeks.

"I like the Beef dip sandwiches here more than any other place I have eaten them. They use real prime rib of beef and the au jus is from the drippings and not that artificial bouillon crap loaded with MSG. You know Monosodium Glutamate, the stuff that gives half of the population either head aches, sever stomach aches or in my case acute breathing problems."

"Oh sure, I have an uncle that is deathly afraid of the stuff, now I know what you mean."

"I am violently allergic to it and when I travel I watch everything I eat. Some people just do not know how to cook any more and so they dump in MSG to get some flavor in the food; mainly fast food joints and big chains who try to keep some kind of flavor in their massively prepared food."

George slid his tray over as Hank spread out his plates, "Did Jerry come in for lunch?"

"No, he was by my office and he kind of let me know how upset he was over the cancellation of the NSR Fast Boat project and told me that he had wanted to put in for some of his vacation time. He is going to leave shortly for some vacation time until after the New Year. He did give me a couple of zingers to chew on."

"I suppose he one can blame him. He has been on this case continuously for over two years. So I know how he feels. I have felt the same way. What kind of zingers did he leave you?"

"It's a little like that song as he put it, 'where have all of the terrorists gone', Carnivore gave us a special list of persons that are of a particular interest and yet they have disappeared. Jerry suggested where they may have gone; across the Mexican border and to the airport to fly back to some refuge and wait. Or instead, if they have gone underground then how are they living and where are they getting money to live on? Two great zingers he said for us to chew on."

"The first one could easily be the case and it is impossible to stop because the politicians want to play politics with immigration and meanwhile the borders are massive human sieves. They go for the vote of all of the illegal aliens and in the shadow of that stupidity, they have set it up so that anyone can come in to this country and go out when ever they want but citizens must check in and out with the authority of a passport. We are in an Asylum and the inmates are in control. What the hell business does a foreigner have to be able to vote in this country? Voting is only for our citizens but no where did the laws foresee that millions of illegal border crashers would come into our country and register to vote as if they were citizens. There is no protection against that phenomenon except that when someone registers to vote they must swear that they are citizens and then they can vote. There is no checking on their statement being true. So what is wrong with our thinking process? They are already law breakers and therefore criminals; why not lie so they can vote and change laws and our government representatives knowing they are not legal allow them to further their illegal actions. An outlaw is an outlaw!"

"I'll buy you a cup of coffee on that one. You hit the nail on the head!"

"Yep, but I can't do anything about it. As to the survival thing, if hundreds of the suspected terrorist in our data bases have gone underground then as far as I am concerned I believe you can take that politically correctness bullshit and throw it in the garbage and intensify the profiling of the most likely person walking down the street, or buying groceries, or going to the mall, or sitting in the park, or just any where. I don't know if I have told you the story of a friend I made at NYU that graduated with a finance major and then moved to San Diego after graduation to enter the mortgage business. He did fairly well and was operating his own small loan shop in El Cajon, California in a small office that was one street away from the main boulevard. Kind of a nondescript older single story line of officers. He told me that a few months after he moved in to his space an Arabic looking person opened a tailor shop next to his office. He said at first he thought it was strange to see a tailor shop that made exclusively men's suites open during an economic slowdown and in that community which was not affluent. Soon he noticed that a number of customers were coming to the shop and they all appeared to be of Arabic decent. During the following six to seven months he could see into the shop from time to time where the suits were being cut and sewed together and then hung on hangers by the front door. He said that many times there would be a gathering of different people in the shop and they would be talking loudly in their native tongue and then laughing and talking and laughing sometimes for hours. It seemed that none the suits were ever sold. Then over one weekend in August of 2001 the shop was vacated and closed. And a few months after 9-11 the investigations had established the identity of those that had perpetrated the attack and some of them were from San Diego and had lived in El Cajon. Trent Green later told me that he was sure that he recognized Ahmed al Ghamdi as being one of the people going in and out of the tailor shop. He later told me he wondered if he should have somehow been more suspicious or told someone he thought that there was something strange in the office next to his. He also said that with the stakes so high since 9-11 he believed that he should at least be curious about any unusual people around him and probably even use profiling. You and I know that if you have ridden any buses or taken any trains you have at one time or another sat with a terrorist, or if you have gone to the movies you have more than likely sat next to a terrorist, or if you have gone to a restaurant you could have been served by a terrorist, and so on. Those whose existence is imperceptible are protecting those that are in need of hiding. We have discussed this before about their ability to just move into any Arabic community and blend in to the extent of being invisible. But that takes money and we have run all of those suspected of terrorist activities through the Treasury Departments bank records section for accounts that are in their names or controlled by them and that information is now in the FBI's data base and ours. We were told that very few have popped up during our monthly cross referencing so what can we surmise from that."

"At first it would indicate that they have left the country waiting for another time, but maybe yes, they could have gone underground. Jerry dropped the zingers on me and I am going to work on them. I've finished, I'll see you later."

'No. Wait a minute. I want to ask for a favor or more like a request. Well what I want to ask you is that I really want to spend some time with my Dad and sister this Christmas. I mean Tiama, Tank and I want to get away and since we have nothing internally pressing and even though Jerry will be gone I am hoping that you can let me take some time off. I need it."

"Hank, I understand. Let me clear it with Human Resources and as far as I am concerned we will be okay here. What dates did you have in mind?"

"Well today is the eleventh so if Tiama agrees the eighteenth to January the second would work for me. That will give me this week to assign my work to a different CI unit and work on your two zingers."

"My zingers? What can you do on those next week?"

"Not anything on the exodus at the border but I have an old college buddy that may give me some insight as to how some one that is under national bank scrutiny can have an account and get money even though their identity and formal identification has been put into the banking clearance data bases."

"Great, who is this person?"

"Howard Slates of Fin-Chk, Inc. He was part of the organization that set up the international financial clearing center for all financial transfers through every bank in the world. It was his company that developed the software to operate the massive interconnection of the supercomputers in the ten major financial centers in the world. He is of course a genius."

"Well I didn't know about the genius but I have heard the name. Any insight he can give us may be one more bit of information that could lead us to those on our list. Let me know that Tiama is happy with those vacation days and I will get it cleared for you tomorrow. Finish that sandwich and relax. See you tomorrow."

"I'm glad you brought Thai food tonight Hon so I don't have to cook or do dishes. I have juice for Tank and Sparkling Cider for us, OK?"
"Sure," Tiama was pouring me a glass as I sat down on the floor next to Tank and pulled the coffee table up close. "I guess you have fed him so he won't be fussy while we eat?"

"He ate a whole bowl of soup and some yogurt, I'm pretty sure he is full."

"I was thinking about the Holidays so I asked George about taking some time off for a much deserved and desired vacation but I told him that you had to agree with the idea."

"What idea?"

"Oh, I didn't tell him my idea. Dad is going to go to Montana to look at either buying a hunting lodge or to find some land and build one. I was hoping you would agree to go with him and we can spend Christmas there. Caroline is going too. He has planned to retire soon and hunting and the outdoors is part of his soul."

"I would love it. The family getting away from the city into the wilds of Montana makes me tingle a little. Tank is still a little young but he'll get a kick out of running in the hills and the woods and eating snow."

"Wonderful, I haven't told Dad about my idea so I'll call him from the office and break the news that he will have company in Montana and get our travel department to book us a flight for the eighteenth. I will be spending longer hours at work the rest of the week so maybe you can lay out all of the things we'll need for the vacation and pull out the clothes I'll need; remember it is going to be cold in Montana and I'll predict snowing and blowing with a wind chill of thirty to forty below."

"Snowing and blowing and a wind chill as low as my age, no way Tank and I are not going!"

"What, you are not going? Honey, I was only joking. The sun will be out and probably no snow and as to wind chill we'll be looking at a temperature about like the chill on a glass of Jack-Seven or in your case a margarita."

"Sure and you think I believe you? I was only joking too. I guess I will go shopping for some Long Johns for all of us."

The operator at International Bank Clearing answered the phone with a surprise greeting. "Hello IBC, may we help you?"

Hank for a moment thought that he had the wrong number so he answered, "I don't know, I am looking for Fin-Chk and an individual named Howard Slates."

"Yes sir, Mr. Slates is our president and our name has been changed. We are no longer Fin-Chk. How may I help you?"

"I would like to speak to him, my name is Hank Brayden and I am an old friend from college."

"Let me transfer you to his personal assistant as I give her your name."

"Thank you."

"Hello Mr. Brayden, this is Mr. Slate's assistant and I will have to find him for you. He took off about three minutes ago and did not tell me where he was going. Give me a little time to find him and I will tell him you are holding or would you like to leave a message?"

"A message will be okay. I am an old college buddy; my number is 206-987-0900 at the Department of Homeland Security. It is important that I talk to him right away."

"I will give him the message as soon as I find him, Mr. Brayden, goodbye."

Hank was on the phone with Tom discussing the family get together in Montana when a call came in on his intercom from the auto attendant announcing an incoming call.

"Alright Dad, we'll all fly in on Sunday to Helena; I'm quite familiar with that airport. I have to go but since you are not leaving until Friday I'll call you before you leave."

"Hello, this is Hank Brayden."

"Hank, this is Howard Slates. Long, long time since we have spoken. I had no idea that you were at Homeland Security. When did you leave the United Nations?"

"About three years ago. I was pretty much bored with the mundane job and lack of any future within the United Nations. I was in the worst of the worst dead-end jobs, security and benefits were excellent but I had hit the plateau in my job position. How have you and Alicia been and how big is your company now?"

"Alicia is more beautiful than ever and a little more mature but still modeling so you would never know she is, let's say, looking at forty.

And if you ever say I told you that then no more reunions. But on to the company, we have grown immensely what with the organization of OHS and our tight union with the Treasury department and of course there is still the growing drug trade which proliferates money laundering. As we expanded we changed the name to International Bank Clearing to stay more in tune with our international operations. Is this a professional call or are you heading up the committee for our next reunion? But first if this is social then tell me what else is going on with your life besides changing sides."

"I never looked at it like that, changing sides, that's a symbol of political confusion, are they for us or against us? A lot of people believe that the U N is a body that is undermining the very basis of Nationalism so I don't get into the politics of it; I just wanted to get back to truly serving my country. But hey, I am married now and we have a little boy. A great wife and my son is a pistol and we live here in Virginia. I would like for us to catch up on everything and maybe we can if you get down here at all. My call is in regards to my job here at NSA. I'm in the CI section and I told our section leader George Meeker that you could probably give us some of you knowledge about how people with out bank accounts or who have been locked out of our banking system can secure funds so that they are able to survive in an underground status in the states. I understand with SWIFT and the Treasury's supervision of international bank transactions that you have more than likely looked at and already evaluated all possible scenarios, so out side of an individual's personal associates giving them money which may not always be convenient or possible, we need to look at what you could tell us."

"Good question and yes we in conjunction with the Treasury have prepared some reports on what the different possibilities might be, as they have taken full control of worldwide money flow analysis. They have a whole department that was set up after 9-11 and they know exactly who is doing what with what. That is why they have found so many organizations here and abroad that have been supporting al-Qaeda and Hezbollah. They have frozen or confiscated millions and millions of dollars from phony charities and businesses that have been a front to support terrorism. I am sure you know about all of that. There are banks particularly from the Middle East that do not give us full cooperation so we can only know account numbers and not account holders identity but we do have access to all bank transaction on an international basis because they must go through the clearing houses and that is where our company and our software come it."

"I knew you could help. Can you give George a call tomorrow and present to him the reports listing the different scenarios. I told him I thought you would be helpful."

"Well Hank I have a manager in charge of the department that can assist George better than I, but one question, don't you people get the information in the Treasury departments IMTR classified memos? I believe all of our findings are listed in those memos. We have been led to believe that all of the government departments and enforcement agencies were sharing reports, memos, and in general communiqués between each other and regularly passing on all information about all terrorist activities. Not to put NSA on the 'hot spot' so to speak. Well you know of course I'll help in any way I can."

"Sad to say Howard but the key phrase here is 'all information', every department is inundated with reports, memos, and communiqués as you put it. No, I don't believe we have seen your memos. Anyway George's phone number is 206-987-0900 so please call him and call me the next time you head to DC."

"You bet Hank, and tell George that a Jason Brown will be calling him shortly. We'll talk soon."

It was on Wednesday morning when Hank told George that a Jason Brown form IBC would be calling him to answer any questions he had on finding out how suspected terrorists were able to use the banking system and to make all of their reports available that had been sent to the Treasury department.

Shortly after noon George buzzed Hank in his office. "Hank, I just talked to Jason Brown at IBC a few minutes ago and he is sending all of their classified memos which he says pretty well covers the gambit of criminal activity that can occur in the banking system internationally, but I feel like I won't need the information. It is going to be for the analysis guys."

"Why, why won't you need to look at them?"

"His call came in as we were having coffee here in my office; that is Jerry, Jeff and Melvin and I and I spewed my coffee all over them when Jason told me what was the biggest loop hole in the money flow system that you could ever imagine!"

"What, what loop hole?"

"It's just like I said the other day to Robert at the FBI, 'is there anyway to stop these people in an open society'."

"What loop hole?"

"Okay, here is the scenario. Hadji Baba who lives in the states and has a green card gets on an airplane and flies to London. There he meets with Abdulla Assam and Abdulla gives Hadji forty ATM cards with individual pass codes on a Bank in Panama for forty accounts under fictitious names which are not on any hot sheets. Could be a Bank in Curacaos, or in the Canary Islands, or in Honk Kong, etc, do you get the picture. Each account has let's say twenty or thirty thousand dollars in it. Then after a few days Hadji Baba gets on a plane back to the States and conveniently distributes the ATM cards to forty terrorist who are living underground. They have the card and the pass word and all the money they need! When he told me that I couldn't hold the gulp of coffee I had taken."

Hank could immediately see how that scenario was possible, "My god, it is so easy and there is no way to know about the ATM cards or the accounts. The accounts are under the radar."

"Walla, and there you have your underground and unidentifiable terrorist."

"Where do we go from here? And the Treasury knew this all along and we had to search it out."

"No, Jason told me that according to Howard all of the information on this scenario and others has been sent to us along with thousands of other reports. They must be archived."

"This is plain 'Bull Shit', does the over-site committee know about this kind of stuff? Does Peter Wing, does Robert Dryer, does Mertoff, does McCain, does Bidben, does Dodd does anybody who can make rational conclusions know about this kind of stuff? We have over one hundred thousand or more radicals running around like little ants in the forest; the forest of 50 states where it is impossible to see them. My god, I fear for our country!"

"Jerry felt the same way if not more concerned, and after he got up and wiped the coffee off he said to me that, 'he was not sure exactly what he was going to do but for sure he said he was going to find this link to Jonathan, this guy named Brada and he was going to find the boats or their final destinations or the C4! And he left.'"

"George, you got two zingers to mull over. I'm sorry that Jerry has left and that I'm going to be gone till after the New Year but it is my humble opinion that everyone at OHS, FBI, NSA, DOD, CIA, and so on need to look it what their jobs are, and that is the safe keeping of the American public. And the hell with the war, the Iraqis don't want us there and they don't appreciate us so come home and protect the homeland. I think we are going to lose it. And that is my zinger to the entire governmental conglomerate of departments responsible for our protection that are swimming in bureaucracy, protocol, and boxes full of reports; well I mean hard drives full of reports – unread reports. Oops, sorry George, no more soap box, but I am disgusted. I'm going to finish my passing of the baton to the other CI units and be leaving early Friday, thanks for signing off on my vacation."

It was Friday and Hank stopped by Jerry's office to tell him to have a Merry Christmas and so on but his office was empty. On the way to the elevator he peered in on Jeff and Melvin to let them know he was taking off till the New Year. "You guys have a Merry Christmas and I'll see you next year. 2007 will be our year!"

CHAPTER TWENTY EIGHT

Ten thirty in the morning as the Continental flight from New York landed in Salt Lake City. Hank helped Tiama with Tank and the small bag filled with flying goodies; the usual small toys, a DVD player and DVDs, the bag of Milk Duds for Tiama's sweet tooth and a couple of paper backs for Hank's reading appetite.

"When we get into the terminal we can relax and enjoy some lunch, you know real food. Our flight to Helena isn't until two this afternoon. I like the bar-b-que and the chicken here, how does that sound?"

"Okay by me but I hope we can find something like a hot dog for Tank."

At Helena Hank stumbled down the exit ramp as he had a quick flash back to the waiting government plane on the tarmac and the moment that he heard the agent say 'hey, Al Sober is dead."

"What's wrong?" Tiama asked.

"Nothing Hon, just a little stumble."

Tom was there at the gate and took Tank so they could get their bags. "I rented a van so we'll have plenty of room. Caroline is waiting at the motel where we'll stay tonight. I don't think I told you but I had my people do research on all of the possible properties that are either available or that I could convert to what I am looking for and one stood out head and shoulders above the rest so tomorrow we will drive up to 'MBS Hunting Lodge' on the plateau east of Great Falls just at the foothills of the Rockies. I think I am sold, Montana Big Sky country, MBS Hunting Lodge. Well we'll see tomorrow, let's go to the motel and get some dinner."

The next day they traveled up U.S #15 and arrived at the turn off to the lodge about forty miles northwest of Great Falls and Jake Harris the owner met them as they drove in on the rock covered road leading from the highway. He signaled them to follow his truck as they wound along the bumpy narrow road to the lodge complex. Getting out of the van Tom stood in awe at the complex, the view of the mountains and grandeur of the spread; it was what he was looking for. A rustic massive lodge with rock and timber siding. From what he could count the main lodge had a least six fireplaces and there were seven out buildings. The largest horse barn he had ever seen and four corals each the size of a football field. This prompted him to ask his host, who just crawling out of his dual cab F350 painted with a Montana Big Sky image and the initials MBS Hunting Lodge on the front doors, about the large horse facilities. He walked over and shook his hand, "Jake Harris my name is Tom Brayden, I am sure pleased to meet you, but first I have to ask; do all of your hunting engagements operate from horseback? I see a grandiose horse operation here. I thought from what I was told that hunting by horse back was a secondary operation."

"Hey it is my pleasure too. Is that your family?"

"I'm sorry, this is my son Hank, his wife Tiama, and my Grandson Tank, and my sister Caroline."

'Well listen, Shorty here will get all of your things and take them to your rooms in the main lodge and we can go in out of the cold and sit by the fire while we get acquainted. It is a beautiful day today and the wind has pretty much gone away."

Tom still was thinking to himself how this place appears to be exactly what he wanted for a place to retire and have a business to boot.

As they sat in the main gathering room Jake explained his hunting programs and described the clientele to Tom. "We have guys and gals coming from all over the country and some foreigners to hunt here. We are not cheap by any means but the experience along with the Montana environment is more than worth the fees we charge. And all of our clients tell us when they leave that the ability to totally unwind while here makes their adventure priceless. The prime hunting trip is by horse back to get to the area where they will camp and hunt for five days. That is the reason for the large stables and the number of horses. We have around sixty well trained for this type of operation. We have eight thousand acres and hunting permits from the Bureau of Forestry on another sixty thousand acres. The live action hunting on horseback is about ten percent of our business. It is rugged and tough. Our clients have to be good on horseback or no go. Hey, any of you want to join Tom and I in a tour of the compound come on and then we can grab some lunch."

That night Tom and Hank sat alone in the smoking room where most of the guns were locked into racks. It seemed like an appropriate room for guys to sit and smoke a cigar and talk about their day of hunting or their ideas on politics or sports or the opposite sex or any other guy thing.

"Hank, I have the money to do just about anything I want to and I have this passion to be close to nature so with out looking any further I am sold on this place. I will have my attorney make Jake the offer and one of my senior accountants scrub the books so that I am satisfied with Jake's numbers and assertion of his clients. What do you think at least at this moment?"

Hank was unhurried to answer. He looked in to the fireplace and slowly drew on the cigar. Then he blew out the smoke as he put the words together. "Dad I think this is the right thing. And I want to add that I would very much like to be a part of this project. I have not told Tiama yet but I am quitting my job at NSA. And before you ask why let me tell you some very confidential and possibly classified information."

Hank took another long puff on his cigar. "A short time ago I had or better let me start this way. I have been involved in a mission we called 'Open Sesame' which has entailed the investigation of the importing of military contraband into the states through the ports on the west coast. We had little or no evidence but a lot of hearsay information and some chatter which is always coming into the agency. It all centered on the possibility that hundreds of automatic rifles and thousands of pounds of explosives had been shipped from the pacific to the west coast in containers for secreted terrorist in the States. After a long and costly investigation authorized by the agency I felt that we were ready for a NSR to be issued, you know a National Security Response priority investigation and all we needed was the hard testimony of a known terrorist that had fled to Canada. Well I was on the team that went to Canada to oust him out of the country to bring him to Washington to be interrogated by the FBI but we had no more than gotten him across the Canadian border and to Helena to a waiting plane when we found that he had been able to commit suicide leaving us with no accomplice. He was our only link to our suspicions. Mertoff could not get us a NSR and I was devastated. Jerry was assigned to a similar mission investigating the probability of the importing of 'Fast Boats' that were laden with C-4 embedded in the hulls. Our estimates are as high as Five hundred thousand pounds of C-4 in the hands of terrorist cells. There are so many of us that know or at least in our minds we believe that the huge number of sleeper cells in this country are getting ready for some kind of massive attacks on our people or our cities. But we can not pass the liberal's block-aid that wants everything politically correct. I am through and I want my family out of Washington. I haven't told Tiama about my fears but I am now waking up at nights and visualizing a suicide bomber blowing up a restaurant or a shopping center where she and Tank are. Dad I fear for our country."

"Has it come to this? Do you think that it has really come to a point that we are not going to be safe in our own country any more! We can weed them out. One by one we can weed them out. There are three hundred million citizens in this country and what, by your estimates only seven or eight thousand radicalized terrorists. We are so much stronger then they are."

"Right Dad, but we are an open society and the politically correct liberals will not let the agencies do their job claiming that everyone has their rights, that is the right to privacy, the right to freedom of speech, the right to not be profiled, and the right to share the same freedoms that all of our citizens enjoy. How can we weed out the cockroaches when there is a protective tent over their refuge? The agencies differ on the number of cockroaches from a low of seven thousand to more like thirty thousand. And Dad, as to our country being a safe place to live, that all disappeared on 9-11."

"I suppose I do not want to lean in that direction but I see the news every day including some of it that never reaches the public. You are probably right. I go into my office sometimes after I hear the fools like Kennedy and Pelosi speak and I cry out in the silence 'Wake up America'! Just Wake Up! Son, don't worry, I'll keep this all confidential and of course as you work out the details with Tiama nothing would make me feel better than to have my family with me in business here. And we know this place will be very secure."

I flew back to Washington and to begin the New Year I returned to work on January the second and handed in my resignation with one month's notice. Most of the friends I had made in the agency wanted to know why I was leaving but they didn't push me for answers. Jeff was sorry to see me leave and wondered if it was because of the busted mission and the lost of a prime participant in our on going investigation. I asserted him that it was only because I was tired of the 'chasing and not finding' and I felt that my service to the government had been fulfilled. George wished me the best and privately told me he was kind of jealous of me getting away from the metropolitan life and moving to the clean air of Montana. My friend Jerry was not around when I announced my leaving.

George had been a great person to work for and as I left his office he motioned down the hall towards Jerry's office, "He is running solo." And in a low hush voice he said, "Jerry has turned his mission into a personal affair operating like a maverick. I have cut him some slack because he is good at operating alone and we track him on the satellite a couple of times a day. I trust him and as you know he is one of our best agents. He may not be back in by the time you leave so the next time he makes contact I'll let him know so he can call you, okay?"

"Well I'll be here for most of a month helping in the analysis section, so let me know."

Dad had been able to close the purchase of the hunting lodge before my month was up and he made plans to take over after the current hunting season was over and move to Montana the first of April. This gave us time so we would be able to handle our affairs and close out all of our ties to DC.

Meantime in Detroit Michigan a key event was unfolding.

The Detroit traffic had slowed down when a blue Toyota pulled up just behind a delivery truck unloading boxes but the car was not able to completely park right in front of the Seven – Eleven. "What are we doing?"

Brada gave his head a little thump and said, "I still have my head ache and you asked for cigarettes. I'll be back, the car is still running."

Inside Brada got his Advil and two cans of Blast, his favorite energy drink. "Excuse me could I get two packs of Marlboro lights?"

"One minute please I have to finish doing my check in."

"Okay, but my meter is running, how much for all of this?"

"Just a minute I'm coming!" The clerk finally rang up the sale, "Nineteen forty with tax. Looks like you have some Christmas tree lights out there, ey?"

"Oh, great, where do I sign and just forget the receipt. What now?" Brada grabbed the sack and stormed out the door, "That's my car officer, what's wrong?"

"For starters you left the car running. This is your car, right?"

"Yes officer it's my car."

"So second you're in a red fire zone! Let me see your driver's license and the car registration. I should give you a ticket for leaving the control of a vehicle while it is running, but parking in a fire zone is a far worst violation so I am writing you for city code 569832 which has a fine of two hundred dollars. I see you are licensed in New York. How long have you been in Detroit?"

"I guess a little over a month."

"Give me your permanent address in Detroit. And I want your signature on that line which is your promise to appear in court. Plus let me remind you that you must get a Michigan drivers license if you are drive here for more than three consecutive months."

Back in DC Hank and Tiama were planning and packing.

"Hank, have you seen Tank?"

"Yes, he is in that packing box by the kitchen door. He wants us to ship him with all of his toys. He is playing mover, packer, shipper and everything. He will be out in a few minutes. His attention span is shorter than my time from the front door to my easy chair when I get home from work."

"I fixed some fruit slices for everyone so let's sit on the porch while we eat and make a bet as to when the rain will come."

"The clouds are coming out of the East so my bet is around ten o'clock tonight."

"What's the bet?"

Hank picked up Tank and said, "I loose and you can go shopping all day tomorrow, What about if you loose?"

"If I loose you can have what ever you want, so I say by seven o'clock tonight."

While they were finishing off the fruit, Tank had snuggled deep into

Hank's arms and fallen asleep. "Hon help me put him on the sofa and I'll get the bowls. We can sit next to him and take a short brake. I want you to be extremely happy in this relocation thing. I believe you are but I want final confirmation before we trade in all the activity of a big city, the restaurants, the malls, the movies, the big parks and vacation spots, you know for the 'wild wild west'."

"OH Hank, I couldn't be happier, I love the out doors."

"Okay that is encouraging in making this decision we have made more positive. I want you to have a look at a web site when you have time. It's www.usawakeup.org which has a lot of information that will add credence to one of the other reasons I want us to move out of the big city. You will see a bevy of articles that present the real threat of the radical Muslims and the advancement they have made in just a few short years. There are headlines after headlines exposing the agenda of a religion that President Cush calls a 'Dark and Distorted Islam'. One of the articles lists the theme of most of the seventeen messages Osama bin Laden has issued since 9-11 and I wrote them down so we could understand my concern together.

> He has praised the attack on the Twin Towers.
> He has praised the attackers.
> He has declared war on the United States.
> He has stated that he will fight until his death.
> He says al Qaeda is on the move.
> He says that he is a Jihadist.
> He says that the Muslim invasion will progress from England through France through Spain through Russia through the Philippines through Indonesia and then Worldwide.
> He says that Iraq is the front of World War III.
> He says that he will not be happy until the world converts to Islam.
> He says that as we use force Islam will use force.
> He prays for all of the Muslims in the United States to advance Islam 'By the Grace of allah'.

I want us where we can be protected from the coming attacks on our country which everyone from the President on down knows is coming. As Chainery and Bates have said it's not if we are going to be attacked it is when! And with all of our power and all of our might and all of our intelligence and all of our agencies set up for our protection we can not stop them."

"Why Hon, this is the United States. We are the greatest nation the world has ever seen."

"You know I love our country more than almost anything except my family, so it not only saddens me, but I know millions of other Americans are deeply concerned of how our open society has been infiltrated by those that would destroy our way of life and try to revoke our freedom and who are encouraged by the foolish and naive thinking of liberals that take no value in looking at past history of fallen civilizations to temper their new world thinking or what some call evolutionary thinking. The idiotic university professors, who impose unproven ideas and philosophies on virgin ears and minds, are at the very root of what will be the fall of the United States. Fools with their faces and worm eaten brains buried in books and writings with no idea of what the real world is all about or what the real needs of a living, breathing moral people are. From all that is available to the public to read and all that I know the decision for us to move to Montana is based on the on coming problems in our government and the advancement of Islam."

Tiama cuddled with Tank as she looked at Hank, "I love you and we will be a tight family, Thank you Hon for your protection and love."

It was April and the first week that all of the Braydens were together in the lodge. With all of the commotion of moving and unpacking and settling in no one's cell phone had been charged so calls from old friends and acquaintances were being missed. Tom had made sure that his New York offices had the number at the lodge since he was not officially leaving UBC until December.

The phone rang at the front desk phone consol and Marylyn the day desk clerk took the call. "Hello this is Montana Big Sky Hunting Lodge, may I help you?" She had only been working during this hunting season and she liked the sound of the name, 'Montana Big Sky'.

"Yes, hello I am inquiring about a hunting trip for a large party in May, of around sixty people. We prefer to go into the hills so that we can practice for about a week in the dense forest. We will all have automatic weapons so will your area be expansive enough to allow us to practice?"

"Uh, who is calling please I will have to ask the owner."

"Yes this is Brada al-Abaji and I am a friend of Hank Brayden."

"Oh alright just a minute please. Hank, Hank, has anyone seen Hank I have a friend on the phone for him. Shorty have you seen Hank?"

"Yes'um, he is checking out the reserve power plant next to the pump house."

"Well would you please tell him that he has a long distance phone call from a friend Mr. Al Jibe, I think Brad Al Jibe."

Shorty took the side door which made the pump house in shouting distance. "Hey Hank, can you hear me? There's a phone call for you, I think Marylyn said someone by the name of Al Jib." He waited a moment for Hank to wave or something. "Did you get that?"

Hank waved at Shorty and headed for the lodge. Inside he asked Marylyn the person's name, he did not recognize what Shorty had said.

She said, "He told me he was a friend of yours, Brad Al Jibe."

"Oh my, you mean Brada al-Abaji."

"I guess so, here's the phone."

"Hello Brada is that you?"

"Brada! Who the hell is Brada? I don't know no Brada and if I did it would be top secret!"

"Top Secre… Jerry is that you? You old coot, what are you up to besides harassing me?"

"I had to pull a lot of strings to find you. I heard that you called it quits but as you know I have still been on my mission. George gave me the freedom to work my own investigation and ever since Jonathan's name and Brada's name were linked together I have not slept. I will find these damn boats or just give up like you."

"Hey my friend, I understand but I did not give up. I had a chance to change my life's direction and I was just tired; no not wrong, let me make that too tired and too exasperated. And my level of concern for the safety of my family rose to a level above my necessity to serve."

"I'm not faulting you Hank, I truly understand. I really wanted to say hello to you and wish you the best and the same for your family. Also, just to let you now, I think I have a lead on Brada. It's weak but I was thinking that he may have stayed in the states and if so I pondered where would he go? Thousands of places correct. So my intuition said no he would blend info a heavily populated Muslim community. I ask the guys in operations to look up the ten most densely Muslim populated areas and then send an alert with his driver's license to all of the enforcement agencies in each area to see if he could have by chance he could of gotten a citation of some kind or be in one of their data bases. Two months ago I get a definite no. Quite discouraging but about three weeks after that Phil called me, you know 'Phil the pill' he is so methodical and detailed that it would take him the entire lunch hour to eat a salad. Well still no citations but in a separate department at the Detroit Central Records where they keep parking tickets Phil got a hit. He had asked all of the police departments from each area to also look up parking tickets. I didn't know this but most were generally reluctant with such a huge volume of tickets but a few did get back to Phil and Detroit said they had a hit. Yes Sir, right there in Detroit your friend and mine Brada al Abaji got a parking ticket for parking in a red zone about five months ago. I've been here for about a week."

"A parking ticket, that's a long shot. Any progress?"

"Here's what happened. There are a number of shops on the street where he got the ticket so I went in to the seven-eleven on the corner and showed the clerk inside a picture of your buddy."

"Not my Buddy!"

"Anyway he kind of remembered that this guy had bought some stuff and then there was a police car behind his car flashing its lights. He said the guy took his purchase and rushed out to talk to the cop. He believes that he got a ticket for something. I asked to see the manager and I had him run the receipts for the date of the ticket and 'Bang' I got a copy of a debit card payment for the purchase. We ran it through the Treasury Dep't and got a confirmation of an account with Scotia bank in Montreal. All they have is an address in New York City but over fifty ATM and debit uses right here in the Dearborn area. He is here somewhere. I am working on verifying where by surveying all of the Mosques that are in the large Muslim community that is semi close to the general location of most of the bank card usages and the location of the parking ticket. Nothing yet but I will find him!"

"Wow, that is great and I know you will. They said that you were the best. I went to college with this guy so Jerry you let me know when you got him. Other than your mission how is everything else going, your wife and the office and our friends?"

"Just fine, when this is over I'd like a little time relaxing at your place. I have to go I'll call you soon."

"The door is open Jerry, come on up to Big Sky Country anytime."

Kansas City, Missouri - April 21, 2007

It was Friday morning when the call came into FBI offices in Kansas City, Missouri from a reporter on the scene at an explosion and fire at a large self storage complex on the northwest side of town. "Hello, my name is Harold French with the Kansas City Star Chronicle newspaper. I need to talk to whoever is in command of the office today; we have an emergency at the Sure/Safe Storage Units near Lou Holland Dr."

"I am agent Granger, what can I do for you?"

"I am at a scene of a large explosion and I would like to speak to the agent in charge."

"Please hold and I will give you to the ATF section." Click, click. "Hello, this is agent Rusk, can I help you?"

"Yes, I am a reporter for the Star Chronicle and I am at the scene of a massive explosion at a self storage facility by the Wheeler Airport off of NW Harlem Road. The fire trucks arrived about five minutes ago and the Captain from station fourteen has said that this is not natural gas related or some kind of normal phenomenon but it appears to be stored explosives that have taken out all of the storage buildings here on Lou Holland Dr. Have you at the agency received any information on this or have you gotten news of the terrible destruction here at the Sure/Safe Storage units?"

"Sir, we first heard of it minutes ago but we are just now getting calls from the fire chief and from city hall; one minute while I get briefed." Two minutes passed before Rusk returned. "What did you say your name was?"

"Harold, Harold French with the Star Chronicle newspaper and the first information I have gotten from the Captain from the fire department is that the source of the explosion is a large amount of some kind of powerful explosive!"

"Thank you Mr. French, we have an investigative team of agents on their way to the scene. If you find out any further information that would be of value to us please call right away."

"Of course, I will stay on the scene until I have all of the facts so I can get back to my offices to complete a story for our afternoon news." The Chronicle owned the UBC affiliate, WUBC in Kansas City and Harold played a duel role as reporter for both the paper and the TV station. "What are the names of the agents headed here from your office?"

"I personally don't have their names as they were dispatched from the 'outside investigations' section of our office and they do the field work. You will know them when they show up, which should be in the next few minutes. Keep in touch with us."

I promised him an immediate return phone call of any new information I gathered and then started looking for the fire Captain again.

At WUBC Harold's report became 'Breaking News' at 1:10 pm cutting into Judge Meyers' courtroom drama. "We have a news bulletin from our reporter Harold French who has been at the scene of a tremendous explosion out by the Wheeler airport near NW Harlan Road." Harold's report was short but chilling as the news cameras panned the area where ten buildings had once housed self storage for businesses and the public. At the back side of the complex opposite the frontage on route 169 was a hole in the ground about twelve feet deep and every building that was within two hundred feet of the center of the blast was pretty much leveled. The rest of the buildings were blown back away from the blast with all kinds of items strewed around the surrounding area; Clothes, parts off furniture, boxes of pharmaceuticals, tools, everything imaginable that had been in the storage units. After Harold's opening comments on the disaster and the video, Harold summed up the short report by repeating the information provided by the fire Captain and the FBI agent that had arrived at the scene. "Authorities will be investigating this most unusual event and hold open all possibilities as to exactly what was the cause of this explosion and who was the responsible person or persons. Some speculation is that it is the work of terrorist but the problem with that probability is the question 'what value would there be in taking out a storage facility'? On the other hand some have speculated that the government had two of the buildings for the nondescript storage of military data from the Air Force NORAD headquarters in Omaha, Nebraska. At this time everything is speculation as the investigation will be going ahead by the FBI and joined by the local police and agents from OHS from Washington."

The news broadcast was seen by a member of the al-Qaeda cell in Kansas City who immediately called Mustafa al-Barak the Kansas City cell leader. "Mustafa, this is Ahmed at the 'Stop and Go' on North Forty Eighth street. I am at work and was watching the TV when a 'Breaking News' bulletin came on channel four WUBC. Have you seen the news on WUBC?

A large explosion at the self storage buildings by the Wheeler Airport has just blown up. Is that important to us?"

"Ahmed are you sure of that?"

"Yes, just turn on your TV and watch for the news."

"I will right now and I'll be back to you after I have seen the news."
Mustafa kept changing channels for over fifteen minutes to find anything on the news report that Ahmed had referred to and then on the
WUBC channel which he kept flipping by he saw what would become
a fiasco for the Kansas City al-Qaeda cell; the storage units where they
had stored their supply of weapons and C4 had blown up. Why? Who
did it? It was a major immediate problem. Mustafa took his cell phone
with him and went on a walk to the corner where there was a bus stop.
He waited until no one was around and he called his contact phone
number in Yemen. Ring – Ring – Ring – Ring – Ring. More than ten
times he listened to the phone ring and no answer. Every one of those
in leadership was told to not use a voice messaging system. All calls
going out of the country gets recorded by Carnivore so he was content
to wait and call a little later. Heading back to his apartment he glanced
at his watch, 4:30 pm and he realized that the national news was now
on the air on the east coast. Many of the members of the organization have probably seen the news and guessed that the catastrophe in
Kansas City is related to the KC cell's storage area. Having all of the
imported materials stashed at secret storage areas had on many occasions prompted thoughts of anxiety by the leaders over the potential of
a problem similar to this or even exactly like this to expose the entire
operation and all cell members. The central people around bin-Laden
had always had a concern and they continuously sent communiqués to
the regional leaders to be extra careful and to make sure the supplies
were secure from exposure. Now the question was how and who!

At that same moment it was 6:30pm in New York and Tom Brayden
who had flown back to New York was in his office for a special executive officers meeting as the news came across on his TV monitor from
his news room about the 'massive explosion' as it was being called in
Kansas City and the speculation that terrorists were involved. The authorities on the case from the FBI, local police and OHS had not discussed the investigation with the media and had gone totally silent.
Tom called up to Ed Rollins the head of the news department to see if
there was more to the story than the feds had allowed to be presented
to the public. "Hello Tom its Ed what can I do for you?"

"Ed what is the skinny on the situation in Kansas City?"

"Well Tom the information so far is that there must have been almost a thousand pounds of explosives in the storage area that blew up and after sealing off the location for about a mile around the blast area the feds have found parts of Chinese MAK-90 rifles but they are not sure how many were in the storage buildings. They think the explosive material maybe C4 and not dynamite so they have rushed some of the debris to the test labs at the Air Force Academy in Colorado. They have told us nothing else but that we must keep a lid on this information as their investigation is moving at a very fast pace and they want no public exposure that could hinder the investigation and the tracking of the persons who rented the storage unit. They feel that just the media coverage of the blast alone will have sent any suspects underground and the speed of their investigation is critical!"

"Thanks Ed, I'm going to stay here tonight. Keep me posted." Tom immediately dialed the lodge to talk to Hank to see what more he might know about the situation.

"Hello this is the Montana Big Sky Hunting Lodge, Tiama speaking, may I help you?"

"Hi, sounds like my favorite daughter-in-law. First tell me how you are and then let me speak to Hank please, it's important?"

"Okay slow down a little, I'm just fine and so is your grandson. Hank is out with the crew bringing in the horses. Anything I can do?"

"No not really. Have you watched the news tonight? It will tell you and Hank why I want to talk to him."

"No we haven't. We are just now coming in from our chores. What should we know?"

"It's pretty important so just watch the news and tell Hank to call me."

At around 12 midnight Mustafa's phone rang and it was Musab with a short conversation. "Go out side and call me on my outer line."

He hurriedly slipped on some pants and a t-shirt and went for a walk while dialing Musab's cell phone. "Hello, this is Musab." Mustafa replied in Arabic, "Follow allah to allah, allah is your eternal peace." Musab waited, then "in paradise." After a short pause Musab began speaking in Arabic, "We know the storage area that blew up was ours and we do not care how. Here are your orders. Contact all of your first echelon members and tell them to get their traveling money and leave immediately. Those with families are to only take the children and a few clothes. Tell them to destroy all evidence and to take their cell phones and head to Canada now. They will be contacted when in

Canada. All of the others will be contacted by the computer in Yemen and provided with instructions. The cell must be dispersed this very night! We are too close to the date of the Jihad and we can not have our brothers or their families around to be discovered by the authorities. Do you understand?"

"Yes it will be done now!" All Mustafa heard after that was the phone call ending. He kept walking and called his five aides who he knew would be suspects in a very short time and gave them the same orders. They had each of them been talking to one another and were already prepared to leave for Canada. Their cars were gassed up and packed with the few things they would need. All of their travel plans were for different areas of Canada and they wanted to be able to cross over early Sunday Morning when most people would be busy with their Sunday church going and relaxation.

In the afternoon on Sunday the cell phones of all of the remaining brothers of the Kansas City cell began ringing with a message from Yemen. Each of them knew that the call would be their instructions on what would be required of them to protect the secrecy of their mission for allah. The message was the same for each, "This is the last call to you. You have served allah well and if by any chance any one should ask you your allegiance you know what to say. You and any of your family must never admit that a union of the Muslim brothers existed in Kansas City and go on about your personal lives in a normal manner. After this message totally destroy this cell phone and your lap top computer. If you have any papers associated with your relationships with the past then burn all of it today. Should you be taken for any kind of questioning and you can not maintain your secrecy then you are to commit suicide in the name of allah. You will be recognized as a martyr and heaven will await you. allah akbar."

It was four o'clock when Stephen Haddle entered the Oval Office to bring the President up to date on the investigation on the Kansas City bombing. "Mr. President, Mertoff and Dryer are here for your briefing, are you ready?"

"Yes let's get started. I need to start my press conference in one hour. Where is Tony? I want him to be alerted on all of the facts so that the statement from my office this afternoon will be congruous with each if your individual comments and any press conferences that come up over the next few days. Michael, bring us up to date and Robert cover anything new that you have learned over the last few hours. Ah, here is Tony now. Go ahead Robert."

"As we are all aware the first FBI team on the scene in Kansas City discovered hundreds of parts of Chinese MAK 90 automatic rifles and the laboratory at the Air Force Academy verified that the explosive material was C4 and maybe as much as one thousand pounds. They immediately cordoned off a thousand foot square area around the site and placed guards on an eight hour rotation to keep the lookie-loue's away. So here is our latest, yesterday we issued an emergency NSR and placed a federal gag order on all the news agencies and national broadcasting stations and newspapers suppressing the facts of this situation in Kansas City until we have completed our extended investigation which we put into full operation shortly after we ascertained that the explosive material in the storage units was C4. From the pieces of evidence that was collected and sent to the labs at the Air Force Academy they found hundreds of bits and pieces of boxes that were joint compound boxes. The kind that premixed plaster comes in. They concluded that the C4 had been stored in these nondescript boxes to keep away any suspicion. With out a doubt this was a terrorist cell's storage location and there are now approximately three thousand agents from all of our combined enforcement departments investigating the entire Muslim community Mosque by Mosque and business by business in Kansas City."

Cush looked at Michael as he pushed his chair back slightly so all could see his expression, "Where the hell did this much C4 come from and in the hands of terrorists? It is beyond belief. We need to get to the bottom of this now!"

"George, I can add that this veil of secrecy that we have right now will not last for long." Robert looked gaunt as he spoke. "Putting a clamp on the news will last for about two days and then somewhere there will be a leak, but what is going to be most obvious is the security that we have placed around the blast site. Further, will be the voice of the Arabic community that will squeal like a banshee when they realize that we are profiling them as the only suspects. They will call on the ACLU and hit the press like an Arizona dust storm. We may have three to four days before their community boils over."

"Tony what do you think. How is the best way to initially approach the public on this disaster?"

"First Uncertainty, let's use uncertainty as our starting point; we do not yet know what the cause of the explosion was but no possibility is being unexplored, stored chemicals, construction company's unauthorized storage of dynamite, liquid gas storage tanks, we just do not know. Second Denial, there is no reason to believe that terrorist had anything to do with the explosion and that there is a reasonable answer to the magnitude of the explosion. Third Confirmation, the OHS is in control and will release their findings and have the answers for the media soon. And last Apology, as some have speculated that terrorists may have blown up the buildings but there is no reason to attack a storage area and there is no evidence that any radicals may have been evolved. "
"Great Tony let's get started and write me a short address to the public."

"Mr. President," Michael had to brief everyone on the work NSA was doing on their side of the investigation, "this investigation is not necessary to substantiate what our CI-4 unit at NSA has declared for almost two years but could never prove. As you have seen from time to time in your PDB's we knew that there are radical Muslims in this country that want to cause sever damage to us however they can. We have believed that there are terrorists inside of our borders with weapons and enough explosives to cause more damage than either England or Spain or Israel have ever experienced. We have been trying to warn everyone but until this event there was no solid evidence. We had a NSR in operation investigating the probability that C4 had been smuggled in through Florida in these large fast boats but we could never get any evidence. I was forced to terminate the NSR due to lack of discovery of any physical evidence and the damn budgetary restraints. However, NSA has directed Agent Ness to continue on with a solo OPT using the unit's own budgeted fund and he is trying at this very moment to get information that could lead us to a suspect who we believe is a top operative for al-Qaeda. And George Meeker at NSA had asked for a NSR to go after containers that his people in one of the CI units believes have been used for a number of years to illegality import contraband for the terrorist cells operating on the west coast. And as I said, with out anything but hearsay evidence we lost our NSR on the investigation on the East coast and never were able to get a NSR for the shipping containers even though the congress had allocated over a billion dollars for investigation and security programs to protect our ports.

Now we have the evidence and I am hoping you will go to Congress to get immediate release of the funding and give the administration's approval for the rapid protection of our ports, airports, trains, subways and other infrastructures. I am going to elevate the terrorist alert to Orange by Monday. Until then we will not want any panic to come from this incident."

"Steven, I want you to set up an immediate meeting for the Vice-president and all cabinet members in the East for one pm tomorrow. I am going to have to sooner or later deal with the facts about this destruction in Kansas City and be prepared to go public with the evidence we have. I believe we need all of the input I can get from my cabinet and advisors to properly go before the people."

"Yes Sir."

"And Steven, I want each of you to hear this. For some time we have all worried about the attacks on our airports, subways, trains, bridges, large buildings, major shopping malls, water supply facilities, chemical plants and government installations. So I am going to ask Robert Bates to transport fifteen thousand of our National Guard personnel home to be immediately assigned to protecting these potential targets. They will have to be extracted from Iraq in air transports at night so as to not alert the enemy there. We will then make the announcement that this is our first commitment to return our troops and to the Iraqi government that if they do not get serious about stopping their internal fighting we will leave them in their quagmire!"

Steven offered his personal thoughts, "I wonder how venerable we are at this moment. I heard Newt Gingrich say that we must complete the mission to eradicate the terrorists or they will spread the Islamic infection like the black plague. And then contrary to that position Chris Dodd said that we are in the middle of a civil war in Iraq between two religious factions that need to sort it out for themselves and that the Iraqis don't want our help. He claims that fifty per cent of them want to kill all Americans."

"I want us to look at both sides since I believe that they are both correct. Okay everyone let's go to work and make the best of this situation and keep calm as we encourage everyone that we have everything under control."

CHAPTER TWENTY NINE

Jerry being absolutely certain that his target was in Detroit had been monitoring the partakers of evening prayer for a few days in a row at each of the three Mosques in the Muslim community knowing sooner or later he would see Brada. The next day after he heard about the explosion of the storage buildings in Kansas City he called his friend Melvin at his office to see what had happened since the news media was being so vague.

"Jerry, the report coming down the internal pipeline from OHS is that it was a terrorist storage area for C4 and weapons to arm the terrorist." And bang, he knew that all of the missions and the intelligence that he and Hank and the CI units had been pursuing was one hundred per cent accurate, this was the catalyzing event every one had hoped for, now there was evidence!

"Melvin thanks for the latest Intel. This is great news, but really it is bad news. Now we have proof and now we have to stop the damn Islamic Fascists before they do to us what they have been doing around the world! This exposure of their possession of guns and bomb making material will cause them to begin their terrorist attacks almost immediately if not sooner. Our vulnerability has gone up one thousand, no ten thousand per cent. What has George said that OHS and the FBI are going to do? Tell George for me that everyone from the top down need to stop being politically correct and profile every S.O.B. in the Muslim community and I hope they all break protocol and go after zinger number two; we know who they are and we must enter every know cell. I am going to find that bastard Brada and bring him in alive even if he is missing parts of his lower torso."

USA: THE SERPENT IS CRUSHED!

Standing near by the Detroit Masjid on Joy Rd, Jerry intently watched as the men moved in for evening prayer. He screamed inside of his head, 'it's him'. He called the night crew at CI unit four for satellite surveillance. "Hello this is agent Ness is Melvin still around?"

"No sir he is in the 'John'."

"When he gets back have him call me on my cell."

"You bet Jerry, this is Phil."

Jerry moved down the street next to a car in a driveway about one hundred feet away from the Mosque. His pulse was not up but he was sweating for some reason. Jerry had been waiting and waiting to find Brada al-Abaji and now the exhilaration was like his first jump from a troop plane and it brought both calm and sweat. Just then his cell vibrated and it was Melvin.

"Hey Melvin I have found him and I am going to follow him until he takes me to where he lives so I need satellite surveillance in case I lose him."

"You got it, where are you exactly?"

"Okay I am in Dearborn an area next to Detroit, you know the car town, and I am about one hundred feet from the building where Brada is now. I am East of the John C. Lodge Freeway and South of the Seven Mile Rd West on 18100 Meyers Rd. I will leave my cell phone on 'T' so you can tract me. Have you got me yet?"

"No the visual is not up yet. Wait a minute the image is coming in now and I think they have you. If you are standing by a parked car in a driveway, then wave at me. I got you, was that your finger or your phone?"

"Very funny. I will pick him out for you when he comes out and as everyone disburses I'll put a small laser beam on him so you can spot him. Then no matter what do not lose him. I have no idea where he might go."

"Ten-four Jerry."

It seemed like hours but finally the men started to exit the Mosque and Jerry strolled up the street trying to not be obvious. There were a lot of trees around so the evening shadows were falling and that gave him a little cover.

"Melvin, have you got the men coming out of the Mosque?"

"Yes, I am looking at you and them on a split screen. Don't worry, as soon as you pin point him we won't loose him. I am going to stay on tact with you. Okay we see the red beam and we have your subject. He is headed south with five others."

"I see them. There were a few people that went down that street before he came out so the other groups are some where in front of Brada. There are some houses on my side of the street and they are walking down on the east side. They have passed Thatcher Street and are headed to Santa Maria, no wait two of them are lighting up cigarettes while they appear to be standing around and talking. Melvin, I am laying back on the other side of the street so they won't see me."

"Right, we see you. The two that are smoking are going towards that building next to those apartment buildings. There were some others from the Mosque that went down to McNichols Rd. and went into a low level apartment building. Might be a compound for a cell or something. You are in a tight Arabic community. Can you see the subject with his two companions? They turned on to McNichols Rd also and they are all going into the second apartment building."

"Yes, I followed them and I am going in now. I don't want to loose him. Stay on line with me. The address here is 20476 McNichols Rd. I will want information on the occupants."

"Jerry, be careful. He is not alone. I don't know if you want some back up but we called for some help and two FBI agents were in the area so they can be there in minutes."

"If they show up in the next few minutes keep them outside until you hear me take him down. I'm in the hall on the first floor going door to door and I don't hear anyone. So now I'm going up the stairs to the second floor and I hear a door opening. I've stopped on the landing looking up the stair well riser to the second floor. Two guys are leaving their unit and walking down the hall to the last door on the right before the back stairs."

"We have you and we see the two moving down the hall. There are two units at the rear. One on your left has a single occupant and the other on your right has only one occupant. The first unit on your left has one occupant and the unit on your right is vacant."

"They have left the door ajar so I'm going on up. I will need to check every unit. I'm starting with the open door then you tell me about each of the other units in the middle. Are you still with me and can you give me a body count unit by unit?

"Okay did you miss my previous transmission? Still here Jerry?; no one in the unit on your right and one person in the unit on your left."

"Have you cross referenced the address of this building yet and do you have the names of the occupants?"

"Data central just gave us the names. Do you want the first floor or just the second floor?"

"I'm on the second floor! Names unit by unit as I go down the hall. Do you see a Brada?"

"No Brada, but here is the first unit on your right, Dave Mallard. First on your left is Al Mohammed and there is a person sitting by the window. At least it looks like he is sitting."

"I got it."

Jerry pushed the door open ever so slightly as he moved cautiously in and extracted his automatic from his hip holster. Al, if that was who was in the apartment was looking out the window when he caught a tiny reflection in the glass and turned right into the mussel of Jerry's gun. Jerry cocked the hammer as he shook his head back and forth and put his finger over his lips uttering a very hush, sh - sh.

"Go into the kitchen now. What are the names of those men who just left this apartment? Speak very, very quietly or you will never speak again! What is your name?"

"I am Saif and the other two are Ali Mohammed and Fazul al-Din."

"Melvin, did you get that? Check out the names. What about the other units?"

"Got them. Four more units and the two in the middle are rented to Hazel Keil on the left and there is no one inside and the one on the right is showing no name and it is vacant. The last two have occupants. On the left there is a tenant named Mason Jackson and he looks like he is watching TV and on the right you have a Khalid Matwalli. And Jerry we ran Ali Mohammed and there are too many in the data based for an ID but Fazul al-Din lived in San Diego at the same time some of the 9-11 terrorist lived there. And now we have the info on Khalid Matwalli. If it is the same one in our data base he has been suspected of operating Islamic Charities to help fund Hamas operations in Gaza and in England."

"Okay Melvin stay tuned this is going to be interesting. Are the FBI guys here yet?"

"Yes and they are parked down the street about fifty yards away. Do you want us to contact them?"

"Yes, I need to cover Ali here while I go down the hall to the last unit. But who ever comes up here to cover for me describe me to him letting him know I have the gun on my suspect and tell him to come in slowly so I don't shoot him and he doesn't shoot me."

He waited until one of the agents came in the door where upon he nodded to him and then turning to Saif and with the gun stuck in his neck he slowly said, "I saw Brada come into this building and go up to the second floor here. Is he in the last apartment with your friends?"

Saif shook his head, yes.

Jerry turned to the agent who was now right beside him as he identified himself, "I'm Jerry Ness and I need him kept quiet while I go down the hall to the last apartment on the right. Did Melvin brief you on my mission?"

"Yes, and I'm Ed Riggs and Agent Jim Acers is down stairs. Are you going to need him up here?"

"I'll let Melvin know as this progresses. I have to take this Brada guy alive so I need to go solo."

Jerry edged out the door and into the hall where he could hear some laughing and guttural sounds coming from the last apartment. As he approached he listened to hear if any sounds were coming from the apartment on the left and it sounded like a TV playing. He thought that was perfect. His entry would not be heard as easily.

The door was not locked, but he was not going to knock anyway. Gun drawn Jerry eased the door knob and opened the door facing three men sitting at a table smoking cigarettes. They were at first stunned and then the two who had gone down the hall got up and moved towards a doorway near the table. "Stop, do not make another move!" Jerry had the two men in his sites as he looked at Brada still sitting at the table. "Melvin I've got him. Send up the other agent to help me hand cuff him and take him in. Well Brada me meet again but on my terms and without the staged environment of a legitimate business in a New York office. Just stay right there till my…….." Melvin saw a figure come out of the apartment across the hall and lift his arm up and point at Jerry; he yelled at Jerry, 'Look out behind you", and then Melvin could hear gun fire and Jerry is down to his knees and crumbles in a heap like his knees had just given out. His ear piece falling to the ground.

The two Fazul and Khalid ran to the door to get out of the apartment but Ed Riggs had used the butt of his gun to knock Ali out and was already in the hall and shouted at Fazul and Khalid to stop as they turned to run down the back stairs. Jim Acers heard the shots and ran in the front door hollering for his partner. "Ed, where are you?"

"I'm up here and I 'm okay, go after the two that just ran out the back. I'll check on the agent from NSA, I think he got shot and may be down."

Ed entered the apartment and found agent Jerry shoot twice in the head and not moving.

Melvin could be heard over Jerry's ear piece, "What's happening? Jerry, Jerry answer me, do you hear me? What's happening? What the hell is going on, Jerry talk to me."

Ed used Jerry's phone to talk to Melvin. "Your agent has been shot and I'm sure he is dead. My partner is chasing the two who ran from the apartment."

Melvin in a hurried sputter started giving orders, "Oh my god no, are you sure? Check again."

"No need Melvin I know dead when I see it; your man is dead."

"Listen closely Ed, there were three men in that apartment and one of them was a Brada al-Abaji who Jerry was there to apprehend. We can see the other two your partner has stopped and there are police cars coming up the alley as we speak, but a third person when out of a side window and somehow got to the ground and went to the front of the building and drove off in a car headed to the John Lodge Freeway. We firmly believe that is Brada and we must get him but you have the shooter across the hall who came out and fired two shots and then went back into his apartment. Be careful. We are directing the police to get there now and capture him and an ambulance is almost there for Jerry. Get after Brada and we will stay with you as we track him. He is a fugitive that we can not lose."

"I'm gone, which way did he go on the Lodge."

"East towards town."

"What kind of a car."

"Blue 2000 Toyota. In one minute we will have the license plate number. Okay there we have it 67jyu 908. It is a Canadian plate."

"I'm on the freeway headed east. How far in front of me is he?"

"We see you and it looks like about three and a half miles. He is passing most cars and appears to be going close to eighty miles an hour. That gives him about a four minute lead on you. Wait a minute he is taking an off ramp and … okay now he is pulling in to a gas station. This is our break, he needs gas. You should be there in about three minutes. It is a Shell station and I think he took the outside pumps but he is under the canopy and we can not see him."

"I'll be going down the ramp in a minute and I see the Shell station sign. Okay I see it, there is his blue Toyota but no one is in it. He must have gone inside."

"No, we have been watching and no one walked into the store from where he entered."

"I'm here and there is no one in the car or around the car."

"Where did he go?"

"I don't know there is no one here but a motorcycle and some people in the store. Here comes the motorcycle rider now. Give me a minute. Hey buddy, did you see the man that drove up in that blue Toyota?"

"Why, who are you?"

"FBI, did you see him or anyone?"

"No the only people I saw were the guys in the pick up. They were getting in their truck as I came in."

"Were they working guys or what? Did you see anything different about them?"

"Nope, except they both got in from the same side of the truck. I guess the passenger's door was broke."

"Melvin are you still with me?"

"Wait a minute the police have the two that ran from the building and we just confirmed with them that it was Brada that got away."

"My guess is he car-jacked the pickup that was here and he has gotten away again. Can you go back and look at the Sat-Intel?"

"Yes, it will take a minute, Wait. We are looking at a black pick up that left about ten seconds before you arrived. We can see it on the tape and if we pull back the image on it until it blends into the surroundings we can see that it went on to the freeway and headed towards town. By now it could be anywhere."

"I'm sorry Mel, I tried. Did your people or the police get the shooter?"

"Not yet, he also went out the window. We did identify the pickup. It is a black Dodge Tacoma but we could not get the license plate. We have asked the Detroit police to do an all points bulletin to stop it and arrest the occupants."

"Okay, I am headed back to the apartments to assist my partner and talk to the police and see about your agent. Keep me informed."

Agents from the NSA and the FBI spent the next two days looking for the pick up and Brada. They felt that he may have taken the number Ten freeway to the border crossing to Canada and gotten on to their freeway 402 to Windsor. Their suspicions were verified when the Canadian authorities found a deserted black Dodge pickup at a motel in London just off of the 402. On the same day the Detroit police discovered a decapitated body in a downtown alley that deadened into the freight dock of a clothing store. The identity was passed on to the FBI and it was the owner of the pickup that Brada had stolen.

George got the call on April 29 from the FBI field office in Detroit. "Hello this is George Meeker, who is calling?"

"This is agent Ed Riggs with the FBI in Detroit. I am the agent that was there when you man Jerry Ness went down. I have information on the person he was after, Brada al-Abaji. He car-jacked a pickup with the owner as a hostage to make his get away and abandoned the pickup in London, Canada. Before crossing the border he killed the owner in Detroit. He cut his head off and dropped him in an alley before going into Canada. Knowing he is a terrorist on the run we thought that he did that to make a statement so we kept it quiet and reported it as a homeless person's death until we can finish our investigation and deal with the family. After that it will be out in the open. It will be your case then."

"Thank you for the report and send me a copy of the case file. Jerry was one of our best agents and a close friend. Our entire department is in disbelief."

"Our condolences, we are a tight family here too."

On Monday, April thirtieth, Tony Snow fended for the President and gave a news brief about the rather secret investigation on the destruction of a storage complex in Kansas City. He spoke slow and convincingly. "Ladies and Gentlemen of the press I have a prepared statement regarding the investigation by the FBI into the explosion of the storage buildings in Kansas City. The outcome showed that a contractor that does demolition work had illegally stored a large amount of dynamite in one of the buildings along with canisters of gasoline and spontaneous combustion had set off the explosives. There was no truth to the rumor that the storage building was destroyed by terrorists. As to the parts for automatic rifles found at the scene it appears that a local gun shop had a small storage unit where they kept some trophy and antique guns stored including a small amount of inventory."

"Mr. Snow, why has the Whitehouse taken so long to talk about this? The public has been concerned and rumors have been flying!"

"Greta, we had to wait for the completed investigation by the FBI."

Tony finished by answering a number of other questions and then closed the press conference.

On May Seventh a call came in to the Big Sky Hunting Lodge at around six a.m. Hank was having a cup of coffee on the porch when the phone rang. He didn't want to get up but no one else was in the lobby.

"Hello, this is the Big Sky Hunting Lodge, can I help you?"

"Hello there, is this Hank? It's George here in Washington."

"George, I recognize your voice. How are you, what is the latest, and no I will not come back, no matter what."

"Sorry Hank but this is not that kind of a call."

Hank's face turned serious knowing by George's tone something was not right. "I needed to call you with some information. Jerry was on the trail of Brada and had him cornered in an apartment in Detroit but he got away and Jerry went down. He took two bullets in the back of his head from a shooter that approached from the rear. He never had a chance."

"Jerry is gone? My impetuous friend is gone……….. Oh my god George this is terrible. I loved that guy. (Pause) Why? Or better how could it happen, he was the most cautious agent in the company. He would never leave himself exposed on his back side. Was it Brada? Did he get away?"

"Here is the story we got from the two occupants in the apartment with Brada when it all happened who are now in our custody. Jerry entered the apartment and surprised Brada and his Muslim companions and as he identified Brada one of their brothers came from across the hall and shot through the open door in the apartment and hit Jerry in the head with two bullets. He had no chance. It seems that they had mini cams placed in a few spots for protection and one was over the front door and they had monitors in their bedrooms and across the hall in the apartment occupied by a person named Mason Jackson. We think that the name of that occupant when Jerry heard it did not sound Arabic so he did not check out that apartment before going in after Brada. But Mason was a Muslim brother with a view of what was going on in his comrade's apartment and opened his door and killed Jerry. Melvin had everything on satellite surveillance and told Jerry that someone was at his back but he was shot just as Melvin told him. Everyone scattered and the two companions from Brada's apartment were captured but the shooter and Brada got away. There is no trace of Brada. We believe that he crossed over into Canada."

"My god what a waste. A great agent and my very good friend. Do you have anything from the guys you have in custody?"

"No and of course we want Brada more than anything now!"

"Well I am in complete shock. Please call his wife and give her my condolences. You've got to get this rat. So an important question, have you gotten anything on the boats? Where are you on the investigation into the boats?"

"Nowhere, Brada would have been our best source for information. We have nothing but the Kansas City incident."

There were some tears in Hanks eyes and his speech became a little wobbly. "From what I know now you would not have gotten anything from Brada. He is a devoted Muslim and would rather be a martyr than give up any information. Mertoff has to put the country on orange alert and tear the Muslim communities apart. We can't let Jerry's dearth go unanswered. I am certain or at least my gut feeling is that the war is about to bust loose all around us and of course we can defend ourselves but suicide bombers will kill a lot of people."

"We are all on the same page and even though the public knows only what the information sector is authorized to put out all of our manpower and effort is to infiltrate their inner sanctum for any clues as to what may be brewing. We need to know not just that we are going to be hit by al-Qaeda but Where, When, and How much."

Hank added in an expression of disdain "Well everyone knows what our unit, Jerry and I thought. They have the commodity and the ambition and their planned objectives so all we can do is wait. I'm glad I am up here with my family but my heart is broken over the news about Jerry. George please keep me in the loop with what ever you can tell me. Say hello to my friends and take care of your self and my God bless and keep you."

"Thanks and you do the same."

Hank went into the dinning room where everyone was having breakfast. "I just got some really sad news from George at NSA. My Friend Jerry Ness who I worked with all of the time I was in the CI unit was killed in Detroit while trying to arrest the suspect Brada al-Abaji, a guy who had been in my class at NYU. You remember him Dad, or at least I mentioned him to you from time to time. At school I knew he was a hard nosed fundamentalist but as Jerry discovered he had terrorist friends and as of late he may have become an operative for al-Qaeda or Hamas. Well I have lost a good friend and a major player in the threat to our country has disappeared into Canada according to George."

"Son, I was just thinking, didn't he run some kind of news journal and consulting operation in New York? "

"Yes, he started the 'World Wide Journal on Hydro Electric Power' and had friends at the United Nations and in the Commerce Department. I understand that he worked with a number of Middle Eastern countries as a consultant on proposed dam projects."

"I guess that gave him opportunities to travel in and out of most Arab countries without any suspicion and what about his access to all of the information on the dams in our country. My first thoughts would be that he has a lot of knowledge about our dams. Has the NSA labeled him as a terrorist and an enemy of our country and if so I would have to think our dams are a prime target for the terrorists?"

"Yes of course, He has been on the radar for some time and I remember Jerry did report to our supervisors about his work in the area of dams and hydro-electric generation and his access to our hydro-electric infrastructure. To calm everyone's nerves if you all are concerned we have been monitoring all of our dams and we have placed military security on most of them. We believe that he was in cohorts with a boat manufacture that was importing contraband into the States"

Caroline raised her orange juice glass. "Let's say thank you and goodbye to one of your good friends, Jerry Ness, and to all of our protectors, both abroad and here at home. May God continue to over see and protect our country."

That kind of broke the somber atmosphere and after Hank finished eating he went to the barn and saddled up his personal horse and rode off into the hills.

Over the next two months the politicians occupied the media limelight as they spent most of their time complaining about the war, campaigning for money and getting ready for the presidential primaries while President Cush was busy defending the military's serge in Iraq claiming it was working. Of course the democrats in congress pointed to the lack of desire of the Iraqi government to quell the violence with no substantial progress on the part of Iraq to reach the eighteen points set by Cush for political change.

At the same time al-Qaeda began a new offensive in Pakistan, Iraq, London and other areas around the world. Their effort was to put out propaganda and increase their terrorist activirty to let the West know that they were not dead or even diminished but were actually growing like an amoeba, growing splitting and then growing more and then splitting and then gro. The terrorist world wide were not all directly affiliated with Osama or his al-Qaeda band but there was no doubt that they were inspired by his image and wanted to further the Jihad under the al-Qaeda banner.

It was June 30th and three different groups of terrorists and some Muslim doctors in London tried to blow up a market place with a car loaded with explosives. The attempt was discovered and foiled. And in Scotland a Muslim doctor rammed his car into a building at the airport and the explosives failed to detonate. Al-Qaeda was inspiring radical Jihadist everywhere.

In July NSA had intercepted many messages from the al-Qaeda camp broadcasted to the world but actually pointed towards the U.S. Threats of many more coming attacks on England and on the U. S. claiming that the devastation will be like Hiroshima or Nagasaki but more frightening. With all of the political unrest in Iraq and the political infighting in the States and the changing of the guard in England; al-Qaeda was unleashing a barrage of propaganda.

The intelligence departments in Washington took the increase in the internet activity and the chatter seriously but many viewed this activity from al-Qaeda more as publicity to attract activist to join their forces. Radicals who wanted to proliferate the Jihad. The noise and chatter on the internet and other communication avenues increased by three fold according to NSA and Homeland Security chief Mertoff called for a heightened security level during the coming Fourth of July holiday and more intense security at the countries airports. At the same time Director of National Intelligence, Mike McConnell said that al-Qaeda has regrouped and is growing and that the United States is going to be attacked at any time by the enemy. Organized terrorist groups are popping up everywhere because they are motivated by the Shia based Islamic clerics. As the world has seen they can use anything as weapons, gasoline trucks, air planes, chemical trucks, bacteria, fertilize and kerosene, or poison and even radioactive waste.

Mertoff summoned the heads of the CIA Michael Hayden, FBI Robert Mules, DOD Robert Bates, NSA Gen. Keith Alexander, and the

President's national security advisor Stephen Haddle to discuss the threats against the States and the possibility of an attack at any time. All departments under the OHS were issued an urgent alert to investigate the minutest Intel that would suggest a terrorist scheme to attack or bomb any public place or for suicide bombers to go to public events and blow themselves up. It had always been the thinking of the President and his people and the OHS that the enemy would use a dirty bomb or attack large buildings, subways, airports, shopping centers or other public areas to cause as much damage and fear as they could. The Fourth of July holiday would be a perfect time and an ironic occurrence if a second homeland attack came on the day of celebrating the countries independence.

It was about two weeks later and the Independence Day holidays had come and gone with not a sign of any terrorist activity but in one of Mertoff's news conferences he said that he had a gut feeling that we were going to see an attack on our mainland very soon. He had no proof to substantiate his feelings; he said that he just had a gut feeling. Later during the week he explained his comment that he just had a hunch and nothing should cause any fear to the American people. That was a real comfort, nothing to worry about, 'that is except fear itself'. A Hunch or Bunch of Hunch or a Crunching Hunch or just a real HUNCH; terrorists around the world have said that they want to destroy the United States; Osama bin Ladin has claimed that he will bring pain and suffering to the States like never before and tens of thousands or maybe more, even hundreds of thousands of radical Islamic Muslims have declared a Jihad against the United States. A damn hunch, he knows better. He has all of the intelligence data and even though the President does not want to talk about it Mertoff hasn't got a gut feeling. He knows it is coming!

The debates and the do nothing congress occupied the calendar until their vacation break and so the rest of the country could take a breather form politics and enjoy slightly lower gas prices and enjoy some sort of a family vacation even if it was just from, 'here to there'. Here to there actually meant a hundred miles or so to a theme park or to the mountains or the beach and for the families on a short budget only a trip to visit relatives.

Summer heat and fires and unusual floods had gently slid the nation into September and Labor Day was just around the corner. Hank sat on the porch taking pleasure in the cool evening breeze coming down off of the mountains and watched as the sun falling behind the mountains continually colored the landscape and hills directly in front of the lodge in an array of magnificent changing pictures. He was in awe of were he was and the beauty of the life that surrounded him. Just then Tom and Tank came out to sit with him. He turned to Tank and said, "Look son how beautiful and how quickly the colors change. Dad, God is surely real and the blessings he has provided to us being able to live up here and feel the security of this open area is truly a gift."

"You are so right son, every day I see the news and talk to my New York office I shutter over what is in store for our country and worst, for the world. Now the Muslims claim they are going to make France and England a Muslim state. And they will not stop until it is done. I know it will never happen here even though we are such complacent people but when the real surge or may I call it an attack on our country and on our culture comes, they will have a huge awakening. They want to take over the world and bring everyone under the rule of Islam and of course that has been their underlying plan for hundreds of years. They have no idea what the 'Bible Belt' really is and they ain't never encountered real 'red necks'. The saving grace in our future is that this country has about a one hundred million man standing army."

"What are you talking about; a hundred million man standing army?"

"You bet son; we have never given up our guns and every God fearing American man, woman, and grownup child will fight for these United States. Thank God the idiots in congress could not supersede the Constitution of the United States and take our guns away. Even that dullard senator from Massachusetts who dumped his car in Chappaquiddick blatantly tried to get our guns from us but he failed."

"Who failed with what guns?" Tiama had come through the door with some chilled fruit juice for her guys and only caught the tail end of Tom's comments.

"Oh nothing honey we were talking about how our guns are a real protection against any bad guys."

CHAPTER THIRTY

September the fifth and the West wakes up to news that some oil tankers had been blown up and sunk in the Persian Gulf. The early morning news programs on the major networks were trying to get the events as accurate as possible and the reports varied from two to five tankers had been sunk and the oil spill was so devastating that no other ships were being allowed to move in the Gulf. Pictures from the scene showed what could be the world's worst ecological disaster ever and an incalculable economic disaster to the worlds oil supply.

On Friday CNN was reporting that oil was now being used by the terrorist to cause financial turmoil in the world economic arena and the Saudis announced that they had captured six of the militants that had taken part in the plan by al-Qaeda to destroy as many tankers as they could to completely stop the flow of oil from the gulf.

The market opened with oil shooting pass one hundred dollars a barrel and market makers suggesting two hundred dollars a barrel if the clean up took an extended amount of time. Within two days gasoline was at six dollars a gallon and the public out cry was deafening. A real turmoil was occurring in the financial markets and the Dow that had risen above fourteen thousand dropped to below eleven thousand in just three days.

On September the Ninth Yassir al-Jazziri's cell rang. At the same time Saja al-Hasi's cell phone rang. And the cell phones of Abu Eisa al-Hindi, Musab Yasin, Amer el-Matti, Abdulla Azzam, Zubayr al-Rimi, Ibrahim

USA: THE SERPENT IS CRUSHED!

al-Mughassil, Faheim Hamad, Omar Bakri, Arabie Ahmed and sixty other cell leader's cell phones rang with the message they had all been waiting for. The message was in Arabic, clear and slow. The voice gave the command, "Each of our brothers have been waiting for 'Operation Ball Buster and Operation Overground Death' and they are now activated. Find a location where you can access an unidentifiable computer and go to http://allahsreward.uk. This web site will only be up for vie at twelve o'clock noon New York time and will be on line for only one hour and then it will shut down. Listen carefully for your personal pass code to open the pages of instructions that are for your own personal mission. Your individual code is tagged to your cell phone number will be repeated at the end of this call three times, memorize it but do not write it down. Then destroy your cell phone and the Sim card. You will first see the nine different types of targets that we have planned to destroy in this attack and then on your personal web page you will each see the specific mission you have been assigned. The nation of Islam will finally be able to make the West suffer like we have suffered for all of these years! Carry out your mission for the pride of allah and if you should die in your battle then allah awaits you with your reward."

On the web site the message was in Arabic and it was clear.

> "To all of my Islamic brothers. The time has come. The world is plagued with financial problems. The supply of oil from the Gulf is halted for a few more weeks and Cush's war is not going well. Pakistan is almost in collapse and all of our comrades are ready. Now is the time to strike. The attacks will begin simultaneously from coast to coast at five am New York time on September eleventh in two days.

> Please read carefully your orders for the attack on the serpent, the satan of the west. Memorize your targets and your battle plans. The instructions are detailed for each target and they have been well thought out. The success of our attack is in your hands, the mighty army of allah and with the blessing of allah, America will be crippled and wither on the vine of self indulgence and pride.   allah akbar, allah akbar."

Like all of the rest of the lieutenants and cell leaders, Musab destroyed his cell phone and pulled the Sim card out so he could put it into some ordinary trash container on the sidewalk and then he went to the public library In Jersey City where he could use a computer and view and review the web pages meant for him.

Musab had returned to the States in August and left his family in Lebanon. He had closed the agency and wired all of his money to his family for their future just in case he should not return. It was still early Sunday morning so only one other person was in the computer section in the library. The computers were set up in small individual compartments and he chose one that would provide the most privacy. Still five minutes to twelve. He had picked up a book off of one of the tables to make it appear as though he were researching some thing on the computer, eleven fifty eight and he went to the web site. http:// allahsreward.uk. The site had been designed by Mustafa Mohammad, al-Qaeda's high tech, guru using the latest web site technology 'Califee-Frmag' known as X force. Totally code protected allowing multiple users to view only their own personal pages. Two thousand four hundred other people were on the web site entering their codes for access.

Here came the categories of targets to be attacked and destroyed by those that had committed their life to allah.

- Hydro-electric Dams: 14 Major dams and 25 Minor dams.
    78 Men and 39 fast boats packed with C4. Two man teams made up of 2 trained scuba divers familiar with welding for each dam location.

- Power Plants: 57 Major Nuclear plants and 200 Co-Generation plants.
    114 Men and 57 trucks carrying 1,000 lbs of C4 for the soft spot on the reactor building and 114 Men and 57 trucks carrying 500 lbs of C4 for the distribution bullpen enclosing all transformers.
    400 Men and 400 trucks each carrying 200 lbs of C4. One truck to destroy the boilers and one truck to destroy the distribution center at each location.

- Major Electrical Distribution Centers: 400 Sub-stations in 50 Major Metropolitan cities.
    400 Men and 400 pickups with 100 lbs of C4 to destroy the eight major sub-stations in each metropolitan city.

- Oil Refineries: 50 Major Refinery Complexes.
  200 Men and 100 pickups to blow up two cracking towers at each refinery.

- Oil Storage Facilities: 1,000 of the Largest Storage Areas in the country.
  1,000 Men and 1,000 cars carrying 200 lbs of C4 to blow up storage tanks in middle of each of the storage yard.

- Power Transmission Towers: 230 kv to 765 kv Towers around 50 Major cities.
  400 Men and 200 ATV's to blow up 2,000 transmission towers at 200 locations. Crippling the 10 Grid Interconnects supplying power on over 156,000 miles of transmission lines.

- Railroad Lines: 24 Main Lines serving coal distribution from mines in six states.
  48 Men and 24 ATV's blowing up train track with 5 lbs of C4 every 1,000 feet for 5 miles.

- Microwave and Satellite Communication Centers: Communication centers in 15 Major Cities.
  30 Men and 15 cars destroying the central communication systems with 500 lbs of C4.

- EDS Main Data Storage Facilities: 6 Cities.
  12 Men and 6 reinforced trucks with 1,000 lbs. of C4 blowing up the company's 6 facilities.

Musab and the other four lieutenants were given the scope of the entire attack including details for the operation of each team and their target. Eighty underground cells made up the implanted army of Jihadist and they had been built over the years since 1998 when bin Laden and al-Qaeda had formulated its massive and horrendous plan to destroy the electrical infrastructure and energy supply of the United States thereby bringing the country to its knees.

The terrorist force numbered more than three thousand which was actually less than one tenth of one per cent of all of the Muslims in the States and was made up of the most loyal cell members who had been recruited by the Islamist and who were fully committed to the Jihad of al-Qaeda and Hamas. Musab knew that the missions would take two thousand nine hundred sixty eight men and one thousand fifteen cars, one thousand six trucks, two hundred twenty four ATV's and 39 boats packed with C4. The planners had done well because the cars and trucks were the personal vehicles of those responsible for carrying the required amount of C4 necessary to destroy the assigned targets. The ATV's had been brought in on the West coast and distributed by Musab's own dealerships. The special boats pack with C4 had been brought in by Jonathan and delivered to each of the dam sites six years earlier. All of the attackers would be armed with MAK 90 automatic rifles and five hundred rounds of ammunition. The guns and the C4 had been distributed and concealed waiting for the command to begin the invasion.

It was five minutes after twelve and Musab had to review each of the missions to confirm their probability of success or at least their percentage of success. He was required to read all of the plans for implementation of each mission and every mission would be duplicated for each of the common targets. As each of the Jihadist operatives entered the web site and entered their personal password to get instructions on their individual mission they could see the orders and procedures they were to follow and the location of their target.

Musab had to read quickly and he began his review with a prayer and praises to allah.

> Mission ONE; BLOWING UP THE DAMS.
>
> A team of two will use scuba gear to find and move the sunken fast boat with one thousand pounds of C4 that had been previously sunk in preparation for this mission. Two inflatable bags are to be attached to the front and back of the boat to give the boat buoyancy and two compressed air driven scooters are to be used to maneuver the boat to the entrance of the penstock. One diver is to cut the bars of the central gate with a tungsten torch and then they are to deliver the boat deep inside the dam through the penstock and set the timer to detonate the C4 at five a.m. New York time.

> Mission TWO; BLOWING UP THE NUCLEAR POWER PLANTS.
>
> A team of four will drive two trucks through the gates protecting the plant and kill any guards that are stationed to pro-

tect the gates. One truck with one thousand pounds of C4 is to penetrate the most vulnerable spot leading to the reactor and then detonate the explosives and the second truck loaded with five hundred pounds of C4 is to drive into the distribution pen where the transformers are located and detonate the explosives all at five a.m. New York time.

Mission THREE; DESTROYING CO-GENERATION POWER PLANTS.
A team of four will drive two trucks through the gates protecting the plant and kill any guards that may be stationed to protect the gates. One truck with one thousand pounds of C4 is to drive into the main boiler area and blow up the boiler and furnaces and the second truck loaded with five hundred pounds of C4 is to drive into the distribution pen where the transformers are located and detonate the explosives all at five a.m. New York time.

Mission FOUR; DESTROYING MAIN METROPLOITAIN
ELECTRICAL SUB-STATIONS.
In 50 designated cities one operative per sub-station in each of the eight main sub-stations is to drive their car as close as they can to the center of the distribution complex approximately five minutes before five a.m. and set the timers for detonation at five a.m. New York time.

Mission FIVE; DESTROYING THE CRACKING TOWERS IN
MAJOR OIL REFINERIES.
A team of four will drive two trucks through any gates protecting the refinery and kill any guards that may be stationed to protect the gates. Each truck will carry two hundred pounds of C4 and take out one cracking tower each at five a.m. New York time.

Mission SIX; BLOWING UP MAJOR GASOLINE AND OIL
STORAGE YARDS.
One martyr with two hundred pounds of C4 in their car is to enter the storage area assigned to him at five a.m. New York time killing any guards at the entrance and drive to the middle of storage area and immediately detonate their explosives destroying or setting on fire as many storages tanks as possible.

Mission SEVEN; BLOWING UP ALL TRANSMISSION TOWERS FOR THREE LENIAL MILE LEADING INTO EACH OF THE ONE HUNDRED CHOSEN CITIES.

Two, two man teams per city are to drive their ATV's or pick-ups as needed along their assigned transmission line of high kilo-volt transmission towers leading into or through the target cites and tape a one pound package of C4 with timers set for five a.m. New York time to each of the four legs of each tower for a distance of three miles.

Mission EIGHT; BLOWING UP THE RAILROAD TRACKS COMING FROM THE COAL MINES.

Two men on ATV's are to place two pounds of C4 on the tracks every one thousand feet for five miles leading from all of the targeted mines with timers set for five a.m. New York time

Mission NINE; BLOWING UP MAJOR METROPOLITAIN TRANSMISSON AND SATELITE COMMUNICATION CENTERS.

Two martyrs in one car with five hundred pounds of C4 are to drive to the main government and law enforcement communications center and detonate their explosives at five a.m. New York time.

Mission TEN; BLOWING UP ALL OF THE EDS COMPLEXS.

Two martyrs in one reinforced truck with steel ramming bars in front and two thousand pounds of C4 are to drive into the main building's receiving area going deep inside of the building and detonate the explosives so as to destroy the two sub basements and all of the super computers and high tech data storage pods at five a.m. New York time.

Musab went to tools and then internet options and first cleared files and then history and then for an added touch he fore-matted the hard drive and closed down the computer. He went out side and lit up a cigarette and sat on the bench along side the corner bus stop. He sat thinking to him self, 'What an ingenious plan. Even if we only succeed seventy percent or fifty percent we will have crippled the monster that has been plaguing the world'. He slowly strolled off to his car and headed for Canada. He knew he would be there when the 'bells would toll for the United States'.

USA: THE SERPENT IS CRUSHED!

Hoover Dam in Nevada.

Based on the increase in the security alert level the FBI had been told to review the security on all major dams and all of the largest electrical power plants. At Hoover dam the National Guard was maintaining an unimposing presence as they visually observed all the cars as they passed over the dam. The two agents assigned for two days to report on the competency of the guards operation introduced themselves to the four guardsmen that were on duty. " We are with the FBI and I believe you have been told we would be meeting with you to do a routine review of the security in place here at Hoover dam. I am agent Holcomb and this is agent Brewster. We will be around for two days so if you can give us any information you think will improve the security here we would appreciate the input. We will just be observers for the next two days." On Sunday evening and at the end of their second day they decided to drive the access road along the lake and see what possible weaknesses they might observe at a distance from the dam itself. About seven hundred yards along the small asphalt road, they came upon a tent with an Arab looking man sitting on the ground smoking a cigarette. It was just dusk as they stopped their car and approached him. He said hello as they came closer and then from behind his partner who had been using a distant tree as a toilet shot the two agents with a nine millimeter pistol and an attached silencer.

"Abu, we must get rid of these two quickly. Who are they?"

"It does not matter. Let's put them in their car and later tonight drive it into the lake. We only have to wait till tomorrow night and we will be finished with our mission."

It was one a.m. on September the eleventh when Kahled and Umar had put on their special underwater gear with two-way voice transmission built into their breathing helmets and entered the water at Glen Canyon dam. They found the fast boat that had been submerged for almost ten years. They attached balloon floats to the front and rear and inflated them enough to provide buoyancy to lift the boat off of the bottom. "Umar we must detonate the explosives at two a.m. our time per our orders so take your underwater scooter and we will head to one of the large water inlet pipes at the bottom of the dam that supplies water down the penstock and to the giant turbines."

"Okay let me put our bags of torches and the detonators in the boat first." Kahled was experienced using the tungsten/magnesium cutting torches and after they made the boat stable by tying it to one of the neighboring gates Umar unpacked them for Kahled. He took one at time and unwrapped each as Kahled needed them for cutting the protecting bars from the inlet pipes. The instant a torch was exposed it reacted to the water, ignited and began burning at two thousand degrees Fahrenheit which cut through the two inch bars like butter.

"Kahled, how long will it take to cut all of the bars and maneuver the boat to its strategic position?"

"About another fifteen minutes and by setting the timers for two a.m. we will have five minutes to get out and make it to shore." Kahled cut through the bars quicker than he had estimated and they both guided the boat down the penstock and deflated the balloon floats. Then they drilled a small hole in the right and left side of the boat and inserted the detonators into the C4 and set the timers. As they reached the shore it was exactly two a.m. and they turned towards the dam to watch the effect of their mission. There was a vibration of the ground along with a muffled sound kind of like a heavy thud and then as the extreme pressure build up inside of the dam a geyser accompanied by a very loud explosion came straight up out of the water rising about two hundred feet in the air. Inside the dam water came gushing into the turbine room from the destroyed inlet pipe and a large crack opened up along the penstock. Mission accomplished and Kahled and Umar walked to their car and drove off towards Page. Umar quizzed Kahled, "How many other dams are we going to destroy today?"

"I can only hope hundreds so that the electricity is cut off very where. allah akbar."

Five a.m. September 11 and all Hell brakes loose across the country in the dark of night on the anniversary of 9-11 as the army of the Islamic terrorists who had waited a long time to carry out a massive attack on the United States at every important facility and operation supplying electrical power began their operation making it possible to shut down the life blood of daily life in the United States; electrical power and thereby rendering the nation terminal.

In San Diego County at the San Onofre nuclear power plant two reinforced trucks drove through the fencing next to the first set of gates as Adallo Alliev used his MAK 90 to waste the two guards standing by their guard shack. The second gate leading to the main reactor building was attended by two guards who were firing at the two trucks when one truck headed off towards the transformer pen and the other drove right over the guard firing at them and then headed straight into the entrance of the reactor building ramming his truck deep inside before he triggered the C4. The other guard had a rifle grenade pointed at Adallo and fired it as Adallo drove through the fence surrounding the power transfer pen. The grenade took out the truck but also blew up the C4 and everything in a one hundred foot radius destroying the entire power transfer system. Martyred and successful.

Other Islamist were attacking facilities at Diablo Canyon, Turkey creek, River Bend, Grand Gulf, Oyster Creek, Three Mile Island, Comanche Peak and the other forty two nuclear power plants.

In Linden New Jersey Mustafa Fadhil and Faheim Hamad from Musab's cell had just crashed through the fence on the west side of the Bay Way Refinery with their trucks and each drove to a different cracking tower. They set their timers for one minute then grabbed their MAK 90 rifles and ran towards the main gate shooting any one that confronted them. The guards that were at the entrance gates positioned themselves behind a truck parked by the entrance and waited to stop who ever had broken into the complex. Unknown to them two trucks loaded with explosives had been parked next to the cracking towers by two terrorist and that an all out attack was under way on the country. As they saw Mustafa and Faheim running towards the gate they pointed the guns at them and yelled for them to stop. Just as they had been trained they stopped running and dropped to their knees and opened fire with their automatic rifles and overwhelmed the guards with their fire power killing them both.

In Georgia, Maryland, Louisiana, Texas, California and other areas oil refineries were blowing up. Power plants across the nation were being attacked and blown up.

In Shreveport, Louisiana two guards on lunch break at the Southern Louisiana Power and Light power station try to stop two trucks from crashing through the gate and one guard is killed by the shooter in the first truck but the second guard is able to stop the second truck and kill both occupants. The first truck makes it close to the furnaces and the driver prematurely detonates the explosives.

One of the two teams in Dearborn, Michigan led by Omar Bakri had left his cell around three a.m. to pick up a brother named Jafar and load up the one hundred twenty packages of C4 they would need for their mission then together they took his ATV to the edge of the Whiting power plant. Their task was to blow up three miles of the first row of 765 kilovolt transmission towers leading from the power plant. At each tower location they taped a one pound package of explosive to each of the four legs of the tower next to the ground and embedded a detonator with wires connecting the timer that was placed on one of the legs. As they were commanded the timer was set for five a.m. New York time.

In Boone county West Virginia out side of Charleston Massed Fadhil and Umar Haddad placed two pound packages of C4 every thousand feet for a distance of five miles along the railroad tracks coming from the largest mine in the county . The timers were set for five a.m. New York time.

And in Plano, Texas Abdulla Nasem and Abu Nasrallah had picked up the retrofitted truck packed with one thousand pounds of C4 and equipped with a massive reinforced ramming front end and drove to the entrance to the EDS facility that housed one of the six top secret computer data storage areas in the country. The gated entrance on the street was not guarded and crashing through it gave them no resistance. It did however trip an alarm and when they approached the seven foot iron gates at the delivery entrance to the facility two guards were waiting with shot guns pointed straight at them. The guards did not expect the on coming truck to have a person armed with an automatic rifle and Abu unloaded on the guards as Abdulla easily crashed the gates and headed right towards the double doors at the loading area. This area was two stories below the main level leading to the sub-sub basement. Abdulla slammed down on the accelerator and plowed through the doors, then through some walls portioning offices and over furniture and then into the area housing the massive data storage units. They detonated their payload and the huge explosion tore the two floors above them up and then brought them down destroying seventy per cent of the one acre facility and sending two martyrs to Hell.

The same scenario at each of the planned targets was happening in unison at FIVE o'clock New York time. The radical Islamist were well trained, well equipped, and well indoctrinated. Terrorist team after terrorist team duplicated the attacks on the ten groups of infrastructure targets that had been the long drawn out plans of al-Qaeda and Hamas.

CHAPTER THIRTY ONE

Five o Five a.m. September 11th 2007

The two security agents stationed outside of the President's bedroom on the second floor had just been alerted by the communications officer on duty at the White House about the attacks on some of the power stations on the East coast by suspected terrorists and were told to awaken President Cush and his wife Laura and escort them to the Presidential Bunker.

Inside the bedroom a bell on the wall next to the double entry doors rang in a random sequence and ever so softly while a red light below the bell flashed rapidly so as to awaken the President and alert him of a pending emergency.

As President Cush set up in bed he picked up the intercom phone to talk to the two agents outside in the corridor. "Alex, what is it? What is the emergency?"

"Mr. President we have just been notified that an attack has been launched against us on the East Coast and we are to escort you and your wife to the bunker immediately. We will go into more detail on the elevator as we go down to the bunker. Please come quickly."

"Oh my god, is it what I have been dreading for so many months?"

Turning to Laura who was now sitting up and rubbing her eyes, "Laura, get up now!"

"What George"

"We have been attacked somewhere on the East Coast, we must go to the bunker now."

After wrapping up in their robes the President with Laura opened the door to the corridor where the two agents were waiting to escort them to the elevator. "Alex what exactly do you know?"

"Only this sir; that some few minutes ago there were some terrorist attacks on power plants here and other East Coast locations and it appears they have destroyed much of the electrical supply for those areas and it looks like our area here in Washington is without power. We were informed that most of the vital government buildings are running on their own back up power but the city is without power. That is all I know. The Cabinet members have been apprised of the situation and they were going to Site 'R' but have been requested by Secretary Mertoff to come to the Bunker and they should be on their way here shortly. Also Mr. Mertoff will be here in approximately 15 minutes. I was told also that Vice-President Chainery is being taken to the underground facilities at Fort Bragg."

The elevator stopped and as President Cush and Laura exited, they were met with the full complement of staff and Marines who had hastily arrived to be in attendance to the Presidents needs. Chief of staff Joshua Bolton ushered them to the dressing area off of the bedroom as he explained that all of the cabinet members were approximately five minutes away and there would be time to change out of his robe. "Your clothes have been laid out for you and there is hot coffee on your desk. I will be waiting outside to go to the situation room when you are ready."

As he emerged from the dressing area George turned to kiss Laura and comfort her with a, "I love you; we'll get all of this under control."

Then Andrew began to present a picture of what was happening based on the most current TIU communications he had received from the night supervising director at OHS. "George, it now appears that we have been hit with bombings at multiple power plants in many states from the East to West coast. There is at this moment vague information that a strike has been attempted at the San Onofre nuclear power plant in San Clemente California and some kind of attack on the Hoover dam in Nevada. None of this Intel has been verified."

Approaching the situation room the Marine Guards stepped aside as Andrew opened the door. Everyone had arrived and they were looking at the map of the states with small flashing red crosses appearing from New England to Los Angeles. Even as the President took his seat additional red crosses continued to pop up. "My lord, what the hell is going on here? Does anyone know what is happening and is this all actually real? Where is this Intel coming from? Is what we are looking at minor incidents or to what level are we under attack and from where?"

Michael Mertoff opened the dialog with an answer to the main question. "Yes, Mr. President this is real and other things are happening as we speak. I have a live feed coming in from NSA communications at Fort Meade and soon we will have visual from our satellites showing the areas that are completely without power. As the satellite photos will show most metropolitan cites are dark from the East Coast to West Coast. I have been told that all of the power stations got hit by the terrorists simultaneously from New York to California and it caused a power grind failure totally across the nation. The distribution stations began to fall like dominos."

Just then the audio from the TIU communications department at OHS came on to report the ongoing developments of the attacks. "Mr. President, Mr. Vice-President, Secretary Mertoff, and members of the cabinet; this is Bob Granger, the night supervising director here at OHS. I am sad to say that the attacks on our nation have been catastrophic. Under the limited authority given us by the Patriot Act we have gone to General Schoomaker and made a request for the army to be dispatched to the areas where we have been hardest hit. Only here in Washington and San Diego have some squads already encountered the enemy and the reports are that we have annihilated around fifty terrorists. They have not yet been identified; however they all appear to be of Arabic decent. It is now O-Five Thirty (am) here and this is the latest Intel we have. At this time we can not accurately tell you when this all started. Only that we saw explosions in multiple locations as we were performing our routine border to border surveillance of the states from the NASCOM satellite at O-Five hundred and then a short time later receipt of incoming calls from a few state enforcement agencies confirming explosions at power plants in their jurisdiction. You can follow this report with visuals on the two monitors set up at each end of the conference table. The feeds are coming from the satellites and Army and Marine helicopters as they survey the damage. Within the past half hour we have found out that terrorists have set off large explosions in ten major dams and the dams may be on the brink of failure. They hit the dams at their weakest spot, deep inside the Penstock. Teams from the Army Corp of Engineers have been dispatched to the dams in question but it will be a few hours before any of them reach their assignment. They attacked fifteen nuclear power plants and we have tactical teams proceeding there now to evaluate the situation. As helicopters passed over some of these facilities they took radioactive readings and no leakage was observed. The worse of their attacks have been the destruction or major damage to more than fifty electrical power plants and the blowing up of many transmission towers leading away from those plants. As you can see from the satellite pictures most cities are without power and many of the effected power plants are shown on your map with flashing crosses."

Secretary of Defense Robert Gates stood up as small flashes appeared on the large overhead, "What are we seeing there at Baltimore and now at New Orleans and Houston and now what looks like fire. Look! There are six more flashes."

Bob then cried out, "Oh My god, those are refineries and oil storage areas. We can see that they have now hit our major oil facilities and it looks like they have been able to set those that you see on the map on fire."

George stood up and screamed at the Cabinet. "What is happening here? Where the Hell is our security? How could all of this be real? We are under a major attack. Robert get on the phone and have the joint chiefs mobilize all military units immediately to destroy these attackers and Michael contact your people at NSA and have them contacting all of the local enforcement agencies from here to California to put their helicopters in the air and shot to kill anyone involved in suspicious activity. Activate the emergency broadcast system and warn the public to stay home. We are in a state of war. Andrew, get me Chainery on the phone."

"Yes Sir, but Mr. President, if I may. It would appear that hundred of thousands if not tens of millions of homes will not have electrical power to see or hear any warnings."

"Oh my god, you're right. Yes, I agree, it is easy to become excitable right now and I am taking a few deep breaths so I can handle all of this in a calmer manner. And please everyone we all know each other quite well so we can drop the formality and use first names. Michael I want answers about how any of this could have happened!"

Bates moved to an area of the room where a separate bank of phones were lined up and picked up the one marked Joint Chiefs. "Hello, this is Robert Bates, with whom am I speaking? Admiral Mullen, good. Have all of the commanders arrived? Let me please speak with General Cace."

"Yes sir, one moment."

"Peter, I am sure the Joint chiefs have been watching the unfolding of events there on their monitors and listening to Bob Granger at OHS. The president wants everybody on standby to wait for his orders."

Andrew stood up again and said loudly, "Listen, Bob is coming on with more information."

"People, without all of the formalities let me tell you that the United States is under sever attack by terrorists from coast to coast. We have now gotten Intel from a number of Military observation helicopters and State police helicopters plus the on going visuals from our multiple satellites that are beaming hundreds of photos into our command center and here is the damage assessment so far. More than twenty five dams have been damaged, fifty nuclear power plants have had some amount of damage inflicted, possibly one hundred of the largest co-generation plants have been bombed, in as many as 40 major cities we are getting reports that major electrical substations have been blown up, if you will look at the various satellite images you will see that there are fires and destruction at approximately thirty oil refineries. I do not need to tell you that all of this is a crippling blow of staggering magnitude to our country."

"This is Secretary Mertoff, Thank you Bob for the on going reporting as bad as it is. We need every bit of Intel coming into your unit fed to us immediately. Stay on our dedicated line and continue to keep us updated. Are all of the agencies feeding you their information as it comes in?"

"Yes Sir, everything is operating according to the departments defined procedures."

"Okay." Michael, grimaced with pain turned to the President Cush and Secretary Bates as he fell back in his chair, "I can't tell you at this moment where this all came from but I can tell you at this time that the reports are ninety percent accurate; the country is in your hands Sir."

Looking at Robert Bates, George asked if the Joint Chiefs were on standby and if the Military was ready for their orders. "Yes Sir." The President stood up and one by one he looked at his friends, his appointees and his comrades. "I am at a loss for words and yet we have all wondered in dreadful anticipation when an attack might come. We were looking for the obvious; a suitcase nuclear device, a dirty bomb, a chemical of biological attack, a poisoning of our drinking water, or multiple suicide bombers at airports, train stations or subways. At the same time we had reports on the vulnerability of our national power grid but the possibly of an attack of this magnitude was dismissed many times because the intelligence reports from our best people in OHS and NSA determined that an organized effort as we have seen this morning was just not probable."

'Sir, excuse me but Bob is coming on line again for an up date on further circumstance around the country."

Cush turned to the speaker in the middle of the table as he spoke to his cabinet. "My friends we must pray that this has stopped. Bob this is the President, go ahead."

"I am sorry but there is more bad news. There are now increasing numbers of oil storage depots showing up on the satellite images as being on fire, we have sent these images to you for your review. Also this is just now coming in to us from the FBI and local state police in Virginia, Tennessee, West Virginia, Kentucky, Alabama, Minnesota, and Wyoming who are reporting that miles of railroad track leading from the coal mines in these states have been blown up. And here is what maybe the worst news of all. In many metro areas we are no longer able to communicate with any of the authorities or enforcement agencies. We believe that their central communication areas housing both microwave and transmission towers and satellite dishes have been crippled or destroyed. Some of our military teams have confirmed this in New York, Atlanta, Houston, Chicago, Denver, and Seattle. Our People as we speak are running test on all other major cities to see if they have also gone silent. We will know the facts and the extent of the lack of coordinated communication in fifteen minutes. By o six thirty you will receive a top secret communiqué with a summation of the damage to our country. I can tell you it is extensive."

The President turned to Secretary Mertoff, "My god Mike what haven't they hit."

"I don't know George! While you were listening to the report from Bob; Robert and I were on the line with our people and I have all of the departments and section heads at OHS, FBI and CIA activated and they are at this very moment putting into operation our emergency plan of action for protection of the country."

"Andrew, have you got Chainery on the phone yet?" "Yes sir, the phone there at your right." "Hello Dick, my friend; draft up the executive order invoking the War Powers act and get it to me immediately for our signatures. I must take complete control of the government at this time. I will keep you informed and I am working with the cabinet to be involved in most of my use of this unprecedented Presidential control. I am going to put our military on war alert world wide; I will not take any risks any where in the world. I am asking the joint chiefs to initiate the alert now. I have ordered all military stateside to begin a search and destroy operation to find anyone who is suspected of being involved in this attack on our country. No holds barred!"

Immediately after Cush had finished his conversation with Chainery, Robert was on the phone with the Chairman of the Joint chiefs, General Peter Cace, reiterating the commands of the President. "George, I have passed on your orders for all of our military to be on world wide alert and all of our stateside military personnel to report for duty immediately. More than half of the alert notification is going to require each of the branches to dispatch messengers to the personnel at their homes. My orders are to send teams to every location of an attack and arrest all suspicious individuals and if they resist then inform them that we are at war and they are to surrender to the military. If at that point they do not surrender then my orders are to shoot anyone resisting arrest."

"Has it all come to this? In just a few hours has it really come to this? I am asking each of you as secretary of a cabinet department to take the next thirty minutes or so while we wait for the damage report from Bob and decide how, based on what we have heard from Mike's people; how we are going to operate this government when it becomes seven o'clock here on the East coast and how you are going to handle the functions of your department to give guidance to those that do appear for work. Mike, OHS was given the commanding responsibility of internal protection of the country and preventing what is now happening to our people from ever occurring. I want you to reach deep inside the performance of the OHS and NSA departments and prepare to give me a truthful evaluation of what was the failure to have not known we would be facing this calamity. I want it by noon today and no punches pulled!"

7:00 AM September 11, 2007

By the time the cabinet members had returned with their hastily compiled thoughts on what each must do. The shock was now gone from everyone's face and there were a few whose faces reflected the fear that they had been holding in. As Cush began to speak, his countenance was as never seen before, eyes sunk in, lips dry, and his jowls drooping as if all of the facial muscles had lost their tension; "Ladies and Gentlemen we have our communiqué from OHS and they have indicated that no more attacks have occurred since they last talked to us at five forty five. We all knew that the terrorists have had only one goal in their mind and now we must have only one goal in our minds, repair, replace, and rebuild in a manner and speed that only the American people know how to do." The cabinet members and staff all stood up and asked if they could say a prayer in unison for the nation and the people? The President bowed his head and offered a prayer of praise to God for the strength He had given to the United States and for mercy for the entire country as it forged through the coming days and weeks. After a few moments of silence he continued, "Okay then, I have each of your reports and we will shortly review them together and make any recommendations as a unified body. I have asked Condolla to start dialog with all of our friends around the world to help us with what ever emergency commodities we might need for our people. I have also asked her to bring in the Directors of both the Brookings Institute and the CATO Institute and meet with them to give us a synopsis of what we can expect from the people who are currently waking up and those across the country as they learn what has happened to us. Before we begin speculation on that subject let's listen to each others observations and plan of action."

"We'll start with you Bob on Defense. Oh and first I have activated the National Guard that we have remaining here at home and placed them under the command of Brigadier General Gordon Toney at the recommendation of Bob. Okay Bob."

"The Marines were first to arrive at most of the locations pinpointed by TIU at OHS and they secured the areas almost immediately. Few suspected terrorist were found, however my last report is that we have arrested around 45 people and killed about 310. What ever their mission was it appears that they hit and then scattered. Our best educated guess is that at least two to three thousand personnel had to be involved in this planned attack and we will probably find out that it could have been twice that. When we look at the targets we now know that it had to have been a well planned attack over many years. Army and National Guard units are going to be in place within the next two hours at ninety per cent of the locations to secure them, to give us an on site visual evaluation of the total damage and to help with putting out fires. We are on top of it."

"Mary, let's hear about the Transportation Department. And I need to add that at six fifty a.m. I declared the country to be in a state of emergency and put out an executive order requiring all citizens to not leave their homes for two days. Please go ahead Mary."

"Our concern is to curtail all transportation temporarily. I have issued orders for all fights to be grounded except military and government. Also our orders are for all railroad and subway transportation to be halted until the safety of such transportation is evaluated and we are trying to implement that as I speak. I have asked that all state highway patrol departments that can be contacted to have their officers stop any and all suspicious vehicles and arrest those who appear as terrorists. Further we are asking that the governors of all states use their state police to immediately put up road blocks on any state or federal highways and stop all movement of trucks and vehicles. The people I have on duty are working as fast as they can to make the contacts and pass on these orders. This embargo will be for four days to help expose any terrorists if they are on the move or trying to leave the country or in general, hide. The problem for us though has been our ability, or actually our inability to quickly establish communication to implement my orders."

"Of course and getting communication to the state and county authorities and to all of the people at large will be vital. We will need all of the methods of communication possible tried as soon as you can get help implementing them."

"Henry, what are going to be the problems as the Treasury Department sees it?"
"We are going to have the Banks and all depository institutions across

the nation to close and remain closed for at least five days. The people will be without the access to money however as power becomes available in various areas to banks or ATMs we will leave the account debit system operational putting a limit of no more than one hundred dollar withdrawal limit per day on each account. This is to keep some amount of order in the system and stop people from panicking. Of course the ability to use the debit withdrawal bank accounting systems will be entirely dependant on the restoration of electrical power to their central computers and to the merchants. Wall Street will be closed indefinably. Another bit of bad news and I do not know the scope of these reports but I am told some of EDS's locations were also in the terrorists list of targets, so pending confirmation of the accuracy of these reports and then the evaluation of the extent of damage if any that may have been done, we may not be able to provide any banking operations to any area for many months and it is possible that even with redundancy in their system's data storage and retrieval capabilities for banking and business records of some of the largest corporations could be lost forever."
"Henry, explain in more detail please."

"Well George, EDS for a long time has been contracted to maintain the data records of county and municipal governments, financial institutions, Wall Street, large corporations, and occasionally requirements of the federal government. EDS has very large capacity for storage of data in mammoth tape and disk recording machines that incorporate cross redundancy, all housed in very secure underground structures at each of their locations. At this point we do not know what if anything may have happened at these locations"

"SO WE HAVE ONE MORE NAIL IN THE ...." The president paused and looked at Dirk. "Dirk, do you have any idea on the scale of the devastation that may exist with regards to our infrastructure?"

"George, I tried to use my understanding of what we heard from the OHS reports and those targets that were attacked by the terrorists while using the overhead map to complete an inventory of what infrastructure suffered damage and how much. While we all will need more information from each of our intelligence sources it is clear that they went after the power grid and that will be number one priority. Rebuilding cable towers and the destroyed distribution facilities will be the immediate order of business and then tying to get the power generation sources that are still operational back on to what will be a make shift grid will be our number two priority. We should be able to get some communities up within a few days and some others in two or three weeks. I would surmise that there will be cities that will not be on line for power for a number of months and then it will be limited usage based on how many power plants are totally lost. I make this evaluation based on the fact that over the course of the next seven to ten days there will be areas where anarchy and complete civil unrest will be the norm. I will wait for the meeting Condolla is going to have with CATO and Brookings in regards to physiological effect on the public and the posture the government needs to take in this regards. We will need a lot of the public's help and their mental stability to rebuild the damaged facilities in every part of our nation. But most importantly we will need the equipment and supplies. I will be asking Carlos at Commerce to get us an inventory of the commercial electrical equipment and supplies that the industry manufactures and suppliers have available.

Nothing is yet too clear on our dams or our nuclear power plants, so at worst case for the damaged dams if they are going to fail we can only let the water out as rapidly as possible to minimize any potential disaster. Then see if they are repairable. I can at this moment only pray that no structural damage came to the nuclear shells. On the other hand the oil refineries are not such a simple matter and we will be looking at a number of years to replace those that have had major damage. The real loss of the oil and gasoline storage areas is a problem that will require rationing of what ever fuel is undamaged and of course we will need to ask for immediate help from our friends and use of the government's emergency fuel storage. The storage tanks themselves can be replaced in a rather short time, maybe within three months. The need for refined oil will have to be supplied by our friends. As to electrical power, I have not yet gotten an estimate of the extent of the destruction to high voltage transmission towers. And last the repair or replacement of railroad tracks is rather easily accomplished and the replacement of many of the communication systems can be done in a month or two, possibly sooner. Will we have to call on all of the public to help us and in what geographical areas we will be able to work is currently the unknown. This unknown is going to be a prime factor in establishing time frames for rebuilding the damaged infrastructure!"

"So far all we have heard about is what confronts us today and what can be expected short term based on our currently information. Carlos can you gives us any uplifting commentary from the Department of Commerce."

"Well Sir, as to what I have to say, I am afraid that this maybe the most fatiguing report of all. I spent time on the phone with our leading economist; that is I mean those that I was able to reach as I prepared this report. Here are the scenarios they presented. Depending on the degree of damage to the countries power grid it is plausible to say that millions and millions of homes and business from coast to coast are now without any power. Commerce as defined by manufacturing and retail business will be at a stand still and as we just heard until the highway embargo is lifted and the rail system proven safe there will be no rolling commerce. Let us look at municipal and utility providers. Water pumping stations will not work and very few of them nationwide have back up generators. Sewage pumping stations will not operate and therefore soon in many areas people will have to vacate their homes. In general all phone systems are not working and of course cell phones have been rendered dead. Next let's look at local or small regional commerce. Generally stores will not be able to open but in the case of grocery stores and markets if they wish they can sell off the food they have but some refrigerated food will only be good for approximately three days. Gasoline stations can no longer pump gasoline and therefore they will not open. And it takes no great imagination to realize what will happen to families who have no electricity, no phone, no refrigeration, no water, and within a few days no food at all. I can not answer Dirk's questions concerning the availability of any of the equipment and supplies we will need to begin to repair and rebuild our infrastructure. I have however already put a team together to contact the multiple manufactures and suppliers to get an inventory of the critical items needed just as soon as they can. This information may take two to three weeks to gather since we have no public phone systems operating or any other communication systems to use for immediate direct contact. I plan to use the military for mobile direct contact."

Cush did not stand as he spoke in a reserved monotone, "My friends, as we hear these comments and look at the situation, it is a very gloomy horizon ahead for our country unless we can come together in a united front and get to the people to assure them that we have a plan and that we can clean this catastrophe up in short order. I was just handed a note by Andrew that a joint convening of the Congress will be ready by ten a.m. and I will be speaking at eleven a.m. so I am asking all of you to prepare your plan of action for your individual department's participation in restoring our country to a condition of equilibrium. Make them condensed and I will need each of you to submit your reports in time for me to prepare for my address to Congress so I can apprise all of them of the condition of our country and especially to those who have not yet seen all of the Intel from OHS detailing the full ruthlessness of the attacks made on us today. It will be important to present each of your department's initial summary of involvement, immediate action proposed, and projected time lines if possible.

Mike do you have anything from the Agriculture Department?"
"George I would say that the farmers and produce growers will be little affected by these events until they run out of fuel. They are generally self sufficient and in the most part they are resourceful and will still be able to provide raw food to us for a while. We will need to make sure it can be transported to areas where needed."

"Excuse me Mr. President but we have a live feed coming in from Al Jazeera Television showing two al Qaeda associates of bin Laden speaking in Arabic about the attacks. They are bragging that Cush and his criminals again know the power of allah. The pictures should be on your monitors now and on another feed from Iran you can see people dancing in the street and carrying signs saying the 'Snake is Crushed'. They are all chanting allah akbar and now from Egypt, Iran, Syria and Saudi Arabia they are all celebrating. The world is just now responding to the news."

Cush's face was blotched with anger and fear, "These damn dark and demented Islamic Jihadist. Now all of the pundits and naysayer's will have to eat their own words and their liberal bylines at the expense of millions of American citizens. Like all of you my heart is so engulfed in sadness for our country at this moment that is hard to think much less command. But we must continue on. Again let us take a few moments for silent prayer."

Michael, can I get some in put on what the Health and Human Services department feels the mental capacity of the public is to absorb this shock as they find out all that has happen today. And even though we will be getting a report from Condolla soon from the experts of psychological shock in the time of war and the probability of civil disorder I want your people's input if you have it."

"George, we do not have any available data to refer to on the circumstances that now exist. We can only refer to historical information from events that have occurred elsewhere. In most cases people first evaluated their situation and then they made temporary plans for day to day existence followed by an attempt to gather together with others for group security. Sharing of personal possessions lasted for a period until food and water for survival became scarce and then the unions broke up and a part of the natural animal instinct took over. Those people then operated as would be expected, every one for themselves. There were in every case those who immediately went into survival mode and an isolationist persona took over as they gathered together as much material goods as they could find to survive. These types coveted their possessions and would kill on the spot to protect them. The first people that became driven by overwhelming hunger became hunters and they were no less lethal in their quest for food. Psychologically speaking the transformation from a law abiding citizen to a lawless fanatic occurred in less than one month and sometimes in less than three weeks."

Once again George paused before he spoke, "Well it appears that we are in for one of the bleakest times in our history, but we will pull through this."

Bob spoke up. "Excuse me Mr. President. I know you and everyone will agree that we must make it a priority to work on a plan of how to feed our people as food begins to run out for thousands across the country. Power of course is critical but right along side of restoring power is feeding the people as hunger begins to set in. Michael and Condolla will both agree that civil unrest will surge as people begin to get hungry. None of us need some kind of report to understand that and we should put that at the top of the list!"

"Bob I agree and when I get back from my meeting with Congress we will all meet with Mike, Mary, Condolla, and Stephen to go over the information we have from them and work on a plan to ward off that problem as best as we can.

The President turned to Alberto who would have the uninviting job of enforcing law and justice over the coming days, "Alberto, can you give us the direction that the Justice Department needs to follow should the worst of the worst be our destiny for the next few months."

"George you now have the ultimate power to rule during coming months and I believe you must announce marshal law and complete confinement of the people for a minimum of the next seven days so that we can get the military and all law enforcement in a position to prevent total civil disobedience. The major cities will be our hardest to secure so concentration on them for the restoration of some power and the supply of food and water will give us a head start on the prevention of an all out rebellion. The justice system can not handle the quantity of violations of the law that will more than likely occur so a certain amount of brute force will have to be used to restrain groups or if I may, gangs that are created. I have been advised that we should prepare a statement informing the people what has happened and how long it will take to return to some semblance of normality and inform them of the government's position on what will be suitable and acceptable conduct as the country mends itself. This statement needs to be printed on a flyer and disbursed by air over every city so that the people know we are still in control and anarchy will not be tolerated. And last George, our department believes that it is necessary to put a price of $250,000 on the head of every participant in these acts of war payable to who ever apprehends them; but only if delivered alive even if they suffer somewhat from resisting capture. We are asking the military to take control of the ones that may become captives to handle interrogation and to get information to help find those war criminals that remain at large."

"Okay, please hand these reports to Joshua. I thank all of you for the enlightenment on the severity of the attack on our country and as I said earlier I am requesting that you give me a short outline with a condensed report on the actions each of your departments will be taking over the next seven days, going day by day. I will be going before Congress at eleven o'clock and I want them on my desk by ten a.m. I am going to retire to my office where I understand Condolla is waiting for me. Also Andrew has information for you on your families. May God watch over us and continue His blessings on our land, our people, and each of you."

Andrew started handing out personal memos to everyone in attendance and began an explanation about the families. "You will note that your memo is personally addressed. You families are now housed at Fort Meade and all members that were transported are listed there. Tell me now if anyone has not been moved to Meade that should have been. Each family has a phone number with an extension number that goes to their personal unit. We do not know if satellite transmission to other areas is operational yet so calling any relatives or friends may have to wait. All of this has transpired according to the government's emergency key personnel protection plan. There is an area where all of you can work and we have some of your assistants waiting, please let me direct you to your individual offices. They are compact but complete in every way. The government phone lines all appear to be working so you can call your families. Back towards the situation room and left down the hall you will find the dining area and there will be food and drinks available all day and night. Please let the aids know about any of your request and call me when the outlines for the President are ready. I will be in his office."

CHAPTER THIRTY TWO

Seven Thirty am. DC Area

"Jeff, darling, the alarm didn't go off and the electricity is not working. It is Seven Thirty, you had better hurry. You will have to get coffee on the way at Coffee Aroma or no I'll go next door to Marylyn's and ask her if she still has some left." Jeff's wife Gloria rang the Horowitz's door bell but no one answered. She saw both of their cars in the driveway so she knocked a couple of times quite loudly and waited for some kind of response.

"Who is it?"

"Marylyn, its Gloria Howell from next door."

"Oh, just a minute I'll be there in a moment. Gloria! Good morning, nice to see you come on in. It's pretty early what can I do for you?"

"I'm sorry to bother you but our power is off and Jeff is late for work so I am hoping that you have some coffee brewed. He needs a shot of caffeine every morning."

"Late for work? I thought that he left around seven."

As Marylyn walked towards the kitchen; Gloria followed behind explaining, "Yes, he does but our alarm didn't go off and it is almost eight o'clock. We have no electricity."

Just then Marylyn hit the light switch and nothing happened. "No lights and look the clock says five twelve. I guess our power is off too. What happened?"

"We don't know, oh well he can just go to Coffee Aroma by the shopping center. Sorry I disturbed you I've got to go, we can talk later after the power is back on."

USA: THE SERPENT IS CRUSHED!

The O'Donnell's in Boston had just sent their daughter off to junior high with her lunch which her mother always prepared the night before. She had asked her husband before he went to work if she should call the power company about the electricity because the food may not keep in the refrigerator. "Yes babe, if the power is still not on by noon you should call them for some kind of estimate when it will be back on plus I think you should take the big cooler and put some ice in it to keep the milk and anything else we need to keep cool until power is restored."

In Boston it was a little after six a.m. and none of the street lights were working and Jake was tied up in traffic. Nothing was moving around the Commons so he wasn't going to make it to work. Some of the other motorists were out of their cars wondering around and asking questions about why traffic was so jammed that nothing was moving. Everyone had noticed that there weren't any lights on in any of the buildings and no signs any where were lit. The guy standing across from him looked at Jake and said, "I thought this was just a localized power outage when I got up this morning and even as I drove on the parkway but now I think it could be a blackout." And the couple in their convertible behind Jake got out and mentioned that it must be a black out because their radio didn't work. "It doesn't?" Jake thought for a minute, and then he said, "That can't be because all of the stations don't just broadcast from Boston! Let me check my radio." By now there were cars honking from all over and it sounded like a bad overture from an all brass band. More and more people began walking around and confusion abounded on everyone's face. After trying the entire dial on his radio, Jake appeared from behind the wheel and acknowledged agreement, "My radio won't pick up any thing and that is weird. I usually get some New York stations. Something is really wrong!"

In New York nothing was moving. Not cars, not buses, not subways, not anything accept people who were already panicking. It took no time at all for news to travel that power was out all over Manhattan and the Burros and people were stuck in trains, subways, elevators, and lights were not on in any buildings or stores. Gangs had already started some looting and the police had no communications to tell their commanders what was unfolding. With the phones out and cell phones not working many small shop owners had already locked their doors not knowing how extensive the power outage was but remembering the massive blackout of a few years past.

Similar events were taking place in Detroit, Chicago, Memphis, Saint Louis, and on and on. Nothing appeared to be working. One station in Chicago had back up generators and was on the air so they were trying to broadcast an emergency news alerts about the power outage in Chicago but they had not been able to talk to anyone at city hall, the power company, or law enforcement and they had no inkling about the attack on all of the states. Their scope of the times was only that there was an emergency in Chicago.

Back at Fort Meade the vice president contacted Kevin Martin the chairman of the FCC and asked him to have his staff start immediately identifying those radio and television stations that had back up power generators. "Kevin I am sure you are aware of the country's situation. I want you to deliver that list to the President and to Alberto Gonzales who are both at the Presidential bunker. Add to the list any information you can about methods of making direct contact with those stations." "Yes sir Mr. Vice-president."

Nine thirty and the President had all of the reports from the Cabinet members and multiple communiqué from the military. Their communication system with the Pentagon and OHS had not been disrupted. "Andrew, help me go through these communiqués and give me a synopsis on their content as I prepare the address for Congress. Also ask Julie to make sure that the security people have been able to contact most all of the senate and house members for the eleven o'clock assemblage of the Congress." "Yes Sir."

After returning from Julie's office Andrew spent about twenty minutes reading what had come in from the various military bases that had reported to the Pentagon. Andrew got the President on the phone. "Sir, we have information from Florida, Georgia, North Carolina, Connecticut, Texas, Colorado, Washington and California. The commander on duty at the Pentagon, Colonel Avery Brown stated that the aerial sweeps over the states along with the satellite imagery has provided us observation of almost eighty percent of the country. Many of the observation teams were able to contact numerous law enforcement agencies in their areas and add their evaluation of the status of their communities to the military's observations. It is not good. The reports on the infrastructure are all pretty much the same and in general, based on an assessment of all of the information here, there may be as many as thirty nuclear plants out of commission, over two hundred power plants totally inoperable, ten grid interconnects and three hundred and fifty power distribution centers destroyed, thirty nine oil refineries rip to pieces, at least six hundred oil and gasoline storage areas on fire with little hope of saving any of them, power transmission lines leading away from the targets are blown down one to two miles from the power plants and some of the interconnects coming from Mexico and Canada may be down and the military observers do not know exactly how many power lines have been attacked. A complete review of the railroad tracks that have been blown up has not been made at this time and the communication centers in a number of the major cities are not operational. We have print outs of many of the satellite photos. Will you want them for your report?"

"What about our hydro-electric dams? Is there information from the Corp of Engineers on the Dams?" "Yes Sir, it was given to the Department of Interior and sent directly to OHS. It is a separate report, I'm sorry to have missed it. Fourteen major dams have had a massive explosion inside the Penstock just before the turbines. The dams have been weakened and with no more generating capacity. The Corp shut them down until further examination can be made."

"Andrew I will need Stephen Haddle to help us put this address together. And I am still waiting for Condolla to bring me the out come of her meetings and the consensus of how the populace is going to act!"

Eleven A.M. - Congressional Assembly

"Ladies and Gentlemen of the Congress, all American Citizens who are able to hear us and the World at large; I come to you in great sadness and I am addressing you at the lowest time in our history since the Civil War. At approximately five a. m. Eastern Standard Time the terrorists we have been warning about and have been pursuing, attacked our nation and declared all out war on the United States of America. From within our borders clandestine Muslim sleeper cells have struck a major blow to out country's infrastructure. In your binder you have an itemized account of the attacks and our latest assessment of the situation at this time with some descriptions of the damage to the various targets that were hit along with pictures. It is not pretty. You will find that each of our Cabinet Secretaries have presented their initial plan on how their departments will affect some amount of normality to our existence and repairing of our nation. And finally a report from a meeting that Condolla Rice had with two of our most perceptive Think Tanks here in Washington. The subject of the report is, 'The Effect of the Chaos of War on People and the Prospect of Civil Unrest from Lack of Basic Human Needs'."

President Cush took a few moments to look at each of the members of Congress as his eyes scanned from one side of the isle to the other. He resisted a tear as his eyes watered. Then he reached for a glass of water to take a drink and regain a certain amount of composure. "I ask that each of you take a few moments for a time of silent prayer before we go forward. Then we will pause for each of you to look through your binders so you will have more detail on the current events and the road ahead."

President Cush sat down and watched as the clock ticked off fifteen minutes. He rose and proceeded, "At seven a. m. this morning I invoked the War Powers Act and placed the country under Marshal Law and on a curfew. I have instructed General Peter Cace to have the Navy surround the Eastern and Western coastline and the Air Force to be on retaliatory alert in case any country would be so foolish as to try an attack on our nation at this time. Further I have recalled a third of our troops from Iraq to buttress up the law enforcement agencies here to both help prevent social disorder and to assist our people in surviving during the coming months. The other two thirds have been ordered to pull back and stay on the borders. You have a detailed report collected from all of NSA's Intel to date. This report gives you a list of all of the areas of our country that have been damaged so in an effort to save time I will not belabor you now to go through it item by item. You need to review after we conclude here. In my next report to Congress we will have a plan outlining the repair and rebuilding of the critical infrastructure facilities and an estimated time line. It is important to realize that we still have an enemy within. I do not find it difficult at this time to inform you that I have ordered all of the agencies to begin a through investigation of all Islamists in our country. I mistakenly gave the benefit of the doubt to them, but not any more. As a heroic NSA agent who is now deceased once said,' It was not Germans, Russians, Filipinos, or

Mexicans who attacked us no 9-11. It was Muslims. And we have the evidence that once again we have been attacked by Muslim terrorists. We leave here asking our friends to send help, to be on the alert for attacks on their countries, and to immediately embargo those Muslim nations that tolerate terrorists; and we leave praying for the people of the United States of America and the God that created this great nation. We are Americans and we will survive!"

Even though the atmosphere in the assembly was bleak all the members rose and gave the President a nod of solidarity and affirmation by clapping of hands.

Back at the situation room it was almost one p.m. and things were popping. "Stephen," George W. was staring at the overhead map of the states, "I want you to get General Steven Blum of the National Guard on the phone and let him know that all of our satellite observations and all of the live videos and audio reports from both the military and civilian helicopters covering our major cities is going to NSA so he and we can be kept abreast of significant events on the ground."

"Yes Sir."

Secretary Gonzales and Secretary Rice had finished the wording they thought was best for the flyer to be dropped on the cities and they were waiting for the President to put his official stamp of approval on it before sending it to the printing office.

TO THE AMERICAN PUBLIC AT LARGE
FROM
PRESIDENT GEORGE W. CUSH

With deep sadness I am having to communicate
to each of my fellow citizens with a leaflet dropped
from an airplane just as was done during WW 2.
Each one of us, our country and our constitution
has been attacked by terrorist who are committed
to destroying us and our way of life.
They have been hiding among us and now they have
used their sneaky and dishonest ways to inflict
considerable damage to our infrastructure.
THIS IS A DECLARATION OF WAR ON ISLAM.
The primary damage has been done to the supply
and distribution of our electrical power system.

Some damage has been done to our ability to
provide fuel for cars and power plants.

We have declared marshal law over the entire country
and we are enforcing a curfew for the next seven days
as we sort out the extent of the damage and install
troops in our larger cities to prevent civil unrest.

I and the members of congress and my cabinet
have all ready begun the road to restoration of the
power grid and the supply of fuel! We will rebuild
our infrastructure in an accelerated period of time.

We are aware that shortly food and water will be
in short supply and we are at this very moment
implementing plans to supply our citizens with a
supply of both food and water.

Each of us is calling on each of you to cooperate
and help each other get through the next few
weeks and if you can provide information on any
suspected perpetrators of this act of war we are
offering a $250,000 reward for their capture!

The FCC is making every effort to get radio
transmission operational so we are asking
everyone who may have a battery operated
radio or some sort of power to run a radio
to keep it tuned to 97.4 FM to hear any updated
news from the Office of Homeland Security.

WE ARE A GREAT PEOPLE AND AMERICA IS A GREAT
COUNTRY, LET FREEDOM RING.
MAY GOD BLESS OUR COUNTRY AND ALL OF YOU!
PRESIDENT George W. Cush

Meanwhile Stephen Haddle and Michael Mertoff had the military's latest information on the geographical areas the power outage encom-
passed and their input on the number of people affected. They were
also reviewing a list their people had put together itemizing the things

in the infrastructure that were not working or were not available due to the power outage. Eighty percent of the nation was affected and approximately ninety five percent of the population was without electrical power. The itemized list of facilities that were no longer operational or were out of service was lengthy; no lights, no motors, no phones, no cell phones, no radio or television, no trains or subways, no water, no refrigeration, no computers, no ATMs, no air traffic, no gasoline, no banks, no factories, no businesses, no basic communications, no medical clinics, no police service, no fire protection, and in many, many areas no hospitals. To be exact anything and everything that needed electrical power had been effected. Andrew took a copy of the list to the President.

The military report also said that some of the transmission lines between Maine and Canada and Idaho and Canada survived, while others carried surges that knocked out some of Canada's grid. In Mexico their shared system with the States was hit hard from the reversed surges that hit their rather antiquated grid system and much of northern Mexico lost their power. There were some connections still working between Texas and Mexico and Michigan and Canada. Both Canada and Mexico were sharing some of their power on undamaged lines leading into those states as of two in the afternoon.

By six o'clock the government printing office had printed five million of the flyers requested by Secretary Gonzales and had a helicopter deliver them to waiting planes to spread twenty five thousand to one hundred thousand over each of the nearest forty cities on the east coast. They would need all night to finish the printing for the rest of the country. Secretary Kempthome's office had estimated that fifty million would be enough to cover most of the country and with word of mouth his people felt that within two days or less everyone would know the real story of what had happened even though rumors would be circulating with a lot of conjecture and a lot of false information.

Once the flyers were totally dispersed the Muslim population would be in jeopardy and their lives would be at risk, or to put it in an American colloquialism 'not worth a plug nickel'.

Stephen returned to the situation room to announce to everyone that NSA was receiving satellite transmissions from overseas from Europe, Asia and Middle East countries about the attacks on the United States.

The news reports and live transmissions would be up on the monitors shortly. Most all of the personnel in the bunker crowded into the situation room to watch the broadcasts as they came in.

In England and other European countries the people were astonished that such a major attack had occurred in the United Sates and live responses from some Muslims stated that they knew the Jihad was coming. Then came more and more live broadcasts from Syria, Iran, Saudi Arabia, Egypt, Indonesia, Sudan and other Muslim nations showing thousands of people in the streets celebrating and cheering for the destruction of the demonic United States yelling, 'allah akbar' - 'allah akbar', and from the Bin Ladin camp al Qaeda was chanting 'the serpent is crushed' – 'the serpent is crushed'! Around the world in country after country in the Muslim communities the same jubilance was seen from millions of the followers of Islam.

CHAPTER THIRTY THREE

It was the Twelfth and dawn broke as usual on the East coast but there was nothing usual about the atmosphere that engulfed all of the cities or the cloud of disbelief that hung over the country from coast to coast. From Burlington Vermont to the Keys in Florida people were stunned and awaking in disbelief. Many had gotten one of the leaflets dropped on their cities and had started spreading the news to anyone who had not heard that the events of the second 9-11 were across the country, from border to border and coast to coast. They moved across yards, streets, roads, farms, highways and freeways like new evangelists but in this case spreading the 'bad news'.

Only the verifiable information about the status of both damaged targets and major cities was coming into the president through communications sent to NSA from the military and law enforcement agencies with their observers in hundreds of helicopters. Visuals were still available from the satellites and were being monitored by all departments of the OHS. Michael had requested that the CIA and DOD transfer over to NSA as many birds for additional satellite transmissions as they could spare without compromising national security so that the FBI and the National Guard could still keep surveillance on all of the large metropolitan areas. NSA had a feed coupled to the vie room next to the situation room in the bunker. Three large screens twelve feet by ten feet covered the front wall with forty flat screen monitors banked two high and twenty across positioned under the large video screens. The operator at the back of the room was perched in a small tower so she could provide any visual requested by the observers including the zooming in or out of the visual on any one the monitors and even a quick review of every square yard of land in all of the states if the president so requested.

At the same time audio was available for listening on every incoming source being received by NSA. All audio reports from any source, military, law enforcement, or civilian that were coming in to the CIA, FBI, and DOD were being sent to NSA for scrutiny and at the same time to the President's bunker. Some of them would come in with a double beep preceding the audio so the operator would know it was extremely important or of a secret content and she could screen the audios as they came in flashing the subject of each one in red on two announcement boards at each end of the room. She would connect them to the overhead speakers based on the level of importance.

Just then from the overhead speakers the room was filled with a live transmission, "This is police chopper Tango X-ray Alpha Tango Seven at fourteen hundred hours over the Boston area reporting an observation of a large gathering of people in the Commons and police cars stationed at the eight major banks downtown. In much of the territory we have covered it appears that people are just out on the streets wandering from area to area and stopping to talk to others. Over on the west side towards Brookline, Newton, and Watertown there have been break ins at banks, department stores, and what looked like jewelry shops but of course we have no idea if any vaults have been compromised. We have noticed that people are gathering in groups at peoples homes. Traffic is very light with parking lots at super markets full. We can not tell if the stores are selling, giving away, or just losing their food. It looks to us like this is happening more and more as the day wears on."

At fifteen hundred hours the operator in the situation room flashed a new report on the announcement board and on the overhead came, "NSA, this is Marine chopper IONT 9 out of Quantico with a report on the Capital area from Baltimore and Annapolis down to Virginia Beach. In most of the areas covered we have observed people flocking to gas stations hoping to get gas and at some locations large groups of them trying to get into the stations and opening the coverings of the underground tanks. Also they are flocking to super markets and drug stores. Most of the stores are closed and in about ten locations they have been penetrated and gangs of people are hauling out all of the food and supplies they can carry. We could say that there is some unrest but not a massive civil disturbance yet. It may very well come by tomorrow or odds are absolutely by the fourteenth. We did observe over one hundred car accidents and in many areas there are cars that have been abandoned. A few of the accidents are bad enough that they are blocking the roads. On the freeways we saw three big rigs overturned and traffic jammed up for miles. Cars and trucks were cutting a new path around them on the dirt shoulders and through fences when necessary. Our onboard cameras are recording our complete mission and if transmission is getting through you can see what we are reporting. We are heading back to base for refueling."

"Can someone tell me how many major cities we have here?" The President knew that civil disorder was only forty eight hours away. "Where is Bultran? He may know. Has any one seen Joshua?" In the situation room he got Dick on the phone. "Dick I wonder if you know how many cities we have that will need military involvement? Can you get Secretary Glutez on the phone and get us some answers so we can mark them on the map and talk to General Blum on how he plans to deploy the troops we now have and then secondly how will he deploy the others as they come back from Iraq."

"No Sir on the first question, but I am working on that as we speak. It appears that we will need the military as soon as you can get them over here. In three days the entire nation is going to be wrapped in fear and every citizen is going to do anything to protect them selves and their families. Food and water being the number one concern and then they will start to seek protection from others. I will call Blum to see what General Petraus has given us for a time frame on the returning troops and then ask him for a written answer to your request for his primary deployment locations and then the secondary locations. George, have we gotten any assessment on how long it will take to provide power to any of our cities and which ones we can be certain will be first?"

"Mr. President," Haddle had just returned to the situation room. At times a casual approach was acceptable and at other times formality was the mood and at this moment Haddle chose to be more formal, "I will have a very comprehensive report from Interior, Transportation, Commerce, and Home Land Security tomorrow after they finish the viewing of all of the satellite visuals and the reports of the observations and the photos taken by our guardsmen who have been personally visiting the damaged sites. All personnel that are available in each department will be working all night to give us their best evaluation. They will provide us with their assessment of where and estimates of when we can expect power to be restored to major metro area by major metro area and to any rural areas. I understand that there are many small power plants that could be operating and shortly we will have a list of areas that could have power in just a few days. A time table for extinguishing all of the fires will be in the report. Assessments of damage to dams, nuclear plants, and the largest cogeneration power plants will take a week or so. And the evaluation of the damage to refineries and storage areas will even take longer."

"Good work Steve. Please make sure everyone gets a personal notice of appreciation from me for their loyalty. We will need to be ready to throw every resource we have at reconstruction just as soon as we know our priorities and establish the plan of action."

"Dick, did you get all of that? I will want you in on the operation of the planning and administration of the general plan for restoration of our crucial infrastructure along with Kempthome, Glutez, Betters, and Mertoff."

"What do you think about bringing Chao from Labor and Blum in on the planning?"

"Right, good idea. Robert! Where is Robert Bates?"

"Taking a break in the Lounge Sir."

"Thank you lieutenant. Please ask him to join us and could you ask the attendant to bring us some hot chocolate and more coffee. We aren't going anywhere tonight."

"Yes Sir."

Robert entered with one of his aides and sat down at his place at the central conference table.

"Ah, Robert, your timing is perfect. We put a radio frequency on our leaflet for the public to tune in their radios for news announcements from NSA. Let me ask you a question. Do you think you can get enough technicians from the Navy to go to our fifty major cities and help the most powerful radio stations get back on the air? I'm thinking we are going to need to communicate with as many people as we can and we will need to be able to broadcast information and announcements to our people. Let's use the same frequency in all areas so that we can get overlap if that is possible. We can do another leaflet drop to tell the people to tune in to the established emergency frequency 97.4 FM when most cities have broadcasting power so that anyone with a battery operated portable radio, a MP3-radio or who may still have power to their home or power from a generator can get information and instructions from us."

"I'll get right on it Sir. I will ask the admirals to issue an emergency order tonight and I am sure we will have all the tech groups required to carry out your request in route by zero six hundred tomorrow. When will the rest of the leaflets be ready to be dropped?"

"Joshua, get with Glutez to verify the schedule for the dropping of the leaflets. I was told by noon tomorrow the planes will begin to drop the leaflets to the rest of the country. Also see if you can contact someone at FFA to work at getting every blimp in the country to use their illuminated signs to get a message to the people over as many cities as they can. Same message as on our flyers, 'TUNE IN TO 97.4 FM'."

It was now late afternoon and hundreds of reports from the military and police departments that had been able to fly reconnaissance missions had come in during the day and the reports were getting worst from coast to coast. On the center monitors under the big screen a continual rolling itemized list of various actions of civil disturbance across the country but mainly in the urban areas of large cities was being reported to OHS.

- Super Markets being raided.
- Gasoline stations being broken into.
- All kinds of stores being looted.
- Some roving gangs in downtown areas.
- More and more trucks and cars deserted.
- Neighbors gathering together for a feeling of security and comfort.
- And on and on.

Generally the National Guard troops were trying to thwart any major civil unrest in the areas they had been assigned to. Up dates were being transmitted every half hour.

Joshua had completed the request of the president to have Glutez get a second leaflet out and was walking into the situation room when George asked him to find Condolla. "Ask her to please meet here with Dick and I in fifteen minutes."

"Okay and the leaflet thing is taken care of."

Steve had been on the phone with John Poles at NSA with an idea that could add some bit of additional communications for the government into pocket areas of hundreds of places around the country. "George, I have received information from our guys at NSA that we have been receiving transmissions from "ham radio' operators and they are telling us that they have a large nation wide membership in the American Radio Relay League and many have battery operated equipment or they are using personal generators to be able to operate their equipment. They also have a satellite called OSCAR which allows them transmission across most of the country. They all want know what they can do to help. We are now arranging for all of the ones who are on the air to be available tonight to listen to a message from you. There appears to be over one hundred fifty thousand 'ham operators' nationwide according to the licensing records."

"Steve, can you get with Dick and compose up a message for me to send to these HRO folks that is short but covers the current events and informs them of our need to use them as carriers of any announcements of emergency situations or vital government notifications. Tell them they will need to go out into their communities if they can and pass on the messages to their friends and neighbors. In the same message let them also know that we want their help to spread the word that we are deploying the military to keep the peace and are already working on rebuilding of the nation's power systems. I think they can be a big benefit to calm down many people where ever they are able to get to the public. Any avenue of communication with the public will help, don't you think?"

"Yes Sir."

Mrs. Rice entered the situation room just as Steven was heading to his office. Knowing the President as she did, she had asked her staff to be ready for some work that may last into the evening. Taking a seat at the table she glanced at the monitor to see if any new civil problems had occurred. Turning back towards George and Dick, "I see things have not worsened this afternoon. I think the reports from the other departments tomorrow will give us some encouragement. We have been receiving offers of help from some of our foreign friends."

"Okay, let us find out who is on the same page with our needs and ready to help. We must call on all of the International Community for their assistance. Every time other nations have had a disaster we have hurried to come to their aid. We have a full blown national disaster and we need to ask our friends for immediate help to bring us food and fuel. I want you to personally make all of our requests. Start with Canada and Mexico. Then call on our neighbors in Central and South America. And then of course call on our European friends. Have your people coordinate the logistics with General Cace because we are going to have to ask that everyone who supplies us with what we need now will use our airplanes and land at our military bases. Fuel will be the hardest commodity to get here rapidly so we will have to start using our emergency supply. Have Samuel Bodman's people get with Mary Betters to allocate our fuel reserves to strategic users. We can only offer fuel supplies to the public for commercial use in an amount that we can safely release and still maintain the amount requirement for national security. After I get all of the reports from Mertoff, Kempthome, Glutez, Betters and Chao we will need your evaluation of how quickly the individual countries will be responding to our requests and a report that itemizes what help we will be getting and a time specific of when that help will be available."

When Cush had finished his message to the HRO's he invited everyone to take time to get some sleep as he took a moment for prayer before retiring to his sleeping quarters.

BIG SKY MONTANA

At the MBS hunting lodge in Big Sky Montana as the first glimpse of dawn appeared over the mountains the Brayden family and all of the crew at the lodge sat on the porch looking as the colors broadcasted across the valley. Tom spoke in a slow kind of prayer like cadence, "Yesterday we thought that the lack of power was due to some kind of blackout. This morning we cranked up the old generator and tried all of our TV's and radios, not a sound. Then Shorty got on the shortwave radio and heard from some ham operators around the country that electric power seemed to be out from coast to coast. Add to the mix Hank's first hand knowledge about many terrorist cells having an arsenal of guns, ammunition and explosives; it is obvious we are under some kind of enormous attack and we do not know anything more than the electrical distribution system from coast to coast has been the focus of the attack and may even be completely shut down. If we can we must see to it that we are able to maintain our ability to preserver and protect our selves. Here is how I see it. Imagining the worst possible scenario that the 'Power Grid' across the entire country has collapsed it will not take too long before people will be needing food and especially water. That need will be most critical in the large metro areas and the available supply will not last long. Again I think that in worst case basis people will become animals very quickly. Then most people will be trying to survive and the strong will protect what they have. I have no idea given a situation like that what the government will be doing to help or even if it can or when it can. I believe we should take action based on the worst possible scenario."

It took a moment for Tom's words to sink in, and then one by one everyone looked at each other and almost in unison they looked at Tom and asked Tom, "What are your thoughts?"

"We are a ways off of the main road so we have seclusion. That is a plus. We have a generator so we can keep our refrigeration going and protect our food. We have a lot of food still in our freezers from the last hunt. We have a radio so we can continue to get information and I am sure the government will be broadcasting on their emergency frequencies soon. We have plenty of guns and lots of ammunition so we must assume the worst and stay vigilant. Anyone want to add anything?"

Shorty looks to the rest of the crew, "Well boss there are a couple of our guys with families in town and they will not be so fortunate."

Tom spoke, "Okay Shorty, get us an accounting of who and how many and we can all vote to decide what help we can give them or if it is plausible we can bring them here."

"Dad I think we should go right now down to town to see if we can buy any thing we may be short of like can goods and staples in case we have to hold out here for more than a few weeks or even a month. We do not know yet what else could have happened. In our projected scenarios at NSA we did analysis of terrorists destroying of the ports, oil supply depots, airports, water plants, railroads, bridges, refineries and the like."

Caroline looked at Hank in total disbelief, "Are you telling us that all the time the government has been anticipating an attack like this on our country and they have been doing nothing. My god what the hell is happening here? How many people are you talking about? That kind of a massive attack would take thousands of people!"

"Maybe six to ten thousand if they wanted to hit us at all the weak spots, sis, but we were never certain about what or when. And we could never get total verification on the how because we had to fight the politics of Washington and the liberals; you know it had to be politically correct or the ACLU and others would stop our interrogation efforts. And as you remember the Congress jumped all over Cush for his eavesdropping on persons that were suspected of any kind of ties to Islamic radicals and for his imprisonment at Guantanamo of radicals who hate our country.. My best friend at NSA, Jerry Ness, was right on top of Brada al-Abaji who I now believe was a planner and possibly, no I am sure he was part of the group that was the master mind for the shut down of our electrical grid system and I lost my best potential lead on the importing of guns and explosives, a Jihadist named al-Sober, when he committed suicide before we could get him to Washington for interrogation. Had that not happened we may have uncovered this horrendous attack."

Shorty stood up and in a rather excited voice had a very important reminder, "I think we had better look at getting some fuel before anything else. We are going to need gasoline and diesel or all of our plans for surviving will only be an unfulfilled dream."

Shorty went to get a piece of paper to make a list of what he thought they would need. But he stopped short of the door to add his personal thought, "And you know what, I second Caroline's thoughts. How could the supposed mighty Cush administration and the department of Homeland Security have let the people of this country down in such a horrendous way? Hank, where has the government been all of this time knowing about how they wanted to attack us? Wasn't 9-11 enough to teach us what they were all about?"

"You would have thought so. I bet the liberals are all hiding now. It's both sides that are at fault. Shorty, ask everyone what they feel we will need and finish your list then let's you and I and Bob take our two trucks and load up all of the empty barrels we have and get down to Cross's Junction to see if we can get gasoline and diesel."

Tom added, "You had better get some oil while you are there if you can."

CHAPTER THIRTY FOUR

September Thirteenth

As everyone awoke on the second day after the day of the attack the continuing bad news was still coming into the situation room in the bunker.

Visuals were being shown on the multiple monitors in the vie room of the fires still burning at power plants, oil refineries, and many gasoline storage areas plus all of the localized fires in city after city that were not only caused by both the terrorist explosions, but now also from looters and gangs.

Audio reports were streaming in from the choppers that were now on their second day of reconnaissance.

Good morning Mr. President, Vice-president Chainery is taking his coffee in the vie room Sir. The Marine guard opened the door to the dining room where the smell of freshly cooked southern sausage and buttermilk biscuits permeated the air. "Thank you sergeant, would you ask one of the attendants to bring me a breakfast tray into the vie room?"

As George entered the vie room Dick rose to greet him with as much of a smile as he could muster, "George, from what we can tell the attacks were limited to the eleventh and we have captured more than four hundred forty plus suspects and they have been taken to Leavenworth where they are under interrogation. The visuals we have been getting from coast to coast show that a number of the power plants, oil refineries, and fuel depots are still burning. There are fires in a number of cities still burning but about thirty five percent of the numbers of fires observed last night have now been contained. We should be getting a detailed report from NSA on the status of any major civil unrest by noon. The sweeping visuals do show pockets of gang activities which we had anticipated, but nothing overwhelming."

President Cush looked up at the center overhead screen reading the current reports from NSA as they were streaming across the big screen. 'The governmental operations are moving forward as directed and the National Guard is in place in the major cities but the forces have been spread thin. People are still venturing out from their homes with no way to enforce the curfew. The plan to stop all vehicular movement has been minimally successful due to lack of communication to almost all law enforcement agencies. Commercial facilities could not be protected and at the same time provide civilian protection. Radio stations are coming on line and the government will be making announcements through these stations by nineteen hundred hours'.

Vice President Chainery had recorded a short announcement of confirmation that the government was stabilizing the country after the unparalleled attack and was working on restoring power to many areas and securing food and fuel from other countries. He announced that the attacks were over and that the operation 'secure and stabilize' was already underway. The message was being broadcast every half hour from all of the ham operators' stations and on all of the commercial stations as they came on line from coast to coast giving confirmation that the government was in control and some comfort to those that could tune in their radios to 94.7 FM.

It was now twelve o'clock and Steven entered to tell George about the comprehensive reports he had requested on the restoring of the infrastructure, "George the four reports from the cabinet will not be ready until later this afternoon. There was way too much video and audio to review to assure a comprehensive analysis of the overall status of the infrastructure without giving them eight more hours. However to review the happenings around the country and our situation after three days, NSA has prepared an itemized list of the major problems facing everyone and it is showing on the big screen."

All or most of the fires will be extinguished by tomorrow night. There are only fifteen percent still burning.

Substations are the biggest problem. Locating and distributing the needed equipment
will be causing delays in repairs and rebuilding.

Rerouting power from plants and dams that can still operate to areas in most need of electricity will take from four days to one month. There will be some smaller rural areas that will have power tomorrow as different parts of the grid is uncoupled from damaged substations and towers.

All Major grocery stores have been vandalized and more than likely the food is all gone.

Reports tell us that meats and milk and other perishables in some warehouses haveeither started to rot or will be totally rotten in two more days.

We have visuals from the satellites that there are thousands of people crossing into Mexico and Canada. The borders are over run with people and cars are being abandoned every where. The freeways and many roads look like junk yards.

Hundreds of thousands of people not close to the borders are exiting the cities and
running to the country.

Gangs are forming from ordinary citizens and they are looting stores and banks. The gun shops have been the first ones to be raided. Armed citizens are banning together for protection.

Steven added to the information on the monitors, "Civil unrest is about to explode and the National Guard can not stop all of it. We will need as many troops here in the next two days as we can get and food for our major population centers. I have asked the secretary of HEW to provide us with what would be an absolute minimum diet that can sustain our people for at least two weeks. Michael Leavitt suggested that we immediately distribute all of the food stored in facilities both private and public that contain no perishables and especially all of the government's stored eggs, cheese, spam and other surpluses to areas where there is no food. This will be a monumental task but in order to salvage those items they must be distributed now!"

Nineteen hundred hours on the fourteenth and evening was beginning to set in on the East coast. The most current damage assessment and status on the populace had been delivered to the President and copies were given to all of the government leaders in the cabinet and the congress for their personal review.

REPORT ON RESTORATION OF COUNTRY'S INFASTRUCTURE AND PUBLICS ABILITY TO SURVIVE

Dams – Ten of the fifteen major dams are structurally doomed to failure and nineteen other dams have collapsed or will collapse in the next two weeks. Water is being released as fast as possible to avoid more disasters from down river flooding.

Nuclear Power Plants – Fifty seven plants were attacked and twenty of them were plutonium fueled and they have critical damage. They will not be restored. The other plants have damage ranging from minor damage to damage that requires complicated repairs and some can be operational in one to month and others may take six months or more. But the power distribution systems are destroyed.

Co-generation Power Plants – There are over ten thousand coal or gas or oil fired plants across the states and two hundred of the largest have excessive damage. Some are too old to repair. The rest will not be on line for more than a year. The smaller plants can operate if they have fuel and those with fuel will be able to provide electrical service to places where the grid is not destroyed. Coal and oil will be a problem.

Electrical Distribution Sub-stations – By last count some three hundred fifty plus major sub-stations were completely destroyed and they in turn caused large water cooled transformers and super condensers in hundreds of other sub-stations to fail. It will be three more days before all of the failures can be identified. A minimum of one month before a few patchwork grid networks will be working. But to have the number of transformers and condensers available to rebuild all of these distribution pens is highly unlikely.

Oil Refineries – All of the oil refineries that were attacked are out of commission for one year to five years.

Oil Storage Facilities – Of the eight hundred storage locations surveyed so far less than half of the tanks survived the fires. In some locations it will take three days to redo the piping and at others up to two weeks in order to reconnect undamaged tanks.

Electrical Power Transmission Towers – Here is our biggest problem area. It will take months to rebuild all of the towers. And the first phase of the rebuilding will be the mapping out of which transmission lines will need the towers rebuilt first so that the spider-web redesign of the grid connections will be able to supply power.

Communication Centers – This reconstruction will be the fastest and the second most important. The military has the ability and the capacity to have ninety percent of the communications in all of the major cities back up in some fashion in two weeks.

EDS – The six EDS central data storage complexes are a total lost. The business and financial records of most major banks, Wall Street firms and the largest American based corporations are lost. It will take more than two years and very likely four years to reconstruct the historical data that has been lost, but then there is no guarantee what percentage of the data can be recaptured and if some of the redundancy is undamaged.

Survival of the Population is shown by weekly nationwide projected deaths. The assumptions are built on the estimates of available food in every household at the time of the attack, the amount of food on the shelves of all of the grocery stores both large and small nationwide, the orderly distribution of food from private and government warehouse and the projection of the amount of food arriving from other countries.

USA: THE SERPENT IS CRUSHED!

WEEK ONE –   Ending September Eighteenth.
              Two Hundred Thousand dead, sick and
              undernourished.
WEEK TWO –   Ending September Twenty Fifth.
              One Million People dead.
WEEK THREE – Ending October Second.
              Possibly Five to Ten Million People
              dead.
WEEK FOUR -   Ending October Ninth.
              A possible Fifteen to Thirty Million
              more dead, with some stabilization
              occurring.

And the very sick and weak will still be dieing at a rate of Five
Million a week.

These projections include the estimate that more than five million people immigrated into Canada and that almost fifteen million people es-
caped into Mexico. We think that the projections are accurate plus or
minus ten percent and that the complete stabilization will occur after
the population has dropped below two hundred fifty million.

Every individual that read the report, the senators, the representatives,
those in NSA, FBI, and the CIA could not believe what they had read.
In the bunker the President and his staff, the Vice-president, and the
cabinet and their staff were overwhelmed at what they had just seen
on the big monitor. Many just sat down in disbelief, some almost collapsed, and there was crying and consoling.

George waited almost ten minutes before he spoke. I would like you
Dick, and you Robert, and General Cace, and Condolla, and you
Michael, and Steven, and Joshua to meet with me in my office to discuss what can be done to mitigate the human suffering and potential
loss of life that this report has forecasted. But first let us pray together.
'Lord God, Creator of the universe and all things, we ask for your wisdom and guidance at this most grievous time. As this nation was built
on the foundation of a Holy and merciful God so then we ask that You
again through Your mercy buttress up our country and our people to
work our way out of this violent assault on our country, our people and
our way of life.' Amen"

"I am not talking to you as the President but as a fellow American." He took a few deep breaths, "Before we can take any kind of rest; I want all of your ideas on what we can do to limit this looming tragedy. Joshua, see if you can get Michael Leavitt to have his people give us a real number for the minimal amount of rice and beans that a person can live on without starving to death. Let's say if necessary for one month, two months, and even three months. Then give us an analysis of the amount of rice and beans we will need daily to sustain the potentially fifty million people projected to die in that report. Carry out the analysis to ninety days from the eighteenth of September. I want Secretary Mike Bohannes to tell us if the farmers will be able to feed the country on a minimal bases after December the eighteenth and how quickly can we get the farmers to plant all of the land currently lying fallow. We will issue a government directive to all farmers that planting is required and will be subsidized. We will need to get food for our people and to transport it to the areas determined to have the greatest need. So Candie, I want you to get with Carlos and contact all of the ambassadors of China, India, Brazil, Vietnam, and any other country that is a large producer of rice and beans and let them know what we need at this time of human crisis giving them the amount of food we will be needing over the next three months if we are to save our people. Have Henry Paulson work on issuing treasury credits for those commodities and get a commitment from each country on dates certain that we can get the first shipments. And I guess for now the last thing will be for you Joshua, to contact General Michael Mosley for us to get our air lift operating from the countries that can have the food available the soonest and then begin a continuing non stop mission until we are confident that we have all we will need for our peoples immediate survival."

"Mr. President, you go and get some rest; we will begin working on your requests and do some of own brainstorming as the evening progresses." Both Stephen and Joshua could tell the President was drained and needed his rest.

CHAPTER THIRTY FIVE

By the fifteenth the Military was arriving in large numbers and were stationed first at strategic locations to protect the country's primary collateral, New York City with its banks and financial district, Fort Knox, the six Federal Mints, major bridges, water facilities, military storage areas, docks, and other infrastructure that was still intact and then finally to the major cities.

The air lift for food was in full s but distribution was presenting a problem. There was not yet a plan on where to keep the shipments that were arriving every few hours from around the world or how to distribute it. The decision had been made to store the pallets of food at airports in each of the major cities and then work on organized distribution. The problem was that the food was now arriving to fast and the operation for distribution was a big SNAFU.

The President and all of the other government officials had left the bunker to return to their normal offices and they were trying to operate in a more orderly routine. There was a battalion stationed around the government buildings and jets continued their air surveillance twenty four hours a day. The families of the officials of the Judicial, Executive, and Legislative departments were protected and were provided all of their needs by the military. Each official was personally chaffered as needed by the military. The President had made sure that the government would be operational at least in the capital buildings even if it would be at a minimum level. The people and the world needed to know that the country was not shut down and that attack or no attack the United States would and always has overcome.

NSA was monitoring the reports coming from around the country from the PBS stations that had become operational. Denver, Colorado – The camera crew for Hawk Rizzer the news reporter for Public TV Station KPBS was operating their sky-cam as Hawk narrated the events taking place in Denver. The president's request to the Navy and the FCC to get as many Public Television stations on the air around the country as possible was moving at break neck speed providing communication to the public and to NSA. They were allowed to use one of the military's birds to send reports via its satellite to NSA giving the OHS additional input on the state of the public's coping with the disaster in their individual areas and report on the unrest in their community and any civil upheaval.

"This is Hawk Rizzer with KPBS in Denver, Colorado with our report for Saturday the fifteenth. People here in Denver seemed to have settled in to local neighborhoods and are sharing their food, supplies, any necessities they can gather together and surrounding themselves with make shift barricades using armed individuals for their protection. As you can see in the downtown area we have people lying in the streets and in the parks and they are either sick or dead. It would appear that they are mostly the homeless and poor who could not find enough food and were quite weak from the beginning. You can see some of the gathering of peoples in various neighborhoods as we past over Westminster here in the northern part of the City. Moving west there are many that have gone into the mountains going as far as they could get with their fuel supply to gain protection from marauding gangs. The gangs, and there are more everyday, have been cruising commercial areas to steal what ever they felt was valuable to them. But here in many areas of Denver we have seen them hunting for food and even killing groups of people for the food and water they may have. We have seen five Mosques burned and maybe a few hundred Muslims, well at least Arabic people killed around the city. As you have seen back at the airport where we had the helicopter parked there is a lot of food piling up and even though it is protected by the Guard it is still not getting out to the hungry. Hawk Riser here in Denver."

Milwaukee, Wisconsin – "This is Sharon Elwell with Public TV station WMPBS making a report for NSA as we make our routine tour of the Milwaukee area. There are still thousands of people trying to get to Canada. Those that have been able to get electric generators and break into the service stations have gassed up and taken extra containers of gas so they can make it into Canada. People are stealing city busses to get to the Canadian border and using the fuel stored at the terminal to fill their cars gas tanks and pack up family and friends to get to the border. It appears in every case they are armed and ready to kill if anyone tries to stop them. We have seen people lying dead along side of their car on the side of the highway and we witnessed a shooting at and from a bus by what looked to us to be a group of ruthless and wildly uncontrollable people who had tried to commandeer the bus. Most of the sporting goods stores and gun shops have been looted and there are some dead people in various places in the city and there has been a rage against all of the Muslim communities. It is our best estimate along with information from people we have on the ground that more than five thousand Muslims in all have been killed in their heavy populated communities. This has been Sharon Elwell reporting from Milwaukee and it looks like civil unrest is taking over our area."

On and On and On reports like these were coming in from city after city.

On Tuesday Michael came into the Cabinet Room with the PDB from the Generals and NSA. "Mr. President, Mr. Vice-president, Cabinet members and staff, I have the latest up date on the state of the nation in a report with as assessed by combination of information from the military observers at all our bases across the country, the many law enforcement agencies around the country and the visual observation of the PBS reporters in all of the cities where we have been able to get satellite transmission operational. Each of you has a copy and when you look at it, it is not pretty. It is however close to our projected status of last week."

Even with the information received from the military and the law enforcement agencies that had been able to reestablished communication channels, no one in the government had a complete picture of what was happening nation wide, not even the Executive department. The satellite visuals and the reports only provided a macro insight into the state of the country. A review of this or that area or one city to another or a report on particulate areas of one state or another; but a real grasp on the status of the nation was still not available. But if micro views from coast to coast inside of the ten thousand towns, and villages and small communities were available they would show the beginning of basic human nature taking control and the impetus of self preservation becoming stronger than the 'help thy neighbor' credo.

Michael tried to be statesman like but the details were too difficult to read without breaking down. With a crackle in his voice he began to read from the report, "This update will correct a lot of our previous reports. First, let's have a look at our infrastructure. All of our major dams... are failing except the Oroville dam at Sacramento. Most of the dams hit east of Colorado are severely damaged but they can more easily be repaired. They are not of the high elevation as are the solid concrete type. Second, we have a number on how many nuclear power plants were hit. It is definitely fifty two and every one of them damaged to an extent they were immediately shut down and any restarting them will be dependant on thorough inspection of all of the damage by the AEC and that will take many months. Third, our reports show that very close to two hundred co-generation plants were attacked and they are all out of commission for at least one year. And now to the countries life blood, oil; I am deeply depressed over the attack on our oil refineries. Forty five of our largest refineries were hit and most of them can not come back on line for two to three years. And we still do not have an assessment on how many oil storage areas were hit but the preliminary estimate is almost one thousand. The only good news in regards to that is in almost all of the areas we were able to save a large number of the tanks. Dirk from interior said that along with the combined effort of all of the power companies and their contractors and with the rather complicated rerouting of power over the national grid the department's consensus is that in two months power will have been restored to about twenty percent of the country and then as work progresses on tower rebuilding power can become available to about fifty per cent of the country in six to eighth months. That does not mean half of the country geographically but rather fifty percent of the nation's users on that kind of complicated spider-web make shift grid. However, even with improvement in the grid distribution we will still need to have the power available. More reconnaissance on the other targets is still being done."

George, before he spoke, looked at the Cabinet with the feeling of the pain of the past seven days on his face and at that very same moment in his mind he felt like he had been disemboweled. "From what I hear from you is that this attack has been successful beyond the enemy's wildest dream and that simply put we could be broken as a nation and brought to our knees. I know that we, all of us here, everyone in the Congress, all of the countries civil servants and the American people will not let that happen. Before we hear the rest of the report from Candie and Stephen I want to present my thoughts and that everyone is in agreement with the continuation of the operation of the government in a 'State of Emergency' and continue with Marshal Law. I propose that we increase the return of our military to sixty percent to protect the country from any possible external attack and any internal deterioration from civil uprising. We have the resources and the man power to rebuild, it is a matter of do we have the time. We will need to know who our friends are and who our enemies are. And as we go forward asking for help if it is the countries with an active Islamic element who shun us and the countries who are predominately Muslim who present problems or interfere with our future survival then so be it. If there is an onslaught of Islamic terrorist's threats then we will destroy them in mass where ever they are; this is their declared war on the United States. They have placed themselves square center in the middle of our sights. I think we will suffer some heavy casualties here at home. We must be prepared for it. History may look at this time as a resurgence of 'The Crusades', but I say to you and to all of our people we will arise to destroy this evil institution with a philosophical foundation of hatred and an agenda to take over the world."

An Amen was heard unanimously around the room.

"Is there any good news or positive developments? Candie, how are we doing with help for food and fuel?"

At that moment before she could answer the President's question an aide to Stephen Haddle entered the Cabinet room. "Excuse me Mr. President but I have an urgent message from a John Poles at Homeland Security. He is having a transmission from the Arabic station in Qatar sent to the monitors here showing a live interview with bin Laden and his lieutenants; look it is coming in now. It is being directed to the whole world and repeated every half hour,"

"Our fighters for allah have begun a major move in the battle against the evil power of the West. The Jihad is now under way and the United States and Mr. Cush have felt the awesome power of allah. We have destroyed their sources of power with the destruction of dams, power plants, oil refineries, and all oil supply. Millions and Millions of people are starving and tens of millions are dieing. This Dajin has been reduced to a third world country and the Kuffers must now come to allah for forgiveness and accept Islam as the true religion of the world. We will move on all nations to accept the truth of allah. All infidels must take the Shadada of our beloved allah." 'All praise goes to allah'.

"As we know", Stephen took command of the moment, "he and the al Qaeda seek the limelight when ever they can get it and they need approval and influence among the Islamic brothers and with our current situation depicted on news outlets around the world he has jumped in with both feet to solidify his organization and at the same time recruit to his army of Jihadist. They have declared their plans to take over the whole world. What he and the rest of the world do not know is how quickly we can restore our lives and how resilient the true American is. We are already on track and give us three to four weeks and al Qaeda and the Islamic world will be quaking in their sandals. Sorry I interrupted you Mr. President. Candie, please go on with your report."

George's solemn look disappeared and his normal Texas smile crept across his face. "Thank you Stephen, we all needed that. Please go on Candie."

"Before I get into hard facts I just want to second what Stephen has just said. Let me emphasize this; 'The world just does not know us, but they will find out. This attack has created a new epoch in the history of the world as will be seen from this moment on'. She stopped to catch her composure before continuing, "Well, the air lift for food is in operation at one hundred cent of expectation. All of the countries we called on to supply rice and beans have filled our request except Indonesia. We are receiving twenty four thousand tons of food per day and we are working on an orderly and systematic plan for distribution. At a sustenance level of eight ounces per day for an adult we can provide nutrition for forty eight million of our people daily. We are planning to double that next week and integrate these numbers with the food supply Mike's reports from Agriculture has projected and learn what the farmers are still able to provide. We will have the numbers on the amount of oil and gas we can get from our friends England, Norway, Mexico, Saudi Arabia, Jordan, Kuwait and others but in the mean time we have opened the National Reserves for the Military and any critical commercial usage."

"Okay, great, some good positive news there. Stephen, our internal security and civil order, how are we doing?"

"Well George, not so good. As we just heard from Michael restoration of power to about half of the population will leave us with about one hundred twenty million people without power. Here are the disturbing numbers. Our best estimates are that ultimately twenty million people will have migrated into Canada or Mexico. We have intelligence that over the next two weeks death squads of radical and irate citizens will have killed almost one million five hundred thousand Arabic people and we can not stop it. Further uncontrolled gangs in every part of the country are growing in numbers and they are plundering businesses and homes looking for any thing of value but especially food and they could kill another ten million people over the next month. We simply do not have enough military to stop this. Finally, even though we are bringing in food to feed those who are without any food our projections are that the distribution into the large populated areas will not be soon enough to save everyone from starvation. We can potentially loose an additional five million citizens more than the projections from illness and starvation during the next thirty days. Even with power everyone will need food. On the slightly brighter side millions of people have banded together in protected neighborhood compounds and armed themselves to keep gangs and thieves away from their food, water, and fuel. We have estimated that these clusters of people by combining their personal resources and what they were able to get on the first two days have enough supplies to sustain their group for up to twenty days if they ration the water and food properly. So between the foods being air lifted and the farm production and efficient distribution we should be able to prevent no more people dieing of starvation than our original projected numbers."

"Dick let us hear the plan we have for restoration. Our plans must have a goal to be able to get us back to a minimum of seventy five per cent of normal business operations and government services in the shortest time possible. What will be the time line for this goal?"

"Aside from what the military and law enforcement must do; the following is the outline for the required tasks that the various departments will have as the restoration plan unfolds. These departments are Transportation, Interior, Energy, Health and Human Services and Agriculture."

- Samuel Bodman's department will control distribution of the national fuel reserve to the military, law enforcement, emergency services, commercial transportation, and farmers. As fuel arrives from our friends his department will take control of the distribution. They will prioritize and coordinate the rebuilding of the electrical cogeneration plants.

- Mary Betters' department has set up the coordination of the transportation of fuel, food supplies coming in from the airlift, farm distribution, and food plant distribution.

- Mike Johanns' department is overseeing the Farm Bureau's authority to have farmers continue their growing by supplying seeds, fuel and supplies and authorizing the planting of all fallow land.

- Michael Leavitt has instructed his people to secure control of all drugs and medical supplies in the hands of the pharmaceutical and medical companies to see to it that they are totally under protective custody and distributed as needed directly to clinics and hospitals that are operational. Emergency fuel and food distribution to hospitals is currently underway.

- Dirk Kempthome has been working with the power companies to get the redistribution of the available power to the most critical areas first. The companies have been instructed to use the power that can still be generated from available sources and what can be supplied from Canada and Mexico for the critical list of users shown below.

- While also having them work around the clock to rebuild the plants that can come on line the soonest and repair critically needed distribution stations and rebuild transmission towers. Here is the list of critical power users in the areas where power will be reinstated shortly or is now available.

> Certain Government Facilities.
> Law enforcement facilities and communications centers.
> Hospitals.
> Water purification plants and pumping stations.
> Radio and Television stations.
> Food processing plants.
> Grocery Warehousing with refrigeration units.
> Banking facilities.

"All of the above has already begun and the Department of Interior has the biggest job requiring it to oversee and implement not only the rebuilding of the power sources and grid but also the low level dams, the refineries, the storage areas, the communication facilities, and the rail lines. The government can not rebuild the EDS systems complexes but Henry Paulson has authorized his department to provide all of its resources to help EDS reconstruct the data bases of the banking systems, Wall Street, and major companies that had their data storage destroyed. That will take many months and then all of the data may never be recaptured."

"Thank you all. I will take the reports, our findings and your projections to congress this afternoon. I will issue an order to shoot on site any persons, groups, or gangs that are attacking citizens. I will ask the military, the PBS stations and the ARRL to announce this order so that we can alert as many as possible of this protective measure. We must be prepared for the amount of deaths that will be sustained and I am asking Michael to set up standards for the record keeping of the identity of the dead and for the disposal of the bodies. This could very well become a major health hazard. Also before we close this meeting I have asked Joshua to prepare announcements every four hours to be broadcast to the entire country over all of our available communication systems and radio and TV stations as they come on line giving them up dates on our progress for the country's restoration. We must keep the people informed and give them the encouragement needed to go through the next thirty days as we head back to a certain amount of normality. Finally, I am preparing a 'Declaration of War' against all Islamic people around the world. Their intent is to destroy the United States and we will destroy them where ever they are; they can not hide and no country will be able to protect them. All people or countries that try to further their cause or protect them will be considered their accomplices and be under our Declaration of War. Any comments let me hear them otherwise we are adjourned."

September 27, 2007, Congress called for a meeting of both houses and invited the President and all members of the cabinet asking the President to speak on the State of the Nation.

"Ladies and Gentlemen of the Congress and our honorable and courageous citizens; the attack on our nation on September 11 has crippled our country for a short time but it has not rendered us vulnerable to the evil forces that wish us to be extinguished. We are in the process of total restoration of the infrastructure that has been damaged by our enemy who we totally now understand. An enemy that many of us knew wanted us destroyed and who the liberals professed were basically good and moral people. Sometimes it takes a hard lesson for foolish people to get the picture. I am here to tell you that the lesson will end up being twenty million Americans migrating to foreign lands, and somewhere between thirty and fifty million Americans dead from illness and starvation. These may generally be the elderly and the weak and yet many will be children who could not survive the trauma. And we have a financial disaster unprecedented in the history of our country but we are resilient and we have the ancestry of true grit.

We have suffered with no food, no water, no gasoline and hospitals overrun with sick people and wild out of control gangs and people acting like animals. The enemy thought that they could bring us to our knees and ultimately reduce us to a third world country. But they did not know who we are; a people who wanted freedom and began a democracy more than two hundred years ago based on right and might. The enemy's philosophy is based on hate and fear. A formula for failure.

I have asked the nations that supply us with oil to continue by our issuing credits for each shipment and I have requested our navy to provide protective assistant with the transportation to our shores.

We have taken the following measures to protect our country. I have recalled from Iraq more than one hundred thousand of our military. I have put all of our foreign bases on alert to protect our country under all circumstances. I have informed every nation that we will not tolerate any act of aggression towards our country at this time when it might appear as though we are completely vulnerable. I have readied the military to use all available force to thwart any act of aggression. And that includes nuclear force. I have informed all Muslim countries that we will take every step necessary to stop the surge of the Islamic ideology and the Islamist desire to rule the world. The Declaration of War on Islam is to stop them in their tracks. I have alerted the Islamic world that their encroachment into the free world is over.

We are operating under marshal law here in the states and that will continue until we have captured every person responsible for the attacks and executed them as enemies of the United States. Also we will continue marshal law until all criminal gangs and individual looters have either been arrested or shot. The civil disorder is not out of control as thousands of our good citizens have helped the police stop the people who are committing these criminal acts. We believe that in three weeks we will have many urban areas back with some electrical power and in certain areas we will have complete power. According to Johanns' of the Department of Agriculture, he has reported that the food supply problems are improving and in thirty days they should be close to being resolved with the air lift now providing enough sustenance for more than one hundred twenty million of our people. The farms and food processing companies will soon have enough food entering the market place to feed another one hundred twenty million people. Water is now starting to flow again in many areas and across the country all of the companies with available tanker-trucks and even the construction people with rolling water tanks have been hauling drinking water to cities where there is no lake, river or stream where people could get palatable water.

I am asking the most dedicated and patriotic peoples on the face of Gods earth; THE CITIZENS OF THE UNITED STATES OF AMERICA, to pitch in and work with all of the agencies and companies to rebuild the damaged infrastructure so as to speed up our recovery. Everyone can do something, construction work, food distribution, help to get plants opening quicker and businesses reopening their doors, general clean up, and even planting vegetable gardens.. Supplies and goods will start to flow again. And when we are back to normal the activation of the War Powers act will be terminated and marshal law will be halted.

I have issued an executive order for all banks and every credit provider to give all creditors a six month period of forbearance on all debt. I have also informed all of our creditor nations that we have suspended payment on any debt. The income for the operation of the government has essentially come to a halt. I am requesting Congress to authorize a one thousand dollar payment each month beginning October the first to every family that had a family income under fifty thousand dollars and continuing until the major bread winner is back to their job or has found work. I am calling this a relief and reward for all citizens to pitch in and help where ever they can. As power becomes available I am asking every business to reopen and begin their commerce. The financial assistance to our people will cost the government an estimated three hundred billion dollars, but it will allow us to recover much faster.

All of the members of my Cabinet who are the heads of the each of the various departments have assured me and so I assure the Congress and my fellow Americans that we will be seventy five per cent restored in six months and fully restored within three years.

I do not pretend that isolationism is the answer but I can guarantee each and every one of you that liberalism is finished in this country. This will never again happen to this country and I will back the second amendment to our constitution guaranteeing our law abiding citizens to forever bear arms and I will from this day forward require that we as a nation and as a people know and recognize who our enemy is. The unabated invasion of our borders is over and I am requesting that the southern border be closed to only those with proper papers and the barrier be finished within one year. I have issued an executive order to Mertoff at OHS and Bates at Defense that there will be no more illegal entrance into our country and we will be a nation that operates under the 'rule of law'.

I thank God for this nation and for all of our citizens and I pray that God will bless the United States of America and I ask that we as a nation Bless God in all that we do and in all that we stand for. Thank you and long live our great nation and its people."

After the meeting with Congress President Cush returned to the White House and retreated to the Oval Office with the Vice-president, Michael Mertoff, and Stephen Haddle.

"Friends, my trusted friends; you have served your country admirably. I have to say this.

May God have mercy on us! We knew .... and yet we could never have known this massive of an attack was looming. We all remained politically correct, better interrupted as <u>Naïve</u>.

'BUT OUR IGNORANCE DOES NOT PROVIDE US WITH INNOCENCE.' We failed the trust...........NO I FAILED MY RESPONSIBILITY!"

THE END...**OR IS IT!**

GLOSSARY OF ARABIC WORDS

ARABIC	ENGLISH
allah	muslim's spiritual being or god.
allah akbar	allah is great
al-salawaat	the blessing
al-tauhid	unity of the faithful
Badr	important ancient battle
Burraq	transportation for prophets, shape of a horse
Dawa	invitation for new muslims to islam
Dajin	demons of islam – single eye of the antichrist
Dajjael	antichrist – the liar
Dua	prayer, always facing Mecca
Fatwa	legal opinion on Islamic law
Hajj	pilgrimage
Halal	allowed
Haq	truth
Haram	prohibited
Hadith	sayings of the Prophet
Intifada	awakening, shaking off, - uprising
Islam	submission
Jihad	striving (many types) personal with weapons
Kuffer	infidel – the unbeliever
Malik	keeper of hell
Miraj	vision
Mosque	place of prayer
Muharram	first month of the year – based on full moon
Mujahedin	radical Islamist

Mu'min	believer
Muhammad	Islamic prophet – died 632AD
Qu'ran	muslin bible or sunnah
Mushbooh	suspect
Rasul	prophet
Salat	prayer , always facing Mecca
Sawm	fasting
Shahada	testimony of faith
Shaheed	martyr
Shaitan	satan
Shariah	divine laws – from mohammed
USA	the snake or serpent
Zakat	religious tax

GLOSSARY OF ACRONYMS

INITIALS	MEANING
ABI	Agencia Brasillia de Intelligencia
ACE	Air Carrier Enforcement
CFR	Critical Field Investigation
CIA	Central Intelligence Agency
CIR	Central Intelligence Review Staff
CIU	Counter Intelligence Unit
DIA	Defense Intelligence Agency
DOD	Department of Defense
DOJ	Department of Justice
EDS	Electronic Data Systems
FBI	Federal Bureau of Investigation
FINCEN	Financial Crimes Enforcement Network –USA
FISA	Foreign Intelligence Surveillance Act
FSIGINTL	Foreign Signal Generated Intelligence
GPS	Geological Positioning Satellite
HRO	Ham Radio Operators
HUMINTL	Human Generated Intelligence
IBC	International Bank Clearing
IDR	Internal Data Review
IED's	Improvised explosive devices
IMGINTL	Imagery Generated Intelligence
IMTR	International Money Transfer Report
JOCC	Joint Operations Command Center
JTTF	Joint Terrorist Task Force
NCTC	National Counter Terrorist Center

NPG	National Power Grid
NSA	National Security Administration
NSD	National Security Directive
NSR	National Security Response
OHS	Office of Homeland Security
OIC	Organization of Islamic Countries
PACK	Pluck a Canuck (Pick up a Canadian)
PDB	President's Daily Briefing
PFI	Priority Field Investigation
SATINTL	Satellite Generated Intelligence
SHIN-BET	Israeli Secret Service - Shabak
SIGINTL	Signal Generated Intelligence
STAL	Suspected Terrorist At Large
SWIFT	Society for Worldwide Inter-bank Financial Telecommunications
TIU	Terrorist Intelligence Unit-NSA
TSU	Terrorist Screening Center
UBC	United Broadcasting Company
WBCC	Worldwide Bank Clearing House
WCTC	Worldwide Counter Terrorist Commission
WUAI	Warrants Unit Analysis & Investigation
WWJHEP	Worldwide Journal on Hydro Electric Power